THE GRANDFATHER CLOCK

DIAL AND HOOD OF EIGHT-DAY
STRIKING CLOCK BY PETER WALKER
LONDON, *circa* 1690
See plates 14 *and* 15 *and Notes page* 221

The Grandfather Clock

An Archæological and Descriptive Essay
on the Long-Case Clock with its
Weight-driven Precursors and Contemporaries

By
ERNEST L. EDWARDES

ALTRINCHAM
JOHN SHERRATT AND SON

First published 1949
New edition, revised and enlarged 1952

Made in Great Britain. Printed at the St Ann's Press
Park Road, Altrincham

And what other thing that has not life could cheer me as it does; what other thing that has not life (I will not say how few things that have) could have proved the same patient, true, untiring friend! How often have I sat in the long winter evenings feeling such society in its cricket-voice, that raising my eyes from my book and looking gratefully towards it, the face reddened by the glow of the shining fire has seemed to relax from its staid expression and to regard me kindly; how often in the summer twilight, when my thoughts have wandered back to a melancholy past, have its regular whisperings recalled them to the calm and peaceful present; how often in the dead tranquillity of night has its bell broken the oppressive silence, and seemed to give me assurance that the old clock was still a faithful watcher at my chamber door! My easy-chair, my desk, my ancient furniture, my very books—I can scarcely bring myself to love even these last like my old clock!

Master Humphrey's Clock
by Charles Dickens

Contents

Acknowledgments

Plates 5, 10, 11 and 12 by courtesy of Mr. G. V. Lancaster, Ulverston, Lancashire.

Plates 19–24 by courtesy of Mr. J. Holt-Haworth, Haslingden, Lancashire.

Plates 27–33 by courtesy of Mr. Robt. W. Sawyer, Bend, Oregon, U.S.A.

Plate 34 by courtesy of Mr. J. W. Needham, Manchester. (Photograph by A. A. Outlaw.)

Plate 53 by courtesy of Mr. G. Mills, Altrincham, Cheshire. (Photograph by A. A. Outlaw.)

Plates 6, 7, 16, 17, and 18 by courtesy of Mr. W. E. Johnson, Sale, Cheshire. (Photographs by A. A. Outlaw.)

The Clocks illustrated by the Plates listed above are the property of those whose kindness in allowing them to be photographed for this volume is acknowledged.

Mr. Lancaster, Mr. Sawyer, and Mr. Holt-Haworth, in addition, have most kindly provided the photographs depicting their own clocks.

The Clocks illustrated by Frontispiece, Plates 1–4, 8–9, 14–15, 25–26, 35–37, 39, 41–52 and 54 are the property of the Author. Photography by Mr. A. A. Outlaw.

Illustrations

The references in brackets are to the pages of Appendix Five where a full
description of the particular clock will be found.

Preface to Second Edition

THE very encouraging reception accorded the first edition (1949) of *The Grandfather Clock* has resulted in a request by my publishers for an enlarged second edition.

If for no other reason than that I have revised my views as to several important dates in horological progress, and that one or two errors in nomenclature may now be corrected, I am glad to be in a position to accede to my publishers' wishes.

In addition, however, it is clear to me that the original book contains an insufficiency of illustrations.

Although it is in no way my wish to make my Essay merely a "picture-book" (several of this type already exist) it cannot be denied that an unfortunate lack of the earlier book is its inadequate display of seventeenth-century clocks, particularly in the long-case form and by south-country makers. These, as I believe, receive due recognition and general description in the text, but the latter is not supplemented by illustrations and descriptions of individual examples. This deficiency has been largely rectified in the present edition, and was due in the first instance to my very strong desire to illustrate only such clocks as have not previously appeared in other books.

Moreover, a work which was originally intended chiefly for the ordinary clock-owner, and which only set out to beguile a few odd hours of the reader's winter evenings (although it is a fact that much more information of a semi-technical nature is included than is usual in similar books) has been accorded the notice of technicians and connoisseurs and, naturally, has fallen short of what might have been accomplished had the aim been different.

In the present version of *The Grandfather Clock* I have kept in mind my original endeavour to render the work interesting to the general reader, and with this purpose as a foundation, I have built thereon somewhat differently than in the chapters of the earlier book. In this edition the reader will find a very much expanded dissertation on the early long-case clocks, including some reflections on the origin of this form, together with a full account of the rival claims of scientists and clockmakers as to this or that improvement in timekeeping or mechanism which affects our subject.

It is nowadays very much the fashion to be an iconoclast. If one cannot, by original research, produce incontrovertible evidence that, say, a cantata or a motet which has been attributed by tradition to Sebastian Bach for generations is not really by him, but by Johann Christoph Bach, or another, one can at least gain a certain celebrity (or notoriety) by publicly questioning its authenticity—the most slender thread will serve on which to hang an " argument "—and then (joyous procedure!) invite " proof " to be forthcoming from those deluded wights who still hold to an " outworn idea ". In the horological world the idol to be destroyed is apparently Robert Hooke (1635–1703) and in his place a monument is to be erected to William Clement, who, it would appear, is to be credited with the invention of the anchor escapement for clocks, upon slender and contra- dictory " contemporary evidence ", the contradictory nature of which, needless to say, is not emphasized by the advocates of " revised ideas ". It is not my intention to enter a controversy in this matter, but in the following pages I have stated the contemporary evidence without comment.

In this edition the errors of nomenclature referred to have been corrected; what I trust may be more mature consideration and experience has resulted in the revision of a date or two in the ascribed period of an invention (or introduction of an invention in its application to clocks) and some additional information has been included in the Glossary.

Moreover, I find that I disagree so strongly with the views expressed by some writers as to the origin of the long-case clock that I have felt impelled (after stating the opinions or assertions) to put forward my own view of these matters. I wish it to be clearly understood that here I am not contesting the *possibility* of the various arguments with which I find myself at variance. I merely find them unconvincing, and exercise the undoubted right of everyone to question their validity. Be it noted here that I am not seeking to contest well-founded traditions for the sake of novelty, and without definite evidence to the contrary, as the opinions or assertions with which I disagree are those of individual writers only, and lack support of any kind other than the deductions and inferences of their authors, writing in modern times.

Now a word as to the long-case clocks illustrated and described in this book. It will be obvious that not all of these are of equal quality or merit. The greater number are serious collectors' pieces—to the connoisseur it will be unnecessary to mention those to which I refer, except to add that not all of these belong to the magical period 1660–1720. One or two will no doubt be considered undeserving a place in a fine collection. But this work is not only for the connoisseur, although such, it is believed, may find some pleasure in its persual and (a rather weak point of many otherwise knowledgeable collectors) perhaps derive additional information relating to the movements. It is intended also—and quite as much—for the ordinary clock-owner; one who may have in his possession a comparable clock to those which, though of little interest to the specialist, are for this reason accorded a place in this work.

Definitely bad examples of clockmaking and case-work—those about which there can be no two opinions—are not illustrated, even for purposes of comparison. These may have proved instructive, but possibly also productive of much rather disturbing revelation. I know personally of several devastatingly ugly clock cases and dials, all of which, as it happens, are in private ownership. The position of an author who requests permission to illustrate a clock-owner's often cherished possession only to condemn it in his book may be imagined! An outline of what to avoid is given in the following pages, and this is so easily explained and recognized that illustration is not really essential.

I wish to stress again the fact that (to the extent of my own knowledge) the clocks illustrated here have not appeared in any previous work—previous, that is, to the original edition. Since the first edition was published in 1949. at least one of the plates has been reproduced, with permission, in another book.

As a reader of antiquarian horological literature, I find it extremely irritating to see the same rather wearisome succession of marquetry and walnut examples appearing with monotonous regularity in book after book. Many of these clocks have a distinct resemblance one to another; moreover, the illustrations themselves are often very small and imperfect, much detail being altogether lost, probably both by the reduction and in the process of block-making.

What one writer[1] has described as " the sheep-like worship of a name "

---

[1] H. Cescinsky. *Old English Master Clockmakers and their Clocks.*

probably accounts for the repetition of clocks by famous makers, particularly Tompion, illustrated in the books to which I refer.[1]

Daniel Quare and George Graham (to mention only two names) were makers who have achieved deservedly high reputations for their improvements to watches and clocks, and occasionally these and other makers made clocks which are exceptional—this is indubitable. Their "standardized" movements (if one may use a term more applicable to modern industry) were no more notable than others by good but lesser-known makers of the same period. This also applies to the products of the case-maker chosen by the horologist to enshrine his movement and dial. It is not to be considered that clock-case makers made special productions for these now famous makers. Undoubtedly the maker of a fine clock would choose an expensive case for it, and the same applies to all makers, not only those to whose normal clocks present-day "experts" have accorded an entirely fictitious pre-eminence.

The above observations are also applicable to clocks and makers of a later period—in fact, throughout the eighteenth century.

Not long ago I was able to examine a movement by John Ellicott, F.R.S. (1706–1772). This maker (like others) attained deserved eminence during his lifetime for his many scientific devices; for his experimental research and his papers read before the august society of which he was a Fellow.

The movement under consideration was a thoroughly ordinary eight-day rack-striking clock, bearing nothing in its appearance and incorporating no feature of construction to proclaim the fame of its maker. The same may be said of the dial and hands; characteristic of the period in both instances, soundly but unimaginatively made. Without the magic of the dial "signature" both clock and case (a walnut example of no great excellence) would probably have passed unnoticed by the collector, but one can be amused by thinking of the "expert" whose mental attitude undergoes a complete change when his wandering eye encounters the name on the dial!

From the foregoing, the average clock-owner (whether or not he possesses a really good clock, and that by either a famous or an unknown maker) will perceive that there is a great deal of humbug spoken and written about clocks, as there is, alas, about many other subjects unconnected with horology, particularly where those concerned have a metaphorical " axe

[1] In this connection, I *do not* refer to R. W. Symonds' *Masterpieces of English Furniture and Clocks* which is magnificent throughout.

to grind". We have all heard of the creation of "corners" in commodities; the process of "cornering" is not confined to what is generally understood by "commodities". I leave it to the intelligence of the general reader, as well as to the undoubtedly sincere section of genuine clock-lovers, many of whom are true experts and discerning collectors in the best sense, to decide as to the fitness and veracity of my opinion in this matter.

A word as to the London makers in particular. There are a fairly large number of early clocks by these makers in museums and private collections throughout the country. There are also not lacking examples of such in the antique dealers' showrooms, the great majority perfectly genuine and altogether admirable. Examples of *similar date* by provincial —and particularly north-country—makers are very much more rare, largely for reasons which will be apparent at a later stage in this book. These latter clocks, then, have every point of rarity in their favour, and should justly be esteemed accordingly.

It should also be remembered that some of the most famous of "London" makers had their origins in the north. It will suffice to mention George Graham, John Harrison, Thomas Earnshaw, and (a very early maker) David Ramsay. Among inventors who were distinguished horologists we may include Edward Barlow (*née* Booth) who has an excellent claim to be considered the inventor of the rack-repeating striking mechanism for clocks, although, as will be seen later, the nowadays somewhat belittled Robert Hooke has perhaps some title to the invention of, at any rate, *a* repeating-work of sorts.

I wish to express my thanks to correspondents who have written to me *via* the publishers, Messrs. John Sherratt and Son, and to those who have made enquiries of me concerning their clocks I extend my wishes that the information I have been able to supply, although in some instances but scanty, may prove of interest and help. I wish these correspondents to clearly understand that when their requests for information are concerned *only with a date* for a particular maker, my details have been derived from the standard works such as Britten's *Old Clocks and Watches and their Makers* and G. H. Baillie's more recent *Watchmakers and Clockmakers of the World* (1947) together with John Smith's *Old Scottish Clockmakers*, any or all of which they may consult for themselves in any reference library. This observation (and clarification of the position) is not intended to discourage correspondence on other details affecting clocks; their design, mechanism, casework and dial-styles, nor indeed on any matter of general historical or aesthetic interest in horology. I merely desire it to be known amongst those who, for lack of a better term, I may perhaps describe as "uninitiated", that I cannot possibly claim to be *au fait* with the approximate dates of individuals in many thousands of old makers. G. H. Baillie in his work lists approximately *thirty-five thousand* names, English and foreign. This kind of book is not often accorded by the general reader the distinction and recognition it deserves. It has not the easy interest of an historical and connected survey of the subject, enlivened by illustration and description, being merely a dry catalogue of names and dates; but its value is incalculable to the horological antiquary and dealer, and should also prove very useful to owners of old timekeepers desiring to verify, at least approximately, their previously conceived ideas as to the dates of their often treasured old clocks. Mr. Baillie (and also others such as the late F. J. Britten) deserve the gratitude of the entire clock-loving fraternity for their painstaking and helpful researches.

In particular, I wish to thank Mr. Robert W. Sawyer, of Bend, Oregon, U.S.A., for the time and labour he has spent in preparing suitable photographs of his fine long-case clock for publication, and also Mr. G. V. Lancaster, of Ulverston, Lancashire, for similar ungrudging co-operation and assistance.

To my friend, Mr. W. E. Johnson, of Sale, Cheshire, I am indebted for permission to photograph two of the interesting examples of both long-case and lantern clocks in his possession, and for his help in preparing them for photography.

My acknowledgments are also due to the following:

Mr. J. Holt-Haworth, Haslingden, Lancashire;

Mr. E. Mills, Altrincham, Cheshire;

Mr. J. W. Needham, Manchester;

Mr. F. G. Rendall, Department of Printed Books, British Museum.

Messrs. E. G. Parker, Ltd., Altrincham, Cheshire;

Professor E. N. da C. Andrade, Hon. Librarian, Royal Society of London.

Mr. W. J. Gilham, Willesborough, Ashford, Kent.

The photography throughout the book, except where otherwise stated, is the work of Mr. A. A. Outlaw, who has taken great pains to make the pictures a success.

I wish especially to record my appreciation of the work of my publishers, Messrs. John Sherratt and Son, who have done everything possible to present this book as I should wish, devoting much care and skill to its production.

Although to one preparing a book such as this, a study of actual clocks in as much variety as possible, together with the writings of Smith, Derham, Hooke, and Huygens, is of most importance, I have felt it worth while to examine contemporary accounts, if only to note the extraordinary divergence of opinion or, at any rate, of statistics(!) displayed in these.

For those readers who may wish to do the same I append the following bibliography.

All the works enumerated I have consulted before preparing this second edition of the Essay.

G. H. Baillie, *Watchmakers and Clockmakers of the World* (second edition, 1947).

A. E. Bell, *Christian Huygens and the Development of Science in the Seventeenth Century* (1947).

Brahe, Tycho, Description of his Instruments and Scientific Work, as given in *Astronomiæ Instauratæ Mechanica* (Wandesburgi, 1598). Ed. and tr. Ræder and Strömgren (Copenhagen, 1946).

F. J. Britten, *Watch and Clockmakers' Handbook, Dictionary, and Guide* (1884).

F. J. Britten, *Old Clocks and Watches and their Makers* (sixth edition, 1932).

D. de Carle, *British Time* (1947).

H. Cescinsky and M. R. Webster, *English Domestic Clocks* (1913).

H. Cescinsky, *The Old English Master Clockmakers and their Clocks* (1938).

J. Charles Cox, *English Church Fittings, Furniture and Accessories* (1923).

W. D[erham], *The Artificial Clockmaker* (second edition, 1700).

N. V. Dinsdale, *The Old Clockmakers of Yorkshire* (1946).

G. F. C. Gordon, *Clockmaking: Past and Present* (1928).

Sir George Grove, *Dictionary of Music and Musicians* (1900).

R. T. Gunther, *Early Science in Oxford*, vols. 6 and 7 (14 vols., 1923–1945).

J. Eric Haswell, *Horology* (1947).

Arthur J. Hawkes, *The Clockmakers and Watchmakers of Wigan, 1650–1850* (1950).

Arthur Hayden, *Chats on Old Clocks* (1920).

W. Carew Hazlitt, *The Livery Companies of the City of London* (1892).

R. Noel Hill, *Early British Clocks* (The *Connoisseur* Booklets, 1948).

Robert Hooke, *The Diary*, 1672–1680 (Edited H. W. Robinson and W. Adams, 1935).

W. E. Hurcomb, *The Wetherfield Collection of Clocks* (1928).

Christian Huygens de Zuylichem, *Horologium Oscillatorium* (Paris, 1673).

Francis Lenygon, *Furniture in England, 1660–1760* (1914).

Fredk. Litchfield, *Illustrated History of Furniture* (1903).
H. Alan Lloyd, *The English Domestic Clock: Its Evolution and History* (1938).
Willis I. Milham, *Time and Timekeepers* (1923).
S. E. Atkins and W. H. Overall, *Some Account of the Worshipful Company of Clockmakers of the City of London* (1881).
T. E. R. Phillips (Editor), *Splendour of the Heavens* (Hutchinson).
J. Drummond Robertson, *The Evolution of Clockwork* (1931).
Dr. Oskar Seyffert (Edited Nettleship and Sandys), *Dictionary of Classical Antiquities* (1894).
J. S[mith], *Horological Dialogues* (1675). (The first English book about Clocks.)
J. S[mith], *Horological Disquisitions Concerning the Nature of Time* (1694).
Royal Society of London: *Philosophical Transactions and Collections* (Abridgment by John Lowthorp and others), fifth edition, London, 1749.
R. W. Symonds, *The Present State of Old English Furniture* (1927).
R. W. Symonds, *A History of English Clocks* (1947).
R. W. Symonds, *Masterpieces of English Furniture and Clocks* (1940).
Kenneth Ullyett, *British Clocks and Clockmakers* (1947).
E. J. Wood, *Curiosities of Clocks and Watches* (1866).

Finally, if any justification is required for the inclusion of the Glossary of Technical Terms in a work which is, perhaps, mainly antiquarian in its interest, such justification cannot be more succinctly supplied than by a quotation from the delightful *Artificial Clockmaker* of Dr. William Derham (second edition, 1700).

Writing " Of the Terms of Art, or Names by which the parts of an AUTOMATON are called," he quaintly observes:

" It is necessary that I should shew the meaning of the Terms which Clock-makers use, that Gentlemen and others, unskilled in the Art, may know how to express themselves properly, in speaking; and also understand what I shall say in the following Book."

Quotations from early writers on Horology have been freely drawn upon in the following pages: In addition to the often very astute and apposite comments of these old authors, their style of expression is frequently remarkable for its freshness and grace in an age not notable for either of these old-fashioned qualities.

E. L. E. 1951

Introduction

So far as I am aware—and I do not claim that my research has been exhaustive—there are no works in existence which deal exclusively with the long-case clock, or "Grandfather" clock as it is more usually termed. In many otherwise excellent horological studies, detailed observations on the long-case clock have had to be curtailed to suit the limits of a normal volume; as a result it has become somewhat inconvenient and expensive to gather together the informative opinions which have been offered about our particular subject. I trust that my modest contribution will help to remedy this state of affairs.

This work is written primarily for the reader with little previous knowledge of horology, and he should find slight difficulty in understanding the initial technicalities, which are simple as compared with the intricacies of radio or the internal combustion engine. For the possessor of one of these fine old clocks I have included a section devoted to the consideration of elementary clockwork, in order that the subject may be studied with considerably increased pleasure and interest.

Particulars of dates, ascriptions of the various inventions, and so on, vary in different authors, and an endeavour is here made to balance the available evidence, in order to arrive at a reasonably correct conclusion. Where I have deemed it advisable, I have included reasons for considering my conclusions those most likely to be free from error. I have not accepted any assertion by previous writers of modern horological works without first checking (wherever possible) the sources of their information. This is mostly derived from early writings such as Huygens' *Horologium Oscillatorium* (1673); Smith's *Horological Dialogues* (1675); the same author's *Horological Disquisitions Concerning the Nature of Time* (1694); Derham's *Artificial Clockmaker* (first edition, 1696, second edition, 1700); and the Diary of Robert Hooke (1672–1680), all of which I have consulted for purposes of verification as well as for those of a more general nature. Dates of inventions and modifications are of primary importance to the antiquary, dealer, collector and auctioneer in determining as accurately as possible, the age and value of any particular grandfather clock, and they are of great help in detecting forgeries and additions or alterations. The rather patent anachronism displayed by fitting a pair of late hands to an early dial is an obvious instance where a knowledge of chronology is useful; there are other somewhat less obvious changes requiring a deeper insight if they are to be quickly and easily perceived.

I recall an instance of a long-case clock with a brass dial, a movement of eight-day duration between windings, and fitted with both hour and minute hands. The dial, an early one of small size, was marked at quarter-hour intervals and engraved with fleur-de-lys to indicate the half-hours, as was customary on early dials. The suspicious factor and, to me, conclusive evidence of alteration, was that *there were no minute marks or numbering*, even though a minute hand was fitted. The only clocks which lacked minute marks were those of thirty-hour duration and they were not fitted with minute hands, in consequence of being without the appropriate mechanism. It was obvious that at some time the eight-day movement, with its hour and minute hands, had been substituted for the original thirty-hour one-hand movement. An examination of the back of the dial revealed marks where the pillars had been altered to fit the pillar-holes in the front plate. Together with other indications, this was ample proof of substitution.

The moral of this anecdote is that the alteration, quite apart from its arrant vandalism, had in no way improved the clock, nor increased its value as a possession. On the contrary, it had very much spoiled and depreciated the piece. In its original state, its fine slender oak case, with a long trunk-door into which was set a "bull's-eye" of convex green-coloured glass, its pretty canopied hood and its quaint movement with a single hand, made the clock an interesting and artistic possession, if not particularly valuable. The unsympathetic conversion had robbed it of all its charm and originality and had turned it into a commonplace affair which would be ignored by a knowledgeable collector or dealer.

Let it not be believed that the only fine clocks are those which bear the names of Thomas Tompion, Joseph Knibb or Daniel Quare. Though most of their productions were undoubtedly excellent, it is true to say that they held no such monopoly of skill and craftsmanship as would entitle their clocks to be regarded as so infinitely superior to others. On the other hand, it must be confessed that an honoured place in the home is frequently given to poor-looking and ill-made time-pieces. In some instances this may be due to sentiment, but in most cases I believe that it is the result of a lack of discrimination. Once a really fine clock has been duly appreciated, it is surprising how intolerant one becomes of others.

The value of a long-case clock is not necessarily determined by its age. Without doubt, the productions of the seventeenth and early eighteenth centuries were, for the greater part, of a very high standard and a really bad one was rare; but no one can dispute that many a clock was made, for instance, *circa* 1770, whose every detail is as well finished as in any made a century before. Preference for different designs of dials and cases is largely a question of taste, and if we prefer a certain clock of, say, 1775 to another of 1675, we are not necessarily showing " bad " taste. When we consider the movement itself, we must admit at once that the earlier clocks were generally superior in finish, often bearing delightfully decorative pillars, hammer tails and springs, ratchet clicks, pendulum cocks, and so on. The early craftsman evidently loved his handiwork and joyed in the creation of an artistic *tour-de-force.* On the other hand, the later wheel-work is usually cut more accurately, for the earliest teeth were sometimes hand-cut, and in any case, the early wheel-cutting machine appears crude in comparison with those later evolved. Although ornamentation is omitted, the later movements by good makers are not generally lacking in finish of a less exuberant kind. Naturally, improvements were also made in other directions.

After about 1780, a definite retrogression began in the making of the long-case clock. First the dial of sheet-iron appeared, painted or enamelled; then (in some districts particularly) the design of the clock-case deteriorated into a monstrosity of extreme width and general heaviness of effect. The movements became more standardized and the old artistry gradually disappeared so that by the opening years of the nineteenth century, it had vanished for ever in most districts and, to all intents and purposes, artistic clock-making was dead in England. The extinction of this painstaking art has been attributed by the late Mr. G. F. C. Gordon[1] to the growth of industry during the nineteenth century and to foreign competition, doubtless consequent upon our decreasing insularity.

---

[1] *Clockmaking, Past and Present,* by G. F. C. Gordon.

Chapter One

The Precursors of the Long-Case Clock

ANCIENT HOROLOGY

PRIMITIVE MAN, and societies of a savage or backward state, doubt-less desired no other measurement of time than that afforded by sunrise and sunset, the meridian position (or greatest height above the horizon attained by the sun) marking the mid-day.

In the course of the centuries, however, an observation of the apparent motion of the sun would suggest the application of the knowledge so obtained to provide some simple instrument capable of determining equal divisions of the day by recording the progression of the shadow of some object exposed to the sun's rays.

We thus have the conception of a sundial of sorts, which was probably the first recording instrument to be used.

Perhaps the earliest reference to a sundial is that in Isaiah xxxviii, 8: " Behold, I will bring again the shadow of the degrees, which is gone down in the sundial of Ahaz, ten degrees backward." This has been attributed by one authority to about 700 B.C.

The use of the Gnomon (the Greek name for a sundial, meaning " an interpreter ") in Greece is said to date from the time of Anaximenes, about 500 B.C.

The first used in Rome (called *solarium*) according to Seyffert, was brought from Catana in Sicily in 263 B.C. A sundial properly adapted to the latitude of Rome was constructed in 164 B.C., and from this date the *solarium* was the normal means by which legislation and all private business was regulated.

There is little doubt that the popularity of the sundial in various improved forms (including portable or pocket dials) lasted well into the seventeenth century. The early mechanical clocks were extremely expensive productions, beyond the means of any but the most affluent members of the

22

community. A few early lantern clocks have been discovered to have doors made from sundial plates, suggesting that about 1630 the makers of sundials were beginning to turn their attention to the new horology.

Of almost equal antiquity to sundials are clepsydræ, or water-clocks.

The name is derived from two Greek words meaning respectively, " to steal " and " water ", doubtless suggested by the gradual " stealing away " of the water contained by the instrument.

Early clepsydræ appear to have been simply globular vessels of known capacity with short, narrow necks, several very small holes being bored into their under surfaces to allow the gradual escape of the water. They would seem to have been adversely affected as regards constancy of period by (a) Temperature, (b) Barometric pressure, and (c) lowered pressure (and therefore less flow) as the water-level in the vessel declined.

The last objection was eventually overcome by keeping the water-level constant in the clepsydra and measuring the volume of water discharged from the device.

Clepsydræ were used in Athenian law-courts to measure the speaker's allotted time. In Roman courts the same use was assigned them. Their appearance in Rome, according to one authority,[1] dated from 159 B.C.

It is said that Ctesibius of Alexandria (who also constructed an hydraulic organ) made a clepsydra about 135 B.C. in which the hours were indicated by the ascent of a little figure pointing to the divisions of a calibrated rod, the rise of the water-level lifting a float to which the index-marker was attached.

Clepsydræ were made until nearly the end of the seventeenth century, perhaps even later in some instances. Britten (*Old Clocks and Watches*) illustrates a fine one made in 1682. It has a 24-hour dial sub-divided into halves and quarters, and the usual single hand found on early lantern clocks, with a counterpoise. An inner circle of the dial exhibits the signs of the Zodiac. A float operates in a brass cylinder attached to the wooden frame-work of the timepiece, to the base of which cylinder is affixed a tap regulating the drip of water therefrom. As the float descends it draws with it a chain passing over a toothed wheel to which the hand is directly attached. At the base of the instrument is a brass plate engraved " John Banks of ye towne Chester Anno Dom 1682." Britten gives its total height as 33 inches.

---

[1] Seyffert: *Dictionary of Classical Antiquities.*

Such examples are extremely rare, as the gradual introduction of mechanical clocks resulted in the eventual destruction of most of these interesting survivals of an ancient system.

Another device of considerable antiquity concerned with the measurement of time is exemplified by the familiar " hour-glass " or " sand-glass " These were often made in sets of three or four, held together in one frame, this framework being frequently more or less elaborately ornamented.

According to Britten, sand-glasses, or " clepsammia " date from about the end of the eight century.

Church sand-glasses, used for timing a sermon, and held in decorated iron frames affixed near the pulpit, are illustrated in the Rev. Dr. C. Cox's *English Church Fittings, Furniture and Accessories* (Batsford, 1923). Several very interesting examples of the seventeenth and eighteenth centuries are shown, including some designed as sets, in one frame, and having differing periods, as 15 minutes, 30 minutes, one hour, and so on.

MEDIÆVAL HOROLOGY

The introduction of mechanical clocks, driven by weights as the source of power, may be ascribed to a very early period. These machines, almost without exception, were what we should now designate " public clocks ", i.e., they were intended for such buildings as churches and cathedrals, or occasionally for a college or local government building, such as a town hall. Their position, often in the tower of a church or similar edifice, has led to their being universally described as " turret clocks ".

The domestic clock, of course, was not provided until very much later, certainly not earlier than the sixteenth century, and then but rarely.

At a period when, as the late Dr. Eaglefield Hull aptly expressed it,[1] " all the art and science of the age was centred in the monk's cell ", it was perhaps to be expected that these same monks should be among the earliest artificers concerned in the erection of " horologia ".

The use of this term has occasioned some confusion, and it may be here stated that when we read in some early chronicle (or extract from such) of a " horologium " we are to understand that this expression was invariably used

---

[1] *Organ Playing: Its Technique and Expression.*

by the monkish brethren to describe a time-recorder *of any kind*. Thus, a sundial, a clepsydra, an hour-glass, and a mechanical clock or timepiece driven by the fall of weights would all be designated " horologia ". Note too that no distinction in nomenclature was accorded striking clocks sounding the hours but without dials, and mechanical timepieces indicating the hours on a visible dial, but unprovided with a striking train. All these were included in the inexplicit expression " horologia ", thus, in the absence of detailed description, we are unable to state with any degree of accuracy what the first mechanical clock was like, or when it was erected.

The subject is further complicated by the fact that some of the early clepsydræ were, surprisingly, capable of sounding the hours. Thus, the Emperor Charlemagne in 807 was presented by the King of Persia with a clepsydra so arranged, one of twelve small doors in the dial opening at the appropriate hour and allowing its corresponding number of little balls to fall consecutively upon a brass drum. Mr. D. Batigan Verne writes of a night-clock said to have been made by Plato, which, he says, was a clepsydra playing on flutes the hours of the night when the index would be invisible. Water-power was employed to actuate a bellows supplying wind to the flutes. Mr. Verne further states that even to-day musical clepsydræ are to be found in some Dutch houses.[1]

There is little doubt, however, that the weight-driven " horologium " provided with an escapement, and with or without a visible dial or striking train, was an invention dating from the " Middle Time ", and it seems reasonable to ascribe its beginnings to the sounding of a bell manually according to the hour indicated by sundial or hour-glass.

A learned Benedictine monk, by name Gerbert, who later became Pope Sylvester II, is said to have constructed a clock for the Cathedral at Magdeburg in A.D. 996. A younger contemporary says of him: " Magdeburg horologium fecit, illud recte constituens considerata per fistulam stella nautarum duce." ("He made a timepiece at Magdeburg, setting it right by looking at the North Star through a tube.")

Here, again, the " horologium " may not have been a *mechanical* clock having an escapement, as no details are given of its construction, emphasis being laid upon the astronomical observation involved in its correction.

Britten refers to a clock presented by Saladin of Egypt to Frederick II

[1] " The Water-Organ of the Ancients." (*The Organ*, Vol. II, No. 7.)

of Germany in 1232, which appears, however, from his description, to have been primarily a planetarium or orrery.[1]

The same authority considers hour-sounding to antedate the provision of dials in mechanical clocks, and mentions a clock at St. Paul's Cathedral. London, prior to 1298, with mechanical figures or " jacks " to perform the striking, known contemporaneously as " Paul's Jacks ". In 1344 the dean and chapter of the cathedral contracted with " Walter the Orgoner " of Southwark to supply and fix a dial, from which the late Mr. Britten logically infers that a previous dial did not exist. The dial was placed below the " jacks ", which continued to strike the hours as before.

There is a well-known tradition that in the reign of Edward I a corrupt Lord Chief Justice was fined the sum of 800 marks by order of the King, and the money so obtained employed to furnish a clock then placed in a tower in Palace Yard, Westminster. This would be early in the fourteenth century. The tower was apparently pulled down shortly after the middle of the seventeenth century.

Wallingford's clock is frequently referred to as the earliest known, but, as Britten remarks, this, again, was apparently merely a planetarium, without an escapement. Richard Wallingford was Abbot of St. Albans about 1326. According to Britten, the account which he himself gave of his " clock " is still preserved in the Bodleian Library at Oxford.

In most clocks constructed during the mediæval period, various puppet-like devices (jacks) were employed for striking the hours, and the mechanism was also often designed to display the phases and age of the moon (an early use of this device).[2] In even more complicated machines of rather later date, such as the successive clocks made for the cathedral of Strasbourg, culminating in the Third Clock (a reconstruction of the Second) originating from 1574, these marionette-shows reached their high-water mark of complexity and ingenuity, and, as some would have it, of futility also. For those interested in such devices, which do not come within the principal study of this work, Britten's book gives full details.

Although the majority of modern clockmakers profess contempt for what they regard as puerilities, preferring the expenditure of skill and labour to achieve greater accuracy in timekeeping, I confess to a certain

---

[1] An orrery or planetarium is a clockwork astronomical machine intended to illustrate the motion of the various planets—Earth, Moon, Mars, Venus, Saturn, etc.—round the Sun and in relation to each other, also their comparative magnitudes and distances.

[2] *See* Glossary.

sympathy with these archaic devices. It must be remembered that the Age which gave them birth was a time of change; the dark of the Middle Ages was giving place to a revival of the classic traditions of civilization and learning, and early attempts in mechanical enterprise were appearing in what was undoubtedly the first machine to give scope to such ingenuity, at a time when the principle of the Steam Engine was a far-distant discovery, and in which the achievements of modern engineering, could they have been suddenly introduced, would have been attributed to witchcraft and direct association with the Evil One, and their perpretrators probably burnt at the stake.

Then, again, we must consider the natural exuberance in the exponents of a new art, that of mechanical clockmaking, and how such would infallibly lead to rivalry, and thus to excessive elaboration in such devices which would then, as indeed they do still, invariably catch the public fancy.

A famous clock of the fourteenth century is that erected in 1370 by Henri de Wyck in a tower of the Palais de Justice, Paris. The clock has an escapement with crown wheel and vertical verge, the control being a horizontal bar with adjustable weights for regulation at each end thereof, attached to the top of the verge. This oscillating bar was known as the " foliot " (*see* Glossary—under Escapement). Both striking and going trains are provided, the striking being controlled by the early device known as a locking plate (Glossary).

HOROLOGY IN THE SIXTEENTH AND SEVENTEENTH CENTURIES

With the opening of the sixteenth century, the spring-driven table clock and the large portable clock-watch of similar construction began to appear.

Some of the table clocks of this period were enshrined in exceedingly elaborate and beautiful cases of pierced and chased brass and damascened ironwork, ornamented with a profusion of small figures and similar detail, excellently worked with file and graver. Even gold and silver were employed for inlaying, etc., in some instances combined with enamel-work of the most exquisite quality and colouring.

Nuremburg and Augsburg craftsmen produced some fine examples of early spring-driven table clocks at this period, which may be regarded as progenitors of the seventeenth-century mantel clocks.

Elaborate movements, showing various astronomical progressions in addition to the time, were not unusual in sixteenth-century clocks, cases in square or octagonal designs frequently displaying four dials. Various automata were often introduced to perform during the striking of the hours; representations of divers acts such as dancing, drinking or actually striking the hour being accomplished by the employment of little puppet-like figures, almost invariably well modelled, but with grotesque jerky movements.

The Connoisseur, No. 380, Vol. XCI (1933), contains an illustrated description by F. H. Green of a remarkable sixteenth-century clock of " lantern " type in his possession. It is a weight-driven chamber clock constructed by " N. Vallin, 1598 ", probably the same " N. V." who is recorded clockmaker to Queen Elizabeth. The maker's name and the date are engraved at the foot of the brass dial-plate. The clock is provided with balance-wheel control, minute motion-work and hand, with dial engraved accordingly, and three trains—the third for quarter-chimes on a carillon of thirteen bells. This exceptional timekeeper is possibly a unique survival. It figured in the Elizabethan Exhibition about the time of the *Connossieur* article, and was " televised " by the B.B.C.

An early chamber clock of the true " bracket " type, weight-driven, presenting a sumptuous case of copper-gilt, richly engraved and ornamented, is that at Windsor Castle, of which an illustration is given in F. J. Britten's work, *Old Clocks and Watches and their Makers*. The arms of England appear on the sides of the case, and also upon a shield held by a little figure of a lion crowning the beautifully pierced and ornamented dome.

According to Britten, the movement now in this case is not the original, but a late seventeenth-century production with a crown-wheel escapement and short " bob " pendulum. Brass wheels of the usual type are said to be in the movement, whereas in an early clock contemporary with the case the wheels would almost certainly be of iron, hammered out and fashioned by hand, as in the later Elizabethan chiming clock just described. Balance control would, of course, be used in an early movement, not a pendulum.

The clock is said to have been a present from Henry VIII of England to Anne Boleyn upon her wedding morning; if so, it dates from 1533.

The late F. J. Britten describes the weights (which are original) to be also of copper, gilt, and engraved with the initials of Henry and Anne, with lovers' knots on one weight, and on both the inscriptions *Dieu et mon Droit* and " the most happye ". The clock measures ten inches in height and is about four inches square.

Britten further records that this historic little clock was purchased on behalf of Queen Victoria for £110 5s. at the sale of the Walpole collection from Strawberry Hill. There is no maker's name upon the dial or case-work, but our authority advances the theory that it is the production of a foreign horologist, most of the clocks of this period being the work of those artists.

Examples such as have been already discussed, however, cannot be regarded as indicating that domestic clocks were at that time established articles in the ordinary, even well-to-do, household. They should be viewed, rather, as made for special purposes to order, or to gratify the skill and creative impulse of the maker himself, as the cost of such clocks must have been enormous in those distant days.

It was not until the manufacture of the weight-driven chamber clock of " lantern " type had become fairly well established that a few wealthier members of the general public became the possessors of clocks for domestic use.

Lantern clocks began to be made in fair numbers in England about 1610, or possibly a little earlier. As they are the direct lineal ancestors of the later long-case clocks, it may be well to consider them in some detail.

The lantern clock, also known as " bedpost ", " birdcage " and " Crom-wellian " clock, was the typical English chamber clock of the seventeenth century, holding this position until quite 1660, at which date the long-case clock and the spring-driven mantel clock began to dispute its supremacy.

The lantern clock, however, did not at once become superseded, and continued to be made in London until certainly the end of the century and in country districts (such as the villages of East Anglia, for example) until about 1750. These latter types were usually of somewhat different appearance from the seventeenth-century examples, and will be discussed later.

The earliest lantern clocks, and some of those made later up to about 1670, had a duration between windings of only twelve hours. Some were arranged to go for twenty-four hours without winding, and the clocks made during the last quarter of the century were almost always equipped with thirty-hour movements. I have read of a clock of this type, by the famous maker Edward East, which was constructed with an eight-day movement, but this must be regarded as an extreme rarity, and as the exception which proves the rule.[1]

The trains of a " lantern " movement are held between two upright bars, which, in turn, are fastened by top and bottom plates, these latter connected by four brass posts or columns, hence the name " bedpost " clock. The striking train is always placed *behind* the going part.

Up to about 1660, the crown-wheel escapement with vertical verge and balance-wheel control was invariably provided; after the invention of the pendulum—or rather, its application to clocks—was established in England, the escapement used was varied. It then became a crown-wheel placed horizontally as to its working plane, beneath a pallet-staff or verge also horizontal and having a short " bob " pendulum attached thereto.

With the general application of the " anchor " escapement to long-case movements (about 1675) some lantern clocks constructed after this date were made with the new escapement and a long pendulum. Many of the existing clocks with the earlier forms of crown-wheel escapement were unfortunately converted to this anchor pattern during the course of the eighteenth century; what is less understandable is that even to-day the practice is not extinct in connection with the steadily dwindling numbers of crown escapements left to us. In particular, it is a matter for the most profound regret that rare examples of the early balance control should be mutilated in this unthinking manner. Very seldom is an old English movement in such a parlous state that a conversion of this nature is a necessity, and the change robs the piece of practically all its considerable antiquarian interest and value.

A few words may not be amiss here as to the recognition of converted examples. In so far as the very early " lanterns " are concerned—those made between, say, 1600 and 1660—the conversions are from balance control to either " bob " pendulum and horizontal crown-wheel or to the anchor escapement with longer pendulum. The latter form of alteration is the easier effected and, unfortunately for antiquarians, probably most often found. The conversion of balance to anchor-escapement clocks was often

[1] This clock is illustrated by H. Cescinsky and M. R. Webster in their book *English Domestic Clocks* (1913).

done in quite early times, even before 1700, the very bad timekeeping qualities of the balance becoming more obvious with the introduction of the much superior anchor escapement.

In all the early clocks with balance control the hammer position is on the *right* of the movement, viewed from a position in front of the dial. Later lantern clocks with pendulums have the striking-hammer placed to the *left*, as in normal eight-day long-case movements of later times. The position of the early striking-hammers in lantern clocks is thus similar to that exemplified by thirty-hour plate-frame movements of the eighteenth century.

The reason for the right-hand position of the hammer may thus be explained:

The main wheel of the clock *has* to turn " anti-clockwise ", so that its pinion may drive the hour-wheel clockwise. The early clocks had a separate rope and driving-weight for each train—" going " and " striking ". The driving-weight for the going train therefore hangs to the *left* of the clock's " centre line ", since it pulls round the main wheel " anti-clockwise ", as stated. Now, in addition to preserving a symmetrical appearance, the balance of the clock, as it hangs from the wall, must be considered. This would be very seriously disturbed if *both* weights were to hang on the same side,[1] so the driving-weight for the striking train is arranged to hang on the opposite side of the middle line, and the " great " wheel is therefore turned " clockwise ". A clockwise-turning great wheel (combining as it does the " pin-wheel " of the movement) would present a certain awkwardness of arrangement with a left-hand hammer, so the latter is placed to the right of the movement, where its " tail " is convenient to the clockwise-turning pins in the rim of the great wheel.

After about 1670, although Christian Huygens (of whom more will be written later) introduced his " endless rope " arrangement, with a single weight for *both* trains in 1658, the main and great wheels were made to turn in the same direction (anti-clockwise) and the hammer then moved to the left of the movement. Some lantern clocks made before this date with the crown-wheel and short " bob " pendulum, and therefore between *circa* 1660 and *circa* 1670 in approximate period, exemplify the right-hand hammer and separately driven trains.

---

[1] Additionally, the two weights would certainly foul each other, both in winding and in " going " and striking.

It should be noticed, when examining a converted movement that it bears evidence of the change in the very usual retention of the bridge (through which passed the original verge on its way up through the top-plate) attached to the middle bar. The original crown escape-wheel arbor had its inner pivot in this bridge, and when the crown-wheel and its arbor were removed, and a new arbor substituted, bearing an escapement of the new type, this too was arranged so as to utilize the old bridge for a pivot-bearing. A specially designed escapement of the anchor type for a lantern clock would have no such bridge, and the 'scape-wheel arbor would therefore be somewhat longer, and pivoted directly into front and middle bars. Below the bridge, again in the middle bar, will be noted either the foot-cock of the original vertical verge, or holes denoting its removal. The top-plate of the movement will also show some superficially mysterious holes where the upper bracket (or " top-cock ") for the verge has once been attached.

In addition to evidence presented by the foregoing details, it should also be noticed that in clocks before the application of the previously mentioned Huygens system of endless rope (or chain) the main and great wheels have " clicks " provided *for each*. After the general adoption of the Huygens system—which, by the way, incorporated a simple and very effective " maintaining-power "—only the great pulley (that of the striking train) bears a click; the main pulley (" going " part) being immovably attached to its wheel. If a clock is being examined which bears all the evidence of conversion mentioned earlier, but which, instead of the usual rope-pulleys, has chains, and pulleys designed accordingly (for the difference in construction *see* Pulleys—in Glossary), then the latter are also substitutions of a later date.

A converted clock, originally made by William Almond, London, *circa* 1640, which I have seen, has its main-wheel " click " removed, and the pulley fastened to the wheel. Chain pulleys have been fitted and also an *endless* chain on the Huygens system. This conversion may be easily recognized, when encountered, by noticing that the *left-hand* rear portion of the chain is that pulled down to wind up the single weight, whereas in original construction, using this method, it is the *right-hand* rear part of the chain or rope which is used for the same purpose. In the instance above, the operation has to be reversed because, when striking, the " great " wheel of the original movement turns clockwise.

PLATE I

PLATE 2

Plate 1

THIRTY-HOUR STRIKING LANTERN CLOCK
WILLIAM COWARD, LONDON, *circa* 1685

Plate 2

MOVEMENT OF CLOCK BY WILLIAM COWARD

See page 211

Plate 3

SMALL THIRTY-HOUR LANTERN CLOCK
WITH ALARUM. ANONYMOUS, *circa* 1710

Plate 4

MOVEMENT OF SMALL ALARUM LANTERN
CLOCK

See page 211

PLATE 5

THIRTY-HOUR FRIESIAN CLOCK WITH
ALARUM. DUTCH, EARLY EIGHTEENTH
CENTURY

See page 212

PLATE 6

THIRTY-HOUR STRIKING AND CHIMING
LANTERN CLOCK. HENTON BROWN,
LONDON, *circa* 1740

See page 213

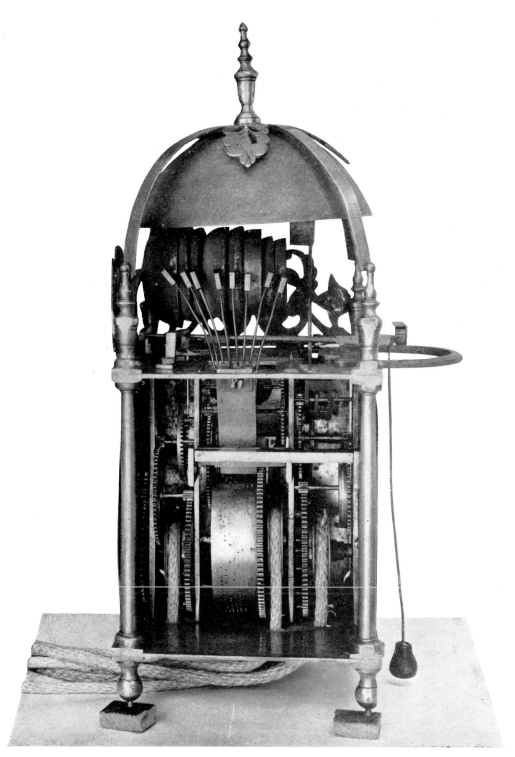

PLATE 7

MOVEMENT OF CLOCK BY HENTON BROWN

See page 213

PLATE 8

THIRTY-HOUR QUARTER-STRIKING
MURAL CLOCK WITH ALARUM
DUTCH, *circa* 1760

See page 214

PLATE 9

MOVEMENT OF QUARTER-STRIKING DUTCH
CLOCK
(THE DIAL-PLATE SHOWN PART-LENGTH)

See page 214

PLATE 10

SMALL THIRTY-HOUR HOODED CLOCK
EDWARD RUSSELL, CATTON, *circa* 1790

See page 217

PLATE 11

DIAL OF CLOCK BY EDWARD RUSSELL

See page 217

Plate 12

MOVEMENT OF CLOCK BY EDWARD RUSSELL

See page 217

PLATE 13
THE AUTHOR

Plate 15

Plate 14

Plate 14

EIGHT-DAY STRIKING CLOCK BY PETER
WALKER, LONDON, *circa* 1690

Plate 15

OPENED TRUNK DOOR OF CLOCK BY PETER
WALKER SHOWS HOLES IN BACKBOARD,
THE PENDULUM AND OLD BRASS-CASED
DRIVING WEIGHTS

See page 221

PLATE 16

EIGHT-DAY STRIKING CLOCK
ROBERT CLEMENT, LONDON, *circa* 1690

See page 223

PLATE 17

DETAILS OF INLAY ON TRUNK DOOR
CLOCK BY ROBERT CLEMENT

See page 223

PLATE 18

DIAL AND HOOD OF CLOCK BY ROBERT
CLEMENT

See page 223

PLATE 19

DIAL OF MONTH STRIKING CLOCK WITH $1\frac{1}{4}$
SECONDS PENDULUM. ABRAHAM FARRER,
PONTEFRACT, *circa* 1695

See page 226

PLATE 20

MOVEMENT OF MONTH CLOCK BY ABRAHAM
FARRER

See page 226

Further, it should be observed that in a converted clock of originally early date, *circa* 1600–1625 (and even in many later clocks up to *circa* 1675 of provincial make), the original arbors are *tapered* from the wheels, entering the latter without brass collets, being " squared " for the reception of the wheels and the latter riveted; and that the new arbor for the different form of 'scape-wheel has a collet provided; also that it is not usually tapered, but parallel throughout its length. The form of collet employed gives us an approximate period for the conversion; the early collets were D-shaped, or rounded, and the later type square-cut or " cheese-headed ". Thus an early conversion, say about 1680, of a balance-control clock of *circa* 1620, would be indicated by a sometimes tapered 'scape-wheel arbor with D-shape brass collet, and an eighteenth-century conversion by an always parallel arbor with cheese-head collet.

Finally, it should be noticed that in early lantern clocks having had the balance form of regulator the main arbor, where it projects from the front bar, has usually a pinion of four " leaves " formed by filing-up the extremity into " pins " which thus drive the hour wheel. The same procedure is adopted for the arbor of the great wheel, where it projects through the rearmost bar. Later clocks have higher-numbered pinions in these positions, the arbors being squared to receive them.

The backplates of early lantern clocks were of iron, not of brass like the sideplates or doors. To these iron backplates were attached the " spurs " or spikes to be referred to later. The later crown escapements with short pendulums rendered the position of these spurs unsuitable, as the pendulum would not have free play during its wide arc. The spurs were therefore moved to the position shown in Plate 4, screwed into the back pair of feet, where they do not foul the pendulum. As with the very much decreased arc of the anchor type of escapement, together with a longer pendulum, these old-type spurs would not be likely to interfere in this respect; it is rather curious to note the almost invariable absence of the original backplates and their spurs from converted clocks. The iron loop or stirrup which was used in conjunction with the spurs is, however, always in evidence, affixed to the upper surface of the top-plate and projecting rearwards.

I have lately examined several lantern clocks for evidence of conversion, and in all of these I have found the above series of " clues " as to alteration. Of those examined, two examples may be cited as instances—

C

one "William Almond, in Lothbury, fecit" (*circa* 1640) and another by William Holloway, Stroud (dated on dial 1675). We have here, therefore, a fairly early and a distinctly late example of balance clocks which have been converted for the sake of better timekeeping, both in all probability at such a comparatively early date that the antiquarian interest and value of their original form of escapement would then be inconsiderable.

Of the quite indefensible practice (now happily becoming less common) of "gutting" a lantern clock and inserting a modern eight-day spring movement, usually of the cheapest description, it should be unnecessary to remark. A more complete degradation of a fine old clock would be almost impossible to conceive.

The bell surmounting the clock was normally provided for sounding the hours, but was occasionally utilized for an alarm. After about the middle of the seventeenth century, the dial was made larger, and projected somewhat on each side of the clock case. The early dials had narrow silvered chapter rings with short, stumpy chapters; after about 1650 the Roman numerals were made longer.

An alarm disc occupies the dial centre in those clocks fitted with an alarum device, which consists of a vertical crown wheel riding upon a stud which also carries the spiked chain pulley. Connection between pulley and crown wheel is effected by the usual "click" to allow winding up of the alarm weight. The crown wheel operates the pallets of a vertical verge, a hammer of special shape being fixed at the top of the verge, which hammer vibrates rapidly against alternate inner surfaces of the bell with the fall of the alarm weight.

The method of setting the alarm is to bring the appropriate hour marked on the disc under the counterpoise of the hand, which acts as a pointer. Provided the interval before the alarm is required is less than twelve hours, the weight can then be wound up, and the device is ready for operation at the time set. After the alarm has been sounded, re-setting of the disc is unnecessary for a repetition of the warning at the same hour the following day, but the weight must not be wound up until within twelve hours of the time at which the alarm is required.

The alarm disc turns with the hour wheel, by spring-controlled friction contact, which causes a pin fixed in one arm of the friction-spring to engage a lever at the forward end of a square arbor passing from front to back of the movement. This lever is thus lifted at the hour set upon the dial disc, raising a second lever at the rear end of the arbor, which latter lever unlocks the alarm by being removed from contact with a pin set in the outer rim of the crown wheel.

Some lantern clocks are provided with the before-mentioned spikes or spurs screwed into the back pair of feet, or (earlier) attached to an iron backplate, and projecting rearward at right angles to the latter. Such clocks also have a loop or stirrup behind the movement, at the top of the clock, or the top plate is extended backward for the same purpose. The intention of these attachments was to allow the clock to be hung from a wall in the absence of a suitable bracket; the spurs fitting into small shallow holes made for them in the wall would prevent its moving laterally. Such fittings to a lantern clock do not, of course, preclude its being placed upon a bracket in the manner usual at a later date.

Occasionally, the pendulum is situated in the middle of the clock, between the two trains of wheels. In these instances, the side doors of the case have slots in them through which the pendulum " bobs " in and out. Britten suggests that the short " bob " pendulum used with the crown-wheel escapement was so called because of this alternate appearance at each side of the clock. In this I think him mistaken, as the term " bob pendulum " probably originated later, when the heavier elliptical " disc " became general, replacing the light pear-shaped weights of the earlier pendulums, which thus became known as " bob " pendulums for distinction.[1] In connection with the middle position of the pendulum are the somewhat rare " wings " or extensions to the case sometimes seen on lantern clocks, enclosing the pendulum during the whole of its progress to right and left of the middle line, and provided with glass or horn windows through which the " bob " can be seen alternately. To certify its appearance the pendulum bob was then made with " flukes " like an anchor, instead of in the more usual pear-shaped form.

A still more unusual position for the pendulum is in front of the dial, sometimes operating a moving figure at the top of the clock. Britten illustrates one such which has the silhouette of a snipe or similar bird arranged to rock with the vibrations of the pendulum.

In most instances where the crown wheel escapement is used, the pendulum of a lantern clock is directly attached to the pallet-staff, without

---

[1] " The *Ball* in long Pendulums, the *Bob* in short ones, is the Weight at the bottom " (Derham, *The Artificial Clockmaker*, 1700).

a crutch, as in the small clock shown in Plate 4. This, however, is not invariable, the larger clock illustrated in Plate 2 being provided with a small crutch and a little suspension spring, both of which are undoubtedly original.

It is strange that the crutch, with independent suspension for the pendulum, was not generally employed earlier than seems the case. Huygens used the crutch from the beginning (1657) as has been proved by J. Drummond Robertson's finding an original clock made by Samuel Coster under patent rights provided by Huygens. This clock (a spring-driven example) was, according to Mr. Robertson, inscribed " Samuel Coster, Haghe, met privilege 1657 " [1] and had a horizontal verge with crown wheel and pendulum suspension by a double thread from a cock, " to which are attached curved cheeks, but these were not yet cycloidal " (Robertson). A wire crutch was employed in this clock, exactly as used more generally at a later period in England.

Lantern clocks were usually made with but one hand, a stout, counter-poised hour-hand, the dials being destitute of minute markings. Except in the very early examples, it was usual to engrave the chapter ring with some such ornament as a cross, diamond, fleur-de-lys, or similar device to indicate half-hours, and short lines dividing the space between two concentric circles enabled the quarters to be also displayed upon the inner edge of the chapter ring.

Very occasionally, clocks with original minute hand and corre-sponding engraving of the hour-circle are to be seen, but these are exceptional.

Minute hands, with the necessary motion-work added to the mechanism, are frequently to be found in clocks which were originally made with a single indicator. In these instances the added hand is betrayed by the lack of complementary engraving on the dial.

In the clock illustrated by Plate 1, a very pretty pair of hands, typical of the late seventeenth century, and obviously dating from the same period as the remainder of the clock, combine with apparently original dial-wheels to give an appearance of complete authenticity to the piece. Here again, however, the chapter ring of the dial is innocent of minute-markings, so we may conclude that the hands are later additions, replacing the original single indicator.

---

[1] A photograph of a later clock gives the name as SALOMON Coster. (A. E. Bell.)

This conclusion is supported by a close examination of the minute-hand. This has had a portion of its length nipped off in order that it may "fit" the dial better. The shortening has disturbed the proportion of the hand somewhat, the decorative part now being relatively too extensive compared with the plain portion. The hour indicator, though not original, has not required this rather clumsy method of adaptation.

The very handsome driving-weight and its pulley should be noted (Plate 1).

The little clock, of which a photograph is given in Plate 4, shows the later-type spurs for attaching to a wall. In this photograph, and also in Plates 2 and 7, the side doors of the clocks have been removed to display the movements. Plate 4 illustrates the vertical crown wheel and verge for the operation of the alarm; this arrangement of an escapement is precisely similar to that employed in the going train of a balance-controlled lantern clock. In this instance, however, the circular balance-wheel is replaced by the hammer, and the operation of the verge is very much faster.

Lantern clocks of early construction and, indeed, those made until nearly the end of the seventeenth century, particularly by the London makers, were almost always excellently "finished". The dials were generally engraved, often with the Tudor or Stuart Rose device, frequently varied or accompanied by the popular tulip decoration, as in the clocks illustrated in Plates 1 and 6. In some of the earlier clocks, the side doors of the case were also more or less elaborately engraved, perhaps according to the taste of the customer; Britten illustrates one made in 1623 by William Bowyer which has a somewhat gruesome engraving of a skeleton upon one door, representing Death, on the other is etched the figure of Time with his scythe and hour-glass, both doors also bearing appropriate inscriptions.

A later example (*circa* 1740) of a clock having engraved tulip decoration on the dial, together with engraving of the side doors, is presented by the Henton Brown clock, illustrated in Plate 6.

The brass pillars connecting top and bottom plates of a lantern movement are terminated at their bases by little turned feet, and finished at their upper extremities by spires also ornamentally turned. In many instances these brass spires and feet are made to screw off, thus facilitating the dismantling of the clock for cleaning.

Between the spires at front and sides of the clock it was usual to provide a pierced brass decoration known as a " fret ", that at the front being also adorned with some slight chasing.

As various patterns of " frets " are said to have been popular at different periods (and also in differing localities) it has been usual to regard these ornaments as supplying an approximate date for any particular clock, sometimes also as indicating roughly its district of origin.

I am not inclined to put my trust in this consideration, chronologically, but will agree that, in conjunction with other features, the frets may help slightly in fixing a probable place or county of manufacture. To make this point clear: certain frets are regarded as " late ", but if I were to see a clock with balance-wheel control ornamented with these " late " frets (should all be obviously original) and had I previously formed any opinions tending to confirm the frets as late, I would then immediately revise such opinions.

As previously noted, the single heavily made hand with counterpoise was used on all the earliest chamber clocks, and the first lantern clocks were provided with a hand very simple in outline, consisting merely of an arrow-headed indicator very substantially constructed and lacking anything in the nature of the elaborate pierced and filed decoration exemplified by the beautiful long-case clock hands of 1690–1740.

As time went on, however, the hands of lantern clocks became less crude in outline and somewhat greater enterprise was evinced in the decoration of the " heart ", which now displayed simple but tasteful pierced designs, similar to the " replacement " hour-hand on the clock illustrated in Plate 1, and already discussed.

The small lantern clock shown in Plate 3 has a single hand with rather unusual style of decoration.

In all lantern clocks with an hour-hand only (which includes the great majority) the hand must of necessity be stoutly constructed to withstand the quite considerable strain imposed when the hand is turned by the fingers to reset the time. In this connection, the counterpoise, besides acting as an indicator for the alarm disc (when this is present) is useful as affording a projection for the thumb, facilitating the controlled turning of a rather stiff hand.

Mr. G. F. C. Gordon (*Clockmaking: Past and Present*) suggests that as the possession of mechanical clocks became more and more within the means of the less wealthy, the fine engraving and high finish of lantern clocks was modified or omitted to lessen the cost, which seems a reasonable supposition. Mr. Gordon's estimate of the class of person on whom fine engraving, etc., would be " lost " is rather amusing; no doubt appreciation of such work would be more restricted 250 years ago than it is to-day, when the general culture of the masses and the artistry of the craftsman are in inverse ratio.

Plates 1, 3 and 6 illustrate lantern clocks standing in going order upon their oaken brackets.

As we have seen, chiming movements for lantern-type clocks were not unknown at the end of the sixteenth century in exceptional instances such as the clock by N. Vallin previously mentioned. A rather late but beautiful example is illustrated (Plates 6 and 7) in the clock by Henton Brown, London, *circa* 1740.

That such elaboration should be accorded the lantern movement and form at a period so comparatively late seems to suggest that in the face of its obvious disadvantages, the true lantern clock still held the affection of many people, and this, too, in the metropolis itself, not only in the provinces. The Henton Brown clock, of course, may have been made to the special order of a country customer, who, however, ordered his clock from a London maker, and therefore was likely to be cognizant of the fashion for clocks of different form.

A new variety of the weight-driven chamber clock, supported by a bracket, or hung from the wall, and provided with a lantern movement true to type, was introduced during the early years of the eighteenth century.

These clocks were known as "sheepsheads" and differed from the earlier form of lantern clock in the shape of dial employed. The "sheepshead" clock had a square dial with arched top, exactly similar to many long-case dials, but smaller. Minute motion-work with corresponding minute-hand and dials engraved accordingly were almost invariably provided. The side frets, doors, and turned decorative spires were all retained.

The great weakness of the lantern clock is its liability to become filled with dust, the case being not at all proof against its ingress. This susceptibility led to the brackets being provided with canopies, often curved to fit closely over the bell, the central spire of the clock being sometimes removed and replaced by a simple nut to enable the canopy to be fixed lower.

It will be appreciated that it was but a step from the canopied bracket to total enclosure in a wooden hood, the brass doors to the movement being dispensed with, together with the frets, spires and other decorative features, and the dial made larger to fit a square aperture at the front of the case. Thus we have the emergence of the mural clock, still with lantern movement, crown-wheel escapement and short " bob " pendulum. *See* Plate 10 (plate-frame movement).

As the mural or wall-clock was the development of the original hood-protected chamber clock of pure " lantern " type, so the early long-case clocks (now popularly designated " grandfather " clocks) would without doubt be evolved from the hooded mural clock.

The appearance of the weights or weight, together with the chain or rope with its pulley, hanging below the case of the mural clock would in time irresistibly suggest their total enclosure in a long case to some progressive minds, and thus we arrive, at last, at the principal subject of this book, that typically English horological production of the eighteenth century, the Long-case clock.

Before proceeding with our chief study, however, and dismissing further consideration of its precursors, we must observe that the mural clock continued to exist coeval with its later development, in both thirty-hour and eight-day forms, and latterly with the plate-frame movement up to about 1790, with a revival for a particular purpose in 1797, when the " Act of Parliament " clock was brought into being. Further, from time to time during the course of the eighteenth century, weight-driven wall-clocks with encased long pendulums in elaborate cases, often with lacquer decoration, were made, but not, apparently, in very great numbers, since they are now comparatively rare. See the example shown by Plates 8 and 9 which, however, is a Dutch clock, and as such not nearly so unusual in Holland as similar timekeepers were then in England. This is explained by the Dutchman's partiality for wall-clocks, evinced over a long period.

Chapter Two

Early Long-Case Clocks, 1660-1740

I AM not convinced that anyone can establish a definite date for the introduction of the long-case clock. Very different ideas in the matter exist.

For instance, we find W. C. Hazlitt in his book, *The Livery Companies
of the City of London* (1892), under "The Clockmakers," writing thus:

"When the Clockmakers' Company was constituted, in 1631, the
science had already made very considerable progress, and the Coffin-Clock
was an established fact *of some standing*." The italics are mine. Mr.
Hazlitt proceeds:

"The earliest manufactures of this type were, no doubt, tentative in
their construction, and destitute of external embellishment; and the richly
decorated cases, which are to be seen in European museums, belong to a
later period. The extensive employment of wood for the coffin-clock
brought the Blacksmiths into contact with the Woodmongers. . . ."

Mr. Hazlitt makes the above rather startling assertion without giving
details, or actual quotations from contemporary evidence tending to prove
that wood *was* largely used for " coffin-clocks " (a not unusual seventeenth-
century term for long-case clocks) at this period.

Merely as an unsupported assertion, therefore, we are bound to
discredit it. *En passant*, the escapement used for clocks in the year 1631
was the early device known as the balance-controlled verge, a variant of
the Continental "foliot" or oscillating bar, the wheel form of balance
being that used in England for domestic clocks, although the " foliot " was
the usual form of turret-clock controller. The idea of a long-case clock
with crown-escapement *and balance control* is so unlikely, though not
impossible, that we really need not consider this particular theory seriously.
It is recorded here merely to illustrate one of the widely differing theories
that have been held at different times, as to the origin of the long-case
form of time-keeper.

Another view is that the " Grandfather " clock—a title, by the way, only applied in recent times, and not used at the period of construction —is of *Dutch* origin.

This theory (for such it can only be) is presented by Mr. Arthur Hayden in his *Chats on Old Clocks*.[1] He says:

" In its decoration *and in its form* the long-case or ' grandfather ' clock is as Dutch as the tiles of Haarlem. As a long wooden case, it was itself an innovation. Being new, it was never at any previous time English, and it started its history under Dutch auspices, as in similar manner the pendulum was introduced into England by Fromanteel.[2] There is no mistaking its origin. It comes straight from the placid canals and waterways, the prim and well-ordered farmsteads, or the richly loaded burghers' houses of the Low Countries. It has become as thoroughly English as the Keppels and the Bentincks."

And again, Mr. Herbert Cescinsky (*Old English Master Clockmakers and their Clocks*, 1938), referring to casework:

" It is more than probable that, in the first instance, these walnut cases were ordered from Holland, and were sent over from that country at about the same time as the Dutchmen introduced another art, that of marquetry cutting."

So we see that there is a distinct body of opinion that the Dutch were " first in the field " with our grandfather clocks.

The whole argument, however, can be very seriously disturbed by one important point.

Many examples still exist of English long-case clocks dating before 1685. Some few can be definitely ascribed to *circa* 1660. Now I have never seen or heard of any Dutch " grandfather " so early in constructional period as this, nor, apparently, has anyone else. The question, then, is " where are the examples of Dutch work in this form of *circa* 1660 or earlier? "

Few Dutch long-case clocks can be described as being much before about 1700 in fabrication, *none* so early as 1660.

There is also to be borne in mind the Report of the Master of the

---

[1] Second Edition, 1920. I have not seen the later editions of this book.

[2] But Fromanteel (although of Dutch descent) was a member of a clockmaking family of that name for some time resident in England, and practising their craft in this country. He visited Holland, and on his return the announcement was made by the Fromanteels of " a new controller " (the pendulum). But this, as is generally held, had only been applied to a clock the previous year (1657, by Huygens) so that the English use of the pendulum differed very little in time from its employment in Holland, and the Dutch are unlikely to have constructed clocks in an entirely new form in the intervening period; the early pendulums, also, were merely short " bob " pendulums up to 1659, at least, and so would not necessarily have suggested the long-case form.

Clockmakers' Company in 1704, quoted in Overall's *History of the Clockmakers' Company.*

"Certain persons in Amsterdam . . . names of Tompion, Windmills, Quare, Cabrier, Lamb and other well-known London makers on their works."

From which it would seem that the gentle art of "faking" was not unknown in 1704, and that our modern age does not hold an exclusive position for instituting forgeries of a horological nature.

The relevance of the above extract at this point is that in 1704 (and probably for some years previously, since the forgeries would no doubt be perpetrated for some time before being recognized as such) the English clocks had attained such distinction that it became profitable for unscrupulous persons in Holland to forge the names of London makers on their dials. Now this is hardly in accordance with there being in existence a well-established school of very high-class Dutch clockmaking (including, of course, long-case clocks) and provides an additional argument for those who maintain, as I do, that the long-case clock is English in its inception.

It is a matter of little doubt that there were English examples of long-case clocks produced as early as 1660.

What must be one of the first pendulum clocks constructed in England has its movement illustrated by R. W. Symonds in *A History of English Clocks.*

It is a spring-driven movement for a mantel clock, "signed" on the backplate "A. Fromanteel, London, Fecit 1658." A weight-driven movement for a long-case striking clock is also shown on the same page, and ascribed (as I believe, quite correctly) to *circa* 1660. Both these movements have short "bob" pendulums with crown-wheel escapements.

That the pendulum should be applied to English spring-driven movements in 1658 by Ahasuerus Fromanteel and not also to the weight-driven type for the long cases (if this form then existed) is not to be considered.

We may therefore fix the date 1658 as being that of the earliest likely instances of long-case, weight-driven clocks and timepieces; at this period all had crown-wheel escapements with the characteristic short pendulums.

If we are to concede that the pendulum was first applied in a practical and marketable way to clocks by Christian Huygens in 1657, unless we accept the statement previously quoted from W. Carew Hazlitt—in which case we are also bound to accept long-case clocks as existing before the application of the pendulum—this would seem the earliest possible date for any long-case example in the present state of our knowledge.

We shall begin our survey, therefore, with this date in mind, as between 1658 and 1670 there were certainly a fair number of clocks made in long-case form.

In the preceding part of this work we have seen how the long-case was evolved from the early English chamber clock and its hooded bracket.

Many of the first examples of the " grandfather " type retained the lantern movements of their predecessors, together with a duration between windings of but thirty hours, pull-up wind by chains or ropes, and, as we have seen, were fitted with the early form of short controller known as the " bob " pendulum. Not having to provide for the arc of a three-and-a-half-foot pendulum (small though this is when controlling the escapement of later invention) the cases were exceedingly narrow, merely enough space being provided to allow the fall of the weight or weights.

With these slender trunks were correspondingly small hoods, made either to lift right off or to slide upwards on tongues projecting from the backboard of the case, the sides of the hoods being grooved accordingly. A spring catch was provided to hold the raised hood in position during setting of the hand (or winding the eight-day clocks) as a hinged door in front of the dial did not exist.

In the clocks with key-wind movements, before the hood could be raised, the long door of the case had to be opened; this action released a trigger-like rocking lever, the lower end of which made contact with the back of the trunk door when the latter was closed, locking the hood by closing the upper extremity of the lever upon its bottom rail or " stile ".

This ingenious device was adopted, not only to effectually prevent unauthorized tampering with the clock, but also to certify the opening of the lower door before the hood was raised for winding. Thus the weights of the movement were exposed to view and could be watched during this operation, preventing accidents due to over-enthusiastic winding causing a broken line, and damage to the case from the falling heavy weight. Incidentally, a movement fitted with the " bolt-and-shutter " maintaining power necessitated the opening of the trunk door before the winding key could be inserted,[1] a cord hanging within the case being pulled to move aside the shutter covering the winding-holes and set the device in

---

[1] Even should the hood be provided with a glazed door.

operation. This, however, was not the primary purpose of the " shutter ", the intention being to prevent winding until the maintaining power was in action. But not all early movements were equipped with this aid to exact timekeeping.[1]

The dials of the early thirty-hour clocks with lantern movements were of small size, being from seven to ten inches square, the hours indicated by a single heavy hand of lantern type, the chapter-rings narrow and having secondary engraving for half- and quarter-hours only. The dial-plates were of brass, the spandrels being engraved, as also were the dial-centres; cast corner-pieces were not used in the earliest of these dials for lantern movements. The narrow silvered hour-circles with the engraving of the chapters and secondary markings filled with black wax were attached by studs and pins to the dial-plates, which latter were treated by the old process known as water-gilding.

It cannot be supposed that the plate-frame movement of longer duration than the lantern type, and with the trains arranged side by side for key-winding from the dial, was an introduction intended primarily for the long-case variety of timekeeper.

Practically coeval with the earliest long-case clocks were the spring-driven mantel clocks with these movements, then very much in the form displayed by these clocks in the eighteenth century, and differing only in the form of escapement employed from such clocks made up to quite recent times.

Ahasuerus Fromanteel, in his advertisements of " a new controller " (no doubt the pendulum) in the year 1658, writes of month and even year duration for his clocks, which implies key-winding and plate frames for the movements.

From these interesting records of an early maker (*see* Glossary— under Movements) we conclude that the early tall-case clocks were hardly in being before the lantern type of movement was superseded by the plate-frame kind, and the duration between windings increased to eight days, a month, or longer. The two types were quite probably coeval in the long-case form, and used as alternatives, the plate-frame type (especially those of month and longer duration) being doubtless very much more expensive propositions to the purchaser!

---

[1] It would seem to have been applied most frequently to eight-day movements, as these would be wound more often than others of longer duration—e.g., month clocks.

Bearing all this in mind, it is certain that the eight-day movement was quite common in long-case clocks before 1670, and that month duration was not unusual.

With the plate-frame movement, wound by a key through apertures in the dial, the long-case clock in substantially the form with which we are all familiar may be said to have become thoroughly established.

For some years the short or "bob" pendulum was still used with the plate-frame movement, until the long or "Royal" pendulum (as it was called contemporaneously—with justifiable enthusiasm) was applied, some time about 1675 in England, although possibly slightly earlier.

There is no doubt that the long pendulum, beating seconds, was first used with the crown-wheel and horizontal verge. Christian Huygens, in his small folio published in Paris in 1673—the full title is *Horologium oscillatorium sive de motu pendulorum ad horologia aptato demonstrationes geometricæ*—illustrates his design with a long pendulum, and we know from one of his letters[1] (dated 1st November, 1658) that he already had a clock with seconds-pendulum for his own use in connection with his astronomical observations. He adopted as standard a heavily-weighted pendulum beating seconds some time about 1659. The seconds pendulum was used, therefore, before the introduction of the anchor escapement (which reduced its arc and improved its timekeeping) and it was also used, as we have seen, by Huygens and his clockmaker, Samuel Coster, with crutch and independent suspension from a back-cock, all as early as the year 1659.

There is no actual proof that long pendulums were used at all generally *in England* until the adoption of the anchor escapement (a distinctively English invention). *En passant*, we may perhaps mention a suggestion put forward by F. J. Britten that the long pendulum was used in this country with the crown-wheel, about 1671, and that, too, in long-case clocks. Britten says that the very large arc thus produced was accommodated in long-cases by the provision of lenticular extensions to the case sides of existing clocks designed for the short crown-wheel pendulums, and that the examples of long clock-cases illustrated by Thomas Sheraton in his book of furniture designs were probably a revival of these "wings" or extensions. I have seen an illustration of a long case enclosing a clock by Daniel Quare, having *two* pendulums: one arranged to record sidereal time and the other

[1] To Pierre Petit (1594–1677), mathematician, astronomer and physicist; friend of the philosopher Pascal.

mean time, in which the case has the little " wings " or extensions referred to above. This must be regarded as exceptional, but accommodation for the arcs of the two pendulums *may* have been suggested by the earlier employment of the extensions as in the instances mentioned by Britten. One of my clockmaker friends told me recently of a clock having a very slender oak case with these " wings " built on to the sides, which he had seen personally, but could not remember details of the escapement— whether crown or a conversion from such to the anchor pattern, as seems most likely. Undoubtedly such instances as this are very rare, and I shall welcome particulars and photographs of any examples in the possession of my readers.

As we find ourselves now at the period of the long (or " seconds ") pendulum and anchor escapement, and as we have read, in the Preface to this work, that these matters are somewhat controversial as to period, and also as to who invented (or first introduced) them, it will perhaps be of interest to examine some of the much-quoted " contemporary evidence ", giving, as far as possible, however, *both sides of the argument.*

John Smith, writing in his *Horological Disquisitions Concerning the Nature of Time*, in 1694 has a passage which I do not remember seeing *quoted fully* in any modern work. As it is quaint as well as interesting I give it herewith.

" At length, in Holland, an Ingenious and Learned Gentleman, Mr. *Christian Hugens* [*sic*] by Name, found out the Way to regulate the uncertainty of its Motion by the Vibrations of a Pendulum.

" From *Holland*, the fame of this Invention soon passed over into *England*, where several eminent and ingenious Workmen applied themselves to rectify some Defects which as yet was found therein; among which that eminent and well-known Artist Mr. William *Clement*, had at last the good fortune to give it the finishing stroke, he being indeed the real Contriver of that curious kind of long Pendulum, which is at this Day so universally in use among us.

" An Invention that exceeds all others yet known, as to the Exactness and Steadiness of its Motion, which proceeds from Two Properties, peculiar to this Pendulum: The one is the weightiness of its Bob, and the other the little Compass in which it plays. . . .

" . . . But the Vibrations of this Pendulum of Mr. *Clement's* contrivance is so very exact and steady, that, when 'tis well in Order, and the Air of the same Consistency, it shall in five hundred or a thousand Revolutions of its Index, keep so Equal a Time, that no Human Art can discover the least considerable Difference in any of its Revolutions, an excellence to which no other known Motion can as yet pretend, and for which I think it will not be improper now, at last, to call it the *Royal Pendulum*."

From which we see that it was, at least, Smith's opinion that William Clement invented that combination of long pendulum with anchor escapement which he calls the "Royal Pendulum". But we have seen that, inasmuch that he alludes to a long pendulum and "the weightiness of its Bob," Clement cannot be credited with the introduction of these characteristics, since Huygens had used them before him, but only with the type of escapement responsible for "the little Compass in which it plays".

So far, then, the evidence of this "contemporary" seems fairly conclusive, but let us look a little further.

The following is taken from William Derham's *Artificial Clockmaker*, second edition, 1700.

Referring to the pendulum, he writes (the reference "he" is to Christian Huygens):

"This excellent invention, he says, he first put in practice in the year 1657, and in the following year, 1658, he printed a delineation and description of it."

The "delineation and description" refers to *Horologium*, a small Latin treatise on the pendulum clock published by Huygens in 1658.

Derham says Fromanteel ["Fromantil"] made the first pendulums "that ever were made here, which was about the year 1662." Remembering the advertisement in *Mercurius Politicus* of 1658, however, we must decide that he is somewhat late here.

Remembering also that in the seventeenth century and earlier it was quite usual to call a person by the name of his birthplace (Huygens was born in Zulichem, or Zuylichem, in Holland) we will proceed with Derham:

"For several years this way of Mr. *Zulichem* was the only method, viz., Crown Wheel Pendulums, to play between two cycloidal cheeks, &c. But afterwards Mr. *W. Clement*, a *London* clockmaker, contrived them (as Mr. *Smith* saith) to go with less weight, an heavier Ball (if you please) and to Vibrate but a small compass. Which is now the universal method of the Royal Pendulums. But Dr. *Hook* [sic] denies Mr. *Clement* to have invented this; and says that it is his invention, and that he caused a piece of this nature to be made which he showed before the *R. Society*, soon after the Fire of *London*."

The records of the Royal Society reveal no very decisive confirmation of Hooke's claim. There is, however, the following very interesting but rather mysterious entry under date *4 December, 1666*, in Dr. Thomas Birch's *History of the Royal Society of London* (4 vols., 4to., 1756 and 1757), vol. II, page 132:

"Mr. Hooke produced a new sort of pendulum made after the manner of a beam, and so contrived, that by placing the beam nearer or farther below the centre of motion, the pendulum may perform its vibrations in any time assigned; in which he affirmed to be one certain depth, beyond which the pendulum would not go quicker, which he had not yet reduced to a theory, but hoped to do it."

Now this is certainly "soon after the Fire of London" (which began on 2nd September, 1666) and the only impediment to complete confirmation of Hooke's claim is the ambiguity of the description. One of the definitions of a "beam" given in Chambers' *Twentieth Century Dictionary* is "the part of a balance from which the scales hang", and we may regard the oscillating steel "anchor" as being in some manner comparable to the "beam" of a balance, and its pallets as taking the position of the scales. Moreover, the reference to "depth" strongly suggests the depthing of the pallets in the 'scape-wheel teeth, and such pallets could have been made adjustable "nearer or farther" below their axis—the pallet staff. The adjustable "bob" was already well-known at this period, so that the description is unlikely to refer to normal pendulum *regulation*.

I have diligently searched Hooke's Diary (which, however, is only for the period 1672–1680) and can find no reference to such an invention by him. It is true that the editors attribute the invention to him in the *Life* (details mostly derived from Waller's Life, together with Aubrey's reminiscences) which precedes the Diary, and attribute it also to the period during which Hooke was at Oxford, or, more exactly, *circa* 1656–1658, but a satisfactory basis seems lacking.

In an endeavour to find some confirmation of a conclusive nature I have consulted Dr. R. T. Gunther's extensive work in fourteen volumes (1923–1945) entitled *Early Science in Oxford*.

D

It is with some degree of surprise that I find Dr. Gunther so far avoiding the subject that he merely quotes from J. Eric Haswell's *Horology* (1947) as " the most recent work on Horology " to the effect that " 1656 is the most probable year for the invention of the Anchor or Recoil Escapement by Hooke, *almost immediately after the introduction of the pendulum.*"

The italics are my own, as the statement seems extraordinary. We have seen that Huygens did not actually *have clocks made* (or thus " introduce " the pendulum) until 1657, and the statement by Mr. Haswell (quoted by Dr. Gunther) is irreconcilable with this.[1] It is possible that the author of *Horology* has had in mind the statement of Huygens in his small Latin treatise on the pendulum clock published in Holland in 1658 and entitled *Horologium*.

In this he gives " *the end of* 1656 as the date when he *first thought out* a new method of measuring time; and *a few months later*, having divulged it in Holland, it could not be doubted but that it would soon spread far and wide, by reason of its own utility, inasmuch as several examples of the new mechanism had already been manufactured and dispatched in different directions."

The italics of the quotation are again mine, and make it increasingly difficult to understand Messrs. Haswell and Gunther, since apparently the " invention " (although it is doubtful whether it should be so called) was not divulged even in Holland until " a few months later " than the " end of 1656 " which would bring us into the following year—1657.

It must be conceded that the general tendency is to credit Dr. Hooke with the invention of the anchor escapement; the diversity of opinion (or should we say " the guesses "?) as to the *date* of its invention is positively bewildering to the layman, who is naturally inclined to credit the first book he reads with authenticity of detail, especially if (as is generally the case here) the dates given are apparently in the nature of assertions.

As to the date of fairly general *application* of the invention, we are once more faced with difficulties and multitudinous " opinions ", again often expressed as assertions so as to lend verisimilitude to the various texts.

The generally accorded date is around 1675, and it must be confessed

---

[1] The previous claims for " introduction " by Richard Harris (1641) and Vincenzo Galilei (1649) are apparently unavailable for comparison, as 1656 cannot be regarded as " almost immediately after " these.

at once that there is much available inference tending to support this. But we must not forget the example of the lantern clock by William Holloway, of Stroud, dated 1675 on its dial-plate, which I have referred to earlier in this book. Here we have a clock made in 1675 as a *balance clock*, and although tradition is strong amongst clockmakers, as in other crafts also, had the clock been by a London maker the inference that the anchor escapement was then either unavailable or only just beginning to be used would have been very decided indeed. But William Holloway was not working in one of the great clockmaking centres of the period, of which London was the chief. He was making his clocks in a little provincial village—as Stroud would then be—and intercourse between such places and London would be difficult and infrequent in 1675. Tucked away in his village, far from the scenes of the " latest inventions ", he probably continued to make clocks as his ancestors did, nor did his customers demand or expect anything different. This instance, then, is decidedly inconclusive, particularly as Holloway neglected the use of even the short crown-wheel pendulum, which was available after 1658.

Taking the opposite standpoint, and searching therefore not *after* 1675, for many but little later examples of the escapement can be cited, but *before* this date, we may see in the Science Museum at South Kensington a turret clock movement in which the anchor escapement is a feature. This clock is said to have been made for King's College, Cambridge, and was transferred thence to St. Giles's Church, Cambridge. In 1926 it was presented to the Museum. It bears on its frame the inscription : " Gulielmus Clement Londini fecit 1671." An illustration (in which it is possible, with a glass, to read the inscription) may be consulted by those interested in Kenneth Ullyett's *British Clocks and Clockmakers* (1947).

Now Drummond Robertson regards this as " positive evidence " and in this I am inclined to agree, at any rate as to date, though others have tended to the opinion that it is either a conversion, or that the clock was begun in 1671 and finished later, with the new escapement. This latter theory I think may be disregarded.

It does not by any means provide " positive evidence " that Clement *invented* the anchor escapement, only that he *employed* it, and that, if the movement be " genuine " (i.e., unaltered) he used it as early as 1671.

I have made very strong efforts to find an earlier instance of the employment of this escapement than that afforded by the above example, but I have not been successful; neither has anyone else, it would appear, and until such earlier instances are discovered we must therefore regard 1671 as the year which provides the earliest known use of the much-discussed escapement.

The success of the "royal" pendulum of true "seconds length",[1] making possible increased accuracy of timekeeping, soon induced makers (Clement among them) to fit pendulums up to five-and-a-half feet long, descending nearly to the bottom of the clock-case, in the base of which there was then provided another door giving access to the "bob" for regulation purposes.

The previously-mentioned maintaining power of the "bolt-and-shutter" type (by which the clock was kept going during the act of winding) was another very early improvement incorporated into the movements of long-case clocks. This device seems to date from well before 1670, being present in many very early clocks by Fromanteel, East, and others.

The early method of controlling the sounding of the hours by the system known as "locking-plate striking" was used in all movements up to about 1675. This had the disadvantage of being progressive in its action, so that should the hands of the clock be moved round the dial without allowing for each successive hour to strike out in full the sequence was disarranged, and the lifting-piece would then have to be manually operated until the sound-signal appropriate to the visual indication was attained. Thus *repetition* of the hour signal (as in "pull-repeat" striking—more common in mantel clocks) was not possible.

In 1676, Thomas Tompion is said to have applied a system of striking invented by Edward Barlow (*see* Glossary—under "Rack") which enabled the hands to be moved round without fear of deranging the sequential nature of the striking, and which also allowed the repetition of any particular hour by merely affixing a cord to the end of the lifting-piece should such a device be required.

Derham, in *The Artificial Clockmaker*, 2nd edition, 1700, says (referring to repeating clocks):

"These clocks are a late invention of one Mr. *Barlow*, of no longer standing than the latter end of King *Charles II*, about the year 1676."

Under date "Friday, November 10th [1676]", I have found in the diary of Robert Hooke this entry:

---

[1] *See* "Pendulum" in Glossary.

" With Dr. Pope at Childs. At Tompions: told him of my new striking clock to tell at any time howr [*sic*] and minute by sound."

Now Thomas Tompion is generally supposed to be the clockmaker to whom Edward Barlow communicated his invention of the repeating-work, and who put Barlow's suggestion (or design) into practice. If this is so, Hooke would hardly tell him of something he already knew about and had constructed, although it is true there is nothing mentioned by Hooke as to the *system* of his repeating-work. Quite possibly, therefore, it was not the " rack " mechanism, as made by Tompion.

The quotation from Hooke is interesting, however, and I cannot remember seeing it previously quoted in any work on antique timekeepers which I have read.[1] I have not been able to find *proof* that Barlow's system was the rack type. Is it not possible that, on the evidence of Derham that he invented repeating work, and the existence of clocks by Tompion, *circa* 1676, or so dated, having this rack mechanism, it has been assumed so?

It is quite probable that Hooke did not develop his " invention "; in fact, he seldom seems to have prosecuted his designs to full perfection, leaving others to modify and improve his original ideas; no doubt, also, these others were in some instances unconscious of Hooke's prior conceptions of many devices.

It may be that Tompion communicated this idea of Hooke's to Barlow, and that Barlow thereupon modified and developed it, but this is unlikely, as Tompion would be quite capable of perfecting an outlined idea himself, without recourse to a third person, and would certainly perceive at once the possibilities of the suggestion. It will be observed that I write of " an idea " of Hooke's. This is because I do not believe " my new striking clock ", etc., referred to an actual clock, but only to a design for such that Hooke had in his mind at the time, and of which it is possible he had made a few rough diagrams.

The instance is a good parallel to that of the Anchor Escapement already mentioned, and serves to emphasize the underlying uncertainty of many attributions in horological invention.

It should be noted that Hooke's invention (if such it were indeed) told " howr *and minute* by sound ". Edward Barlow and Daniel Quare disputed

---

[1] Since writing the above I have found this passage from the *Diary* quoted by Mr. R. W. Symonds in his *Masterpieces of English Furniture and Clocks* (1940). Mr. Symonds draws a similar inference to my own.

the rival merits of their respective systems of repeating-work *for watches* when Barlow made application to patent his in 1686. It would appear that Barlow's watch required two distinct movements in order to repeat hours and *quarters*, whereas only one operation was needed by Quare's example, his watch being therefore adjudged the superior. Quare, in this instance, was supported by the Clockmakers' Company. It remains a matter for conjecture whether Hooke's term " minutes " meant periods of fifteen minutes each (quarters) or actual minutes, as in later examples of repeating-watches. If he really referred to actual minutes, then it would seem that he who is the subject of much modern horological " debunking " has a formidable title to consideration as being decidedly ahead of his contemporaries in this matter.

Even with the rack system it is usually desirable (though not essential) to allow the twelfth hour to strike in full, since otherwise the rack-tail stud passes over the chamfered " step " in the part known as the " snail " and rides upon the surface of the latter until it slips off during the " gathering-up " of the rack itself. There is always the possibility of slight maladjustment of the parts, when instead of the above process taking place the rack tail jams against the snail, sometimes resulting in the fracture of a wheel-tooth or the bending or breaking of the minute hand, should the turning be persistent against resistance.

Of course, if the parts are correctly adjusted—as they undoubtedly should be—the system is fool-proof, but as a precaution it is perhaps better to let " twelve o'clock " strike out in full. This allows the rack tail to assume a position from which it clears the step in the snail, and is ready to slide easily round the graduated circumference of the latter should the resetting of the hands require them to be turned still further.

The earliest form of rack differed somewhat in detail to that used later, this fact providing a valuable indication as to the approximate period in which any particular movement was made.

The " inside rack " (as the early pattern is called) was superseded by the improved type situated on the face of the front plate about 1700 in London, although possibly the earlier variety was still made in the provinces and country districts for a few years after this date.

The calendar, in the early clocks always shewn through a small square aperture in the central portion of the dial, is an adjunct the omission of which is very exceptional in clocks from about 1680–1740. In fact, this device was quite usual throughout the eighteenth century, even mantel clocks frequently displaying the feature. In the twentieth century, with our ubiquitous daily newspaper, we may be slow to appreciate how useful such an addition to a clock would be, at a period when " dailies " were few and the numbers of their regular readers inconsiderable. One writer[1] very sapiently remarks that in the period we refer to, a clock with a calendar, though it had but one hand (and there were many such) would be preferred to another with minute hand, should the latter lack this important accessory. The same author goes on to observe that during the age in which our long-case clocks were made people had no trains to " catch ", reasonably inferring that the extra accuracy of the minute-hand was regarded by many as unessential in those unflurried days, though the date might often be required, being as frequently forgotten then as it is now.

A system of indicating the half-hour by the use of a second and smaller bell of higher pitch was not unusual from about 1660. R. W. Symonds says this was usually employed in table clocks, but there is evidence to show its use in movements intended for long cases also. The second bell received the same number of hammer-blows (by another hammer, of course) as the larger bell at the preceding hour (in Dutch and German movements the *succeeding* hour was sounded) the ear distinguishing between them by the more acute pitch of the half-hour indication.

Mr. Symonds says that this method of sounding half-hours was employed on the Continent, especially by the Dutch, a century or more earlier than in England, but this, naturally, does not infer its use in mantel or long-case forms, both of which would be non-existent in 1560, although elaborate " table-clocks " such as Mr. Symonds no doubt refers to were certainly constructed about this period.

The reference to Holland is interesting, as, by the kindness of the owner, Mr. R. W. Sawyer, of Oregon, U.S.A., I am able to reproduce a series of photographs illustrating his fine Dutch long-case clock by Jacob Hasius, Amsterdam, *circa* 1720.

This clock, illustrations of which will be found in Plates 27–33, has the Dutch arrangement for indicating the half-hour, *the next following hour* being duplicated by the smaller bell. Thus three o'clock would be sounded by three blows on the larger bell, in the ordinary manner, and half-past

---

[1] G. F. C. Gordon—*Clockmaking, Past and Present.*

three by *four* blows on the small bell, i.e., four o'clock "in miniature" or "by diminution": a "lesser four".

Chiming movements are not by any means to be regarded as novelties in 1660, and the early long-case clocks exhibited various kinds.

The number of bells used for any particular movement varied. Some had chimes of six or eight bells; others, properly designated "quarter-striking" or "ting-tang" clocks were provided with but two bells additional to the large one used for sounding the hours.

Bell chimes, when well cast and of good tone-quality, which was almost invariably the case with old examples, produce very charming silvery sounds, really musical in character and creating a decidedly "old-world" atmosphere. One objection sometimes urged against them is that their sounds are somewhat faint and lacking in sonority. Similar criticism is often heard concerning the tone of the viol, recorder, clavichord, and other old instruments of music. The answer is surely that the delicacy of tone is part of the charm, characteristic alike of old instruments and old chimes, and not susceptible to comparison with more modern devices for tone production.

The most usual manner of indicating the quarters in old chiming clocks of six or eight bells was by the playing of the whole or part of a simple diatonic scale for the first quarter, playing the same passage twice for the second quarter, and marking the third by a second repetition.

The method of chiming the hour itself varies with different makers. Occasionally the scalic passage is used four times, with decidedly monotonous effect, to precede the striking. More usually the chime barrel is "pinned" to effect the performance of a little tune, which is often capable of being varied, the barrel sliding laterally in its pivot-holes. The changing of the tune played at the hour leaves the quarter-chimes unaffected, the hammers continuing to sound scales or scalic passages for these.

A system of chiming and striking peculiar to long-case and mantel clocks of the late seventeenth and early eighteenth centuries was that known as the "Grande Sonnerie". In this, at every quarter the preceding hour is first sounded, followed by the appropriate chime for that quarter indicated by the hands.

While discussing chiming clocks, it may be pertinent to observe that

the so-called " Westminster " quarters are never used in really old movements, prior to 1788.[1]

The proper name for this chime is the " *Cambridge quarters* ", as it was
first employed in the clock for Great St. Mary's Church at Cambridge.
The usual explanation of its origin is that Dr. Jowett, the Regius Professor
of Law at Cambridge, was consulted by the university authorities on the
subject of a chime for St. Mary's clock. Jowett took into his confidence a
pupil-assistant of the then Regius Professor of Music (Dr. Randall), which
pupil was afterwards to become eminent as the famous Dr. Crotch, a
musician of considerable attainments as composer and lecturer, and a well-
known authority on English church music, who had been, also, an infant
prodigy.

Crotch was born in 1775, went to Cambridge in 1786, and removed to
Oxford in 1788,[2] so the probability is that this latter date was the year of
the consultation. Crotch, as we are told, took the characteristic descending
phrase from the " symphony " to the soprano aria " I know that my
Redeemer liveth " in Handel's *Messiah*, and expanded it into the form
with which we are now familiar.

These quarter-chimes were copied in the middle of the nineteenth
century for the Houses of Parliament, since when they have been
inexactly known all over the world as " Westminster " Chimes.

The dials of very early long-case clocks with key-wind movements were
invariably square in shape, as were the sometimes earlier dials employed in
the cases having lantern movements.

Separate cast and chased corner-pieces (made especially for the clockmaker by brass-founders) quickly followed the practice of engraving the
spandrels. These corner-pieces, which are generally excellent guides to the
period of the dial, will be considered in more detail in a later chapter.

During the last years of the seventeenth century, the hands of long-
case clocks reached their highest level of artistic design and execution.
Some of the examples to be found adorning the dials of early clocks are

---

[1] It is difficult to say exactly when these chimes first began to appear in domestic clocks.
Probably it was not until their use at Westminster popularized them all over the land. It is
possible, however, that the original Cambridge chime was so appreciated as to create an earlier
demand for their inclusion in house clocks, but, if so, they are hardly likely to have been so
employed much before the beginning of the nineteenth century. Most examples in antique
movements are conversions.

[2] Grove's *Dictionary of Music and Musicians*, 1900. G. F. C. Gordon's *Clockmaking* gives
1793 as the year of Crotch's arrangement of Handel's music, but Crotch was then at Oxford.

simply exquisite. They were equalled (but not excelled) in aesthetic qualities by some of those provided for dials of the early part of the succeeding century.

It would appear to be in the nature of a rarity to find a seventeenth-century long-case clock displaying supplementary movements other than the usual calendar, though such clocks are not unknown.

With the introduction of the arch-dial very early in the eighteenth century, however, makers desiring to use the arch for purposes other than purely ornamental soon began to devise various ingeniously operated indications of more or less useful astronomical or horological progressions.

Early among these phenomena was the device known as the " Equation of Time ". This illustrated the variation between Mean and Apparent time throughout the year, the sun being indicated as slow or fast of the main hands to a maximum of about sixteen minutes either way. Clocks, of course, always show Greenwich Mean Time in England (or should do, if they are accurate). This statement must be qualified when we allow for British Summer Time, but in the eighteenth century no such qualification would be necessary.

True or apparent time refers to that indicated by the sun, by which true noon may be earlier or later than twelve o'clock G.M.T.[1] Equal (or mean) time and apparent (or solar) time agree on but four days in each year, roughly 25th December, 15th April, 14th June and 31st August,[2] on which days true noon and " twelve o'clock " mean time will approximately coincide.

A famous instance of the employment of the " Equation of Time " register is that by Thomas Tompion in the dial-arch of the fine long-case timepiece which he presented to the Grand Pump Room, Bath, in 1709.[3] Daniel Quare was another maker occasionally using the device, as was also Joseph Williamson. The latter maker, in a letter to the publisher of the *Philosophical Transactions* (November–December, 1719) claimed to have made *all* the equation movements " sold in England " up to this date whether for his own clocks or those by (latterly) more famous contemporaries.

An extract from the letter seems to show that Williamson made the clock " with the rising and setting of the Sun " which " Mr. Quare sold

[1] G.M.T. is the *average* length of the year's total of Solar days.
[2] These dates differ slightly because of the varying length of a year—leap year of 366 days occurring once in four, and omission of this adjustment thrice in every 400 years.
[3] Mentioned by Dickens in *The Pickwick Papers*, Chap. xxxvi.

to the late King *William* and it was set up at *Hampton Court* in his lifetime, where it hath been ever since " . . . This contrivance of lengthening and shortening the *Pendulum* I thought of several years before I made any of them. Since then I have made others for Mr. Quare likewise which showed the difference between equal and apparent Time according to the Equation Tables, by a Hand moving both ways from the Top of a Circle; on one side showing how much a clock keeping equal Time might be faster than the Sun, on the other side how much slower." The letter ends: ". . . and I have never yet heard of any such Clock sold in *England* but what was of my own making, though I have made of them so long." Williamson died in 1725. The complete letter may be read in *Philosophical Transactions* (vol. IV, page 394 of the Abridgement by Henry Jones, M.A., F.R.S.).

That well-known feature of many old long-case clocks, the age and phases of the moon, was not very often used for the dial-arches of clocks before 1740, being mainly characteristic of the later examples from about 1760 onwards. Early instances, however, are usually *engraved* upon the revolving disc, the spaces between the two representations of the full moon being filled with appropriately decorative stars (*See* Plate 26). In the later presentations of this device the disc is *painted* in colours, landscapes or seascapes (or both) occupying the spaces between the " moons ". Here, again, the earlier painted types had stellar decoration only (Plate 29).

It was quite usual to provide a subsidiary dial with hand indicating seconds in most of the seventeenth and early eighteenth-century long-case movements, the 'scape wheel arbor being extended through the plate for this purpose, and the small hand attached by means of a pipe fitting over the arbor.

Among other characteristic features of early clocks, sub-dials for chime and strike-silent indications, occasionally for pendulum regulation (more common in mantel clocks), signs of the Zodiac and similar devices to be considered more fully in a later chapter, were not uncommon. All these are more frequently seen in early eighteenth-century movements than in those from 1660–1700 which, as we have already observed, are chiefly characterized by the provision of a calendar and seconds dial only.

When we arrive at a brief consideration of the casework of the clock we have seen that the early cases were notable for their slender outline, added to which characteristic we must mention that of very moderate height, rarely more than seven feet, and often much less.

Hoods were mostly of the "lift-up" type, without a door in front and, if not of the portico-topped (or architectural) kind, were either square topped finished by a straight, moulded cornice, or with the addition of carved scroll-work quite different from the much later swan-necked pediments, which were part of the main structure.

A further variety of early hood was that with the box-like, tiered superstructure above the cornice, sometimes referred to as "cushion-moulded" or "inverted bell-shaped." The latter expression is rather vague, but probably has reference to the fact that the sides of these structures were usually convex in outline, not concave like a bell.[1] This kind of hood was perhaps somewhat later in inception than the types previously described, and no doubt began to be made when loftier rooms induced a demand for a rather taller case, or, more probably, was provided as an alternative to the others, should a case of greater height be required, since the designs of all appear to run practically contemporaneously.

Of decidedly later character, however, dating most probably from the early years of the eighteenth century, is the typical "Queen Anne" hood finished with a plain, rounded top of the "broken arch" variety. Later still, this arch was supplemented by the addition above it of a tiered superstructure, the cases thus being considerably increased in height, especially in those instances where ball-spires or similar ornaments decorated the top of the hood. With this type of case a height of eight or nine feet was not uncommon for important clocks.

As the height of the case increased, the lift-up hood of early pattern would obviously become impracticable, and so we arrive at the provision of glazed doors to the hoods, these latter now sliding forward upon horizontal guides when they were required to be removed for access to the movements. These forward-sliding hoods provided with doors were probably introduced about 1685–1695.

Practically all seventeenth-century hoods, and many later, up to *circa* 1750, had rectangular glass windows in the sides, through which the movement could be seen. (*See* Plate 16.) We find occasional reversion to this practice throughout the eighteenth century, but mostly in casework enclosing clocks by London makers.

At first, the front pillars of the hood were made as three-quarter pilasters fixed to the framing of the hood-door, the latter being hinged upon

[1] The concave-sided superstructure, however, was used for the later cases of the mahogany period. (*See* Chapter III *et seq.*)

pins projecting vertically from the base and capital of the sinister pilaster. A later development of this was to have the door hinged independently, true pillars being then provided for the front of the hood.

In all these early cases, the long trunk door (originally square-topped, but afterwards assuming various shapes) was a salient feature. It tended to become slightly shorter as the eighteenth century advanced, but was still gracefully proportioned as late as 1740.

A prominent feature of many cases of the earlier type is the so-called " bull's-eye " of convex bottle-glass inset into the trunk door, opposite the position of the pendulum-bob. Thus, in the absence of a seconds-dial, an immediate indication was provided as to whether the clock was " going ", since at a little distance the flash of the polished and lacquered brass "bob" would be observed periodically passing this window.

This feature, apparently, was so popular that even in clocks having seconds-dials its inclusion was frequent. The " bull's-eye " was usually surrounded by a circular frame of ebony or walnut (*see* Plates 14 and 17) but some cases of "figured" walnut occasionally display brass surrounds for the window.

The materials used in the making of early cases will be discussed fully in the chapter on casework, but it may be broadly stated here that oak was used from the beginning, mainly in the form of carcase-work for the application of veneers of walnut, either plain (i.e. figured) or inlayed (marquetry).

Solid oak cases, not veneered with walnut or ebony, etc., do not seem to have been very popular in London and Southern Counties (where the London makers were greatly copied), and it must be remembered that London was the chief centre of the clock-making industry at the time of which I am writing. Provincial makers, however, often provided oak cases for their clocks, and occasional examples by London men are known, notably the Tompion timepiece of 1709 at Bath, already referred to in this chapter.

Casework in pearwood, stained a jet black to resemble ebony, and polished (pearwood takes a very high polish) is not unusual enclosing clocks by seventeenth-century makers. Ebony itself, in the form of veneer, was also used by some case-makers in a number of early instances from 1660–1675. Especially was the architectural type of case finished in this way.

There is no doubt that the " architectural " or " portico-hooded " type of clock-case in ebony or stained pearwood is now decidedly rare.

Most of these, the majority dating *before* 1666, must have perished in the Great Fire of London (1666). London was then practically the only clock-making centre of importance in England, since the Scottish and provincial centres, e.g., Edinburgh and Norwich, did not begin producing clocks *in appreciable numbers* until some twenty years later.

Mahogany for long-cases was not used up to 1740, except in very rare instances, and is chiefly identified with clocks made after about 1760.

It is worth while for us to note, in considering the productions of the seventeenth-century clockmakers, how few have been the really important contributions to horological advancement since their time.

True, the dead-beat escapement was left for George Graham to devise early in the following century, together with the mercurial pendulum for combating the variation due to temperature changes, but these are only two important improvements to set against the imposing list of seventeenth-century introductions—maintaining power, anchor escapements, second and second-and-a-quarter pendulums, month and twelve-month duration, rack striking, chiming movements (including the " Grande Sonnerie " system) and the ingenious " Roman Numerial Striking " devised by the famous Joseph Knibb (*see* Glossary—under Movements). Further refinements of this period include various modes of pendulum regulation indicated by subsidiary dial, and a system of plate-fastening without the aid of pins which is at once convenient, neat and effective. In addition, it must not be forgotten that the mantel clocks of the period came in for their own peculiar improvements, some of which were equally noteworthy.

It is not surprising, therefore, bearing in mind the mechanical skill lavished upon clocks during the latter part of the seventeenth century, that these horological equivalents to our modern sports cars and radio-gramophones would appeal very strongly to those of a mechanical bent; those, too, who were able to gratify it by the purchase of what must then have been an expensive article. Charles II (1660–1685) was himself so inordinately fond of clocks (as, indeed, he is said to have been of anything mechanical) that it is recorded that he died in a room wherein no less than sixty-seven of them were ticking!

The reader is advised to supplement this chapter, before proceeding with that following, by a perusal of the articles contained in the Glossary under " Movements " (p. 154) and " Pendulum " (p. 166) both of which contain much relevant information.

Chapter Three

The Later Long-Case Clocks, 1740-1800

I T has been affirmed with considerable confidence by certain authorities on old timekeepers that there were no examples of long-case clocks produced between 1740 and 1760.

In providing a foundation for this remarkably positive assertion the reason usually adduced is concerned with the introduction of mahogany furniture as a fashion following the repeal of the duty on imported timber in 1733.

This vogue of mahogany, it is argued, would make undesirable the earlier long-cases of ebony or walnut, or of walnut inlaid with marquetry, which would " clash " with a furnishing scheme otherwise carried out in mahogany.

An imaginary procedure, based on the alleged intractability of early casework, was that the owners of expensive walnut timepieces would then make gifts of these to their tenantry and to " cottagers " generally![1]

An alternative apparently not deemed worthy of consideration by the adherents to this theory is that the possessors of ebony or walnut clocks should simply place them where they would not cause undesirably violent contrast, or in some apartment not furnished exclusively in mahogany. Then, too, it is surely not suggested that the cult of " everything to match " was prevalent in the larger establishments in 1740; this finicky modernism has apparently never received much attention in the " stately homes of England ", as illustrations of such interiors during various periods from 1660 onwards indicate very clearly. Moreover, we are nearly all acquainted with some of the most artistic smaller rooms imaginable, composed of theoretically impossible furnishings and colour-schemes, yet, the aesthetic effect of the whole has been completely charming.

---

[1] That these early walnut clocks not infrequently gravitated to the humbler abodes is, of course, indubitable. There are, however, many obvious reasons for this unconnected with the vogue of mahogany furniture.

Those who advance the theory of incompatibility as an explanation of the declared cessation in the making of long-case clocks between 1740 and 1760 do not explain why the cases should not have been made in mahogany at the earlier of these dates, concurrently with the demanded mahogany furniture of other kinds, instead of making a belated appearance, *circa* 1760, when mahogany had been in general use for nearly a quarter of a century.

It is argued that the mantel clock took the place of the long-case type during these two decades; we feel bound to enquire—why then particularly, since this type of clock had been popular as an alternative from 1660?

I do not wish to contest the *possibility* that the years from 1740 to 1760 were blank as far as the manufacture of long-case clocks is concerned; I have, in fact, taken the latter year as the real starting-point for this chapter, finishing my survey of the earlier clocks with the year 1740. The particular argument for a hiatus already outlined, however, seems so faulty as to invite detailed criticism, in which, be it noted, I do not claim any measure of infallibility.

If, therefore, a gap in the continuity of our subject occurs from 1740 up to 1760, the reader is invited to consider whether this may not have been due to influences other than that connected with the introduction of mahogany, and such are not immediately apparent. So little is known regarding many of the lesser makers of the eighteenth century that the only guide to an approximate date for any particular clock is that furnished by the details of the movement, dial and casework. Thus, many clocks in mahogany cases ascribed to " about 1760 " might be equally well designated as " *circa* 1750 ". He would, indeed, be a bold antiquarian who would venture to pronounce judgment to within the limits of a decade or so in numberless instances.

We may safely assume that one of the leading characteristics of the later long-case clocks was the use of mahogany for the cases, and this whether we take 1740 or 1760 as the beginning of the later developments.

The *average* height of the complete structure was greater in the mahogany era than with the earlier walnut clocks, although we have seen that these latter were frequently provided with tall casework when such was desired for an important clock. Cases now stood, in an average, about eight feet tall, against the earlier average of about six-and-a-half or seven

PLATE 21

DIAL OF EIGHT-DAY STRIKING CLOCK
AYNSWORTH, LONDON, 1695–1700

See page 227

PLATE 22

DIAL OF EIGHT-DAY STRIKING CLOCK
"JOS. BUCKINGHAM IN YE MINORIES"
circa 1700

See page 227

PLATE 23

DIAL OF EIGHT-DAY STRIKING CLOCK
"WILLIAM TIPLING IN LEEDS FECIT"
circa 1710

See page 228

PLATE 24

HANDS OF CLOCK BY WILLIAM TIPLING

See page 228

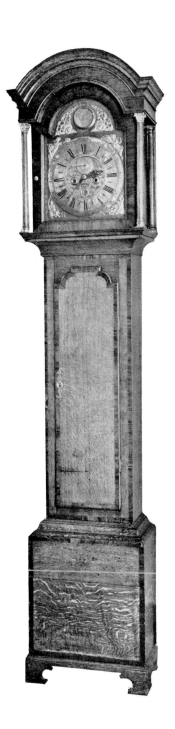

PLATE 25

EIGHT-DAY STRIKING CLOCK
JOHN CLOUGH, MANCHESTER, *circa* 1720

See page 228

PLATE 26

DIAL AND HOOD OF CLOCK BY
JOHN CLOUGH

See page 228

PLATE 27

See page 229

PLATE 29

ENLARGEMENT OF DIAL
CLOCK BY JACOB HASIUS

See page 229

PLATE 30

DETAIL OF CASE
CLOCK BY JACOB HASIUS

See page 229

PLATE 31

MOVEMENT OF CLOCK BY
JACOB HASIUS
SHOWS ARRANGEMENT OF
DRIVING WEIGHTS

See page 229

PLATE 32

FRONT VIEW OF MOVEMENT
CLOCK BY JACOB HASIUS

See page 229

PLATE 33

SIDE VIEW OF MOVEMENT
CLOCK BY JACOB HASIUS

See page 229

PLATE 34

A TYPICAL DUTCH LONG-CASE CLOCK
WITH MARQUETRY INLAID CASEWORK,
circa 1725

See page 231

PLATE 35

THIRTY-HOUR STRIKING CLOCK IN
EARLIER CASE OF ABOUT 1730
JONATHAN LEES, BURY, *circa* 1760

See page 232

PLATE 36

DIAL AND HOOD OF CLOCK BY
JONATHAN LEES

See page 232

feet. It would seem a feature of this later casework, moreover, that the extremes of size were more rarely utilised, there being apparently as few mahogany clocks made under six feet as there were such standing over nine feet in height. From this it may be deduced that a certain standardization had set in, at least as regarding the height of clocks.

Coming to a consideration of the later movements, we notice at once the overwhelming predominance of the eight-day type. Instances of longer duration are much less frequent than in the early clocks, and this may possibly be due to the clock-maker (and his clientele) arriving at the conclusion that this was the best period between successive windings. After all, a week is probably the easiest interval to remember, and winding regularly on a chosen day of the week would impose little strain on the memory; should even this be occasionally forgotten, a day's grace is provided to keep the clock going.

A more regrettable omission was occasioned by the general lack of " maintaining power " in the later clocks. That of the old " bolt-and-shutter " type was a useful refinement of the early eight-day movements, and the Harrison variety cannot be said to have appeared with sufficient frequncy in clocks constructed after 1740. It was quite often applied to movements exemplifying the dead-beat escapement, but many, even of these, were made without it.

Instances of chiming movements occur more often than in the earlier clocks; during the last quarter of the century these developed into the four-train chiming and musical movement, unfortunately necessitating a case of distinctly wide proportions when of moderate height, examples of such never being quite so well-esteemed in these days as when in the form of mantel clocks.

The " seconds " pendulum became the standard for a long-case clock, the old " second-and-a-quarter " length used with a 'scape wheel of twenty-four teeth vanishing from use. As with the early clocks, compensated pendulums were exceptional.

Calendars (often by sub-dial) and lunar records were common, the latter feature involving a *painted* disc occupying the entire arch of the dial. To utilize the dial-arch for the moon's age and phases was probably the most frequently adopted method in the later clocks, but the simple silvered boss, either displaying the maker's name or some apposite motto

E

or engraved decoration, still continued to be used as when first the arch was added to dials. These remarks also apply to the sub-dial for " strike " and " silent " indications.

Tidal indications used with the lunar record became more frequent than during the earlier period up to 1740. Not often were such " universal ", i.e., adaptable for any port. The usual procedure was to indicate the times of high water at a single port, or at most three or four, and the methods varied. That most frequently adopted was to engrave the periphery of the lunation disc with two sets of figures, one set being the numbers for the moon's age in days, and the second (usually inner set) displaying the four series of chapters I to XII which would serve to show the time of high water at some particular place, read off against a central fixed pointer at the top of the dial arch. Variants were a rising and falling plate (coloured to represent the sea)[1], or one or more fixed indicators reading on the revolving " equator " of a globular " Halifax " moon.

Occasionally we find the arch of the dial employed to display various simple mechanical devices, usually operated by the pendulum in a straight-forward manner. These were used throughout the eighteenth century, but perhaps more particularly in the later clocks. Some of the most popular included representations of a tossing ship, a see-saw, an oscillating figure of Father Time, and (possibly the most spectacular of all) a well-painted —usually female—head with rolling eyes, the latter being moved by the vibrations of the pendulum as in the other instances.

Dials became larger as the century advanced, and the chapter-rings were engraved with larger Arabic figures for the minute-numbering. These figures tended to become so large as to occasionally rival in size the Roman hour-numerals or " chapters " themselves, which must be regarded as providing an emphasis unwarranted by their relative importance, and in extreme instances destroying the artistic balance of the dial.

Corner-pieces characteristic of the period were used in the spandrels, but sometimes the very early practice of engraving the dial corners was reverted to.

Dial centres were sometimes matted or " frosted " but more often engraved and silvered; sometimes the attached separate chapter-ring was omitted, the numerals being engraved upon the dial-plate itself and the whole surface of the latter silvered. This was one of the latest chrono-

---

[1] Used in conjunction with a subsidiary dial.

logical developments, brought about by the demand for clarity, since many dials of somewhat earlier date were provided with such elaborate centres that the outline of the hands became lost at a little distance or in a poor light.

Hands, after about 1760, became less elaborate, and the "wavy" minute-hand was generally adopted by makers in all districts, although the straight form was adhered to as a variant. Most of these later clock hands were of good design and workmanship, certainly up to about 1790 or so, but the exquisite creations peculiar to the seventeenth and early eighteenth-century clocks were rarely repeated.

Reverting for a space to the casework of the clock we find that the shape of hood employed in the mahogany period was rather less varied than during the years from 1660–1740.

A type of hood often referred to as "true Chippendale"[1] is that also termed "concave-sided" or "pagoda-topped", the sides of the super-structure above the arch being curved inwards, producing an effect faintly reminiscent of Oriental architecture.

This kind of hood was also frequently used with casework decorated with English or Oriental lacquer, many such cases being made from 1740 to 1790. Lacquered casework, of course, was supplied much earlier than this, perhaps even before 1700, but not with the type of hood designated "Chippendale" or "concave-sided".

Another characteristic design for hoods of the mahogany period, more common in the North of England (where it attained considerable popularity) than in the Southern Counties, was that with the so-called "swan-necked" pediment, also known as 'scroll-topped" or "horn-topped". This seems to me as much a "true Chippendale" style as the "pagoda-topped" hood, since the "swan-necked" pediment is a very characteristic feature of furniture in the Chippendale tradition, as may be verified by observation of the large number of pieces such as bookcases, china-cabinets and wardrobes with their cornices thus decorated. Moreover, at least one clock-case with a hood displaying the horn-top design is illustrated in Thomas Chippendale's *Director*, which would seem ample justification in itself for describing these hoods as "Chippendale" also.

---

[1] Perhaps because Thomas Chippendale illustrated similar patterns for clock-cases in his *Director*, a book of furniture designs published in 1754.

Many of the later mahogany clock-cases with the scroll-topped hood exemplify much fine cabinet-work and excellent design, but a few examples, chiefly in oak, are hardly representative of this high standard; also we cannot but regard the use of the swan-necked type of hood pediment as being more suitable to cases in mahogany, although here, again, it cannot be said that the Chippendale tradition is violated, since Thomas Chippendale himself—or, more correctly, his cabinet-makers—occasionally worked in oak, and may conceivably have considered the scroll-top design as being as well-suited to a piece of furniture in oak as to one in mahogany. The fact remains, however, that those instances of its application to oak case-work for clocks seldom show the same finish and attention to detail as in the mahogany examples, and seem to lack the general sense of fitness so apparent in the latter.

No survey of the long-case clock between 1740 and 1800 would be even tolerably complete without a brief reference to the thirty-hour movement in its later form.

We have seen that many very early clocks were provided with thirty-hour movements of the "lantern" type, but the plate frame was soon applied to the thirty-hour clock, with pull-up winding by chain or rope. Huygens' endless rope or chain (involving a simple maintaining-power) was used in all the later thirty-hour plate frame movements from about the days of Queen Anne to the close of the century, together with minute motion-work and both hour and minute hands.

Although the thirty-hour "grandfather" clock is looked upon with much disfavour by most antique dealers and prospective clock-owners nowadays, because of the nuisance of daily winding, it must be confessed that many examples up to 1770 or thereabouts are very acceptable possessions viewed from the artistic standpoint.

Those instances of this type of movement with graceful, slender cases and handsome square brass dials (often displaying beautifully modelled hands) are, in my opinion, far more desirable possessions than, say, an eight-day long-case clock of *circa* 1800 with a wide case and short (almost square) door in the trunk, reminiscent of a serving-hatch, complete with a painted iron dial of the most common description.

An example of an excellent type of the later thirty-hour long-case movement with fine brass dial and exquisite hands, enclosed in a slender case of pollard oak, cross-banded and very slightly line-inlaid, is illustrated in Plate 35. The dial and hood are shown to a larger scale in the photograph Plate 36.

The case of this clock is not that originally enclosing it. At some—probably modern—period the movement and dial have been transferred to the present case, which would appear to "date" about 1730. (*See* Appendix Five, page 232.)

A discussion of the not uncommon practice of dealers and others of changing cases and movements will be found in Chapter Six (Cases). This clock is here illustrated, not as an example to be acquired by the collector, although personally I think it very pretty, but as providing one which may be consulted (by means of the photograph) in conjunction with the observations contained in Chapter Six.

The introduction of the painted iron dial, which may be regarded as providing one of the earliest signs of decadence in English clock-making, took place about 1780. No doubt cheapness was the primary factor which brought about its inception, but latterly a demand for greater legibility also played a part in popularizing these dials. That clarity only cannot have been the reason for their use is apparent, since the flat brass dial-plate completely silvered was used in the better quality timekeepers, providing equal legibility with greater artistic merit.

Throughout the eighteenth century, and particularly in certain examples of long-case clocks by Dutch makers, the brass dial with painted decoration (often of classical or mythological subjects) is occasionally found. (*See* Plate 34 for a rather early example.) These paintings, however, apart from adorning already fine brass dials, are of quite different aesthetic quality to the usual somewhat crudely-painted posies, birds, or scenes used for the decoration of the typical sheet-iron dials. It is said that the famous painter Johannes Zoffany, R.A. (1733–1810) spent some time in the early part of his career painting clock dials, but this, of course, was before his success as an artist made such work unnecessary to him.

Another indication of the gradual decline of the long-case clock and its aesthetic debasement after the close of the eighteenth century is found in the trend of contemporary casework. Very wide cases with exceedingly short trunk-doors, having broad bases nearly equivalent in height to the length of the trunk portion itself, and surmounted by wide, sprawling hoods enclosing very large painted dials became more and more frequent. This type of case seems to have originated in the Northern Counties, particularly in Yorkshire.

After about 1760, the London makers appear to have lost the lead in the clockmaking industry, *which then passed to the North of England*, where from this date until 1790 or 1795 some really excellent examples of the long-case clock were produced. Many of these clocks emanated from Lancashire, which county had early been noted for the well-designed and carefully manufactured clockmaking tools originating there.

That portion of the preceding paragraph italicized requires the emphasis, as it is often insufficiently realized by the collector who desires a balanced collection. The clock illustrated by Plates 41–44 (for example) is so fine that, together with the earlier dials and movement displayed by Plates 19, 20 and 23 (by Yorkshire makers) the Northern clockmaker needs no further testimonial. The dials may be taken as evidence that *even in an early period* the work of the North Country makers bears comparison with that of the finest London artists in the craft.

After 1800, we may consider the long-case clock to be definitely finished as an art-work,[1] but the form continued to be made until much later in the century, probably lasting well into the early years of Victoria's reign. These latest examples usually took the form of " regulator " clocks, precision timepieces not primarily intended for household use, but often for the clockmaker himself, to set up in his shop as a kind of " standard " clock by which to regulate others.

It is indubitable that *modern examples* of clocks in the long-case form, by good makers, are frequently first class judged by purely horological standards.

The casework, in addition, is quite handsome and well made in many of the better-class modern productions.

It is significant that the best instances of such clocks are generally rather poor copies (*reproductions*, according to the trade terminology) of early cases and dials. As in most " reproductions " the spirit of the original is lacking. I have yet to see an example comparable with the old in æsthetic qualities of case or dial, and much the same applies also to the movements.

These so-called " copies " of fine old cases and dials hardly succeed in deceiving even the veriest tyro, certainly not anyone " with a flair " for

---

[1] With the inevitable very few but noteworthy exceptions.

the antique, even should he have little or no special knowledge of clocks. It is very seldom, however, that such " reproductions " are intentionally designed to be deceptive.

All things considered, it is probable that the most successful efforts of the modern clockmaker consist, not in imitation, but in very accurate and scientifically constructed " regulators " with plain but soundly-made cases. These always include the provision of maintaining power and invar-steel pendulums, and are practically universally " timepieces " only, i.e., there are no striking trains to the movements.

Chapter Four

Mechanical Devices

THE more or less technical explanations involved in describing the methods adopted to effect the operation of the various mechanical devices introduced from time to time by different clockmakers will be found in the Glossary of this work, under the appropriate headings.

It is not intended, in this place, to do more than refer to a few of the many sometimes complicated auxiliaries incorporated by ingenious makers into the movements of long-case clocks and timepieces. Such references as relate to chiming movements, the simple form of calendar, the Equation of Time, Phases of the Moon, Tidal dials, moving figures, etc., will be found in the two preceding chapters; therefore these will not be further discussed here. A few remarks as to some of the more unusual phenomena may, however, be acceptable.

A comparatively rare inclusion in a clock movement of any period is the Perpetual Calendar.

This, as the name implies, automatically compensates for the long and short months, assigns to February its extra day in each Leap Year, and is usually arranged to display not only the day of the month, but also the name of the latter, appearing through an aperture in the dial-plate and moving onward at the expiration of its allotted number of days. As may be imagined, the mechanism is complicated, and when out of order difficult to re-set. It was less infrequently incorporated into the early movements than in those after 1740, but was apparently exceptional at almost any period; no doubt the expense of its provision would preclude its becoming popular with all makers, apart from the skill required by its effective arrangement.

Joseph Williamson was one who seems to have used the perpetual calendar more often than others, but Thomas Tompion employed it in the fine three-months duration long-case clock he made for William III (since known as the " record " Tompion clock).

Occasionally, but very rarely, long-case clocks may be seen with indications of Sunrise and Sunset. *See* Plates 26 and 48 and descriptions of the clocks (Appendix Five). Such are sometimes equipped with perpetual calendars in addition, as the former device is more satisfactorily operated in connection with this mechanism.

The Signs of the Zodiac, normally illustrating the sun's apparent position in the heavens, is another uncommon feature which would seem to be restricted to the older clocks. I know of only one instance of this device dating after 1730, although no doubt there are also other exceptional examples. It is such instances as these latter which, in all horological practices, make generalizations extremely hazardous and dangerous. The beginner, observing a clock to have some such device as that alluded to above, and confidently accepting the apparent assertion of some writer to the effect that its use ceased at a certain date or period, is naturally inclined to regard a much later example as being spurious, whereas such may be, and usually is, a perfectly genuine late employment of the feature.

In the clock illustrated by Plates 25 and 26, the twelve zodiacal signs are engraved around a central *moon* and subdivided nearer the rim of the silvered sub-dial into twenty-four curious anatomically-named divisions, the spelling of these inscriptions being in quaint Old English fashion, e.g., "Brest", "Loyns", etc. The indicator hand is moved once every twelve hours by a stud fixed to the hour-wheel pipe, which also operates the Lunar Record. Two movements give a complete zodiacal division (24 hours).

The twelve signs of the Zodiac are normally used as approximately equivalent to the twelve months of the year (the sun remaining in one "sign" for roughly a month).

It is, however, a so-called "*lunar zodiac*" which is represented here, marking the *daily* stages of the *moon's* progression through the constellations of the zodiac. As, from a particular point in the heavens, say a certain "fixed star" (i.e., not a planet) to an equivalent position again is a journey accomplished by the moon in a period approximating to twenty-seven days (not 29½ days, since this is from a phase to *the same* phase) the relevance of this device is not clear to me, and I should welcome all attempts at an explanation as to why the clockmaker has arranged a complete Zodiacal Cycle in but *twelve days*. Any information forthcoming will be gratefully received, and suitably acknowledged in future editions. I cannot believe that a clockmaker constructing such a fine and well-finished movement as this would insert the device merely as an unmeaning toy.

The seven planets of the ancients—Sun, Moon, Mars, Mercury, Jupiter, Venus and Saturn (the sun being then included as a " planet ") originated the names given to our days of the week, in this order.

The days of the week, with their titles—Sunday, Monday, etc.—were not infrequently displayed on the dials of the earlier clocks, perhaps particularly in those by Dutch makers, who seem to have been rather partial to this movement. (*See* Plate 29.) Accompanying the title of the day was often an engraved representation of the particular pagan Deity to whom it was anciently dedicated, from which dedication we derive its name. Thus Sunday (" Sun's day ") would bear an engraving of Apollo-Phœbus, the Sun-god. Monday, being dedicated to the Moon-goddess (" Moon's day "), would appropriately present the huntress Diana. Tuesday (from " Tiw's day "—Tiw being the Saxon name for Mars) would depict the God of War, while Wednesday (" Woden's day "), Thursday (" Thor's day "), Friday (" Freya's day "), and Saturday (dedicated to Saturn, the God of Time) would respectively portray Mercury, Jupiter, Venus, and Saturn.

Beneath the engraving of the Deity of the Day, and moving with it, would often appear the appropriate symbol or conventional planetary sign. (*See* Plate 29.)

Maintaining power of three types will be found sufficiently described under that heading in the Glossary of Technical Terms.

Before closing this short chapter we must find space to devote a few words to a device which would appear to be peculiar to the later clocks, after 1740, but which is nevertheless extremely rare.

This is an arrangement for indicating the time at various places on the earth's surface, in different countries.

F. J. Britten (*Old Clocks and Watches*, etc.) illustrates a long-case clock by Andrew Padbury attributed to *circa* 1760, which is provided with a twenty-four-hour dial having a revolving centre, to which latter the hour indicator is attached.

Engraved upon the central revolving disc[1] within each of twenty-four divisions are the names of various countries and places all over the world. As the central portion of the dial revolves it will be obvious that not only will the attached pointer indicate the correct hour, but also that each of

[1] This disc turns once in 24 hours.

the twenty-four divisions will point to a time which will be correct for those countries or places the names of which are engraved therein. Of course, the engraving of the centre disc is so arranged as to include only places whose times are in hourly succession. The chapter ring itself is divided into twice twelve hours, noon being at the top, midnight diametrically below, six o'clock morning and six o'clock evening being to the left and right of the centre respectively.

The one weak point in this otherwise admirable arrangement would seem to be in connection with winding the clock.[1]

The winding squares of the movement are in their usual positions, which bring them within the revolving centre. Therefore the winding holes in this central portion are only opposite the squared arbors at a certain time, in this case apparently twelve o'clock noon. Thus the clock cannot be wound except at this time, and that more or less exactly, since a small variation either way would be sufficient to foul the winding key, or prevent its insertion, as the apertures are of but normal size.

A variant of this arrangement of the World Time idea (which has not the limitation alluded to above) is provided in a long-case chiming clock by Thomas Lister, Halifax, *circa* 1780, in my possession. This clock (illustrated by Plates 46, 48 and 49) is fully described later in this book.

---

[1] Additionally, the dial-centre cannot be used for the display of other movements, e.g., seconds and calendar-work.

Chapter Five

Dials and Hands

MANY of the very early dials used for long-case clocks were those fitted to movements of lantern type, these latter being of but thirty-hour duration and almost invariably one-handed.

The brass base-plates of these early dials were always rectangular in shape and of small size, varying from about seven to ten inches square.

Silvered chapter-rings were attached by studs and pins to the dial-plates, and were engraved with subsidiary divisions for half and quarter hours only. Minute markings were not used, as there existed no corresponding minute hand. The engraving of the chapters and sub-divisions was filled with black wax, brought level with the surface of the hour-circle.

The spandrels of the dial and its central portion were usually excellently engraved, often with the popular tulip pattern decoration, and finished by the old method of water-gilding.

An alarm disc occasionally occupies the centre of the dial, but the calendar is usually absent from these dials with lantern movements, and the sub-dial for seconds is not used.[1]

A somewhat later development of the engraved spandrels was the substitution of cast brass corner-pieces, nicely chased with the graver, the early pattern being of simple winged cherub-head form.

These corner-pieces, although costing no more, and perhaps less than the earlier engraving, improved the appearance of the dial to a very great extent, providing welcome relief to the otherwise continuously flat surface of the plate. They were made by brass-foundries specializing in clock parts, and each clockmaker would choose his favourite design, then, until another touched his fancy, would adhere to it for all his clocks.

With the general introduction of minute motion-work and both hour and minute hands we find the chapter-rings engraved with minute divisions

---

[1] It could not be used for normal thirty-hour movements of either lantern or plate-frame type, for reasons explained elsewhere.

upon their outer edes. These divisions were at first large and clear, and numbered at every fifth minute by small arabic numerals engraved *within* the two concentric circles of the minute-band. (*See* Plate 21.) After about 1690 it became the fashion to increase the width of the chapter ring slightly and then "set in" the minute divisions a little distance from the edge, allowing for numbering *outside* the divisions, still at every fifth minute. (*See* Plates 19, 22 and 23.)

Certain authorities consider that this procedure was adopted so that the subsequent numbering of *every minute* from 1 to 60 would be facilitated, should it be required.

Whether this was so or not, we know that the extraordinary method of engraving dials in this manner was occasionally practised during the very early years of the eighteenth century.[1] The expense of engraving a chapter-ring according to this system of "minute-numbering" must have added very considerably to the cost of the clock, which supposition would seem to be corroborated by the rarity of dials thus figured. It is not easy to see the utility of this "minute-numbering", and the device was probably regarded as a mere expensive decoration, the supererogatory character of which would induce few to emulation.

About 1670 the engraving of the dial-centre seems to have been superseded in London work by a "matted" or "frosted" surface for this part of the plate, and this became characteristic of London-made clocks for a long period. A little engraving is sometimes introduced around the aperture through which the day of the month is displayed, this having a very good effect when burnished in contrast to the matted "ground". (*See* Plates 18, 19, 21, 22 and 23.)

The engraved centre, with plain, matted, or silvered "field", continued to be used by North Country clockmakers throughout the eighteenth century, the chronological succession of variants being approximately as given.

It must have been realized at a comparatively early date that some ornamentation of the winding apertures in the dial-centre would add to the decorative effect of the whole.

This decoration was provided by circular brass ornaments to the winding-holes, or a series of concave rings would be turned around these,

---

[1] Britten and Cescinsky both illustrate a clock by Chris. Gould, London, with dial displaying separately-numbered minutes (*circa* 1700).

the turnings being burnished as a contrast to the matting of the centre.

The ringed winding-hole is not, of course, peculiar to dials with entirely matted centres only, although to such may be ascribed its inception. It is frequently a feature of clock dials bearing the names of Northern makers, and such dials often provide fine examples of the highly-engraved centre. (*See* Plate 26.)

As to an approximate date of introduction for the ringed winding-hole opinions differ. I would be inclined to favour 1690–1695.

The earliest type of cast corner ornament was undoubtedly that of the cherub-head pattern, winged, and carefully chased with the graving tool.

This species of corner-piece became more elaborate after about 1685, and the later examples produced during the eighteenth century in London were not always so carefully finished as the earlier castings, often exhibiting a raggedness in their interstices inconsistent with conscientious file-finishing.

The simple winged cherub-head was succeeded by various patterns of corner ornament displaying greater complexity. (*See* Plates 19, 21, 22 and 23.) For some time the winged head remained the *leitmotiv* of these, but it was often varied in the reign of Queen Anne by corner pieces presenting a design of amorini supporting a crown amidst foliage, or by similar figures holding a crown and crossed sceptres or bâtons.

For some time I have been distinctly of the opinion that the particular design of corner-piece displaying the crown, foliage and cherubs (obviously inspired by the Restoration, as witness its employment in the carving of chairs and day-beds of that period) should somewhat ante-date its usually accredited time—the reign of Anne, 1702–1714.

This is confirmed by the clocks in Frontispiece and Plate 18, both *circa* 1690. These, of course, would be of the reign of William III and Mary, but no doubt Restoration enthusiasm and designs would still be in the ascendant at this date, as also in the early years of Anne.

The set of cast "corners" illustrating the four seasons of the year by suitable allegorical figures is of decidedly antique origin, being used in the form of bas-reliefs for the dial of the clock at St. Mary Steps, Exeter, dating from the sixteenth century. In so far as the dials of long-case clocks are concerned, these cast corner-pieces do not seem to antedate those previously described, and in most instances may be regarded as indicating a dial of eighteenth-century production. It is rather curious that their use would appear to be confined to Northern makers, as a generalization; but it will be observed that they appear upon the dial by Edward Samm, Linton (Cambridgeshire), illustrated by Plate 39. An early example of their provision by a Northern maker is that shown in Plate 26, illustrating a fine dial by John Clough, Manchester, *circa* 1720.

The Dutch makers, also, seem to have used this " seasons " type of corner ornament with fair frequency, which has led some writers to the statement that this design is Dutch in character *and inception*. To this opinion I do not subscribe, but it is certainly true to say that it may have been a favourite with the " Hollanders ". I have seen the corner-pieces upon a fine dial by Pieter Moryn, Amsterdam, *circa* 1715, and it will be observed that they appear on the dial by Jacob Hasius, *circa* 1720, illustrated by Plate 29, in practically exact detail to those displayed by the John Clough, Manchester dial of approximately the same period. Many iron dials, later in time and debased in quality compared with the brass dials illustrated in this book, have *painted versions* of this particular corner decoration; in these the classical allusions are replaced by (usually) female figures in the costume of the late eighteenth century, garbed according to the season, and portrayed in appropriate surroundings.

From about 1750 and throughout the reign of George III, corner ornaments of an involved scroll-like type, having a classic head as the central feature, were generally employed. A variant of these was provided by that pattern known as the " flower-and-scroll " cornerpiece, examples of which are illustrated in Plates 39 (arch) and 51.

One of the earliest cast ornaments used for the arch in dials of this type is that known as the " dolphin " pattern. The name is self-explanatory. An example may be seen by referring to Plate 26. This pattern of arch-ornament continued in use until about 1760–1770.

In dials with corner-pieces of the " flower-and-scroll " type the arch ornaments were nearly always of corresponding design. Plate 47, however, illustrates a dial with " classic head " corner-pieces and arch ornaments of " flower-and-scroll " pattern, and Plate 39 displays a dial also having this type of arch decoration combined with corner-pieces depicting the Four Seasons.

A reversion to the early practice of *engraving* the spandrels is illustrated by the dial shown in Plate 48.

Many of the earlier dials exemplified a well-engraved banding, often of " herringbone " pattern, bordering the square and, if present, the arch. This engraved border does not appear on any later type of dial,[1] and would seem to be peculiar to those before about 1740.

Early examples of the sub-dial for indicating seconds were engraved with the seconds-marking around the *inner edge* of the silvered ring, and numbered at every fifth second. Later, the numerals were used at every tenth second, with perhaps a diamond or similar decoration between them, and finally the divisions were transferred to the outer edge of the circle.

A particularly handsome seconds dial is that shown by Plate 39.

The sub-dial itself is sunk below the level of the main dial-plate, so as to give ample clearance between the small hand and the hour indicator. The edge of the plate surrounding the sub-dial is beautifully decorated, and a well-engraved twelve-rayed star ornaments the centre of the small dial.

We have seen how the minute divisions of the chapter-ring were arranged to accommodate numbering at every fifth minute without the figures being intermixed with them.

The arabic numerals were at first of small size, and entirely subsidiary to the Roman chapters. Later, as we have observed in Chapter Three, these arabic characters became much larger, until they attained equal proportions to the hour numerals in many instances. This particular conceit does not appear to be attended by any advantages, since the reading of the time is not helped thereby, and the effect cannot be regarded as being in good taste.

Subsequent to about 1770, the minutes of the chapter-ring were sometimes indicated by a series of dots, instead of by radial lines joining concentric circles. This is illustrated by Plate 48, in which dial it will be noticed that the sub-dials for seconds and calendar are similarly arranged.

On the dial by Edward Samm, Linton (near Cambridge), shown by Plate 39, it will be observed that the minute-circles are disposed in a series of " waves ".

This would appear to be a device of Dutch origin. Not infrequently English watches intended for the Dutch market had dials similarly treated, *circa* 1700 and later. A fine Dutch dial for a long-case clock by Johannes Du Chesne, Amsterdam, is illustrated by Britten (*Old Clocks and Watches*)

---

[1] Doubtless there are the inevitable exceptions!

well exemplifying this feature. This is attributed to about 1750. Another, by Barnish of Rochdale, of somewhat later date, is illustrated by G. F. C. Gordon (*Clockmaking: Past and Present*).

Up to about 1740 the quarter-hours were always indicated on clock dials. The method was similar to that employed for the minute divisions, i.e., concentric circles joined by radial lines marking the quarters, situated near the inner edge of the hour-circle. Half-hours were also marked by an extension of certain quarter-lines into some device such as a fleur-de-lys. (*See* Frontispiece and Plates 18, 19, 21, 22, 23, 26 and 29).

This system was undoubtedly a survival from the days of one-hand clocks, when such indications would be almost a necessity for reasonably accurate reading. It was sometimes used on dials even as late as 1760–70 by those makers displaying reversionary tendencies in their work. (*See* Plates 36 and 42.)

Although its *raison d'être* passed with the general introduction of the minute-hand, it was some time before clockmakers finally abandoned the old method, so strong is the influence of tradition. The later dials, after about 1760, do not generally display quarter-markings; as we have seen, exceptional instances to the contrary exist.

The decoration used to mark the half-hours was the last to go, and may sometimes be seen on quite late dials.

The engraved *and silvered* dial-centre appeared quite early, about 1760. Later, this was succeeded by an entirely silvered dial-plate, lacking both cast corner-pieces and separately attached chapter-ring, this latter being *engraved* upon the flat surface of the plate, together with the spandrels and dial-centre. This development was probably induced by the desire for extraordinary legibility, and originated *circa* 1780.

Also about 1780, or perhaps a little earlier, appeared the sheet-iron dial with painted chapters and decoration. Of these in general we may say that they do not warrant further description, representing as they do the beginning of degradation in clockmaking. A few specimens, however, including those of Battersea enamel, are of greater merit, and the *brass* dials of earlier times adorned with really worthy paintings (sometimes by excellent artists) are mentioned with due appreciation in Chapter Three of this work.

In most of the early dials, the maker's name was engraved in a straight line along the bottom edge of the plate, so that it was not visible

F

until the hood was raised, or the hood-door opened. (*See* Plates 21 and 23.) At this period too, the name was frequently latinized, thus: " Eduardus East, Londini ", or " Johannes Fromanteel, Londini, Fecit ". The word " fecit " (made [it]) was often appended to a signature in English, as " William Clement, Fecit " or Willm. Coward, Fecit " (Plate 1). *See* also Plate 23, " William Tipling in Leeds fecit ".

A variant to the " edge of the dial " position for the maker's name was that in the dial-centre, usually below the hand-collet. It was then often displayed upon a scroll or surrounded with decorative engraving of contemporary pattern.

Later positions for the name of the maker included one such in the chapter-ring just above the minute divisions and to left and right of the engraving for the sixth hour. (*See* Plates 19 and 22.) A favourite and very suitable situation for the inscription (apparently particularly popular with Northern makers) was in a similar position, but outside the minute-band, between the arabic numerals " 25 " and " 35 ", as illustrated by Plates 26 and 29.

It is not very certain when the attached name-plate (as in Plate 39) was first used. It appears to have been a favourite device of Thomas Tompion in his later clocks, *circa* 1710, and an example by this maker is illustrated by Cescinsky (*Old English Master Clockmakers*) which is attributed to a date as early as 1690.

With the advent of the arch-top dial about 1710 the maker's name frequently appeared engraved upon a silvered convex boss flanked by cast ornaments of the dolphin pattern.

Dials from about 1760 onward had frequently a painted Lunar Record in the arch. This species of Lunar Record with *star-spangled firmament* (not the later landscapes and seascapes) may quite possibly be older than the approximate date assigned it here. Mr. Cescinsky illustrates a dial bearing the name of Charles Gretton, London, who was apprenticed in 1662, became a member of the C.C. in 1672, and Master of the Company from 1700 to 1733. which has this kind of lunation disc. It is true that Mr. Cescinsky describes it as a " late dial, *circa* 1790 " but it has many features common to the earlier dials up to *circa* 1740, and, *if really by Gretton,* must of course be some sixty or seventy years before the assigned date.

With the painted lunation disc it was usual to inscribe the maker's name upon a silvered semi-circular plate attached to the top of the dial. (*See* Plates 40, 42 and 51.)

At all periods from about 1715 (Joseph Williamson) the dial centre was used to receive attached scrolling bearing the maker's name, and occasionally inscribed mottoes, often in Latin, a very beautiful and elaborate late development of this idea is illustrated by Plate 51.

A complete book could be written upon the subject of clock hands.

The best exposition the author has seen is that provided by the late G. F. C. Gordon in his book *Clockmaking: Past and Present*, where no fewer than one hundred and three examples are illustrated, in pairs and singly.

For general purposes, however, we shall obtain a sufficiently clear idea of the development of hands by studying the examples illustrated in this book. These range from *circa* 1680 to about 1800, and although neither the very earliest pattern nor the latest possible examples are included, the period covered is adequately representative.

There is little doubt that the earliest type of hand was of arrow-head formation. A simple early pattern, used by William Bowyer for lantern clocks *circa* 1625, displays the shape with curved " barbs ".

From this primitive form of hand a gradual progression leads us to the pattern illustrated by the small lantern clock shown in Plate 3. It will be noticed that the arrow-head shape is retained, but it is now ornamented by piercing, and the surface of the hand is rounded by the file, i.e., the outer edges are " chamfered ". Although measuring appreciably less than two-and-a-half inches overall, this small hand is a solid little piece, of early pattern, although not of early date.

By 1670, the piercing of the arrow-head or " heart " produced a pattern resembling a series of loops, and file-cutting was used to ornament the surface. The hour-hand of the lantern clock illustrated by Plate 1 displays this effect, which was also employed in the hands of long-case clocks from about 1675.

During the latter part of the seventeenth century some exquisite hands were provided by various makers. Examples may be seen in Frontispiece and Plates 18 and 19. It is usually supposed that these beautiful creations were the work of " chamber masters " who supplied the clockmaker according to his fancy. Be that as it may, the fine productions of this period reached a very high level of artistic excellence, which was not surpassed later, although the work of the early years of the succeeding century was destined to equal them in this, and even to exceed them in elaboration.

As an example of the type of work produced during the Queen Anne and early Georgian periods we may refer to Plates 24 and 26. The hands here illustrated represent the culmination of this style, to which occasional reversions were made from time to time until about 1760. Plate 36, which shows a dial by Jonathan Lees, Bury, with beautiful hands, is an instance of this reversionary tendency.

The minute-hand used in conjunction with the type of hour-hand just described was a straight and slender indicator with but little ornamentation.

The earliest minute-hands had a slender S-shaped scroll for their only ornament, situated near the boss. A rather later version of this is shown in Frontispiece. In time this scroll was developed by the addition of various loops and piercings until in the time of Anne it presented the appearance depicted in Plates 24 and 26. Later alterations in the form and size of the loops almost obliterated the idea of a scroll, and about the middle of the eighteenth century we find the serpentine minute-hand beginning to appear. This type had " side-shoots " at intervals up the stem, as illustrated by Plates 47, 48 and 52.

Contemporary with the serpentine minute hand we find the corresponding hour indicator assuming the form shown by Plate 47. This type of hand was never used on dials displaying quarter-hour divisions.

During the latter years of the eighteenth century, when dials had increased in size up to fourteen and even fifteen inches in width, we find the hands correspondingly large and somewhat coarse in comparison with earlier examples.

The workmanship, however, was still good, and the effect not at all displeasing, as may be seen by referring to Plates 48 and 52.

It will be noticed by referring to Plates 47 and 48 (both different clocks, but by the same maker) that the hands are arranged to encompass a larger area of the dial than is the case with those hands designed by early makers (compare these hands with those illustrated by Frontispiece and Plates 18, 23 and 26).

The earlier hands (say up to *circa* 1730) were practically always designed for an exact " fit ", i.e., the hour indicator was of a length just sufficient to touch with its tip the outer edge of the quarter-markings of the chapter ring. The minute-hand, similarly, touched exactly the outer circle of the minute-band, neither more nor less. Occasionally we find some evidence of a slight lack of care in this respect (observe, for instance, the minute-hands on the dials shown by Plates 19, 21 and 29) but the general rule holds good.

The later examples, particularly after about 1750, are variable as to " fit " in this manner. Plate 36, displaying beautiful hands of about 1760, and these distinctly of a " reversionary " character, illustrates the tendency to ignore the old ruling as to the " fit " of the hands in the dial.

Referring again to the hands depicted by Plates 47 and 48, we see that in both dials the minute hands reach quite to the edge of the chapter ring, and the pointers of the hour-hands touch a position at nearly one quarter the entire width of the hour-circle.

I have in my possession a modern gong-chiming mantel clock, made about 1910, in which the hands are similarly arranged. This clock is of the so-called " reproduction " type, and I have noticed that all clocks of this kind which I have seen have hands " spaced " likewise.

It is not apparent that anything is gained by this practice of the later makers; it is, indeed, rather clumsy in its effect, and shows the general trend away from the carefully calculated and highly artistic hands of the fine early dials. That it was not the persistent practice of *all* the later makers is clear (*see* Plates 39, 40, 42 and 51) but it seems to have been fairly common, to say the least.

The assertion has been made that " overlength " hands—as I shall call them for convenince—are replacements; i.e., not the originals.

If we consider this without bias we shall see that the idea is manifestly absurd.

Of clocks dating before about 1730 we may make an examination, and we shall find that our researches result in our ascertaining that practically all these have " fitting " hands.

A similar comparison of later clocks (say from 1760 to 1795) will reveal a very large percentage having " overlength " indicators.

As it is most unlikely that the early clocks, passing through all the vicissitudes inherent in their long life, should nearly without exception retain their original hands, and, conversely, that most of the later movements, logically subject to less disturbance because of shorter existence, should lose the originals, it may be safely assumed that the " overlength " hands (where not obvious replacements judged by other evidence than their length) are quite original.

With the introduction of the completely silvered dial-plate, without separate chapter-ring, we notice the beginning of the " hands to match " fashion. This vogue was further confirmed by the advent of the painted iron dial, 1770–80. Hands designed as pairs were made in either steel or brass, and some of the earlier hand-finished examples are not lacking in artistry, as may be seen by the pair of brass hands illustrated by Plate 54. The " finish " of these is quite good, but the same cannot be said of others produced by means of shearing dies alone, which method is that employed for the making of modern " stamped-out " hands.

The edges of these abominations are left quite untouched by the file, presenting a ragged appearance upon close inspection, and an unpleasant roughness to the touch. In addition, the modern steel hands of this kind are coloured, not by heat, but by a blue lacquer.

The Wall Clock illustrated by Plates 8 and 9 has a really splendid pair of very heavy solid *brass* hands. According to the late G. F. C. Gordon, cast brass hands were a not uncommon inclusion by some early *Lancashire* makers; and here we see their appearance in a Dutch clock. The clock, however, has a brass dial replacing the original enamelled plate.

The small hand used for the subsidiary dial indicating seconds was at first unprovided with a counterpoise. It was straight, slender, and short, since the seconds markings were on the inner edge of the engraved circle. (*See* Frontispiece and Plates 18, 19, 21, 22, and 23.)

About 1720 the double-ended or counterpoised hand appeared (*see* Plate 29), and this type was always used with the later sub-dials, where the divisions were placed on the outer edge of the seconds-ring. (*See* Plates 39 and 48).

With the vogue of " hands to match " previously mentioned, the seconds hand was frequently designed accordingly.

In centre-seconds clocks, the seconds hand is always adequately counterpoised, owing to the great length of the index portion. This latter, despite its extreme slenderness, would certainly stop the 'scape-wheel were it not carefully counterbalanced. An example of this kind of hand is illustrated by Plates 51 and 52.

Chapter Six

Cases

IT cannot be denied, despite its origin as a time-recorder, that a long-case clock is also an article of furniture, and this in the popular and limited sense of the term.

Some go as far as to assert that it is primarily as such that any example should be judged, and, while according every consideration to the horo-logical aspect, it must be confessed that there is much to be said for this viewpoint.

After all, and with but little loss in accuracy, almost equivalent chronometrical results can be obtained by other media. The spring-driven mantel clock had attained a capability for precision not greatly inferior to its more imposing contemporary, even as early as 1680. In addition, these mantel clocks possess the advantage of portability, a point not to be ignored in the days when timekeepers of all kinds were expensive acquisitions, even for the well-to-do.

The undoubted preference given by many to the long-case form assuredly had its origin in the more dignified appearance of the " grand-father " type as compared with other varieties of clocks. It was a piece of some size and importance, often of much beauty also, and worthy to take its place with other considerable furnishings in a room.

All this being conceded, it will be seen with what importance the cabinet-work of our long-case clock is invested. That this was realized by the clockmaker at an early period is supported by the excellence of much old casework.

Although it is indisputable that the clockmaker had his cases made for him by a cabinet-maker, and that the finer points of construction and design must be imputed to the latter artist, we may reasonably suppose that the horologist would select his cases with an eye to their suitability for certain dials, and would exercise some sort of supervision as to general style.

Quite early in the history of English Clockmaking we find mention of " case-makers ". Thus it would appear that a special branch of cabinet-making owed its inception to the clockmaker.

It has been suggested[1] that the early tall cases were of Dutch manufacture, and imported here, but I can find nothing conclusive to support this view. *See* Chapter Two (Early Long-Case Clocks).

As to the *decoration* of early long cases, though not the earliest of these, it can be accepted that the Dutch influence (shewn by early marquetry examples of English work) was paramount.

The exiled Charles II, and his adherents banished with him, probably brought over to England at the Restoration (1660) Dutch fashions and tastes from The Hague, and it is probable that from about 1675 until 1689 examples of English clock-cases were decorated with marquetry in Holland, being sent there for this purpose in much the same way that, at a rather later period, English-made long clock-cases or trunk doors were exported to the Orient for lacquer decoration.

With the accession of William III (William of Orange) in 1689 this Dutch influence would become much stronger, and affect the decorative aspect of the long clock-cases in common with other things.

When Louis XIV revoked the Edict of Nantes, in 1685, many thousands of Huguenots fled France to escape religious persecution, many settling in Holland. It is quite possible that after the accession of William of Orange as William III of England a large number of Huguenot craftsmen came over from Holland to this country, and these would naturally have assimilated, together with the typically French inlay of metal and tortoiseshell known as Boulle (after its originator—André Boulle) the Dutch style of marquetry in wood, if indeed they did not themselves contribute to the development of the latter.

It cannot be supposed that English cabinet-makers would be slow to perceive the possibilities of marquetry-work executed by these immigrant craftsmen, and thus originate what, after a time, became a characteristically English type of inlay, i.e., the so-called " seaweed " and " arabesque " forms of marquetry.

After alluding to " the making of clock-cases becoming an industry " Mr. Arthur Hayden " inclines to the belief that seventy-five per cent of

---

[1] H. Cescinsky: *English Furniture of the 18th Century* (3 vols., 4to, 1909—1911), Vol. I, Chap. 14, where the thesis seems to be that such were also of Dutch *invention*.

them were of foreign manufacture, either in Holland and imported here, or made by Dutch immigrants or French refugees in this country."

My personal opinion is that the tall clock-case being entirely English in its conception (*see* Chapter Two, Early Long-Case Clocks), these were made by English cabinet-makers and very probably—in the instances of examples between 1689 and about 1695—inlaid by Dutch immigrants (or French refugees *via* Holland).

Later examples point to both construction *and inlay* being by our native craftsmen.

Of those cases made before 1689 it is probable that these were either exported to Holland for inlaying or constructed there *from English models.*

The fashion for marquetry did not begin until *circa* 1675, and it is significant that tall clock-cases before this date[1] were usually veneered with ebony all over, in which style I have yet to see or hear of a proved Dutch example in *long-case form.* It must not be forgotten, however, that the cases of Coster's early clocks, and these probably both spring and weight-powered, were apparently of ebony, or veneered with ebony, but these were intended for hanging upon a wall, a distinctively Dutch position for a clock, and we still lack evidence of any " grandfather " clocks of early Dutch provenance with ebonized casework.

It is probable that certain clockmakers favoured particular designs for their case-work; thus, one might shew preference for that type of hood with carved cresting, and evince a partiality for " bird-and-flower " marquetry in panels; another might favour the canopied hood and marquetry of " sea-weed " or " arabesque " pattern, while a third maker would perhaps prefer casework of figured or " burr " walnut with possibly a square-topped hood.

The majority of old makers, however, seem to have varied the case-work of their clocks widely, but always appear to have had in mind that compatibility already mentioned.

One of the earliest materials employed for long cases was oak, nearly always used in the form of carcase-work. Upon this foundation was applied veneers of ebony or walnut, these being occasionally varied by olive-wood, laburnum, kingwood, and pollard oak or yew.

As a general rule, cases finished in solid oak, without veneering except for a small amount of walnut cross-banding at the edges, were not used in

---

[1] Say, in any event, from 1660–1670, after which walnut and olivewood veneers began to be used, to be supplemented with marquetry inlay after 1675.

work of the very highest quality, although this observation is subject to notable exceptions.

For marquetry work, walnut veneer was usually employed as the " ground ", this being inlayed with holly, box, and sometimes ivory, the latter plain or stained green. The yellow colour of the boxwood and holly was varied by burning in hot sand.

The Dutch marquetry was a bold type, the pattern being formed of large floral designs, in which a bird or birds and usually a vase were prominent features. It is consequently often referred to as marquetry of " bird-and-flower " pattern. The design is often displayed in " panels " of ebony, surrounded by walnut, the black background serving to enhance the pattern in different kinds and shades of yellow wood and sometimes white and green-stained ivory. (*See* Plate 14.)

Another type of inlay, possibly of Dutch or Flemish origin, but which was used a good deal by the English cabinet-makers of the earlier marquetry period, was that frequently described as marquetry of " all-over " pattern.[1] An example is illustrated by Plate 16.

This, as the name suggests, was a design of large foliage, etc., completely covering the surface of a piece, sometimes including the sides of a clock case also. It seems to have been employed in England rather later than the " panel " type of inlay. (Compare Plates 14 and 16.)

Two further varieties of " Dutch " marquetry may be mentioned here, they are known as " Star marquetry " and inlay of " fan pattern ". The names are sufficiently self-explanatory. Light and dark woods are used alternately for the " vanes " of the fan and the star's rays, the effect being often of much brilliance, if in rather questionable taste.

These coarser kinds of inlay, after the Dutch model, were succeeded by others of greater complexity and " quieter " effect, founded upon the Italian type of fine filigree work, and representing characteristically English forms of marquetry.

One of these later styles closely resembles the fine scrolled ornament of Boulle, and another, not altogether dissimilar, has been given the name of " seaweed " marquetry. With these types the art of inlaying seems to have reached its climax, and thereafter the fashion for marquetry declined in favour of walnut veneer in " burr " or other figured kinds. (*See* Plates 27, 28 and 30 for illustrations of an example.)

---

[1] Sometimes alleged to exhibit French influence.

A splendid and very late example of marquetry inlay, on *solid* English walnut, may be seen by referring to Plates 41, 42, 43 and 44, illustrating a fine clock by Nathaniel Brown, Manchester, *circa* 1770, the case of which must be regarded as distinctly rare.

During the marquetry period (i.e., up to about 1720) the casework of the clock was distinguished by several features characteristic of the construction then employed.

The trunk door was very long, and rectangular in shape, with a bold half-round moulding, often of ebony or ebonized wood, decorating its edges. (*See* Plates 14, 16 and 17.) The bases of the earlier cases were frequently very short, and were finished by a plain plinth, "feet" of any kind being exceptional.[1]

Although the moulding between base and trunk was of varying pattern, the early cases always displayed a quarter-round moulding immediately beneath the hood (Frontispiece); later, this was changed to a moulding of concave-section. (Plates 18, 26, 28 *et seq.*)

The lift-up hood was invariably employed for the earlier casework, up to *circa* 1685, at which date the height of cases began to increase, making the rising hood an inconvenient arrangement. We have seen (Chapter Two) how the closing of the trunk door was made to lock the hood, by means of a trigger-like catch, so that it could not be raised until the long door was opened. When the glazed door was introduced for the hoods of long-case clocks, another method of securing this door, to prevent winding until the trunk door was open, became desirable.

This was effected by affixing an iron staple to the back of the hood door framing, on the bottom rail and near that corner opposite the hinge. This staple passed through a slot cut for it in the wooden bezel surrounding the dial, thus the hood door could be locked by passing a wooden peg through the staple behind the bezel. The trunk door would then have to be opened in order to remove this peg.

The device just alluded to would appear to have been used until very late in the eighteenth century by many makers, as it is present in clocks known to date from about 1785.

The varying shape of hoods at different periods has been already dealt with in Chapters Two and Three.

---

[1] A few of the early cases, with bases destitute of plinths, had, however, small round feet attached. H. Cescinsky (*Old English Master Clockmakers*, etc.) has discovered that such cases were intended to stand in adjustable "trays" with moulded edges.

The clock case decorated with designs in raised laquer may be said to have become fairly popular about the year 1700.

This is not to imply that examples before this date were not appreciated, but they are now decidedly rare, and we may say that the lacquer cases enjoyed their greatest vogue from about 1700 until *circa* 1730.

Again, however, it is not unusual to see a movement enclosed by lacquered casework dating from almost any time during the eighteenth century; such cases were provided more or less according to choice, but it is undoubtedly true to say that the fashion for *lacquered furniture generally* began to decline *circa* 1730.

Rather curiously, this decline in favour did not affect the clock case to anything like the extent applicable to other domestic articles, and to this we can perhaps attribute the comparatively large number of tall clock-cases decorated in lacquer which survive at the present day, in various states of preservation.

It has been stated with some show of fact that many clock cases to be ornamented by " japanning " (as lacquer-work was generally called in the seventeenth and eighteenth centuries) were sent to the East to be so treated, and that frequently—no doubt in response to a demand for cheaper styles —only the *trunk doors* were sent for lacquering in the characteristic relief patterns of the Orient. The remaining portions of the casework would then be decorated in England with comparatively crude designs by stencil. the " lacquer " used being little more than paint. The trunk-doors in these instances were usually made of oak, the remainder of the case of deal.

In those instances where a clock-case is ornamented by lacquer-work of the highest class, the embossed or relief designs are used not only for the long door, but also for the base and practically the entire front of the case, sometimes even extending to the trunk sides and those of the base also. Qualities but little inferior and distinctly more common than the fore-going type restrict the relief-work to the more expansive surfaces, notably the trunk-door and the base, but evince a certain artistry in the application and arrangement of the stencil patterns elsewhere.

The raised portions of a design in lacquer-work were formed by a white composition applied to the carcase, over which composition the " ground " was applied in many successive " coats ", the whole process being a compli-cated and lengthy one, very much related to the characteristic patience and traditional lack of time-consideration implicit in the Oriental nature.

The finished work was finally completed by a thin coating of a very fine translucent varnish.

Those readers who may be interested in a very detailed description of the way in which a *smooth* lacquered surface was obtained in China by artists in the medium we are considering should consult the account of M. Jacquemart, quoted in Litchfield's *Illustrated History of Furniture*. Chapter Five (The Furniture of Eastern Countries).

The colours of the grounds employed in lacquer-work varied. We will take " English " lacquer for examples.

The most common is, perhaps, black; blue and green are rarer, still more so is the red ground, and (according to R. W. Symonds in *The Present State of Old English Furniture*) the buff ground is the most uncommon of all, genuine examples being extremely scarce.

The introduction of furniture in the " Chinese Taste " (*cf.* Thomas Chippendale—chairs of his period designed in this manner being fairly common) brought about the clock-case having a hood now often described as " pagoda-topped ". (*See* Chapter Three.)

Several such designs for tall clock-cases are illustrated in the book of furniture designs by Thomas Chippendale, published in 1754 and entitled *The Gentleman's and Cabinet Makers' Director*. A rather less ornate variant in actual construction became quite popular from about 1760.[1] until *circa* 1790, and this type of case, often made of mahogany, was also the subject for lacquer treatment. Its form, suggestive of the East because of the concave-sided superstructure to the hood, seems rather appropriate to lacquer decoration.

Mr. Arthur Hayden, *Chats on Old Clocks*, quite reasonably objects to the typically Western architectural features displayed by the rounded tops of the trunk and hood doors, etc., frequently employed at this period, in conjunction with the Oriental effect imparted by the lacquer ornamentation. In parenthesis, it may here be observed that many such solecisms and anachronisms are perpetrated by case-makers, and indeed by cabinet-makers and designers generally. Thus we have the Chippendale " Gothic " designs *in mahogany*, for instance, and clock-cases of the same material are not unknown which display *together* the Gothic and Oriental idioms!

A school of artists in lacquer became established in Holland, as also in England, towards the end of the seventeenth century, no doubt inspired by the imported Oriental work.

[1] The early cases of this type date from *circa* 1740. Most are of later date.

This "Dutch" and "English" lacquer, as it is now called, was often of high quality. The designs were still mostly *Oriental in character*, as is fitting for the medium, and the clock-case bearing "japanned" ornament in relief is frequently attributed to Eastern art when the lacquering is, in fact, native to England or Holland in its production.

Some skill is required to identify genuine old lacquer (whether Oriental or European).

Much of the lacquer-work upon old cabinets-on-stands of the Charles II period is modern English work "faked" to represent genuine old lacquer.

There is insufficient evidence to indicate that much is done in this way applicable to clock-cases, original examples of these being much more numerous than the cabinets referred to above. The faker's incentive to reproduce lacquer examples is therefore largely removed.

Many lacquered cases for clocks are to-day in very bad condition. For one case in anything approaching its original surface state and brilliance a dozen may be seen which, although objects not lacking in interest to the collector or student, serve very little decorative purpose.

Lacquer is most seriously harmed by exposure to continual strong sunlight; extremes of dampness or a very warm and dry atmosphere have also a baneful influence.

The repeal of the duty on imported timber in 1733 undoubtedly gave a fillip to the manufacture of domestic furniture in the much-admired mahogany, which was first used in the "Spanish" or San Domingo variety —hard and heavy wood of close grain and little "figure" but of very rich brown colouring, turning darker with age.

Later, Cuban mahogany was used as a variant, this being enriched with a fine curly grain of intriguing appearance, still having the predominantly brownish shades, but being (while still of closely-grained texture) somewhat lighter bulk for bulk than the San Domingo or "Spanish" variety.

Last of all the different kinds of mahogany employed for furniture-making in the eighteenth century was that known as Honduras mahogany (from its place of origin) sometimes referred to in the trade as "baywood". This was altogether a cheaper and lighter kind of wood, but often exhibiting a well-marked "figure" was much used in the form of matched veneers for panels and the larger surfaces. Both this and the Cuban variety do not perceptibly darken with age, the Honduras mahogany being also of a much redder cast than either of the earlier-used kinds.

"Spanish"[1] and Cuban mahogany was mainly used up to about 1770, after this date the Honduras variety seems to have held the field, the reason sometimes advanced involving the difficulty of transporting the San Domingo kind from the interior to the ports, as the supply of more easily procurable timber became less. No doubt, also, "baywood" would be a less costly timber, apart from the transportation charges. As far as the island of San Domingo is concerned, it occurs to the present writer that the confused state of racial and political opinion prevalent there at this period, and for many years afterwards, may possibly have provided no inconsiderable deterrent to prolonged journeys into the interior!

The mahogany-cased clocks of the period 1760–1795 included many choice examples, regarded both horologically and as "furniture". Plates 45, 46 and 50 may be consulted in this respect, all illustrating fine clocks.

Unfortunately, this same period saw the production of many monstrous caricatures of the graceful old cases, which regrettable effusions have been referred to elsewhere in this book.

Mention must here be made of the clock cases sometimes seen which are constructed of oak throughout (a rare variant is teak) and enriched by *carving* in a style analogous to that produced in the seventeenth century as a decoration upon other domestic furniture such as coffers, buffets and cabinets.

Britten alludes to these in his well-known work on clocks, and proffers his opinion that such cases are probably not of construction contemporary with the clock, but substitutions at a later date "to replace inferior or worn-out existing cases" and made by "enthusiastic artists in wood".

To this opinion I feel strongly inclined to subscribe, as a correspondent has recently furnished me with evidence which I have derived from an example in his possession, proving incontrovertibly that in this instance, at least, clock and case are not contemporary.

The clock in question has an *arched dial*, and yet the case is *dated* 1701!

I have for long had more than a suspicion that these carved cases

---

[1] San Domingo (better known as Haiti) together with Cuba and the other islands of the West Indies was discovered by Columbus in 1492. The island of San Domingo seems to have remained in Spanish possession (at least partly) until 1795, when it was ceded to France. Later, independence was proclaimed by the natives.

originate around the eighteen-sixties, when much imitation Jacobean carving was done on various kinds of furniture in the " exhibition " style.

Mr. H. Cescinsky has a reference (". . . clockcase of oak, in the later Carolean manner . . . a monstrosity . . .") which possibly refers to this style of casework, although the intention of the reference is somewhat obscure, as the writer seems to infer that he has never seen an example by his qualification " if such were possible ". It may be, of course, that he regards such cases as impossible *in the later Carolean period*, and, if such is the correct interpretation of the passage, I feel disposed to concur in this.

There is little doubt that Charles Dickens (*Master Humphrey's Clock*) was at some time acquainted with a clock in carved casework, and that he must have been impressed by it is suggested by his reference to the clock in his story: " . . . a quaint old thing in a huge oaken case curiously and richly carved."

The novelist's description " quaint " (though doubtless intended for the *clock*) is exactly applicable to these carved cases. One would hesitate to describe them as " handsome ", yet " handsomely carved " would not be inappropriate. They have certainly no claim to be called " beautiful ", and some people might perhaps consider " ugly " to be a more fitting adjective!

From which it will be seen that personal taste must decide as to the suitable nature of this kind of casework for a clock. There can be little purpose served by attempting a defence (if such is required) of carving in high relief on a clock case. One either likes it (or perhaps regards it as " quaint " and rather interesting, which is my own view) or one cannot bear it at all, and there we must leave the consideration of this not very common type of casework. An illustration will be found at Plate 53.

Before leaving the subject of cases altogether, I wish to write a few lines which may prove useful to the amateur upon a subject which has not, apparently, received much attention.

I refer to the not unknown practice of dealers and others in exchanging movements (with their dials) and cases.

It is well known that certain movements with sheet-iron dials painted or enamelled in the later style were enclosed in mahogany casework of excellent proportions and finish. The details and quality of workmanship in some of these later cases are in every way admirable; the selection of mahogany as to its " figure " and colouring is also frequently irreproachable.

PLATE 37

EIGHT-DAY STRIKING CLOCK
EDWARD SAMM, LINTON, *circa* 1760

See page 232

PLATE 38

EIGHT-DAY STRIKING CLOCK. JOHN ALLEN
MACCLESFIELD, *circa* 1770

See page 233

PLATE 39

DIAL AND HOOD OF CLOCK BY
EDWARD SAMM

See page 232

PLATE 40

DIAL AND HOOD OF CLOCK BY JOHN ALLEN

See page 233

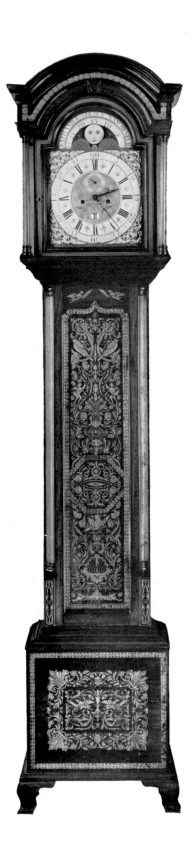

PLATE 41

EIGHT-DAY STRIKING CLOCK
NATHANIEL BROWN, MANCHESTER
circa 1770

See page 233

PLATE 42

DIAL AND HOOD OF CLOCK BY NATHANIEL
BROWN

See page 233

PLATE 43

DETAIL OF INLAY ON TRUNK DOOR
CLOCK BY NATHANIEL BROWN

See page 233

PLATE 44

DETAIL OF INLAY IN BASE OF
CASEWORK
CLOCK BY NATHANIEL BROWN

See page 233

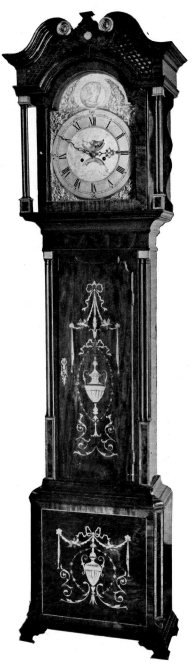

PLATE 45

EIGHT-DAY STRIKING CLOCK
THOMAS LISTER, HALIFAX
circa 1780

See page 236

PLATE 46

EIGHT-DAY STRIKING AND
CHIMING CLOCK. THOMAS
LISTER, HALIFAX, *circa* 1780

See page 237

PLATE 47

DIAL AND HOOD
STRIKING CLOCK BY THOMAS LISTER

See page 236

PLATE 48

DIAL AND HOOD
STRIKING AND CHIMING CLOCK BY
THOMAS LISTER

See page 237

PLATE 49

SIDE VIEW OF EIGHT-DAY STRIKING AND
CHIMING MOVEMENT BY THOMAS LISTER

See page 237

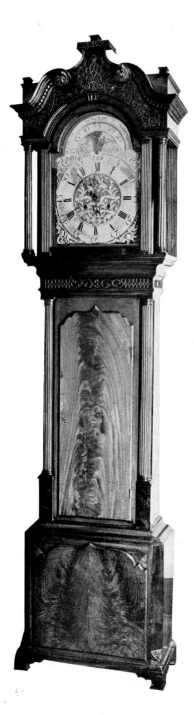

PLATE 50

EIGHT-DAY STRIKING CENTRE-SECONDS
CLOCK. PETER FEARNLEY, WIGAN, *circa* 1790

See page 240

PLATE 51

DIAL AND HOOD
CLOCK BY PETER FEARNLEY

See page 240

PLATE 52

EIGHT-DAY STRIKING CENTRE-SECONDS
MOVEMENT WITH LUNATION TRAIN BY
PETER FEARNLEY

See page 240

PLATE 53

A CLOCK-CASE OF CARVED OAK,
ENCLOSING A THIRTY-HOUR,
LATE EIGHTEENTH CENTURY
MOVEMENT. LOMAX, BLACKBURN

See page 241

PLATE 54

A SIMPLE TYPE OF THIRTY-HOUR LONG-
CASE MOVEMENT SHOWING BRASS HANDS
DESIGNED FOR A WHITE DIAL (LATE
EIGHTEENTH CENTURY)

The white dial being unpopular with collectors (it is, of course, generally the first thing that one learns to avoid!) dealers in old clocks are very strongly tempted to replace the movement with another, possibly from a less distinguished case having the same dimensions of dial-aperture, which latter movement has a brass dial of good quality. The white-dial movement is then put into the second (mediocre) case, and, behold! The fine case has then a nice brass dial, very tempting to the strolling clock-lover.

Provided that the transferred movement has its dial an exact fit for the " married " case, and that *the periods of case and dial are approximately coincident* the change is practically impossible to detect, and, in fact there must be many such instances of " married " movements and cases in the possession of very estimable collectors all over the country, proud of their " original " clocks and happy in the state of ignorance which is proverbially said to be bliss!

A word of comfort to such unconscious owners of " married " examples may now be offered.

Originally, as should be realized by everyone, the clockmaker bought his casework from the casemaker; he *never* made it himself. Even in such instances of obscure country workers as did their own dial-making and engraving, the local joiner was always responsible for the case.

This being so, I cannot see any possible harm in such instances of transferrence as I have mentioned, *always provided that due regard be given to coincidence of period and style.*

The latter point—" style "— is best exemplified by illustrations.

One often finds an elaborate dial enclosed by comparatively plain casework, *see* Plate 25; still more frequently an elaborate dial in correspondingly elaborate case—Plate 50; *very rarely indeed a plain dial in a " fancy " case,* since the guiding principle of artistic clockmaking is, or should be, that the dial should provide the central feature of the entire " clock ", and be as it were the focus towards which the eye of the beholder is at once attracted.

This " artistic principle ", consciously or unconsciously, seems to have been followed in the main by all the old makers in the selection of their casework, and its absence may therefore be regarded (lacking qualifying details) as strongly suggestive of substitution in the manner already described. It may be objected that the white-dial clocks in splendid mahogany cases previously mentioned as supplying instances of transference

G

are, *in their original state*, examples of plain dials in elaborate cases. But here the " plain " dial receives due accentuation by its treatment, as do also those *brass* dials which are entirely silvered, so that we are here provided with the " qualifying details " referred to above, and the general application of the artistic principle still holds good.

If there should be exceptions to the employment of this principle (and it will be noticed I have alluded to its being followed " in the main ") they are provided by clocks in marquetry cases.

The latter are not infrequently of such brilliance that the " artistic principle " we are using as a guide is confessedly broken. These clocks in marquetry casework are therefore a law unto themselves, and I do not propose to discuss here their artistic fitness; they must be accepted as being peculiar to their period and only to be judged by standards applicable to themselves alone.

When considering a possibly " married " movement in a marquetry case we must be guided by " period " only in this matter. It should be noticed, however, that even here one seldom finds a very plain and simple dial and hands enclosed in such a case; originally, that is to say. Walnut veneer of the " figured " type was most frequently used for the cases enclosing these dials and movements, the very earliest of which were encased in austerely beautiful coverings veneered with ebony. The gilding and silvering of the dial plates, chapter rings and corner-pieces would here provide the requisite emphasis.

An example of an exchanged movement and case is illustrated by the clock shown in Plates 35 and 36.

We may, perhaps, consider this in some detail.

The dial exemplifies somewhat " early " characteristics in the provision of quarter-markings, and decorations of conventional type at the half-hour positions. The arabic minute numerals, though not small, are not sufficiently enlarged in relation to the chapters to distinctly " date " the dial as a " late " example, but the tendency should be duly noted.

In the corner-pieces we have an altogether more trustworthy guide. These are of the pattern used after *circa* 1760, in the George III period, during which they were deservedly popular. On this dial the particular corner-ornaments are very nicely cast and carefully and effectively " chased ". This suggests that they are *early examples of the type*; many later corner-pieces of varying pattern are notable for rough casting and poor finish, which certainly cannot be said of those ornamenting this dial.

The really beautiful hands, in their form and workmanship strongly suggesting an early date, do not, however, " fit " the dial in the sense that they *overlap* the quarter- and minute-bands. (*See* Chapter Five—Dials and Hands, for a full discussions of this characteristically " late " practice). They are, therefore, of *circa* 1760, like the corner-pieces.

On glancing at the movement itself, we find the form of wheel-collet employed, together with other indications, is such as to confirm our attribution of *circa* 1760 for this clock.

Now let us give our attention to the *case*.

The hood has a superstructure, variously described as " cushion-moulded " or of " canopied " or " tea-caddy " type; an early design originating about 1685. The hood-door, however, is made without " pilasters ", true pillars being provided at front and rear. It is, therefore, *not* an early example of the form. The hood-sides, moreover, do not contain glass windows, which in the early hood were very usual; these windows, however, seem to have been a distinctly London fashion so that too much importance should not be attached to the lack of their provision here in so far as " period " is affected by them.

Passing to the trunk of the case, it will be observed that the large moulding immediately beneath the hood, upon which the latter is supported, has not the quarter-round section employed in the very early cases, nor is the trunk-door square-topped, or surrounded with the usual small moulding of the early types. The form of hinge employed (a strap hinge *lacking decorative finials at the joint*) is the early pattern, and the oaken back-board of the case bears therein many holes as evidence of frequent change of ownership over a long period.

The base has been cut down at some time, and a new plinth fitted, displaying very neat work having dovetailed joints at the front edges. Its depth, however, is probably much too great, and the cut-down portion now too short, destroying the original proportions of the base. The cutting-down of the original base was in all probability necessitated by the rotting of the woodwork at the bottom of the case, caused by the latter having stood at some time upon a flagged floor which has been periodically swilled with water, this water being responsible for the damage to the original base.

As the case is not a tall one, it is unlikely that its original height overall had anything to do with the mutilation of its base.

Now all these indications, and the inferences we may logically draw from them, help us to fix with tolerable exactitude a date for this case of around 1730, and we have already analysed the dial and movement as being *circa* 1760.

If final and irrefutable proof be required that case and movement are not contemporary, it is provided by opening the long door of the trunk and glancing within.

It will then be observed that the case sides have small " scooped-out " portions in their surfaces at positions coincident with those of the pendulum bob at either end of its arc, and that this " bob " has itself been modified in shape from the circular by the flattening of its right- and left-hand segments. This was done, of course, to allow an unimpeded arc in the narrow trunk, although its necessity does not seem apparent, as there is sufficient space available in the trunk to allow a free swing of the pendulum without the expedients adopted, but only just sufficient. It may have been done as a safety-measure, but in any event proves conclusively that the movement is not in the case originally intended to receive it.

This substitution has been quoted, and described at length, because it is one which (apart from the adaptions just mentioned) is not glaringly obvious.

No serious collector, however, should consider himself anything more than a mere tyro if he cannot with confidence decide a matter of this nature by an exterior examination only; even adequate photographs should suffice to arouse suspicions.

The question may now arise in the reader's mind—is a clock of which case and movement are known to be of different periods worth possessing?

The answer must be a qualified one. Certainly the movement and its dial illustrated by Plates 19 and 20 would be very well worth possessing without a case at all, or with almost any kind of case which affords protection; the same remarks apply to several movements (with their original dials) illustrated or described in this book. But possession of these, under similar circumstances, would only be a satisfaction to an enthusiast who already owned at least one complete timepiece with original case, and that of really good quality throughout.

For the ordinary clock-owner, possessing but one example of the long-case clock and desiring nothing further, it is to my mind essential that this single example be a worthy one, original as to both movement and case so far as can be determined.

Moreover, a very ordinary example of an eighteenth-century movement enclosed in an equally undistinguished case of different period would hardly commend itself to anyone if its anachronisms were known, for obvious reasons. In other words, either case or movement, and if not both, much preferably the latter,[1] must possess some features of more than usual interest to become acceptable as an entity when the periods of each are clearly not contemporary.

There are not lacking in existence to-day clocks in which the necessary conditions for complete acceptance and appreciation are entirely fulfilled, in despite of the sometimes very obvious chronological disparity of their movements and casework.

A very distinguished instance is provided by a clock by Thomas Tompion now in the possession of the Earl of Leicester at Holkham.

This famous clock (it would be more correct to refer to it as a "time-piece", since it has no striking train) was constructed in 1676 for John Flamsteed (1646–1719), the first Astronomer Royal. The $17\frac{1}{2}$-inch square dial has an original black velvet facing covering the brass base-plate, and at the bottom portion of scrolled decoration around the winding-hole bears the inscription "Sr. Jonas Moore caused this Movement with great Care to be thus Made Ano 1676 by Tho. Tompion". Engraved at the top of the scrolling is MOTVS ANNVVS, a reference to its being a *year movement*, perhaps Tompion's first of this kind. This gift of Sir Jonas's to Flamsteed has a replica at the British Museum and both were fitted originally with 13-foot pendulums (beats of two seconds). An old print of the Octagon Room at Greenwich Observatory in Flamsteed's time shows the two identical dials in the wall-panelling, set side by side. (*Historia Cœlestis* by J. Flamsteed, 1709.)

The "Holkham Tompion" has now a seconds pendulum with corresponding escape-wheel and is enclosed in an early eighteenth-century long case of plain oak.

A complete description (with illustrations) of the Tompion movements which were at one time in the Greenwich Observatory may be consulted by referring to the excellent article by Mr. H. Alan Lloyd which appeared in the *Horological Journal* for December 1948 ("The Clocks of John Flamsteed").

---

[1] By the term "movement" I include the dial and hands in this connection.

Chapter Seven

Eminent Makers: Their Characteristics and Improvements

THE very high standard of mechanical accuracy and constructional
ingenuity displayed by such horological machines as Harrison's
Marine Chronometers could hardly have been attained had it not been
for the pioneer work of the earlier craftsmen, working in cruder forms.
Indeed, it may be stated that the art or craft of clockmaking in England
began with the gradual introduction of that early type of chamber clock
to which the name " lantern " has been generally applied.

Even in this comparatively imperfect expression, opportunity was not
neglected by progressive early makers, as may be observed in those rare
examples of the lantern type in which *chimes* were introduced, as well as
in the more common instances of striking trains, alarums, and minute
motion-work.

During the period 1630–1730, which includes both the earlier lantern
clocks and the " walnut veneered " type of long-case timepiece, we find
many famous names.

Fromanteel, East, Jones, Knibb, Tompion, Graham and Quare
flourished during the years of that century, together with many a lesser-
known maker of doubtless equal ability. Of this latter class we may
perhaps especially choose for mention the names of Nicholas Coxeter,
William Bowyer, Peter Closon, Thomas Wheeler, Joseph Williamson,
William Clement, Christopher Gould, Joseph Windmills, Peter Garon,
George Etherington, and Charles Gretton.

Quite early in the history of English clockmaking appears the name
of Fromanteel, variously spelt ' Fromantil ", " Fromantel ", and
" Fromanteele ".

There were apparently several makers of this name from about
1630–1720, including three or four with the same name of Ahasuerus, of

whom the earliest is first mentioned in 1630 in connection with the guild known as the Blacksmiths' Company. The members of this Guild who were clockmakers were later admitted to the Company of Clockmakers, upon the incorporation of the latter in 1631. Another Fromanteel, by whom several early long-case clocks exist, was John or, as the name usually appears upon clock dials, Johannes Fromanteel. At least two other persons of this name, Abraham (C.C. 1680) and Louis are mentioned as being clockmakers, and a partnership under the names of Fromanteel and Clarke produced many fine clocks in the latter part of the seventeenth and early years of the eighteenth century. The family of Fromanteel was of Dutch origin, but early settled in England, later attaining some degree of celebrity as being responsible for the introduction of the pendulum into this country (*see* Pendulum, in Glossary).

Apart from the important innovation mentioned above, clocks by the Fromanteels exhibit many refinements representative of the best work of contemporary makers, among which features may be included bolt-and-shutter maintaining power, second-and-a-quarter pendulums, month duration and three-train movements.

The Clockmakers' Company was incorporated by Royal Charter of Charles I in 1631, as previously observed, and consisted of a Master, three Wardens, and at least ten Assistants, these forming the " Court ". Upon being admitted a member of the Company, the particular clockmaker was then known as a " freeman " of the Guild and was from thence at liberty to practise his craft by setting up in business on his own account. Clockmaker members of other City Guilds in being before the incorporation of the Clockmakers' Company were admitted to the latter as " brothers ".

The qualifications necessary for admittance to the Clockmakers' Company were the serving of the usual term of apprenticeship with a master who was a member of the Company, a further two years (normally) as " journeyman ", and the production during this latter period of a " masterpiece ", i.e., a work testifying to the suitability of the applicant for " freedom " to practise his craft and to take apprentices in his turn.

The powers of the Company were exerted to advance the repute of the " art and mystery of clockmaking " by regulating the conduct of the trade throughout the realm, with particular reference to those persons practising in the City of London or within a radius of ten miles thereof. The Company had power to confiscate and destroy, or cause to be amended, any bad or faulty work, and to this end were empowered to search premises " with a constable or other officer ". The expenses of these searches were provided by a quarterly contribution from each member of the Company.

As with the other and more ancient Trade Guilds, it will be apparent how the system tended both to protect the public and to promote the interests and reputation of the clockmaking craft in general.

The Clockmakers' Company does not appear ever to have possessed a Hall of its own, most of the meetings necessary to its business being held in taverns during the seventeenth and eighteenth centuries, although occasionally use was made of a hall belonging to another more fortunate Guild. During more modern times the City Guildhall has been used for meetings, by permission of the Corporation, where also the library and museum of the Clockmakers' Company have had their home.

The anchor escapement, perhaps invented by Dr. Robert Hooke at some time between 1656 and 1666 (both dates inclusive), may have been first generally applied to clocks by William Clement, to whom, indeed, the invention is ascribed by some writers, probably chiefly on the authority of John Smith in his *Horological Disquisitions* of 1694. Clement was a London clockmaker who was admitted to the Clockmakers' Company as a " brother " in 1677, the appellation signifying his previous membership of another and probably older Guild, very likely the Blacksmiths' Company.

Clement's use of the anchor escapement has been generally accepted to date from 1676, but there is evidence that this date should in all probability be 1671, if not earlier. The turret clock by Clement for King's College, Cambridge, *dated* 1671 and with anchor escapement has been referred to in an earlier part of this Essay. The provision of this type of escapement made possible the " seconds " pendulum *in a narrow case,* so that the chronometrical advantages of extra length in the pendulum were then accorded immediate acceptance.

William Clement, who, like many other early makers, often latinized his " signature " on a clock dial,[1] may have been the first to use the after-wards practically universal suspension *spring* for the pendulum. He was Master of the Clockmakers' Company in 1694, and appears to have been a most progressive maker.

[1] Thus: "Gulielmus Clement, Londoni, fecit."

Thomas Tompion (1638–1713) to whom, with rather questionable justification, has been applied the title of " father of English clock-making ", was born at Northill in Bedfordshire. He was the son of another Thomas Tompion, who was apparently a blacksmith by trade, and who is recorded as being one of the churchwardens at Northill.[1] Thomas Tompion (the clockmaker) would appear to have been a bachelor. His niece Margaret (a sister's child) married Edward Banger, who was after-wards associated in business as a clockmaker with Tompion, several clocks being extant which display the names of *Tho. Tompion and Edw. Banger* upon their dials.

Tompion was acquainted with some of the most prominent men of science of his day, including Dr. Robert Hooke (1635–1703) and Rev. Edward Barlow (née Booth) who was born in 1636 and died in 1716. Several horological improvements invented or suggested by these virtuosi were first employed in practical form in clocks or watches made by Tompion.

Of these inventions, one said to have been by the ingenious cleric Barlow (or Booth) was applied by Tompion to clocks about 1676. This was the device known as the rack repeating mechanism, for striking (*see* Glossary). It was first used in the early form, between the plates of the movement, only later (*circa* 1700) assuming the arrangement now most frequently found. It is questionable, however, whether Tompion obtained the idea for repeating work from Barlow (as generally stated) or Hooke. (*See* Chapter Two.)

To Thomas Tompion and his successor " honest George Graham " was accorded the honour of burial in Westminster Abbey, sufficient indication of the esteem in which horologists of eminence were held in those days.

George Graham (1673–1751) was apprenticed to Henry Aske in 1688, admitted to the Clockmakers' Company in 1695, after which he became associated with Tompion, apparently as a kind of advanced pupil-assistant.

Graham married another niece of Tompion's, daughter of the latter's brother James, which explains why both Graham and Edward Banger are often referred to as Thomas Tompion's " nephews ", which, of course, they would only be by marriage.

On the death of Tompion in 1713, George Graham, who was one of the executors, and to whom Tompion had left all his stock, took over the

---

[1] *See* " The Rise of the Tompions " by Miss E. Simcoe in *The Connoisseur*, November 1931.

business, which he had managed for the older man for several years before the decease of the latter.

Graham's name is chiefly remembered for his two inventions of the mercurial pendulum and the dead-beat escapement. These have been fully described in the Glossary of this book.

The contributions of Graham to horological advancement in all departments were considerable; he modified and improved the cylinder escapement for watches, previously introduced by Booth and Tompion, and in his later years devoted much time to the improvement of clocks for astronomical purposes. He was elected a Fellow of the Royal Society in 1720, and sat on the council of the Society in 1722. According to F. J. Britten (*Old Clocks and Watches and their Makers*) Graham contributed twenty-one papers to the *Philosophical Transactions*.

On Graham's death in 1751, Tompion's grave in the Abbey was opened to receive the remains of his former friend and pupil, the stone slab placed in the floor of the nave on the South side commemorating both these eminent men.

Britten records particulars of a sale by auction in 1765, when two of Graham's clocks were sold for what would now seem paltry sums. One appears to have been a month clock (i.e., of 30-day duration between windings) displaying equal and apparent time, with a perpetual calendar and compensated pendulum, this bringing £42 10s.; while another month clock, also showing mean and solar time, and with a mercurial pendulum, but apparently without the perpetual calendar, realized but £34 2s. 6d., both being acquired by members of the nobility. It is interesting to note that these prices would to-day be multiplied by ten, at least.

Working at a rather later period, horologists like John Harrison (1693–1776), John Ellicot (1706–1772), and Thomas Mudge (1715–1794, Graham's successor in business) all produced inventions and improvements many of which were of lasting value to their craft.

Harrison's name will be best remembered for his efforts to improve marine timepieces, and his celebrated series of four chronometers for use at sea, by which he won awards totalling some £20,000 offered by Parliament through the Board of Longitude for a timepiece sufficiently accurate to be capable of determining longitude at sea.

In so far as the long-case clock is concerned, Harrison's chief contribution would appear to have been that particular type of compensating pendulum which relies on the differing expansion and contraction of rods composed of brass and steel. This pendulum has since been known as the " gridiron " (*see* under Pendulum, in Glossary).

In addition, he fitted his invention of the " grasshopper " escapement to several timekeepers in the long-case form; one such was to be seen at one time in the Guildhall Museum.

An invention of Harrison's which is to this day generally found in superior weight-driven clocks of the long-case type, especially when such are fitted with the " dead-beat " form of escapement, is the " going ratchet " or " Harrison's maintaining power ". A description and illustration of this device will be found in the Glossary and Diagrams to this work.

John Ellicot, previously mentioned, also an F.R.S. (1738) like Graham before him, invented still another type of compensating pendulum and was responsible for many useful experiments tending to improve the performance of clocks and watches.

Mudge, Dutton, and Arnold were all excellent horologists of the later eighteenth century, their improvements and inventions chiefly relating to watches and astronomical clocks and instruments rather than to the long-case variety in particular.

Reverting for a space to a consideration of the characteristics of the early makers of long-case clocks, we find that one of the most strongly individual was Joseph Knibb, who was admitted to the C.C. in 1670.

Joseph Knibb was one of a family of clockmakers, of whom Samuel Knibb was admitted a Fellow of the Clockmakers' Company in 1663, Peter in 1677, Edward in 1700, and Joseph Knibb, jnr., in 1717. Joseph (senr.) would appear to have been at one time resident in Oxford, but afterwards moved to London.

Clocks bearing upon their dials the inscription " Joseph Knibb att Hanslop " or " Joseph Knibb of Hanslope " are mentioned by Britten, and are by the elder and more famous maker of this name, as Britten records one as dating from about 1705, and another as possessing that system of striking apparently peculiar to this maker. Mr. G. H. Baillie (*Watchmakers and Clockmakers of the World*) states that Joseph Knibb (senr.) *moved from London to Hanslope, circa* 1700, *and died circa* 1711.

Hanslope is a village in Buckinghamshire, near Stony Stratford.

That system of striking on two bells known as " Roman Numeral Striking " is usually regarded as being peculiar to clocks by Joseph

Knibb. It is true that Daniel Quare used the same device at least once; a long-case clock by him is illustrated in Mr. Cescinsky's book, *Old English Master Clockmakers and their Clocks*, which has this method of hour-striking. The invention of the system, however, is almost certainly to be ascribed to Knibb, who apparently used it frequently not only in long-case clocks, but also in spring-driven mantel clocks.

Another peculiarity of Knibb's work is the frequent provision of a striking bell shaped like a Chinese gong, i.e., flat-topped or nearly so, with straight, sloping sides of skirt-like form. Knibb's dials and hands are also fairly easy to recognize as indicating his work, and he seems to have been particularly fond of movements giving a greater duration than the normal eight days. As with other makers, he often provides the bolt-and-shutter maintaining power and occasionally uses the extra long or second-and-a-quarter pendulum. Chiming clocks of three trains by this maker exist, providing early examples of this kind of movement.

Except for the usual calendar (in some clocks even this is omitted) Knibb does not appear to have employed such devices as the Equation of Time, perhaps because he worked before the arch-dial period, the arch encouraging the provision of some such movement as this, or the Phases of the Moon.

Knibb's dials are often extremely plain, the frequent absence of both calendar and seconds dial, together with the narrow chapter-ring and plain, matted centre giving a certain chaste austerity to the whole. This simplicity is accentuated by the form of hands employed, which, although of fine design and workmanship, do not exhibit any tendency towards the rococo or flamboyant style.

Probably no other maker displays characteristics quite so easily recognizable as those of Joseph Knibb, who, in this respect, is in a class by himself. The applications of Clement, Tompion and Graham, although possibly restricted to their own productions for some years, have since become the common property of all makers, perhaps because the superior nature of these innovations was early perceived by both trade and public. In the case of Knibb's square-topped bell, however, this would have nothing to recommend it beyond its unusual shape, any difference of "timbre" being of insufficient importance to warrant a general departure from the more usual form.

With regard to the Roman Numeral Striking system, one can easily understand that tradition, even so early as the latter part of the seventeenth century, would oppose its acceptance in a general way. Let the reader imagine himself endeavouring to teach some rather stupid individual how to recognise the time by this system; it would be much easier to impart to a child who had never heard the more usual mode than thus to contend with the respective strength and weakness of tradition and perception.

Chapter Eight

Conclusion

FOR those readers of his book who may have had their interest in old long-case clocks sufficiently stimulated to consider the acquisition of a good specimen, the author has felt impelled to add a few remarks, which, he trusts, may serve as a help in this eventuality.

The introduction of purely commercial considerations with regard to antiques is usually avoided by writers on this subject.

However laudable this detached attitude may be, as separating art from materialism, we cannot but regret the consequent lack of guidance to a prospective purchaser.

The quotation of excessive prices obtained at famous auction sales for extreme rarities, or altogether special productions, can hardly be regarded as a guide to more modest aspirations, although such information is not without interest.

In our own subject, an example of the extreme nature referred to in the last paragraph is afforded by the story of the so-called "record" Tompion clock.

In 1904, the Duke of Cambridge's sale took place at Christie's, and according to a Press report, an old "grandfather" clock had been left behind, forgotten, in one of the bedrooms. It was removed hurriedly, catalogued in two lines, and sold for 125 guineas.

At the Dunn sale (Peter Dunn, Woolley Hall, Maidenhead) in 1911 at Christie's, it reappeared, and was sold for 380 guineas.

On the decease of its last English owner—the late Mr. D. A. F. Wetherfield—in 1928, it was sold for *approximately £4,000*. It is now in America. It was held for a long time in the hope that it might be acquired for the Nation by the Victoria and Albert Museum.[1]

It is a three-month clock, with perpetual calendar, in a burr-walnut

---

[1] These particulars are transcribed from a volume devoted to the Wetherfield Collection of antique timekeepers, by W. E. Hurcomb.

ormolu-mounted case of great magnificence, bearing the monogram of William III, for whom it was made. At one time the clock stood in Hampton Court Palace. The height over all is 10ft. 6ins.

Instances of the acquisition of fine clocks by noted makers for absurdly small sums are also not wanting. These testify not only to the perspicacity of the buyers, but also to the ignorance of the vendors, an ignorance which is becoming so rare as to be almost a negligible consideration in these times.

In many ways the most desirable, and certainly the rarest and most valuable form of the long-case clock is that exemplified by the inlaid walnut-cased productions of the late seventeenth century. These, by makers such as Tompion, Knibb or Quare, are seldom procurable under three or four hundred pounds apiece, and, if in any way unusual, sometimes command much higher prices. Similar (and, let it be said, in every way comparable) clocks by less-known makers are usually to be had for very much less, say, from about one hundred pounds upwards according to their importance. The prices quoted are those charged by reputable dealers in antiques, not those of auction sales, which are obviously unreliable indications of real value in many instances.

The high prices obtained for clocks of the period just mentioned have nothing whatever to do with their comparative merit as horological instruments. Informed present-day taste has decided that the slender and severe outlines of the casework, beautiful proportions, and often small height of seventeenth-century clocks, together with their figured or inlaid walnut veneers and simple, dignified brass dials with fine hands, should constitute the ideal. Incidentally, the added charm of an existence beginning, in many instances, some two-and-a-half centuries ago must be allowed for, though far be it from me to impute mere antiquity as the sole reason for the undoubted pre-eminence of the seventeenth-century clock in the collecting world.

Generally speaking, long-case clocks of the mahogany period, including those in the later examples of lacquered casework from about 1740 to 1795, unless by very famous makers, can be obtained at prices comparing favourably with those in the preceding category. Such extra refinements as are unusual or very rare have to be paid for, of course, but a good clock in a fine Chippendale mahogany case of excellent proportions, dating from about 1760–70, and in perfect original state, can often be acquired for as little as fifty or sixty pounds. Chiming clocks, in original condition and having the movements untampered with, bring rather higher prices, say, seventy-five to one hundred and fifty pounds according to quality and maker.

I have endeavoured to quote prices which should be representative of neither the famous London antique showrooms, with their high rents and other charges, nor the very small dealer in a little provincial industrial town; but which should be typical of the average good-class dealer with a reputable business.

It frequently happens that the foregoing prices can be considerably reduced—by a lucky private purchase, for instance, or by happening to find a dealer whose knowledge of clocks is not extensive! In the latter eventuality, however, it has been the author's experience that such men are unlikely to possess anything of interest to a connoisseur; their lack of knowledge precludes their acquiring really desirable clocks.

The actual choice of a clock is largely a matter of personal taste, at least in so far as the casework is concerned. In this connection, the author is acquainted with several persons to whom marquetry (especially of the more brilliant, larger type) is simply " showy " or " spectacular ", and lacquer-work merely " quaint " if not actually distasteful. To such people, clock cases of plain " figured " walnut or the later mahogany almost invariably appeal most strongly, and one can imagine their selection of a clock accordingly.

There are certain features, however, which confer greater value upon the clocks which possess them, and it is well that such should be recognised without much difficulty by a possible purchaser.

One of these features, not unusual in seventeenth-century clocks but sufficiently rare in the later productions, is maintaining power. In clocks up to about 1740 this is usually of the " bolt-and-shutter " type, in which the winding-holes in the dial are closed by the " shutters " until the pulling of a cord swings them away, and sets the device in operation (*see* Glossary).

Another valuable feature, again found mostly in early clocks, is month (or longer) duration between windings.

The easiest way to ascertain whether the clock has a longer duration than the normal eight days is for the tyro to look at the driving weights when he opens the trunk door. A month clock has much heavier (and therefore bigger) weights than one designed for eight-day duration only,[1] and the very rare three, six and twelve-month clocks and timepieces are provided with really enormous weights.

If the clock is without weights, these being stored elsewhere, or missing, the movement should be examined. Four wheels from main to escape wheel denote the eight-day movement. Month clocks have five wheels in their going trains, and year timepieces six or more. Movements of six or twelve-month duration are practically never fitted with a striking train; thus, technically, they are not " clocks ", but " timepieces " only.

Should it be impossible to adequately inspect the movement owing to its position or other inconvenience, the winding key should be tried —or the barrel turned by the fingers—and the direction in which the clock winds noted. If the winding be clockwise (the usual way) the movement is almost certainly of eight-day duration; anti-clockwise winding nearly always indicates a month movement. The reason for the variation is that the 'scape and centre wheels *must* turn clockwise, so that the main wheel of an eight-day movement turns anti-clockwise, and the barrel therefore winds *clockwise*. With a month clock, an extra wheel is interposed between the main and centre wheels, and as the latter must turn clockwise, this extra wheel turns in the reverse direction. The main wheel again reverses the motion to clockwise and, of course, the barrel winds anti-clockwise in this case. Movements having a " train of six " will wind like an eight-day movement, i.e., clockwise. Their superior duration can only be ascertained by examination, but a glance should suffice.

Original driving-weights on good-quality clocks are brass-cased, but differ from the modern variety in shape, and usually bear evidence of their age, often being indistinguishable from lead in colour, until scraped slightly with a penknife.

The original brass-cased weights are often replaced by lead or iron monstrosities after the former have been lost, mislaid, transferred to another clock, or sold separately. It is a fact that month clocks are more often found with their original brass-cased weights than are eight-day movements, for obvious reasons.

Chiming clocks of all periods are undoubtedly of more value than those which merely strike the hours, but here caution should be observed.

Many chiming movements are alterations of ordinary eight-day

---

[1] The respective weights are (approx.): 8-day—12–14 lbs.; month—28–35 lbs.

H

striking clocks, the trains being re-set in a pair of new plates and a new dial-centre being provided, with *three* winding-holes coincident with the new positions of the squared arbors. This fake can be readily detected by an examination of the back of the dial and the plates and pillars of the movement.

The purchaser should be wary of the "Westminster" chime in an old long-case clock; these have usually an alternative for eight bells. These chimes generally indicate a converted movement, or, at least, an altered chiming part in an otherwise original clock. The subject has been dealt with in an earlier part of this book.

The hands and dial of the clock should be carefully examined. If the dial requires re-silvering and lacquering, and if the black wax is disappearing from the chapters, etc., this is of no consequence, as the dial can be satisfactorily restored at a very small charge. Missing parts, such as a hand or corner-piece are serious, and although not insurmountable obstacles, should give the purchaser pause. In an otherwise perfect and very valuable clock it would be worth while to accept the risk of suitable replacements being procurable, but not in the case of a more ordinary timekeeper.

Broken hands, providing there are no missing pieces, can be satisfactorily and imperceptibly repaired by silver solder; the proper person to take them to is a spectacle-maker, who is used to fine work which must be also very strong and reliable.

Small repairs to the casework of the clock are perfectly amenable to the attentions of a good cabinet-maker, and should not be regarded too seriously, provided there are no missing parts. Missing fret is more serious, as this is not possible to reproduce with the accuracy required, and generally removal of the old work and its replacement by a complete new fret is necessitated. When these replacements are extensive, and in prominent positions, the value of the clock as an antique is rather badly affected. This is particularly true of Chippendale cases, with their decorative applied frets and crestings.

To conclude this final chapter, I have thought it not irrelevant to include a few remarks concerning the fixing of a clock, its winding and general periodic attention.

There is hardly any other article of furniture which is so naturally insecure as the long-case clock, neither are there many pieces exceeding the value of a choice example.

This being so, one is surprised to note that no attempt is generally made to secure the clock from accident, and to increase the convenience by which it may be wound and dusted.

I regard it as an essential to have a clock properly fastened to the wall. It can be accomplished quite neatly and innocuously by the method of screwing a short board to the previously plugged wall behind the clock-case. The board should be the same thickness as the skirting-board, and a little less in width than the clock-case at the trunk. The case is then screwed to this " wall-board " by two one-inch screws through the backboard, spaced about six inches apart, according to the width of the trunk. It will usually be necessary (and always desirable) to drill the backboard for the screws, and provide the latter with fair-sized washers, so that their heads shall not bite into the wood of the back when the case is screwed up to the wall-board.

Long-case clocks placed crosswise in a corner of a room may be fixed quite easily and neatly with the exercise of a little ingenuity, and the gain in convenience for dusting, polishing, winding, etc., is immeasurable. We are then also quite sure that any vibration likely to be transmitted to the case by the periodic oscillations of the pendulum will be largely nullified. Should the owner's house be near a busy highway, the traffic along this will not tend to disturb the accuracy of the clock to the same extent as would this if the case were unsecured in any way. Incidentally, many a fine clock, standing in a somewhat awkward position—say on a small landing with steep stairs below—may conceivably be saved from almost complete destruction.

" Moreover, take care that the clock be fix'd fast and firm, that no Violence may justle [*sic*] Him out of his Place . . ." (John Smith, *Horological Disquisitions concerning the Nature of Time*, 1694).

In winding thirty-hour clocks, such as " lanterns " and early long-case types, the ease of winding and life of the mechanism will both be considerably increased if the weight is helped in its ascent by pulling *up* the part of the chain or rope on the left hand, above the weight, at the same time as the right hand pulls *down* that portion of the chain to the right.

To hoist away vigorously at one part of the chain or rope without endeavouring to ease the strain on the arbor in any way seems to me an almost inconceivably brutal way in which to treat any small mechanism such as a clock movement.

When winding eight-day movements *always* first open the trunk door of the case and watch the ascent of the weight while using the key. In this way the rising weight can be guided—by the left hand—from any temporary obstruction, such as the edge formed by the cut-away woodwork of the case at the top of the door-aperture. Sudden violent contact with this edge, or with the bottom of the seat-board, may cause the gut line to break, with resultant damage by the falling weight. This will be avoided if the weights are watched in winding.

In clocks not fitted with maintaining power, it is a good plan to arrange for a gain of about one minute per week, which is sufficient to allow unhurried winding without subsequent alteration of the hands. The striking or chiming trains should not be wound when the clock is about to sound the hour or quarter.

If the movement is in good condition and clean, oiling once per year will be quite often enough. Only the best clear clock oil should be used for this purpose, and it should be applied very sparingly, taking care to oil only the pivots of the arbors and the pallets of the escapement. In addition, the studs of the dial-wheels may receive a spot each, as also the pivots (studs) of the various lifting-pieces, rack, etc., and it is often a good idea for a spot of oil to be placed on that portion of the pendulum which passes through the crutch-fork, in the event of any slight rub here. A creaking sound coincident with the motion of the pendulum is most frequently caused at this position. Avoid useless extravagance of oil; it will only serve to collect dust and make the movement filthy in a short time. Do not drop oil upon the barrels, where it will contact the gut lines, and avoid touching the dial front whilst oiling.

Perhaps one of the most convenient forms of oiler for the amateur, and not the least effective, is a piece of thin wire which, when dipped into the oil just beneath the surface, carries away a drop upon its extremity. This is sufficient, if correctly placed, to oil one pivot of the movement, and the wire has the property of being easily bent in order to reach awkwardly-placed positions in the clock.

It is a very natural and excusable procedure for one not especially acquainted with the particular conditions under which a clock movement works to oil (in addition to those portions of the mechanism referred to) the *wheels and pinions*. This should not be done.

In all the horological works with which I am acquainted, *where the antiquarian interest is uppermost*, as distinct from purely technical disquisitions on clockwork from a manufacturer's or repairer's viewpoint, this important reservation remains unmentioned. It is true that instructions about oiling, if present at all (and this is rare) carefully refrain from allusion to wheels and pinions in this connection, and it cannot but be suspected by the technician who reads these works that this reticence may be the result of a desire to avoid the consequential explanation which would appear to be called for. This explanation is as follows:

A clockcase is never absolutely dust-proof, as to be so it would also have to be practically air-tight. Dust-laden air is therefore entering and leaving the case continually, often over a very long period. Now this air-borne dust carries within itself particles of grit, and this adheres to the teeth and leaves of wheels and pinions much more strongly if they are oiled; moreover, the movement of the wheels transforms the mixture of oil, dust and grit into a kind of abrasive paste, in which the gritty particles are prominent.

A grit-particle will embed itself (consequent to the before-mentioned movement of the mechanism, and the contact between tooth and pinion) into the comparatively soft brass of a wheel tooth, to which it does no further damage. With every revolution of the wheel, however, this embedded grit-particle scores or scratches the steel leaves of the pinion, thus, whilst damaging the brass wheel-tooth only once, it scores the pinion many times, until itself worn away in the process.

It has been said that a hundred years of "going" with dry wheels and pinions will show very little wear in the movement, only a "polished" or bright appearance of the pinion leaves where the wheel-teeth have engaged them; whereas with pinions which have been oiled a very much shorter period suffices to provide evidence of serious wear in these.

We do not, as collectors, care to contemplate the time when our particularly treasured example will pass to other hands. Still less, no doubt, shall we desire to overhear in imagination the exasperated comments of some future connoisseur of a fine old movement, attributing the worn pinions to a probable indiscriminate use of oil by some previous owner.

There are, of course, clockmakers (and expert restorers of old move-ments) together with those who are just competent repairers. There are also more or less untrained " clock-jobbers " and I have seen many move-ments which have been through hands of the last category bearing undoubted evidence of oiled pinions; occasionally the entire movement has been simply smothered with lubricant! *Verb. sap.*

The beautiful surface condition of old, well-cared-for furniture is one of its chief attractions. The lustrous, bronze-like " patina " of old oak and mahogany is something quite different to the cold, glassy surface produced by French polishing, which tends to obscure the natural figure of the wood by filling in the grain and " evening-out " the colouring.

A clock case which has been French polished or varnished[1] should be avoided, as careful scraping of the entire surface of the casework, down to the bare wood if necessary, will be required to restore its proper character. It is sometimes possible to scrape off the polish or varnish little by little until the original oil or wax-produced surface is arrived at, but then, of course, this will be damaged by the business of removing the glaze, and will need restoring, a lengthy process involving much patient treatment, first with raw linseed oil and finally with wax polish. It should be clearly understood that nothing but time, with its constant exposure of the surface to the light and air, and continual handling and polishing (in the very early days with linseed oil, and later with beeswax and turpentine polish) is responsible for the wonderful patina of old oak, walnut and mahogany furniture.

Given the possession of the original surface, however neglected, dirty or dull, a fine clock-case may be speedily transformed into a thing of com-plete beauty by the sparing application of a good wax polish together with a sufficiency of manual exertion. Most of the better wax polishes now offered for sale are also effective as cleaners when applied vigorously, obviating the need for treating the surface with some form of dirt-remover before applying the wax.

Regarding the brass ball-spires and other ornaments of a clock-case there is a type of mind which apparently envisages antiquity as necessarily involving cobwebs, rust, and pitted metalwork. There is no earthly reason

---

[1] A distinction should be made between the thick mastic varnish often applied in later times (usually by amateurs in an endeavour to " brighten up " a rather dingy case), and a fine translucent varnish similar to that used in violin-making. This latter is often original, applied when the case was made.

why the brass spires, escutcheons, etc., should not be clean and bright; certainly this does not make their form and construction partake of another period, and the gain in appearance is striking. Once cleaned and polished. these fittings can be lacquered by the heat process, thus they will retain their colour indefinitely.

Should very bright brass-work be reasonably objected to as being in too violent contrast to a sober case, the finish may be that known as " antique ", which is perhaps preferable in all instances.

Missing spires, when the hood has obviously had them originally, should be replaced by a set of approximately the correct period. Old ones of suitable pattern can occasionally be obtained, and should be procured if possible, failing which, modern reproductions will have to be employed. These latter are provided in various sizes and patterns, and are sufficiently well-made not to disgrace a good clock. The best of the old spires, however, as those illustrated on the clock by E. Samm in Plate 39, are superior in appearance, solidity and finish to any modern ornaments I have yet seen.

The pendulum " bob ", which is usually a lead weight " faced " by brass, should also be clean and bright, especially in those early clocks where a glass window in the trunk door is designed to display the movement of the pendulum. Incidentally, the rating-nut under the bob, placed there for regulation of the clock, is often inconveniently small, sometimes making fine corrections impossible by working up under the lower edge of the brass covering in certain positions of the nut. It should be replaced by a nut of suitable size.

It is in every way desirable that a clock-case should be perfectly " plumb ", i.e., quite upright viewed from front or sides. It is a fact that nothing looks worse than a tall object which is not exactly vertical.

Such objects become sources of intense irritation after a time, even should the error be small, and passed over in the first place. Again, a point of importance, it is well that the pendulum, when at rest, should hang quite vertically, so that it may not tend to encounter during its arc either the backboard of the case, or the driving weights when the latter, in the course of their descent, reach a point immediately in front of the pendulum bob.

Having fixed the case perfectly upright, and secured it in the manner before mentioned, the owner should see that the seat-board of the movement fits well upon the extended sides of the case. It should not tend to rock at all on these, and of course should be quite level, if only because of the resultant effect of the dial. It should not be fastened by screws or nails.

Regarding the setting of a clock " in beat ", the method is known to all having much to do with long-case clocks, but for the benefit of those perhaps setting up a clock for the first time, and unacquainted with the quite simple process, it is therefore given here.

The " crutch " (*see* Glossary) of a long-case movement is of comparatively soft iron wire, quite easily bent.

Occasionally a hard steel crutch may be found fitted to the rear end of the pallet-staff. This is incorrect, and probably fixed by some amateur repairer to replace a damaged or missing original. It is very difficult to set in beat a clock with such a crutch, and it should be removed and replaced by one of the proper type if practicable.

The movement being in the case, and the dial showing its correct position in relation to the wooden bezel of the hood, the pendulum should next be attached and then the driving-weights hung upon S-hooks from their pulleys.

A slight push is then given the pendulum, from the bob or near it (the hearty swing often accorded it is absurd, and fraught with some danger) and the movement should then function.

It will probably be found, on listening carefully to the beat (" tick " is the popular term), that one side of the arc described seems to receive additional accent or emphasis, and that after the click of the arrested wheel-tooth the " bob " travels a greater distance, measured by the eye (as most old clocks have no degree plate) on this side than on the other.

The effect is uncomfortable in the extreme, when pronounced, and but little mollified by a reduced error. Some people are curiously impervious to errors of beat, others with a strong rhythmic sense suffer acute discomfort when subjected to them.

Having ascertained on which side the error lies—say " short " on right —the crutch should be *very slightly* bent by the fingers *in the opposite direction*; in our supposed instance, therefore, to the left. If the operation is carefully carried out it is quite unnecessary to remove the pendulum or anything else, but, of course, the clock should be stopped until after the bending of the crutch.

When the movement is set going again, an improvement should at once be noticed. Quite probably the process will require repeating several times (always *very little* bending of the crutch) but eventually the beat will be perfect, or at least as near perfection as the particular owner's ear and eye are capable of approaching.

It is perhaps as well to advise the operator to wait until the clock has "settled to its beat", good or bad, before again stopping the movement and effecting further bending of the crutch. A minute or so should be ample, providing the pendulum is given an initial impulse producing an arc comparable with its normal, and not greater.

Should a clock-owner find it necessary or desirable to fit new lines to his movement, the following hints may prove of service.

Before taking a movement from its case (either for this or any other purpose) the driving-weights should be wound to a position in which the pulleys are about three inches from the top of the trunk-door aperture.

The weights should then be carefully removed so as not to disarrange the lines on the barrels, and *a small weight* (about two pounds is sufficient) then attached to *both* pulleys, its hook passing through the pulley-loops, these being brought together to facilitate this, or the "S-hooks", may be used for the same purpose. This will prevent the lines varying from their correctly coiled positions on the barrels, and the weight is so small that it does not add appreciably to that of the movement and dial.

Some form of improvised "horse" for the movement which allows the lines to remain taut should be prepared before actually removing it from the case. (See that this impromptu "horse" is secure.)

After fitting new lines, these should be wound again to a suitable extent and the small weight affixed as before, the movement then being transferred to its case. This method will be found particularly convenient in the event of *wire* lines being used, as these are most intractable things, especially when new.

Before fixing the new lines, it is as well, if possible, to remove from the barrels any old knots carelessly left inside at previous periods.

One of these may at some time work itself out, and, wedging between the barrel and plate, perhaps stop the clock or render inoperative the striking, afterwards being difficult to dislodge.

A line of gut or wire, when completely wound, should be of length sufficient only to exactly fill the barrel-space. If it is longer it may possibly leave the barrel (some barrels have very shallow rims to the end-plates) during the act of winding, and the resultant shock by the sudden fall of a heavy driving-weight may cause serious damage somewhere; additionally, the line will then transfer a portion of itself to the barrel-arbor, very likely wedging tightly between barrel and plate in its progress, if the clearance is small.

Some further information about the fitting and choice of lines will be found in the Glossary, under Lines.

In adding the appendices I hope they may be found of interest by the general reader. Appendix Five, it will be noted, contains a few details relating to the clocks forming the illustrations to this Essay.

To the best of my belief, no clock depicted in this book has ever been illustrated in any previous work; it will be observed by the collector that more illustrations and greater space in the text are devoted to the later clocks than is usually apportioned to them. This is because I feel that such clocks, particularly those by Northern makers, have been rather sketchily dealt with in some other works on the subject, and also because I believe that clocks such as those shown in Plates 38, 40, 41–44, 45, 46, 47–49, and 50–52 are worthy to rank with the undoubtedly fine seventeenth-century productions in every way. The style is different, it is true, but the same high craftsman spirit is discernible in the movements, dials, and cabinet-work; each displays that singular perfection and individuality found only in the hand-created thing, to which the mass-produced examples of our modern era are strangers.

Should any who read this book have an interest in old long-case clocks aroused where such did not previously exist, or find their appreciation of these antique timekeepers encouraged, and, perhaps, their store of knowledge concerning them increased, then will I regard my labour as not expended in vain, and my reward as the privilege of increasing the number of those to whom

"A thing of beauty is a joy for ever."

Appendix One

Glossary of Technical Terms

Alarm, or Alarum

Most frequently this device is applied to lantern movements (and spring-driven clocks of the " mantel " or incorrectly designated " bracket " type) but it is not unknown incorporated in the plate-frame long-case movement, as, for instance, in the Dutch clock illustrated by Plates 27–33. Its action and construction will be found described in Chapter One (*Horology in the Sixteenth and Seventeenth Centuries*).

Anchor Escapement

A particular type of recoil escapement. Perhaps invented by Robert Hooke sometime between 1656 and 1670, although William Clement is claimed by some as its originator. (*See* Chapter Two, *Early Long-Case Clocks*.) The present writer is inclined to favour the claim of Hooke (as recorded in Derham's *Artificial Clockmaker*) to be its inventor, *circa* 1666, but for a discussion of this *see* Chapter Two.

In the *Brief Lives* of his contemporaries by John Aubrey, F.R.S. (1626–1697), edited by O. L. Dick, under " Robert Hooke " we find no mention of the anchor escapement as being invented by Hooke, which could certainly be an argument against Hooke's authorship of the escapement were it not that Aubrey mentions his intention of procuring from Hooke a list of the latter's inventions, and refers to the difficulty of getting people to do themselves justice. Aubrey further states that Hooke estimated the number of his inventions to be a *thousand*.

J. Drummond Robertson, in his excellent book *The Evolution of Clockwork* (1931) refers to the records of the Patent Office, and states that no horological patent is recorded as being granted between March 1665 and March 1694, from which it would appear (as this was a time particularly fertile in horological progress) that it was not the general practice of clockmakers to seek patent rights for their improvements during this period. We know that Hooke was also prone to leave his claims as to various improvements and introductions until some other, probably unconscious of Hooke's previous work in similar fields, announced a claim, which thereon became the subject of sometimes very bitter protests by Hooke, who did not hesitate, on occasion, to brand as plagiarists of the worst type those whom he considered he had anticipated in their designs. It must be confessed that Hooke had frequently only himself to reproach in these matters; his characteristic lack of interest in the perfecting of a design, or, at least, his indifference or inability to bring it to a practical conclusion can be regarded as providing the real basis of the misunderstandings and disputes which arose in this connection.

From the foregoing it will thus be seen (as Robertson very justly observes—*loc. cit.*) that there would be nothing to prevent Clement or any other clockmaker from adopting the anchor escapement if he were so inclined; the more so as Hooke seldom seems to have been at any particular pains to keep secret his inventions and ideas once they were fairly " under way " (cf. his frequent conversations with Tompion and others as recorded in the *Diary*, in which the phrase " Told Tompion the way of . . ." occurs quite often).

The anchor escapement consists of the employment of an escape wheel which works in a vertical plane (hence it is often rather ambiguously referred to as " the vertical escapement ", which was also the crown-wheel used with a balance) above which 'scape-wheel oscillates a steel lunette (the " anchor ") with pallets or checks at each end. The anchor is fitted to a horizontal arbor between the plates, variously called anchor-arbor, pallet-arbor, pallet-staff, or verge. From one end of this the pendulum receives its impulses through a crutch attached to the arbor. The teeth of the 'scape-wheel are released or " escaped " by each alternate pallet of the anchor. *See* illustration—Fig. 3.

Arbor. [*Latin:* " Tree " hence " axle-tree "]

A steel shaft or rod, round in section and pivoted at both ends, which is fitted between the plates of a movement, sometimes (as in the case of the main or barrel-arbors) projecting through the front-plate. To it is attached its wheel, the pinion-leaves being frequently at the opposite end. Many arbors, particularly the older types, are tapered from the wheel positions.

It is a custom to refer to the complete arbor (with its pinion) merely as a "pinion". This is because all but early types were produced from "pinion-wire", made and supplied to the clockmaker with "leaves" continuous along whatever length was required of any particular type and leaf-number. The leaves were removed by the clockmaker where not required, and the pinion proper thus provided at the correct position. Very early arbors have the pinions formed from the solid rod of the arbor itself by file-cutting by hand.

The term "arbor" is also applied to any shaft pivotted between the plates, e.g., those arbors which carry "lifting-pieces", locking-hooks, the striking-hammer, etc. In a perhaps particularly apposite sense (as "tree") it is also sometimes applied to the *vertical* shafts carrying the pallets and balance of the true verge escapement, and the crown-wheel of the later pendulum-controlled "verge".

Balance

An early regulator used before the invention of the pendulum. The earliest was the "foliot", a crossbar attached to the top end of an upright verge, and made to oscillate first one way and then the other by pallets projecting from the verge and worked by the teeth of a vertical crown wheel. The "foliot" was provided with adjustable weights at each end of its length, for rough regulation. This "foliot" was not used in England,[1] where a circular balance wheel of iron with a single arm served the same purpose.

Barrels

The brass drums fixed to the main arbors, to which latter the key is fitted when winding. They are often grooved for the gut lines, though some are plain, and are provided with a ratchet and "click" through which the weight delivers its power to the main wheel on the same arbor. When winding, this ratchet allows the barrel and arbor to turn without moving the "meshed" wheel, thus winding the line on to the barrel and drawing up the weight.

Bob. See Pendulum.

Bolt and Shutter Maintaining Power. See Maintaining Power.

---

[1] Not, at any rate, for *domestic* clocks.

Bridge

The brass crosspiece fitted over what is usually the centre arbor, and provided with a tubular projection to carry the hour wheel and its pipe. It is fixed to the front plate by screws, and assumes a bridge-like form because of the situation beneath it of the cannon wheel (often referred to as " cannon pinion "), whose pipe passes through the tube of the bridge to carry the minute hand.

Bush

Where the pivot-holes in the plates of a movement are worn, the remedy consists of re-drilling the hole larger, and providing a circular brass inset known as a " bush " which bears in it a hole of the correct size.

Calendar

The " perpetual " calendar makes automatic adjustment for the long and short months, and also faithfully records the extra day of leap year. It is a rather unusual and complicated refinement, and a knowledge of its action is perhaps outside elementary requirements. The usual calendar found in long-case clocks has to be altered for those months of less than 31 days by hand, apart from which its action is automatic. Calendar movements are of two kinds—those worked by the clock every twelve hours, and those whose date is changed every twenty-four hours. In the case of the twelve-hour calendar, the indicator is moved half-way to the new date in the first twelve hours and completes its indication of the correct figure at the expiration of the second period of twelve hours. The mechanism is simple, and usually consists of a stud attached to the hour-wheel pipe, which every revolution (twelve hours) engages with a tooth of the calendar disc and moves this onward. Sometimes the stud in the pipe of the hour-hand is varied by a pin projecting from the face of the snail, which, however, works in the same way. The twenty-four-hour type of calendar is a little less ingenuous. It consists of an extra wheel placed on the hour pipe between the hour-wheel and the snail, and turning, therefore, once in twelve hours. Engaging with this wheel is another having twice its number of teeth and therefore turning once in twenty-four hours. In this latter wheel is a pin which engages every revolution with a tooth of the calendar ring, thus moving this on to the new date. It should be noted that the kind of calendar which is moved every twelve hours has usually a disc indicator, of which a segment is arranged to show through a lunette or fan-shaped aperture in the dial. The earlier (and better) twenty-four-hour type of calendar is provided with an engraved ring of large diameter, with teeth cut on its inner edge, and working on small rollers which are fitted by studs to the back of the dial. The ring is engraved with figures for each day from one to thirty-one and these are caused to appear separately through a small square or round opening in the dial. The effect is that of "framing" the particular date by the sides of the aperture, with enhanced legibility. The calendar indicating the day of the month by means of a hand from the centre of the dial is worked by the twenty-four hour arrangement, and a fourth variation of the calendar idea is to display the days of the month on a subsidiary dial of the same approximate size and general appearance as a seconds-dial, with a pointer similar in shape to a seconds hand. This is worked by the twelve-hour arrangement in most instances, the stud or pin connecting with the usual toothed disc, which, however, is now completely covered by the dial-plate, the attached hand or pointer projecting through the dial to indicate the date.

Calendar Circle

The brass ring, ratchet-toothed on its inner edge, and engraved on a silvered surface with numerals from one to thirty-one, which appear through a square or circular aperture in the dial. Used in conjunction with a twenty-four-hour wheel. (*See* Calendar.)

Calendar Wheel

A wheel which is worked from another on the hour-wheel pipe, having double the number of teeth, and turning, therefore, once in twenty-four hours. In its face is fitted a pin which works the calendar ring or circle. (*See* Calendar.)

Cannon Pinion

A term sometimes used to indicate the *cannon wheel*, the expression "cannon pinion" being more corrrectly applied to pocket-watch mechanism.

Cannon Wheel

The cannon wheel is provided with a sleeve or " pipe ", squared at its extremity for the attachment of the minute hand. Wheel and pipe are placed over the centre arbor, the fit being close but not tight, so as to allow the pipe to be turned on the arbor when re-setting the hand. Contact with the turning centre arbor is maintained by a slightly bowed brass spring, with a round or square hole in it, which is slipped over the arbor to a position near the front-plate, against a step or " shoulder " made in the arbor immediately after its emergence from the plate. The cannon wheel on its pipe (often referred to by watch *and clock* makers as the " cannon pinion ") is then fitted over the centre arbor. The bowed ends of the spring touch the back of the cannon wheel near its teeth-roots, and the spring is then compressed slightly by the wheel being pushed towards the front-plate and held there by the hand-collet and pin. This results in connection by friction between the arbor and wheel, the friction, however, being only sufficient to establish a coupling of the turning movement, a slight push on the minute hand readily overcoming it, so that the hand may be moved round the dial without difficulty. Sometimes, as before mentioned, the round hole in the spring is varied by a square opening, according as to whether the arbor is correspondingly squared at the point where the spring is compressed.

When the movement is dismantled, the spring is often wrongly re-assembled. The *back* of the " bow " should be towards the plate, not its extremities, which should bear on the cannon wheel. The other way it will not turn with the arbor when the train is working, its extremities pressing against the front-plate, and its pressure-bearing on the wheel being exerted at the wrong position for the requisite turning power. This fault is quite frequently the cause of the minute-hand remaining stationery, although the clock " goes " (i.e., the " watch " or going train is correctly functioning otherwise). An alternative cause of this trouble may lie in the spring-pressure, although correctly applied, having become very weak. In both instances the remedy consists of dismantling the parts concerned and, in the latter case, giving greater curvature to the pressure-spring. A spasmodic movement of the minute hand, together with very little resistance indeed to the finger, or a minute indicator which is inclined to fall suddenly by its own weight from " twelve o'clock " towards " six o'clock " suggests the same fault and a similar remedy.

The term "minute wheel" is often applied to the cannon wheel (or "cannon pinion") since both the cannon wheel proper and the wheel with which it engages have equal "numbers" (i.e., both have the same number of teeth) and therefore turn in the same time, but in opposite directions. Both, then, are quite truly "minute wheels". (*See* Minute Wheel, Cannon Pinion and Bridge, also Dial Wheels.)

Centre Wheel

The wheel attached to the centre arbor of the movement. Its arbor projects well through the front-plate, and over it is fitted the cannon wheel on its pipe, the end of which is squared to receive the minute hand. The forward end of the centre arbor is drilled at its tip for the collet pin which secures the hands. The centre wheel itself is driven through a pinion (the centre pinion) on the same arbor by the main wheel, which receives its power from the weight through the barrel and ratchet. The centre pinion has usually 8 leaves and the centre wheel 60 teeth.

Click

The small lever pivoted to the side of a main or great wheel, and engaging with the ratchet teeth on the barrel, by which the weight power is transmitted from the barrel to the wheel. The click is held in contact with the ratchet teeth by a curved "click spring" riveted at one end to the main wheel, and with its other end bearing upon the click itself. The click can then be raised from the ratchet, against its spring pressure, if it is desired that the gut line should be allowed to unwind quickly from the barrel, in the event of its becoming twisted, for instance. Many of the older clicks, and some few of the later, are provided with a little curved extension, nicely file-cut, which greatly facilitates disengagement from the ratchet. For a late example *see* Plate 52, illustrating a fine movement by Peter Fearnley, Wigan, *circa* 1790.

Clock

In the technical sense, this means the striking train of a timekeeper, as distinct from the going train, which is known as the "watch". For the use of the latter term in the sense of describing a *timepiece* only (not a "clock") it is interesting to note the inscription near the Tompion "clock" in the Pump Room at Bath (mentioned by Dickens in *Pickwick*). This inscription refers to a "watch and sun-dial", meaning a timepiece with

I

an equation-of-time register showing the difference at any period of the year between "Sun-time" and "mean-time" (Greenwich time). The aforesaid Tompion "clock" is unprovided with a striking train, but the going part or "watch" is of one month duration between windings. It is, therefore, a *timepiece* and not a *clock*, the latter appellation always signifying a striking train. Note that "glocke" (German), "clocca" (Latin), and "cloche" (French) all signify the same thing, that is "a bell", and our English word "clock" (probably derived from a mixture of the other languages) should therefore be used as implying the *sounding* of the hours.

Cock

The brass bracket, attached by two screws to the back-plate of a movement, from which the pendulum is hung by means of a suspension spring carried between "chops" or "jaws" in the extremity of the cock. The cock is drilled to receive the back pivot of the pallet-staff or verge, and this can be removed from the movement by first detaching the pendulum and removing the cock, and then drawing the pallet arbor away by manœuvring the crutch through a large hole in the back-plate. The older cocks were usually slightly ornamented by file-cutting into curved surfaces; they were also provided with rather less bearing surface on the plate than the later cocks, and were, therefore, generally somewhat smaller. This observation would also appear to be true of some of the later cocks by London makers.

The employment of a pendulum cock undoubtedly dates from 1657. In this year Samuel Coster's early clocks, made under the patent assigned to him by the inventor, Christian Huygens de Zuylichem, and bearing the inscription "met privelege 1657" all had back-cocks and pendulum suspension therefrom by a double thread. *See* also the illustration in the *Horologium* of 1658. The arrangement is always fundamentally different from that wherein a back-cock is used merely as a pivot-bearing and support to the old horizontal verge, since the main purpose of the pendulum cock proper is to support the weight of the pendulum; it is only incidentally and for convenience that a part of the cock is utilized as a rear pivot-bearing for the verge or pallet-staff. In the drawing shown by Huygens in *Horologium* the back-cock is entirely for the purpose of supporting the pendulum, no other function being assigned to it.

In clockwork, any bracket (other than a "hang-down" bracket) may be described as a cock.

Collet

(*a*) A small brass disc, driven, brazed or soft-soldered to an arbor for the attachment of the wheel. The early collets were brazed to the arbor and often ornamented by lathe turning. The later collets were soft-soldered or simply driven on to the arbors, and were free from ornamentation, being usually cylindrical in shape.

(*b*) A somewhat similar brass disc, usually slightly ornamented, or "dished" to a convex form, used for the attachment of the hands. A "collet-pin" secures the brass collet (and the hands) by being driven into a hole drilled in the extreme forward end of the centre arbor.

Contrate Wheel

In a crown-wheel escapement with "bob" pendulum this is the wheel next below the escape wheel, engaging with the crown pinion. It is the third of the train in a 30-hour movement, and the fourth wheel of an 8-day movement. "Contrate" because of its working-plane compared with that of the crown wheel.

Crown Wheel

So called because of its resemblance to an Early English crown. It is the escape wheel, and may be either vertical or horizontal as to the plane in which it moves. The former kind is used in conjunction with a controller of the "foliot" or "balance-wheel" variety, and the horizontal crown wheel is found with the short "bob" pendulum.

Crown Wheel Escapement

An early (probably the earliest) form of recoil escapement. Used in two forms, vertical and horizontal, from the plane in which the crown wheel works. Let us take an early balance-controlled lantern-clock for illustration. The main wheel (rope-driven by a weight) drives the "third" wheel (in this case the *second* of the train) through a pinion. The main arbor extends through the front "bar" of the frame and has a pinion driving an hour wheel riding upon a stud, to the pipe of which wheel is fitted the single hand—attached outside the dial. The "third" wheel drives (through a pinion) the escape wheel or crown wheel, fixed vertically on a horizontal arbor. This crown wheel engages during its revolutions with two " pallets ", " beds " or " checks " projecting from an upright arbor called the " verge ", to the top of which is fitted a large wrought iron ring with its rim attached by a single arm—the balance. The teeth of the crown wheel engaging with alternate pallets produce a to-and-fro motion in the verge and balance, thus the crown wheel is alternately stopped and released, producing the necessary periodic advancement of the train and hand.

The horizontal form of crown-wheel escapement is similar in action, but requires a different arrangement of the wheels and arbors, as in this case the crown wheel is fixed horizontally (really like a crown) to a vertical arbor, and engages into pallets projecting from a horizontal verge or pallet staff to the back end of which a short " bob " pendulum is directly attached as a controller.

Crown-wheel escapements are found only in the very earliest long-case clocks, before the application of the anchor escapement (q.v.) and therefore are practically certain to date before 1675. The " bob pendulum " (introduced by Fromanteel in 1658) is always used, never the earlier balance wheel, which is found only in early lantern clocks, before the pendulum was applied (by Huygens in Holland in 1657). The crown wheel, however, was used with the short pendulum in *mantel clocks* throughout the eighteenth century. The reasons for this properly belong to a disquisition upon mantel clocks, and are outside the scope of our particular horological study, which is intended to deal with long-case clocks only, with a short consideration of their precursors for the sake of a full understanding of their evolution.

Crutch

The attachment fixed to the pallet staff for the connection of the pendulum. The stem should be made of soft iron wire, so that it may be bent easily for the setting of the clock "in beat". The lower portion is formed into an elongated loop known as the crutch fork, bent at right-angles to the stem, for the reception of the pendulum. This loop is more often replaced by a steel attachment with a slot in it, to which the crutch stem or rod is riveted.

The employment of the crutch dates from 1656 or 1657. At this time it was used by Huygens and exemplified in clocks made under his assigned patent by Samuel Coster of the Hague. As previously mentioned in this Essay, it is strange that English clockmakers should continue for a good many years after this in their use of the direct attachment of the pendulum to the verge; the independently suspended pendulum to which impulses are transmitted *via* the crutch approaches much more nearly the ideal of a " free " pendulum, i.e., one which is not mechanically connected to the escapement in any way.

The crutch was also known in principle, at least, to Leonardo da Vinci (1452–1519), as it is sketched by him in one of his notebooks, together with a very advanced application of the pendulum. (*See* Pendulum in Glossary.)

Dead Beat Escapement

This escapement was invented by George Graham (1673–1751) probably about 1715. It was (and still is) much used for the best type of " regulator " timepiece, and is often found in conjunction with maintaining power, either of the bolt-and-shutter or Harrison kind. Centre-seconds movements with this escapement, however, do not appear to have maintaining power incorporated, probably for the reason that the seconds hand would foul the winding-key during its travel, if its motion were uninterrupted. The pallets of a dead-beat escapement are sometimes jewelled with insets of some such semi-precious stone as agate. The escapement is often known as a " repose " escapement, from the fact that there is no recoil of the escape wheel after the pallet has arrested a tooth, which may be verified by watching the small seconds hand on a clock with this type of escapement. It will be seen that the hand moves without visible shudder, in distinction to the seconds hand on a clock provided with the older anchor escapement. It may be well to mention here that the writer has not seen a *centre-seconds* dead-beat escapement that was entirely without a slight shudder of the seconds-hand; but this would be magnified by the length of the seconds-hand of centre-working type. Possibly the inertia of a rather badly-balanced long seconds-hand would also exaggerate the apparent recoil, owing to back-lash.

In spite of its somewhat greater accuracy as compared with the anchor escapement, the dead-beat type is not so well adapted to endure unfavourable conditions as the former pattern. It has to be kept perfectly clean and with a film of oil always on the pallet-faces (unless these are jewelled), which oil must not be allowed to become gummy or the timekeeping will inevitably suffer. In addition, the pendulum must be perfectly " in beat " if the best results are to be obtained. It is possible for a good restorer of old clocks to reface pallets of the anchor type, or to make a new anchor if necessary, which will be nearly dead-beat in action and produce results for all practical domestic purposes equal to the dead-beat escapement, without its liability to derangement.

Dial Pillars

The round, bar-like projections from the back of the dial, into which they are riveted. They fit into corresponding holes drilled in the front-plate of a movement, and are usually rather short for the sake of rigidity, only enough space being left between the dial and front-plate as will suitably accommodate the dial wheels, rack, and striking mechanism. The dial is secured to the movement by pins passed through the ends of the dial pillars, behind the front-plate.[1] There are usually four dial pillars, but movements are quite often found with only three, in which case the arrangement is in the form of a triangle with its apex inverted, the single pillar being thus at the bottom of the dial.

Dial Wheels

The minute wheel, cannon wheel, hour wheel, and calendar wheels (if any) comprise what are usually known as the dial wheels, since these are placed on the front plate between that and the dial. The calendar circle or disc and the moon disc if there is one, do not, properly speaking, belong to the dial wheels,[2] but if there is a special lunation train (*see* Trains) this would no doubt be regarded as coming within the definition, as nearly all the wheels are fitted to the front plate of the movement.

Equation of Time

The employment of this indication in the arch of a clock dial has been referred to in Chapter Two. The *reason* for its provision in certain rare examples of eighteenth-century movements can be here briefly stated as follows.

[1] But see the movement by Jacob Hasius, *circa* 1720, illustrated by Plate 33, where the latchet system is used both here and for the plate pillars.

[2] In spite of the fact that they are actually *on the dial*, which the others are not!

During the period in which these long-case clocks were originally constructed there existed no easy method of setting a clock to correct Greenwich time, such as we enjoy to-day by means of the radio transmission of frequent daily time-signals.

In the case of one living in a country district, far from a reliable public clock, the only method of checking a domestic clock was by the sundial. Now sundials, of course, record Solar or Apparent Time, and we have seen that this differs from Greenwich Mean Time ("clock" time) to a maximum of fifteen or sixteen minutes either way.

For many years during the latter part of the seventeenth and early eighteenth centuries there existed publications in the form of equation tables showing the daily variation throughout the year in minutes and seconds. These tables would appear to have been printed for the clockmaker himself, for him to distribute to his customers.

The procedure, therefore, was to ascertain Solar Time from the sundial,[1] find its variation, slow or fast, from G.M.T. for that particular day of the year, make an adjustment for the local meridian, and then set one's clock accordingly.

The mechanical substitute for the published equation table, exemplified by the arch indicator of a clock or timepiece, is something of a rarity; the cost of its inclusion no doubt accounts for the very small number of extant examples.

Escapement

See under the various kinds, as Anchor, Dead-beat, and Crown-wheel escapements. There are other kinds of escapements, such as the gravity and the pin-wheel escapements, but the first is practically never used in long-case clocks and the latter very rarely.

Escape Wheel

Often referred to "in the trade" and in works of horological technology as the "'scape wheel". The fourth wheel (reckoning upwards from the main wheel) of an eight-day movement, and therefore at the top of the going train or "watch". It is the third of a 30-hour train, and the fifth

---

[1] A "dyall" for checking purposes, together with the "equation table", was usually provided by the clockmaker for his customer; his "dyall" in all probability being a pocket sundial. Two such are illustrated by F. J. Britten, *Old Clocks and Watches and their Makers*, 6th edition, 1932.

of a month train, but still at the top. Above it swings the anchor and
pallet-staff, or the pallets and verge of the older escapement, in which case
the escape wheel is of the " crown " variety. Escape wheels used with an
anchor or dead-beat escapement vary in number of teeth. The usual is 30
teeth, in which case the pendulum beats seconds in a long-case clock. It
may, however, be occasionally provided with 24 teeth only, and used in
conjunction with an extra long pendulum nearly to the floor, and in this
event the pendulum will beat an interval of $1\frac{1}{4}$ seconds and the
subsidiary seconds-dial—if there be one—will be divided not into 60
divisions, but into 48, as $48 \times 1\frac{1}{4} = 60$ seconds. The escape wheel is stopped
and released by alternate pallets of the pallet-staff, thus providing a
periodic (usually a seconds-length) interruption in the otherwise continuous
movement of the train and hands. The exact and unvarying preservation
of this particular length of period results in perfect timekeeping. Actually,
there is no such thing as an exact and unvarying periodicity, as will be
seen during the course of this book, therefore absolutely perfect timekeeping is in any event an impossibility.

It should be noted that the teeth of an escape wheel used with an
anchor are cut the reverse way to those of an escape wheel designed for a
dead-beat escapement.[1] Also that the teeth of the latter wheel have their
fronts " undercut " some ten degrees from the radial. This causes only the
tips of the teeth to contact the curved locking surfaces of the pallets. In
early escape wheels, the escape pinion on the same arbor often had fewer
leaves than those in use later, and the wheel itself was comparatively small
and light. This was especially so in clocks of three, six, or twelve months
duration between windings, since the weight required to drive the clock
would be affected by such details. Britten records particulars of a twelve-
months timepiece by Daniel Quare in which all the upper wheels of the
train were pivoted into a separate small plate attached by diminutive
pillars between the main plates of the movement, the arbors, therefore, being
very short and light, with extremely fine pivots.

Another name for the 'scape wheel (but somewhat unusual, perhaps)
is the *swing wheel*, which nomenclature is used in the interesting account
by Britten mentioned above. This appellation is no doubt derived from
the pallets which " swing " above the wheel, and which engage its teeth.

---

[1] Except in 30-hour movements, in which the 'scape-wheel teeth are set in the same direction
as those used for a dead-beat escapement; this because a 30-hour 'scape wheel turns *anti-clockwise*.

In the examination of an old movement, it is an interesting fact that the hardened steel pallets of an anchor nearly always show considerably more wear than the teeth of the escape wheel, which are of comparatively soft brass. The reason for this has already been given during the explanations about " oiling " in Chapter Eight, but of course, in the instance now before us, the pallets *must* be oiled slightly, unless they have jewelled acting-faces, in order to reduce friction as much as possible at this important position. Badly pitted pallets can be re-faced by a good restorer of old movements, or an entirely new " anchor " made, if necessary. (*See* Pallets.)

Finally, the escape wheel and pallets provide the answer to the child's question—" What makes the clock *tick*? " The " tick " is the clicking sound made by the periodic impact of tooth against pallet and, according to one authority,[1] should be almost inaudible with a good escapement at a little distance from the clock.

Fly

The fly is situated at the top of the striking train or " clock ", immediately above the highest wheel (the " warn wheel "). Its purpose is to equalise and steady the hammer blows upon the bell, by providing a slight resistance to the weight-power owing to the rapidly revolving vanes meeting with air-resistance in their travel. It may, in fact, be regarded as a kind of governor, tending to keep the speed of striking constant under slightly varying conditions of frictional resistance in the train. It will be at once appreciated that the greater the area of the fly, and the more rapid its speed of revolution, the more effective will be the governor in producing a slow and perfectly periodic series of hammer blows upon the bell. It is usually agreed that the requisite area or mass of the fly is better produced by a short fly with comparatively broad vanes than by a longer fly of narrower construction. The reason for this is obvious when we consider that air-resistance to the fly of broader type will be greater than that to a fly of equal area but with narrower vanes, revolving at the same speed.

It is essential that the fly should not be heavy, and that it should not revolve too slowly. The older flys used in long-case movements were sometimes rather small, but always very light, and revolved at high speeds, carrying on their arbors pinions often with only six leaves, and therefore

---

[1] G. F. C. Gordon, *Clockmaking, Past and Present*.

revolving very fast. The result was a *slow* strike, which served to emphasize the pleasant, well-sustained sound for which most of the bells of 1680–1720 were deservedly considered as eminently musical.

Foliot

The foliot was an early form of regulator, before the application of the pendulum, which took place in England about 1658. Except for "turret-clocks" (church clocks and the like), however, the foliot was not used in this country, where the circular iron balance wheel took its place. The foliot consisted of a straight bar placed across the top of an upright verge. The bar was toothed, ratchet-style, at each end, and provided with small weights pendant therefrom; the attachments of the weights could be moved into different teeth to roughly adjust the regulator. Neither foliot nor balance wheel are ever found in the movement of a *long-case* clock, since these only appeared after the pendulum was established, the very earliest long-case clocks dating from about 1660. *See* also under Balance.

Gathering Pallet

The number of blows delivered to the bell by the hammer is regulated by a contrivance known as the rack (q.v.) in conjunction with a cammed plate termed the snail. In early long-case 8-day movements, and in practically all the 30-hour movements made early or late, this rack is displaced by the older device known as the locking-plate. In connection with the gathering-pallet, however, it is with the rack-striking that we have to deal.

After falling to a position determined by the snail, and thus beginning the release of the striking train, and during the period in which the clock is striking, the rack is gradually returned to its original position, where it can again perform the duty of stopping or "locking" the train by means of the usual pin fixed into its surface. This return of the rack, or "gathering up", is performed by the gathering-pallet, which is a steel cam fixed or fitted to the arbor of the pallet wheel (the third wheel of an 8-day train) and engaging, with every revolution of this wheel, into a tooth of the rack, thus "gathering" this step-by-step (or blow-by-blow of the hammer) back to its original position, against the light pressure of the rack-spring. The rack-spring pressure is replaced by the force of gravity in the case of the earliest racks, which were fitted horizontally between the plates of the movement, not vertically on the face of the front plate, as was usual after about 1700. The gathering-pallet is frequently filed out from the arbor of the pallet-wheel, about midway between the plates, in the earlier type, or assumes the form of a pin projecting from the pallet-wheel collet. In the later rack-striking movements (after *circa* 1700) the gathering-pallet is fitted to that end of the pallet-wheel arbor which projects through the front plate, which arbor is squared to receive it, and usually the gathering-pallet has an extension or " tail " which is designed to fall upon the rack-pin when the latter comes into position, thus stopping the clock striking by locking the train again. The first " outside " gathering-pallets were unprovided with this " tail ", the locking being accomplished by the rack hook (*see* Rack) itself; in fact, it was not until many years after the introduction of the outside rack that the tail to the gathering-pallet was added. The locking of the train in the old inside-rack movements was effected by a pin in the pallet wheel engaging with a projection from the side of the rack, or in some similar way.

Great Wheel

The great wheel is the main wheel of the " clock " or striking train. This designation is used to distinguish it from the main wheel of the " watch ", or going part, which latter is strictly that which ought to bear the appellation " Main ", since it must be regarded as of prior importance, in so far as the provision of a " watch " is primarily required in order to release the " clock " train at determined intervals.

Nomenclature, however, is often somewhat vague in practice, *both* wheels being usually referred to as " main wheels ", frequently without qualifying the term as " main striking " or " main going " wheels, which lack of definition tends to obscure a discussion. In this book, therefore, for the sake of clarity, the main going wheel and the main striking wheel will be constantly referred to as " Main wheel " and " Great wheel " respectively.

The great wheel is usually smaller than its counterpart in the " watch " —the main wheel. In the early clocks the great wheel is often very noticeably less, the usual number of teeth being 78 as against 96 in the main wheel. Later, this proportion was modified, the great wheel frequently being provided with 84 teeth, with 96 in the main wheel.

The teeth of the great wheel gear with the pinion leaves of the wheel next above it, which in an 8-day movement is the " Pin " wheel. In a month movement an extra wheel is introduced between the great wheel and the pin wheel, known as the " second " wheel.

For an explanation of the way in which the great wheel " rides " upon its arbor, and of the method by which the weight power is conveyed to it, see under Click, Main Wheel, and Ratchet.

Hoop Wheel
See Pallet Wheel

Hour Wheel

The hour wheel is fixed or detachably fitted to a tube or " pipe " which bears the hour-hand, the pipe being squared at the end so that the hand may be firmly fitted. Some of the later movements had the pipe made with a " step " in its circumference at the end, producing a pipe of less diameter for about ⅛ inch, and had a pin projecting from the face of this " step " or shoulder fitting into a corresponding slot or " keyway " in the hand, thus forming a method of attachment.

The hour-hand pipe also carries the snail (q.v.) in a rack-striking movement, and frequently another toothed wheel situated between the snail and the hour wheel, which functions in connection with the separate calendar wheel, the teeth of this latter being engaged thereby. The hour-hand pipe, complete with its hour wheels and snail plate, is fitted over the bridge-pipe (*see* Bridge) and in its working revolves thereon. The teeth of the hour wheel are engaged by the leaves of the minute pinion (q.v.) and the wheel is driven by this in the proportion 12 to 1, as the minute pinion revolves once in one hour and the hour wheel once in twelve hours. It will be noted that to attain this relative movement the hour wheel must have twelve times as many teeth as the pinion has leaves, so if, as is usual, the latter has 6 leaves, the hour wheel must have 72 teeth.

The term " hour wheel " is doubtless used because its pipe carries the hour hand, which indicates the hours on the dial. This name for it is universally used both in the clock trade and by writers on clockwork, and I follow the usual practice to avoid confusion throughout this book. I am of the opinion, however, that the term is misleading, and an inaccurate description of a wheel which makes a complete revolution in *twelve* hours, and therefore would be more justly described by the admittedly rather clumsy name of " twelve-hour wheel ". The preceding remarks also apply to the usual nomenclature accorded to the wheel whose pipe bears the minute hand, and to the minute wheel, both of which are always referred to as " minute wheels ", whereas they both complete a revolution in *sixty* minutes, and consequently should be logically known as " hour wheels ", but here again custom makes this description dangerous.

Jaws
> *See* Cock.

Leaves
> *See* Pinions.

Lifting-piece
> The lifting-piece is the steel lever with two arms, one of which is the lifting-piece proper, and the other the " tail ", It is pivoted to the front plate at the junction of the arms. The extremity of the tail is engaged every hour by a pin projecting from the circumference of the minute wheel, which pin pushes the tail lever to the left, thus raising the lifting-piece. The end of the lifting-piece is bent at right angles and projects slightly within the plates, a slot being cut for it in the front-plate. The purpose of this projection is to engage with a pin in the " warn wheel " of the striking train, which engagement locks the train after its initial move-ment or " warning " until the lifting-piece drops again, which it does after the pin in the minute wheel clears the tail, releasing the train for its striking run. When the lifting-piece rises, its extremity also raises the rack hook (q.v.) from the teeth of the rack, allowing this to fall and the train to move until it is again temporarily locked by the pin in the warn wheel, and finally released as explained above.

> The levers of the lifting-piece were frequently made objects for slight ornamentation, in early long-case movements, but not, apparently, to quite the same extent as was the case with some of the early bracket-clock movements.

> The lifting-piece is often made with a short prolongation at the pivot, which extension frequently has a hole drilled through its extremity. This is a suitable position for the attachment of a cord to hang within the clock case, or even to be brought outside the case through a small bushed hole, a little decorative drop handle of bone, ivory or similar material being attached to the end of the line. The purpose of this cord is then to

provide a means of repeating any hour by pulling gently on the line, and thus raising the lifting-piece. The hour repeated will always be the last hour struck by the clockwork, unless the hand be close to the following hour, when the snail will be in such a position that the hour struck on pulling the cord will be the next to be sounded in the ordinary way. It will be obvious, therefore, that with an ordinary striking clock (not a chiming clock) the aural indication will only be approximate, and that very roughly—to an hour, in fact. Nevertheless, it provides a means of ascertaining very approximate time in darkness, or when the dial cannot be seen, and might be convenient if the clock were situated in a bed-room, the pulling string could then hang within reach of a person in bed. It is interesting to note that the same idea was used in the early bracket clocks; the time in this case would be given with a lesser margin of error, however, as these clocks were nearly always quarter-chiming, and the pulling of the cord was arranged to sound the last hour in full, before the quarters past were given (*see* also the "*Grande Sonnerie*"— Chapter Two, *Early Long-case Clocks*).

Lines

These are the gut or stranded wire cords from which the driving weights are suspended in movements of 8-day duration and longer. A line is attached to the barrel (q.v.) by means of a small hole drilled in the latter to receive it. The line is then knotted securely so that the knot is inside the barrel and prevents the line being pulled out by the weight. A larger hole is provided in the end of the barrel near its edge, opposite the small hole, to facilitate attachment and removal of a line. After leaving the barrel the line is passed through a rectangular gap in the seatboard (q.v.) and round the weight-pulley, and rises again to the seat-board, through which it should pass by a *small* hole, to be secured on the top by a strong looped knot large enough to make it impossible for the line to be pulled through the hole. Pieces of wood, nails, etc., used as cross-pieces in this position are unsightly and unnecessary if the knot is large and strongly tied. In a few instances, however, the holes in the seat-board will be found in the correct position, but so large that a knot would be impracticable. Some form of cross-piece is then, of course, a necessity, unless the holes are plugged.

Lines should *never* be attached by hooks under the seat-board. If these hooks are in the correct position for the weight to fall properly, they will almost certainly catch the edge of the pulley, if the weight be wound high, causing a nasty burr in time, which will finally have the inevitable result of fraying a gut line badly.

The holes in the seatboard where the lines are fastened should be so placed that when the weights are about half-way down the case the flats of the pulleys are in the same plane as the dial and front of the clock-case; that is, their flats should be seen when the trunk-door is opened, not their edges. Also, the distance from the line where it leaves the barrel on one side to the point where it enters the seat-board on the other should be about the same measurement as the diameter of the pulley. The adoption of this method of attaching the line will tend to prevent the weight revolving during its descent, which would twist the two parts of the line together, and thus stop the clock. The line should not be allowed to rub on the seat-board where it passes through from the barrel.

Lines are made in more than one thickness; the thicker lines are used for clocks with heavy driving weights, such as month clocks, or chiming movements. Some people prefer wire lines for the heavy weights of chiming clocks, but if these are used they should be of good quality. Mr. G. F. C. Gordon, in his book *Clockmaking*, says they should consist of a three-ply wire rope composed of about forty strands of fine steel wire. These, he says, are as cheap and flexible as gut and last for ever. To save the line becoming untwisted after cutting, the same authority suggests applying a small gas flame to the place where it is to be cut, softening a length of about one quarter of an inch, twisting the line a good deal at this position and then cutting it. Of course, wire lines should invariably be used for movements of extra long duration with enormously heavy weights, i.e., three-, six-, and twelve-month clocks and timepieces.

A gut line is often broken by careless winding, the weight not being watched in its ascent, and vigorous winding causing the pulley to be brought into sharp contact with the bottom of the seat-board, thus breaking the line and possibly causing considerable damage if the weight is a heavy one. A badly frayed gut line should on no account be tolerated, but replaced at once, for obvious reasons.

Regarding the life of lines, we have seen that the wire variety, if of good quality and not subjected to maltreatment, is practically everlasting. The gut line, under good conditions of service and used in a favourable atmosphere, should last about forty years.

Locking-Plate, or Count Wheel

This device for controlling the striking of the clock is very ancient in horological history. It is probably the earliest contrivance ever used, in fact, as it is employed in the oldest mechanical clocks of which we have any trustworthy details available. It was present in the lantern clock of the seventeenth century, and when this form of " chamber clock " began to be superseded by the long-case type about 1660, the old well-tried striking control was transferred to the new timekeeper, being retained even after the early form of " lantern movement " had given place to the plate-frame type.

Locking-plate striking was not wholly abandoned for eight-day long-case movements until well into the early part of the eighteenth century.[1] Even then, the earlier locking-plate persisted in 30-hour movements for long-case clocks throughout the eighteenth century.

The locking-plate consists of a flat brass disc, turning like a wheel (it is often referred to as a " locking-wheel ") with eleven notches cut into its edge, at unequal intervals according to the number of blows required upon the bell. Into these notches drops a steel hook known as the " locking-hook ", the fall of this causing a lever fixed to the same arbor, but between the plates, to engage a pin in a wheel of the striking train, thus locking the train. During the time the locking-hook is riding upon the edge of the revolving locking-plate, and while the clock is striking in this period, the lever between the plates is held clear of the pin in the wheel, but after the requisite number of blows have been given, the locking-hook drops into a slot, the lever falling also, as it is on the same arbor, and engaging the pin, thus bringing the train to rest. It will be seen, therefore, that the locking-plate, while controlling the striking, does not actually lock the train by itself, but because of the drop afforded the locking-hook (and therefore to the lever fixed to the same arbor) when one of the notches is entered, is the means by which the locking of the train is accomplished. In this connection, it will be noticed that only *eleven* notches are formed in the locking-plate. The eleventh notch, which is somewhat wider than the others, serves for both twelve and one o'clock, as the train has to move so slightly for the single stroke of the hammer that the mere unlocking and almost immediate re-locking of the train by a flick of the lever away

---

[1] F. J. Britten (*Old Clocks and Watches and their Makers*) states that the celebrated Thomas Tompion applied the rack *about 1676*. These early racks were always fitted between the plates, certainly until well after 1700.

from the pin in the wheel, followed at once by its return to position is enough to allow the wheels to revolve sufficiently for one stroke of the hammer.

Locking-plates are found in different positions. Some are situated between the plates, attached to the side of the great wheel, and these are known as "inside locking-plates". Others, the earliest, are placed at the rear of the backplate and driven by a pinion from the pin-wheel arbor, and are called "outside locking-plates". According to G. F. C. Gordon, this type was particularly favoured for month movements. A third variety, next in evolution to the last mentioned, was attached to the arbor of the great wheel,[1] which arbor then had to be divided inside the barrel to allow of winding. The form employed here obviated the necessity for the cutting of an extra wheel and pinion, which Mr. Gordon thinks was probably considered more serious two-and-a-half centuries ago than the work entailed in dividing the barrel arbor.

Still another form of locking-plate, similar in kind to the second described, inasmuch as it revolves on a stud behind the backplate, is driven by a pinion on the great wheel arbor, and this type was used for most 30-hour movements during the whole course of the eighteenth century.

In the locking-plate system, the striking is progressive with each successive release of the train, and consequently any particular hour cannot be repeated; further, if the hands be moved round the dial, each hour must be allowed to strike out in full, the neglect of this resulting in lack of coincidence between the visual and aural indications. After an error of this kind, the striking can be brought coincident with the hands by raising the locking-hook manually as many times as are necessary to arrive at the correct hour.

The rack system is not susceptible to either of the above limitations, as repetition of any particular hour depends merely on the position of the snail (and therefore of the hour hand) and, as a corollary, moving the hands does not disturb the concurrence of the bell, though they be moved past successive hour positions without time being allowed for striking. (But *see* Rack for a qualification of this, and a full explanation.)

The old form of striking work, with locking-plate attached to great wheel, was occasionally employed for the later eight-day striking trains. This usually varied from the early type in one small detail, which,

---

[1] Another "outside" type.

K

together with obvious differences elsewhere in the movement, is sufficient to indicate the period of construction. This detail is shown by the form of the third wheel in the striking train. In the early locking-plate movements this is the *hoop wheel* (q.v.), which designation accurately describes the form of locking employed. Those movements of later construction using the old system for eight-day clocks have substituted for the " hoop " *a pin*, which performs the function of the former.

I have seen an excellent movement by James Sandiford, Salford (Manchester), period 1790 or thereabout, in which the old locking-plate striking is used for an eight-day clock, but in which the variation referred to above is introduced.

Lunation Train
      See Trains.

Main Wheel
      As explained under the heading *Great Wheel*, the term " main " is often rather loosely applied to *both* large wheels the arbors of which bear the barrels and transmit the weight-power to the going and striking trains of a timekeeper. In accordance with the principle already advocated, it is proposed here, when discussing the " main " wheel, to restrict this designation to the chief wheel of the movement—that which drives the upper wheels of the " watch ", or going part.

The main wheel is fitted closely, but not fixed, to the arbor on which it " rides "—the main arbor. The forward end of this arbor is squared to admit of the temporary attachment of the winding key, and protrudes through the front-plate of the movement very nearly to the surface of the dial, in which appears a corresponding circular aperture, often finished with an ornamental ring or an incised decoration. Immovably attached to the main arbor is the barrel (q.v.) upon which the gut or wire line bearing the weight is wound.[1] The main wheel " rides " or turns loosely upon the arbor, close to the rear of the barrel, and is provided with a " click " (q.v.) engaging with a ratchet on the barrel, so that the turning of the latter by the weight may also turn the main wheel. The purpose of the ratchet is to allow the main arbor and barrel to be turned in the reverse direction when winding up the weight, which is also the reason for the main wheel being " free " on the arbor.

[1] For the method of attaching the line and weight *see* " Lines ".

Engaging with the teeth of the main wheel is the pinion of the wheel-arbor next above—the centre pinion. Now the centre arbor, in a normal 8-day movement, bears the cannon-wheel on a pipe to which is attached the minute hand, and has obviously to turn once in sixty minutes. Since the barrel and main wheel are usually arranged to turn once in twelve hours, the centre pinion is given eight leaves (turning once an hour) and the main wheel, therefore, has $12 \times 8 = 96$ teeth.

As in the case of the great wheel, an extra wheel is interposed between the main and centre wheels of a movement intended to go a month between windings, which extra wheel is then known as the " second " wheel (*see* Movements).

Maintaining Power

When the " watch " or going part is wound, the power of the driving weight is temporarily removed from the train, as the barrel is turned backwards, thus ceasing to transmit the weight-power to the main wheel through the ratchet and " click ". In consequence, the escape wheel, instead of tending to drive the pendulum through impulses given to the pallets, becomes powerless, and tends to be driven in reverse by the pendulum, through the pallets. With an anchor escapement, the 'scape wheel does, in fact, move backwards when the gut line is wound up, as may be verified by observing the seconds hand on the dial, which then moves anti-clockwise for as long as the winding continues.

It will be seen, therefore, that although the pendulum still vibrates and beats seconds, the onward motion of the train *recording* these beats is arrested, and the timekeeper " loses " to an extent proportionate to the time taken in a reasonably careful winding, usually about a minute.

Now this error, though small, is about twice that of a clock with well-adjusted pendulum and reasonably good train *in a week*. If the variation of the movement from strict time be a half-minute *loss* per week, then the winding will increase this error to a loss of one-and-a-half minutes in the same period, if the minute hand is not re-set to compensate. To obviate the inaccuracy due to winding the " maintaining power " was introduced, which is a device to keep the train working normally during the time of winding, when the weight power is inoperative.

A very old system of maintaining power is that known as the " bolt-and-shutter " type. The date of its introduction appears uncertain, but it was used in many of the very earliest long-case movements, both of eight-day and month duration, about 1660–1665. Possibly it was a transference to the domestic clock of the method applied to church or turret clocks, which were similarly weight-driven.

It consists of an arbor between the plates, the forward end of which, passing through the front-plate, bears a weighted lever.[1] This lever has two projecting flats or "shutters" which are arranged to cover each winding-hole from the back of the dial. The shutter for the "clock" winding-hole is merely to preserve a balanced appearance from the front, as it is obviously unnecessary to provide maintaining power for the striking train, as nobody winds a clock when it is striking, or about to strike. A second lever is fixed to the arbor, but between the plates this time, and when the former lever is lifted to expose the winding-squares, the other engages the teeth of one of the train wheels (usually the centre wheel) by means of a "click" or bolt. The centre wheel is then driven by the weight on the outer lever, until the bolt works itself out of engagement, the shutter gradually dropping back to its former position, closing the winding-hole. Ample time is allowed for winding by this means, as the centre wheel turns comparatively slowly—once per hour, in fact. The lifting of the weighted lever is usually accomplished by a cord hanging inside the clockcase.

A later method of keeping the train going during the act of winding was invented by John Harrison (1693–1776). This is often referred to as the "spring going-ratchet", which describes it well, or by the name of its originator, as "Harrison's maintaining-power", which is not so explicit.

The spring going-ratchet was largely used in dead-beat escapements of clocks made after about the middle of the eighteenth century, when the older bolt-and-shutter system appears to have been discontinued in favour of Harrison's method. This was probably due to the fact of the going-ratchet being more compact, which will be apparent when we consider its construction. Also, it does not seem to possess any serious liability to faulty operation, and one trouble with the bolt-and-shutter type is the possibility of the "click" or bolt becoming wedged in a tooth of the wheel, when it stops the train altogether, and has to be freed before the normal weight power will again perform its duty.

---

[1] The weight-loading is frequently varied by a *spring-powered* lever, but the principle of both is the same.

Harrison's maintaining power is to this day much used in very accurate timepieces of the "regulator" type, for special purposes, and in most modern productions of the long-case kind, with movements chiming on tubes, and glass-fronted trunk-doors.

The device consists of a second ratchet wheel riding on the main barrel-arbor next the main wheel itself. The "click" of the barrel-ratchet is attached to this second ratchet wheel, not to the main wheel directly, as is usual. Connection between the main wheel and the weight-power on the barrel is provided by a curved spring attached at one end to the large (second) ratchet wheel and at the other to the side of the main wheel. The teeth of the barrel-ratchet and those of the large or "going" ratchet are cut in reverse directions. Into the teeth of the going ratchet drops (by gravity) the end of a long lever or click pivoted at its other extremity to an arbor between the plates. When the train is being normally driven by the weight, the turning of the barrel and its ratchet also turns the going ratchet, through the agency of the barrel-ratchet click, which latter, it will be remembered, is now attached to the side of the going-ratchet. The long click-lever simply slides over the teeth of the last named, which transmits the turning movement to the main wheel in the same direction, by means of the spring before-mentioned, *which is compressed into tension by the process*.[1] When the weight is wound up by turning the barrel-arbor with a key, the barrel-ratchet allows the barrel to be turned in the opposite direction to that of going, but the long click-lever prevents the going-ratchet turning the same way, by engaging a tooth, and the stored energy of the spring is then expended in driving the main wheel in the direction of going, by its gradual expansion.

As this later kind of maintaining power is not so susceptible of intelligible verbal description, in so far as its operation is concerned, as the old bolt-and-shutter type, a drawing of Harrison's maintaining power mechanism will be found at Fig. 6. This should be studied in conjunction with the foregoing explanation of its working.

Christian Huygens (1629–1695), a Dutch mathematician and physicist, who is usually accredited the first horologist to apply the pendulum as a controller in a thoroughly practical manner (1657), was responsible for the introduction of what is now a third variety of maintaining power. The precise date of its appearance seems a fairly certain conclusion, for in his

---

[1] The tension of this spring is equivalent to the force exerted by the driving-weight.

Horologium of 1658 (a small treatise in Latin describing his new pendulum clock) Huygens illustrates the system applied to a clock having its pendulum-crutch operated by a segmentally-toothed "contrate" wheel. It is fully described by Huygens in his folio work *Horologium Oscillatorium*, published at Paris in 1673. It may be reasonably inferred, therefore, that Huygens used it in his clocks of 1657.

Briefly, the mechanism consists of two pulleys, with spiked rope-grooves, one pulley on each main arbor. The pulley in the going part is fixed to the side of the main wheel; that in the striking train is connected by a "click". Passing over the pulleys is an endless rope attached in the manner shown in Plate 7. The same weight is utilized for both going and striking, and the winding is effected by pulling down that portion of the rope farthest from the weight, an operation facilitated by the "click" on the striking side. It will be seen that during the period of winding the weight-power is still effective on the going train, though not, of course, on the "clock" part. The latter fact is immaterial, as the striking is not required to be continuous, and winding is never performed during striking.

The rope originally employed becomes worn by the spikes in the pulleys, designed to prevent it slipping, and eventually fills the movement with fluff. Because of this fault it was not many years in general use before it was superseded by a steel chain, the pulleys being modified in form to suit the links.

Huygens's maintaining power was employed in thirty-hour long-case movements throughout the eighteenth century and, used with a chain and pulleys in good condition, is perfectly satisfactory. It is not suitable for eight-day movements, with their heavier weights.

Minute Pinion

The cannon-wheel (often called the "cannon-pinion", from its application to watch-work) which is fixed on a pipe fitted over the centre arbor, drives another wheel with exactly the same number of teeth. This second wheel is known as the minute-wheel, or as a reversed minute-wheel, since it moves the opposite way to the cannon-wheel—which is another "minute-wheel" in reality—i.e., anti-clockwise. To the centre of this minute-wheel is fixed a projecting pinion, known as the minute-wheel pinion, or simply as " the minute-pinion " whose leaves engage with the teeth of the hour-wheel (really the *twelve-hour* wheel, as it makes one complete revolution in twelve hours). As the cannon-wheel turns once in 60 minutes, the minute-wheel and its pinion do likewise, but in the reverse direction. If the minute-pinion is provided with six leaves, therefore, the hour-wheel with which it engages must have 12×6 teeth $= 72$, as it has to turn only once in 12 hours. The direction is again reversed in the contact of the pinion with the hour-wheel so that the motion of the latter is once more clockwise.

Moon's Phases, or Lunar Record

The phases of the moon, and often its age in days, shown on the dial by some form of internal mechanism, is a very early horological device. It was one of the first of the many subsidiary movements which, in addition to the main arrangement for indicating the passage of time, distinguished the remarkably complicated "horologia" of the fourteenth century.

F. J. Britten, in his book *Old Clocks and Watches and their Makers*, illustrates the dial of a clock said to have been made by one Peter Lightfoot, a monk of Glastonbury, for the Abbey Church there, provided at the expense of the Abbot, Adam de Lodbury, who was appointed to the abbacy in 1322. The abbot died in 1335, which year, according to Britten, was about the time that this ancient piece of mechanism was constructed. It exhibits, together with various other movements, the phases of the Moon displayed through a circular opening in the dial-plate, and indicates the age of the luminary by figures on a revolving ring, marked by a pointer from the edge of the aperture.[1]

The lunar record was also frequently included in the dial arrangements of early complicated watches; one by Jan J. Bockelts from the Schloss collection is also illustrated in Britten's fine work, dated "anno 1607"; another, by Thomas Alcock, is a splendid English calendar watch, indicating the moon's age by means of a central revolving disc with an encircling ring of figures, the phases being displayed through the usual circular aperture, near the edge of the rotating disc. The date of this watch is about 1635.

Most representations of the moon's appearance take the form of an

---

[1] This story of Peter Lightfoot's clock has since been discredited. It is now even supposed doubtful whether Lightfoot ever existed! There is little doubt, however, that the dial is at any rate late fourteenth-century work. *See* R. P. Howgrave-Graham: *Peter Lightfoot, Monk of Glastonbury, and the Old Clock at Wells* (Glastonbury, 1922).

engraved or enamelled human face on a toothed rotating disc. The early " moons " were usually engraved and silvered, upon a star-spangled background, but the later types were more often painted in colours, Luna frequently acquiring a somewhat rubicund " complexion " in this manner! The background of the painted variety is usually in the form of a landscape, sometimes a landscape followed by a seascape, as the revolving disc carries *two* " moons " and two sets of figures, since the disc turns only once for two complete lunations.

The mechanism employed to actuate the moon-disc is ordinarily of simple description. A double-armed lever is pivoted to the dial-plate at the back. The arms are usually provided with jointed tips, spring-controlled, and the lower arm engages with a stud on the hour wheel pipe, or with a pin from the snail, thus every twelve hours the arms vibrate. The upper arm engages, with its spring tip, the teeth of the moon-disc, moving this onward half-a-day, or one click. The disc is positioned by a spring click or " jumper " acting against its toothed periphery. After performing their function, the levers drop back against a supporting stud projecting from the back of the dial-plate. The different forms of moon disc almost invariably occupy the arch of the dial, but occasionally the dial centre is utilized for the display of this feature. This latter position is, of course, obligatory in the somewhat rare instances of a square-dial clock with a lunar record. The rotating disc principle is occasionally found operated by a special train of wheels—a lunation train, as it is called—in which case the movement is continuous, not intermittent as with the lever-controlled method. For a description of this system see under Trains; and for an illustration, see the example shown by Plate 52.

A second variety of the lunar record is that employed in " Halifax clocks ", so called because they were popular in Yorkshire during the eighteenth century.[1] This consists of a rotating *globular* " moon " particoloured black and white, actuated by a nearly vertical shaft worked from the dial wheels by a system of gearing using bevel or " mitre " wheels.

[1] The famous *seventeenth-century* clockmaker Fromanteel, however, employed this device nearly 100 years earlier than the " Halifax clocks ". Britten illustrates a hanging clock by " A. Fromanteel, London " in ebonized casework, in which this arrangement occupies a separate little case with a glass door to it, placed intriguingly on the top of the main case. The rotating globe representing the moon surmounts two revolving discs which have their edges towards the front, the rims of each being figured with the days of the lunar and calendar months respectively. This beautiful example of early work had been made into a long-case clock when the late Mr. Britten saw it.

In conjunction with the lunar record, a method of indicating the time of high and low water was used by some eighteenth-century makers in districts where journeys involved the crossing of a tidal river. This was most frequently indicated by a second set of numerals in Roman type added to the moon disc, in addition to those in arabic characters showing its age. Where the spherical or "Halifax" system of phase indication was employed, the time of high water was often displayed by means of a plate in the arch, coloured to represent the sea, rising and falling with the tides, in conjunction with a subsidiary dial and pointer giving the hours of high and low tide, but sometimes a secondary system of *Roman* numerals was used on the globe itself. Occasionally the times of high water for *several* places are indicated, especially in the "Halifax" type of record, and in this a series of fixed pointers mark off on the secondary (Roman) numerals of the revolving globe the appropriate times.

The methods employed in long-case clocks to illustrate the moon's phases, such as described in the foregoing paragraphs, are only approximate to the duration of an actual lunation.

A lunar month is a period of 29 days 12 hours 44 minutes and 3 seconds exactly, or rather *more* than 29½ days.

A "lunation" according to the moon-disc of a clock with this apparatus is 29½ days; hence, over a period of twelve lunar months the clock will gradually build up its error so that at the end of this time it will be 8 hours 48 minutes 36 seconds short of the real age of the moon. This lapse will be altered slighly, plus or minus, with any variations in the timekeeping of the going train itself, over the same period. It will be noted, however, that the inaccuracy is not really serious—less than a half-day per year. Such a divergence can be easily corrected by moving the disc one click forward (one half-day) at the expiration of a year. This, of course, will not be an exact compensation, but is sufficient for all practical purposes.

The appended extract from the Diary of Robert Hooke, under date Monday, January 29th, 1677, may be of interest as illustrating the ingenious doctor's many horological conversations with the famous Thomas Tompion, as also bearing upon our subject of the Lunar Record:

" To Garways.[1] Met Sir Ch. Scarborough. Taught him the way for

---

[1] Or Garaways, as sometimes spelt by Hooke. A well-known coffee-house in Change Alley, Cornhill. According to the editors of the " Diary ", whose information is from various sources, tea was first sold there.

the shell to turne about the Moon at. the top of the clock and to show how the shadow hides the parts and spots of the Moon, advised him to have also a moveable horizon, the way of both which I shewed Tompion next night."

Movements

Among the earliest long-case movements were adaptations of those used in the older type of chamber-clock, therefore known as Lantern movements. They were invariably of 30-hour duration or less between windings, pull-up wind on cords, and the wheels of the trains were arranged as in lantern clocks proper, i.e., the arbors pivoted into three upright bars or strips of metal, the going and striking parts one behind the other. A short " bob " pendulum was used as the controller, with a crown-wheel escapement. An hour hand of rather massive construction provided the only index, the dial being divided into quarter-hours exactly corre-sponding to the earliest of the lantern clocks. The striking was on the locking-plate principle (q.v.).

Even at this early period makers such as Fromanteel (1658) began to produce movements capable of a greater duration than thirty hours. About 1660 the eight-day, month, and even year movements became established, both for spring-driven mantel clocks and weight-powered long-case time-keepers.

These movements inaugurated the plate frame, which was to become standard practice to the present day for all kinds of clocks. This made key-winding from the front of the dial possible, the trains now being set side-by-side, and led to the introduction of the gut or wire line winding on to a brass " barrel " or drum.

" Bob " pendulums with a crown-wheel escapement were still used, with locking-plate striking first of the " outside locking-wheel " type (*see* Plate 20—with *anchor* escapement and $1\frac{1}{4}$ seconds pendulum), and later with the locking-plate attached to the great wheel. Bolt-and-shutter main-taining power was often applied, particularly in eight-day movements. The calendar, shown through a small square aperture in the dial, became an almost invariable adjunct (it must have been used occasionally in the thirty-hour lantern movements, but this may have been rare). Minute motion-work and a minute hand now became standardized in the best clocks, although there were notable exceptions. Joseph Knibb introduced his peculiar system of striking on two bells, known as Roman Numeral striking. This striking-system, which may be regarded as the especial attribute of certain clocks by Joseph Knibb, was occasionally used by other makers, notably by Daniel Quare.

It consists of the emploment of *two* bells, one of high pitch, the other of deeper tone.

At "one o'clock" by the hands, one stroke is given on the smaller (high-pitched) bell, two strokes on this bell serving for "two o'clock" and three for the following hour, as usual. "Four o'clock" is generally indicated on the chapter-ring by the Roman numeral IV and not by IIII in clocks having this method of hour striking, and here the system changes from that used normally. For the "I" of the Roman numeral "IV" one stroke is given on the smaller bell, followed by one on the larger, this latter sound being always understood to represent the numeral "V". Similarly, at "five o'clock" one blow only is given, and that to the larger bell. At the next hour (VI) both bells are sounded, first the larger, then the smaller—one stroke each. At seven o'clock the larger bell is first sounded once (for the "V" of the numeral VII) and then the small bell twice. Ten o'clock is indicated by *two* strokes on the deeper-toned bell (representing twice "V", or X, and XI and XII are correspondingly aurally interpreted by each having two strokes on the large bell followed by one and two respectively allotted to that of more acute pitch.

The Roman numeral striking-system was undoubtedly devised to reduce the number of hammer-strokes required over a period of twelve hours, as by this method only thirty blows need be given during this time, whereas the normal mode would require seventy-eight. A greatly diminished weight-fall was thus secured for the striking train of a month movement, for instance, without the necessity of an additional wheel in the train, with its consequent frictional disadvantages.

It will be observed that in this interesting system both aural and visual indications are very closely co-ordinated.

There are, of course, two hammers (one for each bell) and two sets of lifting pins, arranged each side of the pin wheel, each set actuating its own hammer. The locking-plate system is used to control the striking.

The "royal" pendulum (a long pendulum *with the anchor escapement*) was established by *circa* 1675. After this, one-and-a-quarter-seconds pendulums were occasionally used in an endeavour to obtain still greater accuracy. *See* under Pendulum in this Glossary. Chiming movements began to become popular about 1690.

An eight-day movement has a going train of four wheels, which are, in order and beginning from the lowest wheel, Main, Centre, Third and Escape wheels. A description of each, with an explanation of its purpose, will be found under the corresponding heading in this Glossary. The striking train has similarly four wheels, which are known as Great, Pin, Pallet or Hoop, and Warn wheels. Each is described fully under its own heading.

A month movement is equipped with an extra wheel, situated between the main and centre wheels of the " watch ", and then known as a " Second " wheel. The interpolation of this wheel necessitates the turning motion of the main wheel in driving to be reversed, since the centre wheel *must* turn " clockwise ". This causes a reversal of the usual winding motion, which now becomes anti-clockwise. The striking train of a month clock has also five wheels.

Three, six and twelve-month movements were constructed at a very early period, as long ago as 1658, as is proved by A. Fromanteel's advertisement in *Mercurius Politicus* of October in that year.

This interesting advertisement—often quoted in horological books— is given again here for the sake of those not wishing to acquire or consult other works than this, bearing in mind, also, that one of the primary purposes in the writing of this book was to obviate the necessity for a multiplicity of reference works.

Mercurius Politicus, 27th October, 1658

" There is lately a way found out for making Clocks go exact and keep equaller time than any now made without this Regulator (examined and proved before His Highness the Lord Protector, by such Doctors whose knowledge and learning is without exception) and are not subject to alter by change of weather, as others are, and may be made to go a week, a moneth [*sic*], or a year, with once winding up, as well as those that are wound up every day, and keep time as well, and is very excellent for all House Clocks that go either with springs or weights; and also steeple clocks that are most subject to a change of weather. Made by Ahasuerus Fromanteel, who made the first that were in England. You may have them at his house on the Bankside, in Mosses Alley, Southwark, and at the sign of the Mermaid, in Lothbury, near bartholomew lane end, london."

This advertisement also appeared in the *Commonwealth Mercury*, of Thursday, 25th November, 1658. The reference to the "regulator" (pendulum) should be noted.

Six- and twelve-month movements are almost invariably *timepieces* only, not clocks (i.e., they have no striking trains). The number of wheels in the "watch" of any of these movements is six, viz., Main, First, Second, Centre, Third and Escape wheels. The "first" and "second" wheels occupy positions between the Main and Centre wheels, hence (bearing in mind the necessity of a clockwise-turning centre arbor, and the alternate reversals of motion in the wheels below it) the main wheel drives anti-clockwise, as in an eight-day movement, and the main arbor and barrel winds normally—clockwise.

After the introduction of the plate frame, before-mentioned, the 30-hour movement broke away from the lantern tradition,[1] and became similar to eight-day clocks inasmuch as the trains were now fitted side-by-side between plates. The pull-up winding system, however, was retained for the great majority of these movements, the rope being generally superseded by a chain. In the Wetherfield collection was a 30-hour clock in a long case of walnut by Thomas Tompion (1638–1713) attributed to *circa* 1675, fitted with both hour and minute hands, and with a *key-wind* movement. This instance, however, is very rare in 30-hour long-case clocks, and cannot be regarded as representative.

The thirty-hour movement was used throughout the eighteenth century with very little or no change after the provision of the plate frame, and the adoption of the long pendulum with the anchor escapement. Minute motion-work and both hour and minute hands now became standard practice by makers of these clocks. Because of the pull-up winding the movements were differently arranged in detail compared with eight-day clocks. A typical example of a thirty-hour long-case movement of the later kind will now be described.

---

[1] In country districts this change in the 30-hour form took many years to accomplish. Even as late as 1750, long-case movements of lantern form with small square brass dials (but usually with anchor escapements) were still being made in rural parts of England. The best guide as to period in these instances is the style and engraving of the *dial*, should this be obviously original, since this would bought from a dial-maker in one of the larger towns, where fashion was more studied and observed.

The going and striking trains show a reversal of the usual arrangement for eight-day clocks, the striking part being on the right and the going train on the left. The main arbor carries a pulley with sides or "flanges" of large diameter, fixed immovably to the main wheel, and turning with it and the arbor. This pulley is grooved and spiked in a special manner to accommodate the links of the chain and prevent it slipping. The forward end of the main arbor projects through the front-plate and carries a wheel and pinion, both on the same pipe, arranged to transmit power by friction through the medium of a spring and pin, but susceptible of being turned on the arbor if need be. The wheel engages the leaves of another pinion made with a long pipe which carries the minute hand at its extremity and turns upon a stud fixed in the front-plate. Over this cannon-pinion pipe is slipped the hour wheel, on its pipe carrying the hour hand; the teeth of the hour wheel engage the leaves of the pinion on the main arbor previously mentioned. The hands are thus driven from the main arbor by means of a wheel engaging the cannon pinion, and a pinion engaging the hour wheel. There is no centre wheel as usually understood by this term, the main wheel teeth engaging a pinion on an arbor carrying the third wheel. The third wheel drives an escape pinion and wheel in the orthodox manner; above the 'scape wheel swing pallets of the anchor pattern.

Proceeding to the striking train (on the *right* of the movement from the dial) it will first be observed that the cannon pinion carries a cam attached to its back, which, turning once in sixty minutes, raises the usual type of lifting-piece pivoted to the front-plate. Inserted in the rim of the great wheel are the pins for actuating the hammer, since there is no separate "Pin Wheel" in the eight-day sense. The main arbor, to which the great wheel is attached, also carries another spiked pulley, but loose on the arbor this time, and provided with a " click " for winding purposes. The great wheel teeth engage the pinion of the hoop wheel arbor, and the hoop wheel in turn engages the leaves of the warn wheel pinion. There is the usual " fly " above, worked from the warn wheel through a fly pinion.

For the system of striking, which is controlled by a locking-plate riding on a stud affixed to the "outside" of the back-plate, driven from the great wheel arbor by a pinion outside the plate, *see* Locking-Plate. See also under Maintaining Power for an instance of its application in these movements.

The thirty-hour movement is distinguished from the eight-day by having only *three* wheels in each train, as explained in the foregoing description. The wheels of the " watch " are, in order, Main, Third, and Escape; those of the " clock " are Great, Hoop, and Warn.

The driving weight used for a thirty-hour clock need not be so heavy as those usual in eight-day movements, owing to the lower gearing of the upper wheels in each train, and the reduction of friction occasioned by the presence of only one wheel between the driven and the driving wheels—the 'scape wheel and the main wheel. With a train (or more correctly, trains) in good condition an eight-pound weight is generally ample, against the twelve or fourteen-pound weights of eight-day clocks, and the thirty pounds or more of month movements. Six-month and year movements (which are very rare) have an enormous weight for the " watch "—there is usually no " clock "—as much as 100 or 130 pounds.

About 1740, centre-seconds movements began to appear, in the great majority of instances applied to eight-day clocks.

These have a long seconds-hand using the minute divisions of the chapter-ring as seconds-markings. This long hand is worked (with the hour and minute hands) from the centre of the dial. Shortly after its introduction various makers combined it with a calendar, the indications for which occupy the inner edge of the chapter-ring, the index being a pointer again from the centre. Thus *four* hands are used, all centrally operated, differences in shape, length, and material or colour providing distinction from each other. The seconds-hand, for instance, is extremely slender, plain and provided with a counterpoise. The calendar hand is usually rather stouter, but still plain in form, and made of brass, lacquered or gilded.

The provision of centre-working seconds-hands necessitated a slightly different arrangement of the wheels and arbors to that used for a normal eight-day movement.

The main wheel drives a " centre " arbor displaced from its normal position, passing through the front-plate and carrying a minute-wheel on a pipe which is capable of being turned independently of the arbor, but driven from it by the usual arrangement of a bowed spring and friction. This wheel engages the teeth of the usual minute-wheel, which in turn drives another (third) minute-wheel in the ordinary central position, having a pipe carrying the minute-hand working through the usual bridge-pipe.

This bridge-pipe takes the weight of the minute-wheel, pipe and hand on its inner surface, the outer portion of the pipe bearing the weight of the hour-wheel, snail and hand on their own separate pipe. Passing almost through the central minute-wheel pipe to a point about ¾ inch from its end (which is a circular orifice) is the escape-wheel arbor, worked—through a pinion—from the third wheel as usual. It will be noticed that the 'scape-wheel arbor assumes the position of the displaced centre arbor, which in an ordinary movement would occupy this situation. The forward end of the 'scape-wheel arbor (hidden within the pipe) is tapered for the attachment of the long seconds-hand by means of a small pipe fixed to its boss. The pallets work above the 'scape-wheel in the usual manner. It will be noted that there are *three* minute-wheels (including the cannon-wheel) in all in a centre-seconds movement, not two, as in a normal eight-day movement.

The seconds-hand has always a counterpoise, as balance is of primary importance, the 'scape-wheel being very easily stopped by a slight resistance to its turning movement, as it is at the top of the train, where the power is weakest.

The striking train is arranged normally.

Dead-beat escapements (q.v.) are frequently applied to centre-seconds movements, indeed, this form of escapement appears to be almost invariably used with them.

The calendar hand is fitted outside the dial to the pipe of a separate wheel which rides upon the hour-hand pipe and which is worked by a pin or a cam on the 24-hour calendar wheel. This last, upon a stud from the front-plate, is driven from another (12-hour) calendar wheel placed between the snail and the hour-wheel (*see* Calendar).

We now come to a consideration of quarter-chiming movements.

These, as mentioned earlier in this article on Movements, were frequently provided in long cases by 1690, and were made with various numbers of bells giving different chime-tunes. One of the earliest systems is that known as the " ting-tang quarter-strike ". This, strictly speaking, is not really a *chiming* movement, since to be such the striking must be on at least four bells.

The quarter-chime idea is of considerable antiquity, being used in exceptional chamber clocks of the sixteenth century, but does not appear to have been applied to long-case clocks until some years after the advent of the plate-frame movement. An early example of a *three-train* (going, striking and " ting-tang ") movement is provided in a long-case clock by J. Fromanteel which was in the famous Wetherfield collection. This clock, dating from 1680 or slightly earlier, strikes the hours upon four bells of differing pitch, using four hammers on one arbor, thus sounding a chord at each blow from I to XII. Two separate bells are used for the " ting-tang " quarters.

Six- or eight-bell three-train chiming movements were not unusual by about 1700, in many instances incorporated with other features such as month duration, second-and-a-quarter pendulums and so on.

A further feature, not infrequent, was the system of chiming known as the " *Grande Sonnerie* ". This, before every quarter-chime, repeats the previous *hour* in full, so that the sound-signal shall be perfectly explicit. The " *Grande Sonnerie* " seems to have been peculiar to the early clocks, about 1700–1730, as it would appear to be very rare indeed in the later chiming movements of the eighteenth century, if not altogether discarded.

The tunes used for old chiming movements varied. One of these " tunes " in use about the middle of the eighteenth century was simply a diatonic descending scale on eight bells, the scale being repeated for the second quarter, used thrice for the third and four times for the hour. If the bells are good and the " tempo " (speed of striking) fairly quick this is not so dull as might be imagined, a pleasant " pealing " effect being produced, but it cannot be regarded as an ambitious effort.

The so-called " Westminster " quarter-chimes are never found in a genuine old movement, made prior to 1788. It was in that year they were first used, for the clock of Great St. Mary's Church, Cambridge.

Musical clocks, having a chiming train utilizing a large barrel, and provided with a complete chromatic scale of thirteen bells (or almost any number of bells up to twenty-four) appeared in long-cases about 1770.[1]

The systems of tune-playing varied. Some were arranged to play a melody at each quarter, others *chimed* the quarters and played a tune at the hour only, after the hour itself was chimed and struck; still others played musical compositions at twelve, three, six and nine o'clock, chiming and striking the intermediate hours and quarters only. In most, a tune indicator was arranged somewhere, a favourite position being in the arch of the dial, often accompanied by subsidiary dials for " strike silent " or

---

[1] Such movements were a much earlier feature in spring-driven bracket clocks, in which they were used as early as 1710–1715.

L

"chime silent" and "music silent". The titles of any number of tunes up to about a dozen were engraved upon the indicator, a pointer being moved to select any particular one.

Chiming clocks are very frequently produced from ordinary (old) eight-day striking movements by modern fakers, new plates being provided and a chiming train added, in order to supply the public demand for "chimes". See the body of this book for a full discussion of the subject.

Old chiming movements have a locking-plate (q.v.) controlling the chimes and a rack for the striking part, or (in very early examples) a locking-plate for both trains. If a movement is found with a small rack for the chime part it may almost certainly be regarded as modern, or a modern conversion. This particularly if the fly (q.v.) is brought outside the back-plate, the back pivot of its arbor working in the pivot-hole of a large bridge screwed to the outside of the plate, and the fly itself provided with long arms for extra efficiency, or a double-fly employed.

Regarding the operation of the chiming train, the release is usually effected by four pins in the rim of the minute-wheel. At the completion of each quarter a pin engages the tip of a lifting-piece, the other arm of which operates another double-armed lifting-piece; the end of one arm of this latter is bent to work inside the plates through a slot. This bent portion releases the train by its removal from a pin fixed in a wheel on the chime-barrel arbor (the third of the train). The locking-plate then revolves until the next notch is reached, when the lower arm of the second lifting-piece drops into this, causing the upper arm to engage the pin in the wheel with its bent part again, thus bringing the train to rest. At the completion of the fourth quarter-chime, a pin in the face of the locking-plate raises (through the media of two double-armed levers) the main rack-hook and so releases the hour-striking train, as previously described (*see* Lifting Piece).

Chiming trains have four wheels and a fly forming the complete train, as in the hour-striking part or "clock"; the chime-barrel is attached to the arbor of the third wheel. In this brass barrel or cylinder are inserted "pins" which, as they revolve with the barrel in which they are fixed, contact the bottom portions of hammers, causing these to strike in the order determined by the position of the various pins in the barrel. *Two* hammers are provided for some or all bells in musical clocks, so as to allow the rapid repetition of a blow, otherwise impossible because of the lifting-time of the hammer. The series of hammers is fitted into a block or frame positioned between the plates of the movement, and each hammer is provided with a separate spring.

Musical barrels were from early times made to move longitudinally in their pivot-holes so as to present a different set of pins to the hammer-tails, so varying the melody played. A tune-indicator, before-mentioned, was provided in connection with this movement on the dial.

Although, as we have seen, the painted iron dial was primarily introduced to cheapen production, the cheapening process did not necessarily extend to the movement also.

I have seen several movements with painted dials in which the mechanism and construction is quite equal to most of the earlier productions with far more artistic brass dials.

One such is a movement by "Barnish, Rochdale" (late eighteenth century) having a very commonplace white-enamelled iron dial, much the worse for ill-considered attempts at cleaning at various times, but having a really excellent movement, an unusual feature of which is the method of operating the Lunar Record.

This is effected by a large, delicately-constructed wheel, situated on a stud placed towards the upper right-hand corner of the front-plate. This wheel has the same number of teeth as the large hour-wheel, with which it meshes, and is provided with a pin which periodically engages the teeth of the lunation disc, thus moving the latter onwards twice in every twenty-four hours in the usual way.

Both the moon-wheel and the hour-wheel in this movement are made with four arms and narrow rims, a charming effect of lightness and grace being thus imparted to the wheel-work, adding considerable interest to the appearance of the movement.

In this clock the calendar was operated by the very usual pin projecting from the face of the snail, but at some time the complementary wheel at the back of the dial, bearing a pointer indicating on a sub-dial at the front the day-of-the-month has unfortunately been removed. This regrettable piece of vandalism is often practised, even by those who should know better, merely because the mechanism is suspected (rightly or wrongly) of stopping the clock.

If this should be so, then obviously the proper course to pursue is to adjust the arrangement so that its action shall not prejudice the normal working of the movement in any way, an alternative which one would think unnecessary to mention to any with the slightest regard for a fine old clock-movement.

In the case of one who feels incompetent to adjust the movement correctly, a simple and non-damaging course to adopt is to slightly bend the operating pin so that the particular motion is put out of action *for the time being*.

In the instance I have mentioned, the hole in the dial through which the calendar hand should be operated had been plugged *with wood* (!), but perhaps not by the individual responsible for the loss of the missing wheel and hand.

Pallets

These are the projections from the "verge" or pallet-staff which periodically check the turning of the escape wheel by engaging a tooth, thus causing the train to move onwards intermittently instead of continuously. A pendulum, connected directly or by means of a crutch to the verge, or pallet-arbor, is employed as a regulator, to which impulses are transmitted in alternately opposite directions by the action of the escapement. (*See* Escape Wheel, Pendulum, and the various types of escapement, as Anchor, Dead-beat, and Crown Wheel.)

The pallets of crown wheel escapements, used with short "bob" pendulums in very early long-case clocks, are filed into shape from the solid rod of the verge, being afterwards case-hardened and polished. They form an angle of about 90° to each other, and are actuated by opposite sides of the revolving crown wheel, or, more correctly, they check the wheel (and receive impulses from it) by arresting and releasing teeth on opposite portions of its periphery.

Pallets of the anchor[1] type are attached to the pallet-staff by means of a brass "collet" (q.v.) which is brazed or soldered to the arbor, and to which the anchor is screwed or riveted. In this case the pallets should have convex acting-faces, the curve of the entrant pallet being exterior and that of the exit pallet interior. These curved faces tend to reduce the "pitting" of the pallets by the wheel teeth; most old pallets are, however, formed practically flat as to their acting-faces. The sliding motion of the 'scape-wheel teeth along the acting surfaces produces the impulse before

[1] So-called because the steel lunette carrying the pallets has roughly the curved shape of a conventional anchor, but inverted, the pallets being where the "flukes" of the anchor would be.

mentioned. The case-hardening and polishing of pallets, and the exact adjustment of their position relative to the swing wheel is of supreme importance in the provision of a good escapement.

The most obvious differences shown by the dead-beat variety of pallets is in the shape of the pallet-arms, which are formed like a triangle, the apex being at the collet and the pallets at the base. The teeth of the 'scape-wheel are set the reverse way to those employed with pallets of the anchor type.[1] Their points are also usually "undercut" about ten degrees from the radial, so that only the tips of the teeth touch the locking faces of the pallets. (*See* Fig. 4.) These latter differ in form from those of the anchor pattern, which have continuous "faces". A dead-beat pallet is provided with *two* acting surfaces, a "dead" or resting face and an impulse face. The "dead" faces are formed as portions of a circle struck from the centre of the pallet-staff, and the impulse faces should be tangents to the impulse "tangent-circle". The result of this formation of teeth and pallets is to cause the 'scape-wheel tooth to repose on the "dead" face without recoil until the return movement of the pendulum, lifting the pallet-arm, allows it to slide along the impulse face, giving a slight impetus to the pendulum as it does so. The period of rest compared with the time of movement of the sceonds-hand varies with different clocks; it is usually considered that a short impulse and a longer rest is the best arrangement, as this tends to reduce friction.

Pallets of the dead-beat pattern were sometimes jewelled—both to reduce friction and to avoid the necessity of somewhat frequent oiling, the oil becoming gummy occasionally and causing faults in the timekeeping until cleaned off and new oil applied. Sapphires or rubies were considered to be the best for the purpose, but agate was often used instead.

Pallet Wheel

In an eight-day rack-striking movement this is the third wheel of the "clock" or striking train. Its arbor is prolonged through the front-plate and carries a cam known as a "gathering-pallet" (q.v.) at its extremity, from which the wheel takes its name. In early rack-striking movements the pallet is carried upon the arbor in a position between the plates, or takes the form of a pin in the wheel-collet itself, actuating an "inside rack".

[1] Thirty-hour movements of the later type, however, have 'scape-wheels (used with pallets of the anchor kind), having teeth set in the *same* direction as those used in dead-beat escapements. This is because the 30-hour swing-wheel revolves *anti-clockwise* (*see* Trains).

In locking-plate movements this wheel is known as the "*hoop-wheel*", because of a circular band of brass which is attached to its rim. This band or "hoop" is not continuous, but has a wide gap in its circumference; one edge of this gap is utilized to lock the train by engaging the end of a lever from an arbor between the plates, which drops when the hook-shaped outer arm on the same arbor enters a notch of the locking-plate.

A pin often replaces the hoop as a locking medium, especially in thirty-hour movements of the late eighteenth century.

Pendulum

The origin of the pendulum used as a controller for clocks is involved in a certain amount of obscurity.

For the time-measurements involved in astronomical observation clocks were very faulty *media* before the introduction of this nearly ideal regulator, although it is certain that the Dane, Tycho Brahe (1546–1601), employed the very imperfect mechanical clock of his day (with "foliot" controlled escapement) for his astronomical observations *circa* 1580. He is even said to have employed a *pendulum*.

In the *Bibliotecta Ambrosiana* at Milan (according to J. Drummond Robertson) there exists—or existed—a volume, undated, known as the *Codice Atlantico,* in which are bound up some sketches by Leonardo da Vinci (1452–1519) attributed either to the late fifteenth or early sixteenth centuries. Among these sketches is one (reproduced by Robertson) which apparently exhibits a crown-wheel escapement with horizontal verge *and pendulum.* It remains a matter for conjecture whether Leonardo ever constructed such a device, but such is not an impossibility, having regard to his great and all-encompassing genius and abilities.

Galileo (Galileo Galilei, 1564–1642), the celebrated astronomer, in 1581, while watching the oscillations of a great bronze lamp swinging on chains from the roof of the Cathedral at Pisa, observed that its vibrations were all executed in equal time, although the range of their arcs varied. This led him to the discovery of the principle of *isochronism,* which is, briefly, the fact that a pendulum of given length will always preserve the same time of vibration whatever (within limits) the arc through which it swings. Actually this needs qualification, a qualification discovered later by Christian Huygens, of which more hereafter.

In 1649, Galileo's son Vincenzo had made a timekeeper from a design dictated earlier by his father (then blind); a working model of the original design is to be seen at the South Kensington Museum.

There are many illustrations of Galileo's original design, in various books devoted to the evolution of clocks; it is only necessary to state here that it consists of a train of wheels (whether originally intended for spring or weight drive—or either—is not clear) culminating in what is probably the very earliest example of a "pin-wheel escapement", which conveys impulses to the pendulum. There is no recording apparatus of any kind, the beats being apparently *counted* to determine time-measurements.

Much controversy was excited by the claims of the Accademia del Cimento of Florence in 1662 on behalf of the clock said to have been constructed in 1649 for Galileo's son Vincenzo Galilei, as being the *first pendulum clock to be constructed*.[1] They have been accused of "moral bias" in referring to the "construction" of a clock which was, in fact, never actually completed, and of illustrating the clock in such manner that its unfinished state was not apparent.

Vincenzo Galilei died of fever in 1649, and shortly before his death, appears to have conceived an intense hatred of clocks; in the paroxysms of his illness he would appear to have destroyed all (or nearly all) the uncompleted examples in his possession.

Fortunately, however, on the death of his widow in January, 1669, the inventory of her effects (which is said to be still preserved) disclosed an entry referring to "an iron clock, unfinished, *with pendulum*, the first invention of Galileo."

This "unfinished iron clock, with pendulum" may surely be taken as lending very strong support to those who maintain that Vincenzo Galilei had anticipated the adoption of the pendulum by Christian Huygens de Zuylichem by some eight years.

In addition, it must not be forgotten that the Danish astronomer Johann Hevel (or Johannes Hevelius—the name is variously given) born in Dantzig in 1611 and dying there in 1687, records in his *Machina Cœlestis* of 1673 his experiments with pendulums applied to various types of clocks during the period 1640–1650.

Huygens, then, cannot be said to have been the first to apply the pendulum to a clock *in an experimental manner*.

There is also the claim of an Englishman, one Richard Harris, to have

---

[1] Made for Vincenzo Galilei by Domenico Balestri, of Florence.

antedated all the above-mentioned instances by actually applying in working order a pendulum for the clock he constructed for the church of St. Paul, Covent Garden, since destroyed by fire.

An engraved plate in the vestry of the old church bears an inscription from which the following is an extract:

"The clock fixed in the turret of the said church was the first long pendulum clock in Europe, invented and made by Richard Harris, of London, A.D. 1641 although the honour of the invention was assumed by Vincenzo Galilei, A.D. 1649, and also by Huygens in 1657."

This plate was affixed by Thomas Grignon, clockmaker, as a memorial to his father (also a Thomas Grignon) who made a clock for the church succeeding that of Harris, and also to Richard Harris himself. The clock by Grignon Junior was made—together with the bells—in 1797, according to the inscription.

It is opined by Britten that Harris's claim is inconclusive, the reason adduced being that "his application of a superior controller should have remained a solitary instance for twelve years or so, and have evoked no attention from scientists and others interested in the subject."

Finally, there is our ubiquitous Robert Hooke, who may also have some claim to be considered in this connection. It has been suggested that he employed a pendulum (perhaps with the controversial anchor escapement) in his third year at Oxford (1656) when asked to take part in some astronomical observations which were then being made. He himself states (though the intention of the reference is irritatingly obscure) that he successfully "contriv'd a way to continue the motion of the *Pendulum*, so much commended by *Ricciolus*[1] in his *Almagestum*, which Dr. *Ward* had recommendede [*sic*] me to peruse."

There can be little doubt that the pendulum was first applied to clocks *as a commercial proposition*, and not merely as an experimental device, by Samuel Coster, clockmaker of The Hague, Holland, through a patent assigned him by the designer—*Christian Huygens de Zuylichem*, in 1657. (*See* Chapter Two, Early Long-Case Clocks.)

---

[1] The reference here is to Riccioti (Ricciolus), a Jesuit, born at Ferrara in 1598. He did much to advance the study of astronomy, less by his own discoveries than by his accurate and detailed accounts recording those of others. Believing that the findings of Copernicus (1473–1543) were irreconcilable with the teachings of the Church, he rejected the Corpernican theory ; notwithstanding, his works are both extensive and informative. His *Novum Almagestum* is a collection of observations, opinions, and physical explanations of phenomena, and contains all the methods of astronomical computation then known. The names he gave to the principal features of the moon are those still in use by astronomers.

Coster died at The Hague in 1659. The famous London clockmaker, Johannes Fromanteel (who was of Dutch descent) made a contract with Coster dated 3rd September, 1657, under which he entered Coster's service until 1st May, 1658. This was doubtless with a view to acquiring the necessary facility in the making of clocks with Huygens' pendulum, since we find Fromanteel advertising clocks made by him with the new controller in October and November of the same year. The introduction of the pendulum into England may therefore, with complete confidence, be ascribed to this Johannes Fromanteel, and the date with equal certainty be fixed as 1658.

Early English clocks with pendulums were provided with the crown-wheel escapement, and the pendulum was usually directly attached to the rear end of the horizontal verge, the later "crutch" not being used, although from an illustration in Huygens' volume *Horologium Oscillatorium* (1673) depicting his "standard" clock of 1659, he used a crutch very similar in form to that adopted later for the English clocks with anchor escapements, and also a "seconds" pendulum with heavy "bob" which he employed for his own use as early as 1656.

Crown-wheel movements of English make with short "bob" pendulums and plate-frames were used in the earliest long-case clocks from about 1660 onwards. The next change was to the "royal pendulum" (a "seconds" pendulum with anchor escapement) sometime about 1675, this date being approximate for its general use.

With the application of the anchor escapement the pendulum of a long-case clock was sometimes increased in length up to some 65 inches (61.155 inches exactly from the bending-point of the suspension spring to the "centre of oscillation"). This gave a "beat" of $1\frac{1}{4}$ seconds duration, and therefore vibrated but forty-eight times in one minute, instead of sixty times as with a "seconds length" pendulum (39.1393 inches).[1]

Now with a train in perfect condition and with friction reduced to a minimum (assuming temperature and barometric pressure to be constant) any error in timekeeping must be due to a pendulum inaccurately adjusted, i.e., of incorrect length. It follows, therefore that in a pendulum of nominal seconds length, any error will be multiplied sixty times in a minute, or 3,600 times in an hour, and 86,400 times in one day. In a pendulum beating but

[1] These lengths vary slightly with the latitude of the place, the "pull" of gravity lessening near the equator, owing to the Earth's rotation, and the fact of its being an oblate spheroid.

once in 1 ¼ seconds, however, any error will be multiplied forty-eight times only in a minute, or 69,120 times in a day. Obviously, therefore, the sixty-five inch pendulum gives better results than one of the usual "seconds-length", and the seconds-length pendulum must be superior to the short "bob" pendulum, if all are equally well adjusted, since absolutely correct timekeeping is impossible, owing to several causes, friction and temperature (both variable) being the chief of these.

As will be seen from the foregoing, pendulum times are dependent upon their lengths, but not in direct proportion, since a pendulum to beat once in two seconds must be 156.5572 inches long, *not* 39.1393 inches × 2 = 78.2786 inches. Actually, the times are as the square roots of the lengths; in other words, to double the time one must quadruple the length.

The effective length of a pendulum is the distance from the point of bending of the suspension spring to a point approximately in the centre of the "bob", referred to as the "centre of oscillation". If this measurement be 39.1393 inches exactly, then the pendulum must beat seconds, or would do but for the considerations we have already noted.

The arcs of a pendulum are not strictly isochronous unless these are small. Very large arcs are only really isochronous (should these vary) when the "bob" follows a cycloidal path. Huygens, therefore, using the crown-wheel-and-verge escapement, with its necessarily large arcs, tried to overcome this objection (not realized by Galileo) by the fitting of cycloidal "cheeks" to the pendulum cock, these tending to cause the pendulum bob to follow a cycloidal path, not a circular one, in its travel.[1] The cheeks are shown in the illustration in *Horologium Oscillatorium* of his clock of 1659. Prior to this, in *Horologium* (1658) he had used a peculiar form or variant of the crown escapement by which the arc of the pendulum was reduced. The form shown in *Horologium* depicts a *vertical* crown wheel engaging the pallets of a true (or likewise vertical) verge, to the upper portion of which is attached a pinion engaging the teeth of a kind of contrate wheel (with teeth on half its periphery only) which "contrate" wheel has the crutch attached to its arbor. There are no "cheeks" to the back-cock, from which the pendulum is independently suspended as in the later clocks of *Horologium Oscillatorium*.

---

[1] A " cycloid " is traced by any particular point in the circumference of a circle if this latter be rolled upon a straight line. It will be appreciated that the segment of a circle is only coincident with a cycloid for a small distance at the bottom of its arc.

The "cycloidal cheeks" were used in England by the Fromanteels in their early clocks; after the application of the anchor escapement, with its much reduced arc, the necessity (or desirability) of their provision vanished.

Robertson (*Evolution of Clockwork*) considers the idea of cycloidal cheeks ingenious, but in practice "not only unsuccessful, but actually detrimental on account of friction and 'banking'."

From time to time efforts have been made, with greater or less success, to combat the variation due to temperature. Our ancestors relied in general on a pendulum rod of iron wire, which, though susceptible to temperature change, expanding when warm and contracting when cold, nevertheless gave a good *average* performance, as temperature changes are liable to cancel each other over a period of twenty-four hours, more so over a longer period, say a week.

As the old makers were always striving after greater accuracy of time-keeping, however, it was natural that various kinds of compensation should be applied to the pendulum.

One of the earliest of these compensating pendulums was that devised by George Graham (1673–1751) between 1721 and 1725. This consisted of a glass jar containing mercury used as a "bob", held by a stirrup at the bottom of the rod. When an increase of temperature caused the rod to lengthen, it also made the mercury rise in the jar, this having the effect of raising the bob by altering the centre of gravity of the pendulum. The converse action provided for contraction of the rod through cold. Normal regulation was effected by a sliding weight fitted on the rod well above the top of the stirrup.

In Volume 6 of the *Philosophical Transactions* (Abridgment) for the years 1719–1733, edited by Eames and Martyn, will be found (page 297) Graham's Paper which he read before the Royal Society—"A Contrivance to Avoid Irregularities in a Clock's Motion by the Action of Heat and Cold upon the Pendulum" (1726).

In this he refers to his "trials about the year 1715", but gave up these trials, after establishing that steel, brass, silver, etc., varied in their degree of expansion under heat, coming to the conclusion that the differences were too minute to be utilized for correction.

Whilst making some experiments with "quicksilver" in December 1721, he was impressed with its great capacity for expansion. Thereafter he began his "trials" anew, using a glass jar containing mercury as a pendulum "bob". He ascertained the required height of mercury by experimenting until the upward expansion of this altered the centre of oscillation of the pendulum sufficiently to counteract the effect of expansion in the rod.

Graham gives an account of a comparison effected from June 1722 to October 1725 between an ordinary good timekeeper and his mercury-compensated clock, in which the maximum error of the latter was one-sixth that in the other clock.

The well-known "gridiron" pendulum was the invention of the celebrated chronometer-maker John Harrison (1693–1776) about 1726. The device is founded upon the fact that of two bars, one of steel and the other of brass, the brass bar has the greater reaction to heat and cold, its expansion and contraction being in both cases more than that of the steel bar. The ratio of reaction to temperature between brass and steel is as 100 is to 60. Accordingly the "gridiron" (from a supposed resemblance to such) pendulum has nine rods, five of steel and four of brass, each type compared in total length approximating to an equivalent of the ratio quoted. The nine rods are carried in frames, the pendulum bob being attached to the central (steel) rod. Each set of rods is arranged to react in opposite directions, i.e., upwards and downwards, so tending to cancel each other's expansion or contraction.

John Ellicott (1706–1772), like Graham a Fellow of the Royal Society and a famous watch and clockmaker, invented (circa 1738) a type of compensating pendulum also based upon differing expansion and contraction of brass and steel, utilizing two bars, one of brass sliding upon another of steel in response to temperature changes. The brass bar, when it expands under heat, depresses levers which raise the bob, and vice versa.

Some "regulator" clocks, which were mostly for shop use by the clockmaker, and which were always well-made in plain but tasteful case-work, were provided with a much simpler type of pendulum, not "compensating" but designed to resist as far as possible the effect of varying temperature. This took the form of a varnished rod, usually oval in section, made of some straight-grained wood not much affected by temperature, such as pine. The "bob" was large and heavy, disc-shaped and nearly always of lead. Because of this large and weighty bob, the wooden rod provided a much more stable suspension than the slender iron or steel rod of the ordinary type of pendulum, which would have been more liable to twist under the influence of such a bob, encouraging a particularly bad fault of certain pendulums, in which the bob describes an arc accompanied by a twisting or wobbling motion in itself.

Occasionally one may see old long-case clocks of the later type fitted with pendulum "rods" of flat steel measuring about an inch in width, or others where the rod is formed with a convex front and flat back, the width in this latter instance being usually somewhat less, about half-an-inch. Then, too, pendulum rods of this kind are frequently found painted, usually black. Whether this was done when they were made, or later, as a protection from rust, is a matter for conjecture; at least, I have no definite information on this point.

The pendulum is hung from the back-plate of the movement by means of a brass "cock". This "cock" is screwed to the back-plate near the top, and is made to form a bridge in which the rear pivot of the pallet-staff has its bearing. The "crutch" (q.v.) is attached to the pallet-staff so as to hang from within this bridge, its lower end or "fork" projecting to the rear at right angles to the crutch-stem. The pendulum cock has a further rearward projection from the bridge, having "chops" at its termination formed by the cutting into the brass-work of a fine vertical slot for the reception of the suspension spring. The suspension spring itself is equipped with brass terminations, the lower and larger of these being "tapped" to receive the rod and that at the top providing a means of hanging the entire pendulum from the cock. The suspension is so arranged that the brass piece at the lower end of the spring passes through the fork of the crutch for about half its length, a connection being thus established for the communication of the escapement impulses.

As has been already indicated, the pendulum rod in the vast majority of old long-case clocks is made of iron or steel wire—the gauge varies slightly with different makers. A flattened extension, also of iron, usually slightly wedge-shaped and about six or eight inches in length, is screwed, brazed, or otherwise fastened to the lower end of the rod so that the "bob" may be attached and made to slide upon this either up or down. A fine screw-thread is cut upon a round termination to the flattened portion, and a "rating-nut" provided by which the bob can be moved either way in small gradations so as to alter the "centre of oscillation" of the pendulum, and so bring the clock to time.

The pendulum " bob " is usually a circular lead weight of elliptical section, faced with brass. Occasionally copper appears to have been used instead of brass for the covering, and sometimes the bob is made of iron in the same form, in this case without the brass or copper facing. Bobs of cylindrical shape were the exception in old " grandfather " clocks. The same may be said of the various kinds of compensating pendulums previously described, the vast majority of the old makers did not use these devices, despite the often extremely complicated character of their movements.

A form of pendulum regulation sometimes provided in long-case clocks (often used in contemporary mantel clocks) was the so-called " up-and-down " regulation by a hand and sub-dial. This system consists of a cam working inside the movement, operated by the hand on the small dial, which cam (usually snail-shaped) raises and lowers the suspension spring in the jaws or " chops ", much in the manner of some modern movements. A month timepiece in a long-case by William Clement which was in the Wetherfield collection has a little separate dial fitted between the plates of the movement, facing sideways so as to be visible through the glass panel in the side of the hood. This dial has a single hand like that of a miniature lantern clock, acting upon a similar mechanism to that described above. The dial is very prettily engraved and has arabic numerals from 1 to 12 in a chapter-ring of the normal kind. An illustration of this movement and its handsome little regulator is given in Britten's work. Possibly this early arrangement of the idea is unique, as in later versions of the same device the subsidiary dial was incorporated into the design of the main dial, a favourite position for it being in the arch. It is, however, a somewhat unusual feature of the " grandfather " clock, being much more frequent in " bracket " or mantel clocks, its place being filled in the long-case clocks by the " strike-silent " dial and hand.

To conclude this short article on the pendulum I append a few further historical details which may interest the horological antiquarian.

William Derham (*Artificial Clockmaker*, 1700 edition) records that Tycho Brahe (1546–1601) is said to have used a *pendulum* clock for his astronomical observations, according to Dr. Johann Joachim Becher (1635–1682), a German physician and chemist who visited England, and who, in his treatise *De Nova Temporis Dimitiendi Ratione Theoria* (dedicated to our Royal Society in 1680) relates that " one Caspar Doms, a

Fleming, and Mathematician to *John Philip a Schonborn* (the late Elector of *Mentz*) told him that he had seen at *Prague*, in the time of Rudolphus the Emperor,[1] a Pend. clock [*sic*] made by the famous *Justus Borgen*, Mechanick and Clockmaker to the Emperor : which Clock the great Tycho-Brahe used in his Astronomical observations " (Derham).

This, of course, is possible, as Tycho Brahe, sometime after the publication of his famous *Astronomiæ Instauratæ Mechanica* (1598) proceeded to Prague. If, therefore, he did in fact employ a pendulum clock by Borgen or anyone else for his observations it must have been during the closing years of his life, as Hevelius in his *Machinæ Cœlestis* of 1673 states that Tycho had *vainly* attempted to get clocks to keep accurate time.

That Tycho did not use pendulum clocks up to the publication of *Astronomiæ Instauratæ Mechanica* in 1598 is certain, as during the description of his Mural Quadrant in this work he refers also to clocks which, he says, " are constructed in such a way that they give not only the single minutes, but also the seconds, with the *greatest possible* accuracy, and imitating the uniform rotation of the heavens." The italics are my own. Tycho goes on to observe that " it is necessary to have two clocks of this kind so that one can correct the other if necessary." He further states that he had at his disposal " four such clocks ". Nowhere in this short reference to his clocks does he mention the pendulum as a controller, a then novel device upon which he most certainly would comment had such been employed in his clocks.

However, Borgen (Burgius, Byrgius, or Burgh—the name is variously spelt) would appear to have constructed a clock controlled by a pendulum which was at some time (and may still be) in the Vienna Treasury, striking hours and quarters, displaying Moon's Phases and Day-of-the-week. This has been attributed to *circa* 1612. Justus Borgen (a still further variant of the name is Jost Bürgi) was of Swiss origin, born at Lichtensteig in 1552, becoming " Mechanick and Clockmaker " to Rudolph II in 1602 or 1603, and dying in 1632.

Pillars

The round brass bars which hold the front and back plates of a movement together. They are riveted into the back-plate, the front ends of the pillars fitting through holes in the front-plate, and having their

---

[1] Rudolph II, " Holy Roman Emperor " 1552–1612.

extremities drilled for the insertion of pins to fasten the plates together. There are usually four such pillars in movements made after 1700. Prior to 1700 the number of pillars was often six, and the system of pin fastening was frequently varied by the provision of hooks or catches pivoted on the front-plate engaging into slots cut into the ends of the pillars to correspond, thus fastening the plates together.

For a rather late example of this very convenient system, applied to both plate and dial pillars, see the movement by the Dutch maker Jacob Hasius (*circa* 1720) illustrated by Plates 32 and 33.

The form of pillar used is of some little assistance (in conjunction, of course, with corroborative details elsewhere) in helping us to fix the approximate age of a movement. Prior to the middle of the eighteenth century the pillars were more or less ornamental as well as utilitarian. Many of the pillars of 1720 and earlier were really beautiful things, slightly engraved around their circumference, and with four raised fins turned upon their surfaces, the middle portion of each pillar being decorated with a nearly spherical enlargement. Brightly-polished plates, and pillars of this kind also well burnished, combined with clean and bright steel-work, including sometimes file-cutting of hammer shafts or hammer springs and buffers, made the early movements more attractive in appearance than most of the later types. Again, the earlier plate-pillars were usually drilled and "tapped" in the centre spherical portion of those at the bottom of the plates to receive the seat-board screws, which secured the movement to the board. This is unquestionably a neater arrangement than that most frequently employed in the later types of movement, in which the pillars were not drilled, and where the movement was fastened to the seat-board by steel hooks clipped round the pillars. This change, which was not an improvement, but saved drilling and tapping the lower pillars, took place about 1750–60 when plainer pillars became the usual practice.

Pinions

A pinion has a few broad and shallow teeth which are known as *leaves*. Clockmakers and writers of horological works very frequently refer to " pinions " when they really wish to indicate " pinion *arbors* ", which is somewhat confusing to the amateur unless due regard be given to the context, which usually supplies the clue to the real meaning. This indefinite expression probably originated through the practice of forming the arbor and its pinion from a length of " pinion wire ", i.e., a thin steel bar having continuous " leaves " formed by drawing lengths of steel rod through a " draw plate ". When received by the clockmaker these lengths of pinion wire are fashioned into complete arbors, with pinions and pivots, by his removing the leaves where not required. The early pinions were formed by file-cutting from the solid steel rod of the arbor itself, this being left thicker for the purpose at the position of the pinion. All pinions are case-hardened and polished before use in the movement.

A pinion may be either driven by a wheel or made to drive a wheel. Examples of the former kind are supplied in both going and striking trains of a movement, and an instance of the latter type is exemplified by the minute-pinion, which drives the hour wheel.

All pinions were case-hardened and polished when made, and badly worn pinions are the source of much of the trouble experienced with some old movements. A worn centre-pinion will often be the cause of a movement requiring a driving weight of excessive size, and frequently even this will be ineffective in making the clock " go " satisfactorily if the pinion wear is considerable. The same remark is applicable to the striking train where the pin-wheel pinion is badly worn.

The early makers—*circa* 1700—used pinions with fewer leaves than those employed later, i.e., " low-numbered " pinions, particularly in the upper part of the " clock " train. Thus, where a train made in 1790 or 1800 has seven and eight-leaved pinions, the train of 1700 will usually be found to have pinions of six and seven leaves only. These early movements require more driving-power than the later types, apart from questions of wear, because of the less easy action of their low-numbered pinions.

In thirty-hour movements for eighteenth-century long-case clocks it was an almost invariable practice to use the six-leaf pinion throughout for both trains.

Pin Wheel

In a normal eight-day movement this is the second wheel of the striking train. It carries a series of pins fixed around its rim, the purpose of these being to contact the tail of the hammer shaft, and so, with the revolution of the wheel, effect the movement of the hammer in striking the bell. The number of pins used is decided by the " leaf-number " of

M

the pin-wheel pinion (*see* Pinions); as this has usually eight leaves there are also eight pins in the wheel.

This term is also used to describe the *escape-wheel* of a pin-wheel escapement. This is very rare indeed in a long-case movement, but there may be examples here and there, perhaps mostly of an experimental nature. It is only mentioned here for the purpose of being fairly comprehensive in our definitions.

The number of teeth in the pin-wheel is governed by the number of pins and the leaf-number of the pallet-pinion. This latter has to make one turn for each blow of the hammer, as the pallet itself "gathers up" the rack one tooth after each blow. Thus if, as is usual, eight pins are used in the pin-wheel and the pallet-pinion has seven leaves, then the pin-wheel must have $8 \times 7 = 56$ teeth.

Thirty-hour movements of long-case clocks have a combined pin and great wheel, the pins, thirteen in number, being set in the rim of the *great* wheel. Six-leaf pinions are used throughout these movements and thus the great wheel (pin-wheel) has 78 teeth, exactly as the normal great wheel of an eight-day clock.

Pipe

A pipe is a tube or "sleeve", generally of brass, varying greatly in diameter and length according to the purpose for which it is employed.

Pipes are used in two ways:—

(*a*) Arranged to "ride" *upon an arbor*[1] as the cannon-wheel pipe upon the centre arbor) or *upon another pipe* (as the hour-wheel pipe upon that of the "bridge").

(*b*) Arranged to fit over the end of an arbor, friction-tight, as the pipe of the seconds hand over the end of the escape-wheel arbor.

Pivots

The wheel and pinion arbors of a movement are held between the front and back plates, these forming a frame in which the arbors revolve. Both ends of each arbor working in this manner are diminished for about ⅛ inch, these extremities entering holes bored for them in the plates. The diminished ends of the arbor are known as "pivots", and the bearing in the plate as a "pivot-hole". The formation of a pivot results in a step

---

[1] With or without a friction-contact spring.

or " shoulder " on the arbor, and there being two such shoulders prevents " end-play " and thus obviates the possibility of a narrow pinion working " out of mesh " with the wheel below.

A pivot being case-hardened steel wears better than its pivot-hole in the comparatively soft brass of the plate, and thus, in old movements, we frequently find that the pivot-holes have been drilled out and re-bushed (*see* Bush).

In movements where economy of driving force is more than ordinarily essential, such as those designed to go a year between windings, friction is reduced as much as possible by the pivots being as fine as practicable, with correspondingly minute pivot-holes. This observation does not, of course, apply to the pivots of the main (barrel) arbor, which have to be substantial in view of the enormous weight necessarily used for driving the long train of such a movement.

Plate Pillars
See Pillars

Plates

The frame in which the pinions and wheels of a movement are fitted is formed by a pair of brass plates, each about ⅛ inch thick, held together by connecting horizontal " pillars " (q.v.). The height and width of these plates vary with the type of movement; the six wheels, pallets and fly of a 30-hour clock requiring smaller plates than the ten wheels, etc., of a month striking movement, a 3-train month chiming or musical clock providing about the maximum size of plate usually found in antique movements. Occasionally, however, one finds very large movements with correspondingly expansive plates for rare examples of four-train movements; going, striking, chiming and musical parts being contained within the plates.

The plate frame superseded the earlier lantern type of movement in which the trains were held between three upright strips of metal, each strip not much more than an inch in width, one train behind the other. This development took place about 1658, roughly coincident with the introduction of the eight-day movement, and enabled the trains to be arranged side-by-side, so as to permit key-winding from the front of the dial. For the methods employed to fasten the plates together, *see* Pillars.

Pulleys

(*a*) Driving Pulleys. The special grooved and spiked wheels with flanges, fitted to the main arbors of a thirty-hour movement for the attachment of the driving weights or weight on its chain (or earlier rope). (*See* Movements.) It should be noted here that a driving pulley designed for a *chain* has the spikes projecting from a narrow middle groove which has "lands" (to borrow a term used in gunmaking) on each side. This groove accommodates the edgewise links of the chain, and the alternate flat links thus lie upon the flanking "lands". A *rope* pulley, whilst still preserving the spikes, has these latter set within a plain, rounded groove with no "lands", conforming to a section of the rope employed. By carefully noticing the type of pulley used one may ascertain whether chain or rope shall be fitted to a particular movement, a matter (judging entirely by observation!) which seems to provide something of a puzzle for not a few dealers and owners.

(*b*) Weight Pulleys. The brass wheels from which the driving weights themselves are directly hung by means of a steel or brass loop riveted to the axis of the pulley, into which loop an S-shaped hook is inserted from the weight. The gut or wire line passes round the weight-pulley on its way from the barrel (q.v.) above to the return position in the seat-board. A weight-pulley for a thirty-hour movement is grooved for the chain or rope (differently for each as above) but not spiked.

Pull Repeater

See Lifting-piece.

Rack

The system of striking used before the introduction of the rack was that controlled by the device known as a Locking Plate (q.v.).

This controller works well, but will not allow the repetition of the hour last struck, being progressive in its action. Also, it has the disadvantage of requiring each hour to be allowed to strike out in full if the hands are moved forward several hours; neglecting this causes non-coincidence between the hour shown and that sounded.

The "snail-and-rack" striking (which is not subject to either of the above limitations) is said to have been invented "about the year 1676" (Derham) by an ingenious cleric who was also a noteworthy horologist—

Edward Barlow (née Booth) 1636–1716. The celebrated Thomas Tompion 1638–1713), however, is usually accorded the credit of applying the device to clocks, which be accomplished *circa* 1676.

As in most horological ascriptions, there is some slight doubt about Barlow's credit for the invention. I have found a passage in Hooke's diary which strongly suggests that *he* may be the real originator of repeating-work (*see* Chapter Two, Early Long-Case Clocks).

It would appear (by actual examples) that the use of the rack was mostly confined to spring-driven mantel clocks until after about 1710, as the great majority of long-case clocks before this date exemplify the locking-plate system.

The early racks were invariably fitted between the plates of the movement. For convenience, however, and because most rack-striking movements of long-case clocks likely to be examined will exemplify this pattern, we will begin our consideration of the subject with the " outside rack ", which came into use about 1715–1720.

The rack itself is a flat steel object, having two arms which are frequently set almost at right-angles to each other, the lower and longer arm is the vertical stem, and the more horizontal upper portion is found as a segment of a circle, having ratchet-type teeth cut into its upper edge. The two arms described are fashioned from a single piece of steel, the toothed portion being integral with the plain stem. A short tube or " pipe " projects from the bottom of the vertical arm, on which pipe the rack is pivoted, and to the forward end of this pipe is attached a third arm, most frequently found set roughly parallel with the segmental portion. This third arm is known as the " tail " of the rack, and has a short pin or stud projecting inwards from a point near its extremity. The stud (in the first form of this pattern) was spring-controlled to engage the cams of the " snail " or slide over its surface, but later (according to the late Mr. Gordon, about 1720) makers introduced the flexible brass rack-tail. The complete rack is pivoted on a stud projecting from the front plate. The vertical rack-stem has a hook-shaped termination below the pivot, which prolongation is utilized as a pressure-point for the rack-spring, which is riveted or screwed to the plate in a suitable position. Pivoted to another stud from the front-plate is the lever known as the " rack-hook ". This assumes slightly differing forms with various makers and according to its position, but all have a projection or " hook " usually at a point about midway in the length of the lever, which drops by its own weight, or is impelled by a spring, into the teeth of the rack.

Yet another lever, double-armed in this instance, is pivoted on a stud from the plate, this being known as the "lifting-piece" and its "tail". (*See* Lifting-piece.)

The end of the lifting-piece engages the rack-hook, and the tail is engaged by the pin in the minute-wheel.

For the sequence of movements involved in the actual striking of the clock, *see* under Lifting-piece and Gathering Pallet.

The snail, which is an indispensible adjunct to the rack system, is a helical plate with twelve cams, fixed to the hour-wheel pipe in front of the wheel, and revolving with it.[1] The snail is so arranged that the deepest cam (that for twelve strokes of the hammer) is coincident with the twelve o'clock position of the hour hand, this cam being then in a position diametrically opposite, i.e., at "six o'clock". As the hour-wheel and hand advance, the various cams on the snail come into the correct places for the rack-tail to engage them, thus allowing a rack-fall only sufficient in number of teeth to provide for the striking of the appropriate hour as the revolving "gathering-pallet" gradually returns the rack to its original position, "tooth-by-tooth and blow-by-blow".

This "gathering-pallet" performs two functions—(*a*) returning the rack ("gathering up"); and (*b*) locking the striking train in later examples of this system. For a detailed description of the pallet and its working *see* under its own name.

The early pattern of rack (that between the plates) also has its operation described under "Gathering Pallet". The snail for such a rack is situated and operated exactly as described above, the rack tail being connected outside the front-plate to an arbor passing between the plates, which arbor carries the rack inside the movement. The lifting-piece communicates with an inside rack-hook through an aperture in the front-plate.

Rack Hook
   See Rack.

Ratchet
   The ratchet is universally employed in long-case movements as the

---

[1] There is another kind of snail, fitted to a "star-wheel" upon a separate stud, and worked from the minute-wheel at every hour, positioned by a "click" or "jumper"; but this is very seldom employed for long-case movements.

medium whereby the weight-power is transmitted from the barrel (or driving pulley of a thirty-hour clock) to the main (or great) wheel.

Some such device was imperative from early times, as both a fixed pulley and main wheel would not allow the process of winding up the weight to be effected, once it had descended to its full extent, since the wheel would be "in mesh" with the second of the train, and therefore could not be moved backwards.

We will first consider the embodiment of the arrangement in an ordinary eight-day movement, taking the going train for illustration, as the application of the ratchet is precisely similar in the "clock" part.

That portion of the barrel nearest the main wheel is provided with a toothed periphery, and the barrel itself is firmly fixed to the main arbor, which last is squared at its forward end for the application of the winding key. Arranged to "ride" (i.e., turn loosely) upon the arbor is the main wheel, and the toothed portion of the barrel lies against the side of the wheel, but not, of course, fastened to it in any way except in that to be explained. Upon the rim of the wheel is screwed or riveted a small steel arm or lever known as a "click", having its pivot at the rivet and kept in contact with the teeth on the barrel by means of a semi-circular spring (the "click-spring") riveted firmly to the side of the wheel-rim at one end and bearing at the other upon the "click".

The teeth of the barrel-ratchet are so arranged as to direction that when the weight is driving the train its power is transmitted from the barrel through the "click" to the main wheel, thus turning this and thence operating the entire train. When, however, the winding key is applied, the barrel may be turned in the reverse direction since the teeth of the ratchet will then be "escaped" by the click, the main wheel remaining stationary upon the turning arbor.

Various ingenious mechanisms have been devised to keep up the turning movement of the main wheel upon the train while the winding-up is in progress, and thus avoid the consequent slight inaccuracy of time-keeping. (*See* Maintaining Power.)

In the thirty-hour movement a "click" is always applied to the driving-pulley of the striking train or "clock", the pulley on the "watch" side being a fixture[1] to the side of the main wheel and this to their arbor. The click-pulley runs loosely upon its arbor and transmits the weight-

---

[1] Unless *both* pulleys have clicks, and separate driving-weights, as in early lantern clocks.

power to the great wheel by means of a type of spring click peculiar to these movements, engaging with an arm of the wheel, and passing these arms when the pulley is turned in the reverse direction on pulling down the chain or rope to wind up the weight.

Rating Screw or Rating Nut
     See Pendulum.

Recoil Escapement
     See Anchor Escapement and Crown Wheel Escapement.

'Scape Wheel
     See Escape Wheel.

Seat board
     This is the wooden platform which forms a base for the movement. It rests at each end upon the extended sides of the clock-case and is occasionally found screwed down in this position. With a well-fitted seat-board of *suitable width* this screwing is not necessary, since the driving-weights, movement and dial all tend by their combined weight to keep the position of the clock unchanged.
     The movement is (or should be) fastened securely to the seat-board by screws passing through or into the lower pillars, with nuts and washers beneath the board; or by steel hooks clasped around each lower pillar and similarly secured beneath the seat-board, which is bored accordingly. This latter arrangement is usual in the later types of movement, wherein the plate-pillars are seldom tapped for screws.
     The seat-board is provided with rectangular apertures in suitable positions beneath the barrels of the movement for the free working of the lines (*see* Lines), which lines (after passing round the weight-pulleys below) return to the seat-board and, passing through, are firmly secured by a suitable knot. *Hooks* beneath the seat-board for fastening the lines should not be tolerated upon any account (*see* Lines).
     The back of the seat-board has usually a cut-away portion to allow the swing of the pendulum.
     It should be almost unnecessary to remark that a badly-split, rickety or worm-eaten seat-board should be repaired or replaced, but, as in all antiques, what seems to be the original ought to be retained, if this is possible without danger, but certainly not otherwise.

Snail
    See Rack.

Suspension Spring
    See Pendulum

In this place, however, it may be of antiquarian interest to remark that, according to Mr. H. Alan Lloyd " the *spring* suspension *with verge escapement* was first used by *Tompion* about 1675–1680 " (my italics).

I cannot confirm this statement, but it seems reasonable; it will be remembered that the fine lantern clock by William Coward of London (Coward was apprenticed to Johannes Fromanteel in 1673) has this arrangement for its pendulum. *See* Plates 1 and 2, and Description of Clock, Appendix Five.

Clement's name has always been associated with the introduction of the spring suspension, but he may not have employed this *with the verge*, retaining for this escapement the directly-attached pendulum.

Swing Wheel
    See Escape Wheel

Teeth
    The media of transmission cut upon the rims of clock wheels, engaging either with a pinion or with another wheel, are known as " teeth " in distinction to those of different shape used in the construction of pinions, which are known as " leaves " (*see* Pinions).

It has been said that toothed wheels for transmitting energy were used by Archimedes sometime about the third century B.C.

Very early wheels have file-cut teeth of remarkable accuracy, formed and finished by hand, as may be found in early lantern clocks. Such wheels are usually somewhat clumsy, being large and heavy, and this may be observed by comparing the wheels of an old lantern clock with those of a typical long-case movement of *circa* 1760, when the wheel-cutting machine was universally employed for teeth-formation.

Dr. Robert Hooke (1635–1703) is usually credited with the invention of the first wheel-cutting " engine " about 1670. Before this, a semi-mechanical device was used to mark out those numbers of teeth in general use upon a " blank " which was afterwards filed into shape entirely by hand, as previously noted.

The earlier wheel-cutting machines merely cut slots into the blank, the teeth being still finished or "rounded-up" by hand with the file. This practice was apparently continued for a very lengthy period. It was not until much later that "engines" were constructed to perform the complete operation mechanically, and entirely automatic cutting of several wheels at once is of recent introduction, being used in modern clock-making factories.

If two perfectly plain rollers be placed in contact, and one of these then revolved, the tendency (accentuated by roughening their surfaces) will be for one to turn the other. Those portions of a *toothed* wheel and pinion which, when in engagement, correspond to the contacting surfaces of our plain rollers are known as the "pitch circles", and that part of a tooth or leaf which projects beyond the "pitch circle" is referred to as the "addendum" of such tooth or leaf.

The addenda of wheel teeth are usually formed to resemble a Gothic arch, and those of pinion leaves sometimes in a rounded or semicircular shape, comparable to a Roman arch. There is, however, nothing designedly fanciful in these forms, as we shall see later.

The parts of the teeth and leaves which lie *within* our "pitch-circles" (not projecting therefrom like the "addenda") are referred to as the "flanks". The "flanks" of the pinion leaves are radials from its centre, thus producing a "club-shaped" leaf. Wheel-teeth have flanks which are also radials from the axis, but the club-shape is not so apparent because of the greater diameter of the wheel as compared to a pinion.

Not all old movements have wheel-teeth and (especially) pinion-leaves shaped as above; variation from the strictly "cycloidal" formation are not infrequent. It would appear, however, that long before the system was mathematically demonstrated as a theory of clock gearing, the old makers were producing what have been called "wonderfully accurate approximations" to it.

The chief variation (from my observations) seems to have been in the shape of pinion-leaf employed by most of the old English makers. In this the flanks are radial but the addendum of more "pointed" formation at its tip.[1] This should be verified by an examination of several old movements, when it will be noticed that the wheel-teeth display the formation

---

[1] i.e., "cycloidal" (see later), similar to the wheel-teeth.

referred to earlier, whilst the leaves of the pinions generally follow the same shape.

From the moment a wheel-tooth begins its pressure upon a pinion-leaf until the instant that it leaves this the turning-motion should be maintained in a perfectly continuous and steady manner. Moreover, the succeeding wheel-tooth must take over the next pinion-leaf quite smoothly, without "drop", i.e., it must not fall on to this through a space, but begin its contact before the preceding tooth is approaching the termination of its pressure.

It may be argued that as the going-train of a movement proceeds by a series of "stops-and-starts", by reason of the limiting action of the escapement, this continuous and even turning movement is superfluous, provided some kind of turning-motion exists. The fallacy contained in this view is exposed when we remember that uniformity of *power* is an essential to any going-train, since without it there will be an inclination for the train to "hold up", and thus stop the clock. Now uniformity of power is not possible without a similarly unvarying *motion*, and hence we arrive at the necessity for not only good formation of the teeth and leaves but also for accurate "depthing" of these.

The "line of centres" is an imaginary line joining, say, a wheel and pinion at their axes. In all horological practice it is regarded as preferable that *most* of the turning-action shall take place *after* the teeth and leaves have passed their line of centres, because the friction is then much less. Friction before the line of centres is termed "engaging friction", that after it, "receding" or "disengaging friction". A homely illustration is provided by a yard-brush held at the usual angle, but quite loosely. Pushing the brush gives us an example of "engaging friction", pulling it, of "receding friction".

A "high-numbered" pinion is one with relatively many leaves, and a "low-numbered" pinion, conversely, one having comparatively few leaves.

The advantage of "high-numbered" pinions (with ten or more leaves) is that with these it is possible to have all the action after the "line of centres" which, as we have seen, is very desirable. Few *old* makers used pinions with such high leaf-numbers in their general work, and it is a fact that the eight-leaf pinion gives an action beginning so near the line of centres that "engaging friction" is negligible. The seven-leaf pinion gives an action commencing much before the line of centres, and was never used by old makers as the *centre pinion* for an eight-day movement, but was frequently employed higher in the train, i.e., for the escape-pinion. The six-leaf pinion was mainly used in the " clock " or striking train, for Hoop (or Pallet), Warn and Fly Pinions, and its employment in this manner would appear to have been confined (as a generalization) to the earlier makers of long-case movements, before *circa* 1750. Much greater driving-power is required by a train having low-numbered pinions than is necessary with a high-numbered train, provided always that the latter is well made.

By " depthing " we express *the amount of engagement* between teeth and leaves; shallow or deep.

A pinion which is " too deep ", i.e., one which is so positioned that its leaves are inserted too far into the spaces between the wheel teeth, is perhaps (except in extreme instances) not so great an evil as one which is too shallow. In the latter case—if the depth be *very* shallow—there is a decided tendency for the action known as " butting " to take place, in which the pinion-leaf " butts " against the addendum of the oncoming wheel-tooth, thus stopping the train. Even should this " butting " be absent, a shallow depth will cause action before the " line of centres " and thus produce engaging friction.

Pinions much too deep encourage action by the *tips* of the addenda, as the contact of the outgoing wheel-tooth is unduly prolonged.

Badly worn pinions will produce the " butting " referred to above, as the leaves assume a formation which results in the production of " pits " in the wheel teeth where the worn leaves are contacted, this combination then producing particularly favourable conditions for the " butting " fault.

A badly worn centre-pinion is frequently the cause of a clock stopping when all else is in order.

We have mentioned the " gothic arch " formed by the addendum of a tooth designed on the cycloidal system. As the term will frequently be encountered in horological works of a technical nature it may be well to state here that this " arch " formation is known as an " epicycloid ".

An epicycloid is produced by rolling one circle upon another. If we take our " pitch circle " and roll upon it another much smaller circle, the curve traced by any particular point in the circumference of this smaller circle during its progress will be an epicycloid, corresponding to the formation of the addenda of the wheel-teeth.

The flanks of the pinion leaves which, like the addenda of the wheel teeth, are the "acting portions", are *hypocycloidal*, produced by *the same* small circle.

A hypocycloid is formed by rolling one circle *within* a larger one (in this case the pitch circle of the pinion) when the line traced by a particular point of the smaller, or "generating circle" will be straight and radial, corresponding to the flanks of the pinion leaves.

A suitable size for the generating circle used for forming both wheel-teeth and pinion-leaves is half the pitch diameter of the pinion.

The following definitions are added for the convenience of the reader.

"Circular pitch" is the distance between the middle of one tooth and that of the next, measured over the pitch circle. In wheel-work the teeth usually occupy equivalent portions of the pitch circle to the space-measurement between each, but the leaves of pinions are less in width at the pitch circle than the spaces between them, to permit the essential freedom in action when wheel and pinion are in mesh. It is, of course, essential that two wheels having to engage each other should be of the same pitch.

The "roots" of the teeth or leaves are their bases, parallel to the pitch circle. They are usually formed with angular corners, although occasionally rounded roots are employed for driving wheels, as this formation increases the strength of the tooth.

The varying number of teeth upon the different wheels of the trains will be found discussed under the relevant headings and also under "Trains". It may be desirable, however, to mention here the teeth of the well-named "Star-wheel", sometimes used for certain motion-work in connection with such dial-indications as day-of-the-week, day-of-the-month and month-of-the-year, and also for the operation of a special kind of snail (*see* Rack, footnote). Such teeth are long and acutely pointed, and appear as star-like rays from the wheel-centre. There are always as many teeth as there are motions desired for that particular indication; thus, a star-wheel for the months of the year would have twelve teeth; that for the days of the week seven only; and a star-wheel operating a snail for controlling the hour-striking would have twelve teeth, as there are a similar number of cams on the snail itself. The star-wheel is positioned by a spring-loaded "click" or "jumper", acting into its teeth.

Damaged or broken teeth on a wheel belonging to an antique movement should be replaced by others of correct form *brazed* on neatly, and if this is carefully done by a competent repairer the new tooth or teeth will be almost indistinguishable.

We often find, however, such repairs executed indifferently; a very usual method is to drill a small hole into the rim of the wheel at the position of the broken tooth, inserting a pin or spike therein to act as a tooth. This practice, although it may serve to effect the continued operation of the train, cannot be regarded as being in the best tradition of craftsmanship, and is eschewed by really good and conscientious repairers of antique movements. Still less to be desired is the brazing to the side of the wheel-rim of a complete segment of more or less suitable teeth to replace consecutive broken members; an entirely new wheel is better than such an expedient if the movement is of a rare and valuable character. This last device (that of the attached segment) of course cannot be employed where two *wheels* mesh, but only in the case of a wheel engaging with a broad pinion.

Third Wheel

In an eight-day movement, this, as its name implies, is the third wheel of the going train or " watch ". However, as there is no " centre " wheel in a thirty-hour movement, in this case the so-called " third " wheel is really the second of the train, which is composed of Main, Third and Escape wheels only.

Similarly, in a movement of month duration, the " third " wheel is number four in the train of five wheels; and in a three-month or year train it is number five in a train of six.

It will be noted, however, that the " third wheel " always preserves its position *relative to the escape wheel*, so that it is always the wheel next in order below this[1] (*see* Trains).

The third wheel was almost invariably provided with 56 teeth, certainly throughout the eighteenth century, and driven by the centre wheel through an eight-leaf pinion, except in the thirty-hour movement, where it is driven by the main wheel through a " pinion of six "; the third wheel has usually 72 teeth in these movements.

[1] Except in movements having a crown-wheel escapement with short pendulum (e.g., lantern clocks and very early long-case movements prior to 1675) where the wheel next below the escape (" crown ") wheel is the " contrate wheel " (q.v.).

Trains

A series of wheels transmitting power from one to another in succession, usually through "pinions", and in a certain order, is collectively known as a "train".

The most obvious instances are afforded by the Watch and Clock parts of a movement, which are each composed of a "train" of wheels for going and striking, respectively.

There are, of course, other kinds of "trains" used in clockwork, notably that for the chiming part, if there be one. Most of them will be found discussed under "Movements", and the peculiar functions of the various wheels comprised in the trains are described under their own particular headings.

The centre wheel, which operates the minute hand, must clearly turn "clockwise" and therefore the wheel next above it (the third wheel) will turn in the reverse direction, and the 'scape wheel again clockwise, since it is next above the third wheel. This is true of all going trains that have a "centre wheel", which includes eight-day, month, and three-, six-, and twelve-month movements.

The thirty-hour movement, however, has no centre wheel, the minute hand (if provided) being worked by a friction-contact wheel on the main arbor (which is brought through the front-plate) engaging a pinion turning upon a stud, to the pipe of which pinion the minute hand is attached.

There being no centre wheel, the next in the train or "number two" (counting upwards from the main wheel) is the so-called "third wheel" (q.v.), which still retains its name and, as the main wheel turns (in going) anti-clockwise,[1] the third wheel turns in the reverse direction. This being so, the next wheel above, the escape wheel, has to turn *anti-clockwise* in one of these movements, and this is the reason why one never sees "seconds-hands" on normally constructed thirty-hour clocks, these hands being always attached to the 'scape-wheel arbors of movements to which they are applied.

In the striking train of the thirty-hour movement, the great and pin wheels will be found combined, the great wheel carrying pins around the side of its rim. Number two of the trains is therefore not the "pin wheel",

---

[1] In order to drive the minute-hand clockwise.

as usual, but the "hoop wheel",[1] with the warn wheel as the last of the three wheels of the train.

A special kind of train, rarely found, is the so-called Lunation Train. This is a series of wheels coming into the category of dial-wheels (q.v.), since they are carried, not between the plates, but on the face of the front-plate, which is extended higher than usual in order to accommodate them. (*See* Plate 52.) The purpose of this Lunation Train is to operate the moon disc in the arch of the dial (*see* Moon's Phases) and the degree of accuracy and certainty of working is greater with this arrangement than with the usual system of jointed levers, the wheels being always in mesh and the movement therefore continuous,[2] though very small.

It is questionable whether the ordinary lunation train was worth incorporating, since the accepted period of lunation was still the nominal 29½ days, which is, of course, only an approximation, so that perfect accuracy was still not possible. However, it is an interesting and rare feature of a movement, conducive to unfailing operation of the lunar record, and must have added considerably to the original expense of a clock, as the wheels would have unusual teeth-numbers, to mention only one characteristic.

An *exactly-calculated* lunation train can, of course be constructed, but I am not aware of an instance of such in any antique movement, although it is possible that they exist. It would be interesting to know how many of these can be found, and where they are now; examples must be very rare.

I give some details so that the possessor of a movement so equipped may recognize it and record its existence.

The first pinion of the train may be placed on the centre arbor, there-fore revolving once per hour, and if of, say, 6 leaves, should engage a wheel of 91 teeth, this having a 9-leaf pinion engaging another wheel of 91 having a pinion of 37, lastly engaging a wheel of 171, this final wheel carrying the moon-disc upon its axis.

This arrangement will give the correct duration of a lunation, viz., 29 days, 12 hours, 44 minutes and 3 seconds, to within a fractional part of a second. The pinions and wheels may engage in any order, provided their "numbers" remain the same, or, at least, their proportions.

[1] Its counterpart in movements of longer duration after about 1720 is the "pallet-wheel" (q.v.).
[2] "Continuous," in this connection, is really a relative description as compared with the twelve-hourly imeptus given by the more usual arrangement. Actually a very tiny movement should occur in some part of the train with each beat of the pendulum.

The following table shows the order of the wheels in the going and striking trains of different movements, reckoning *upwards* from the Main or Great Wheels—

Going Trains				Striking Trains	
30-hour	8-day	Month	3, 6, and 12-month	30-hour	8-day
Main Wheel	Main Wheel	Main Wheel	Main Wheel	Great (and Pin) Wheel	Great Wheel
Third ,,	Centre ,,	Second ,,	First ,,	Hoop ,,	Pin ,,
Escape ,,	Third ,,	Centre ,,	Second ,,	Warn ,,	Pallet ,,
	Escape ,,	Third ,,	Centre ,,		(or Hoop Wheel)
		Escape ,,	Third ,,		Warn Wheel
			Escape ,,		

Six- and twelve-month movements are very seldom provided with a striking train; in fact, the author is not aware that an example of such is in existence, having never seen or read of an instance.[1] One does, however, occasionally hear of rare examples of three-month clocks (an instance is that of the "record" Tompion clock made for William III mentioned earlier in this book) and month striking clocks are not exceptional. The extra wheels in these movements are disposed similarly to those in the going trains, i.e., between the Great and Pin wheels.

Verge

The name "verge" originally signified a staff or wand of office, and the "vergers" in churches did at one time carry white staves as a symbol of their office. From the verger's custom of carrying his white wand upright before him the name "verge" has been applied to the balance staffs of watches and early clocks, and, by association (though with less reason, since such are not upright) to pallet-staffs and anchor-arbors in the horizontal position.

Early continental clocks of all kinds with "foliot" control, and English chamber clocks of the "lantern" type with the balance-wheel regulator (all before the general introduction of the pendulum) were provided with a true "verge" (*see* Crown Wheel Escapement).

---

[1] Since the above was written the present writer has been shown what must be a very rare example of a long-period movement by Jno. Wyatt, Altrincham (Cheshire). This is provided with a separate striking train, has a round, white dial with centre-seconds hand and counterpoised minute-hand, 24-hour dial-markings, and goes for about 9 months between windings. The date is about 1810. (In the possession of Mr. J. Kinsey, Hale, Cheshire.)

N

In long-case clock movements—always of the pendulum type—the terms "pallet-staff" or "anchor-arbor" are more correct when referring to this part of the mechanism (*see* Pallets).

Vertical Escapement

This is usually another name for the anchor or dead-beat escapement, but there is a type of crown-wheel escapement which also has a vertical 'scape-wheel. This is the crown-wheel used with a true verge and balance-wheel as in early lantern clocks. It is never found in long-case movements, however, where the crown-wheel is always used horizontally, under a "verge"—properly, pallet-staff—likewise horizontal and with a "bob" pendulum (*see* Anchor, Dead beat, and Crown Wheel Escapements).

Watch

In clockwork, this term refers to the going train of a movement. As to the application of the terms "Watch" and "Clock" in horology, see under "Clock".

Warn Wheel

This wheel, at the top of the striking train or "clock" (*see* Trains) has its operation described under "Lifting Piece" (q.v.).

Wheels

From Derham (*Artificial Clockmaker*, second edition, 1700): "The parts of a *Wheel* are, the *Hoop*, or *Rim*: the *Teeth*: the *Cross*: and the *Collet*, or piece of Brass, soddered [*sic*] on the Arbor, or Spindle, on which the Wheel is rivetted." The peculiar punctuation of the passage is the author's, as in the original.

Appendix Two

The Long-Case Clock

For a full understanding of the foregoing Glossary, the reader is advised to study the diagrams, in which I have tried to illustrate the inter-relation of the various parts as clearly as possible. *I wish to emphasize that they are nothing more than diagrammatic representations* and should not be regarded as working drawings.

Figs. 1 and 2 are lettered and numbered similarly, so that corresponding parts may be identified; but they are *not* different views of the same movement.

To avoid undue complexity of appearance, only the teeth and leaves of the dial wheels and minute-pinion are shown in Fig. 1, and these but segmentally. The interior wheels and pinions are displayed as "pitch circles", touching where they are supposed to engage or "mesh". An exception is made in the case of the escape-wheel, of which a toothed segment is illustrated.

The centre wheel of Fig. 1 is expressed as a broken (or "dotted") circle. It is that wheel lying nearest to the backplate of the movement, as also is the corresponding wheel in the slightly differing movement of Fig. 2.

Appended is a Key to the Diagrams.

The reader is urged to examine an actual clock movement, in conjunction with the Glossary and Diagrams.

Should he not care to interfere with a cherished possession, it is possible to secure for a small sum an old separate movement, and so long as it is in reasonable condition, he may derive amusement and edification from atttempting to make it "go".

Once the names and functions of the various parts are generally understood, practical experience is of inestimable value and interest, and little difficulty will be found in understanding even the most complicated of movements.

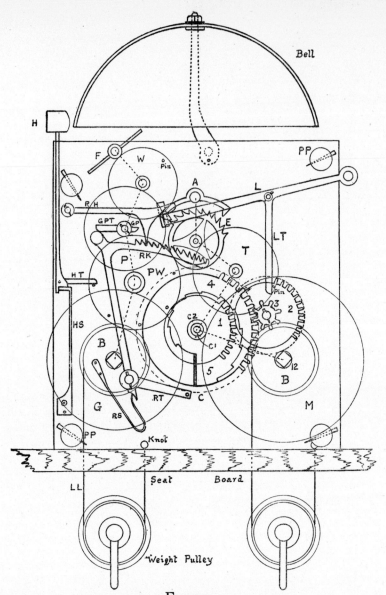

FIGURE 1
Eight-day Long-Case Movement
Front View, showing Striking Train, etc.

KEY TO FIGS. 1 AND 2

A—Anchor	F—Fly	L—Lifting Piece	RH—Rack Hook
B—Barrel	G—Great Wheel	LL—Lines	RK—Rack
C—Centre Wheel	GP—Gathering Pallet	LT—Lifting Piece Tail	RS—Rack Spring
C¹—Centre Arbor	GPT—Gathering	M—Main Wheel	RT—Rack Tail
C²—Centre Pinion	Pallet Tail	P—Pallet Wheel	T—Third Wheel
D—Dial Wheels	H—Hammer	PP—Plate Pillars	W—Warn Wheel
DP—Dial Pillars	HS—Hammer Spring	PW—Pin Wheel	
E—Escape Wheel	HT—Hammer Tail	R—Ratchet	

1 Cannon Wheel	6 Bridge	11 Hand Collet	16 Pendulum Spring
2 Minute Wheel	7 Hour Wheel Pipe	12 Winding Squares	17 Pendulum Rod
3 Minute Pinion	8 Seconds Hand	13 Pendulum Cock	18 Seat Board Screw
4 Hour Wheel	9 Hour Hand	14 Crutch	
5 Snail	10 Minute Hand	15 Crutch Fork	

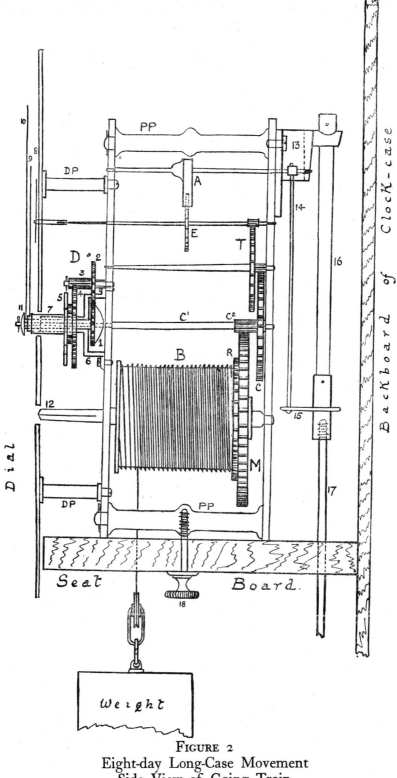

FIGURE 2
Eight-day Long-Case Movement
Side View of Going Train
197

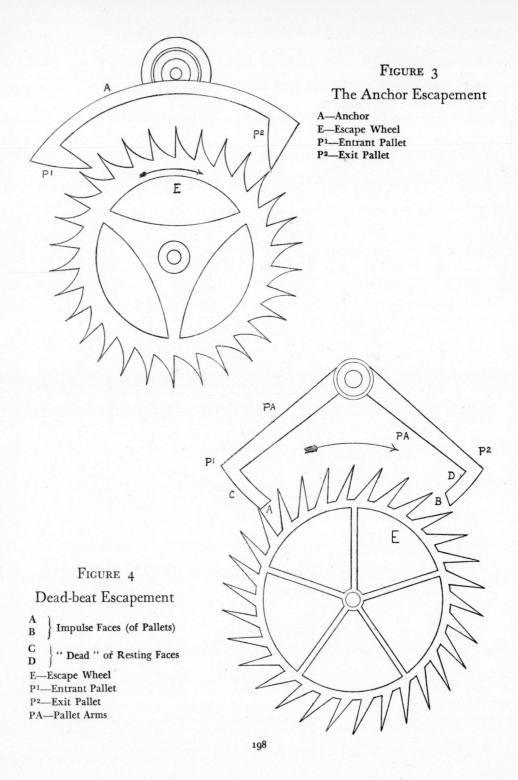

FIGURE 3

The Anchor Escapement

A—Anchor
E—Escape Wheel
P¹—Entrant Pallet
P²—Exit Pallet

FIGURE 4

Dead-beat Escapement

A
B } Impulse Faces (of Pallets)

C
D } " Dead " or Resting Faces

E—Escape Wheel
P¹—Entrant Pallet
P²—Exit Pallet
PA—Pallet Arms

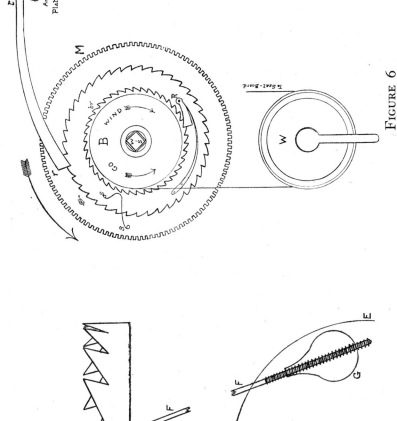

FIGURE 6

Harrison's Maintaining Power
or The Harrison Going Ratchet

B—Barrel	R—Barrel Ratchet " Click " and Spring
br—Barrel Ratchet	rt—Going Ratchet Click Lever
gr—Going Ratchet	ss—Spring
M—Main Wheel	W—Weight Pulley
	WS—Winding Square

Note that the connection of the Spring at SS drives the Main Wheel M in the ordinary going of the clock

FIGURE 5

The Crown-Wheel Escapement
(With Horizontal Verge and "Bob" Pendulum)

A—" Verge " or Pallet Staff	E—Contrate Wheel
B—Crown Pinion	F—Pendulum Rod
C—Crown Wheel	G—Pendulum " bob "
D—Pivot Bracket	1 and 2—Pallets

N.B.—The Crown Wheel Escapement (always exclusively in the form shown in this diagram) is used only in the very early long-clocks, dating from about 1660. (See Glossary, " Crown Wheel Escapement ".)

199

Appendix Three

Dates of Importance in Horological History

700 B.C. (*circa*). Mention of Sun-dial in Isaiah xxxviii. 8.

340 B.C. (*circa*). Berosus, Chaldean Astronomer, (constructed a dial "hemicycle"). Was in use for centuries.

135 B.C. (*circa*). Ctesibius of Alexandria. Clepsydra or Water Clock.

A.D. 807. Clepsydra of bronze inlaid with gold presented to the Emperor Charlemagne by Shah of Persia.

A.D. 1326 (circa). Richard Wallingford, Abbot of St. Albans. Clock (really a planetarium or orrery, not having an escapement). His own account of the machine preserved at Oxford. (Bodleian Library.)

A.D. 1370. Henri de Wyck (Wieck, or de Vick). Clock at Paris, in the the Royal Palace (now the Palais de Justice). Foliot escapement.

A.D. 1372. The first Strasbourg Clock. Many ingenious "motions".

A.D 1480. Clock at Exeter Cathedral. Presented by Bishop Courtenay. A view of the movement of this clock may be seen by consulting Cox's *English Church Fittings, Furniture and Accessories* (Fig. 179). In this the original escapement has been altered at a much later date to what is apparently one of "anchor" type.

A.D. 1533. Anne Boleyn's Clock. Said to have been presented to her on her wedding morning by Henry VIII. This is a *domestic* clock of "lantern" type. Was in the collection of Horace Walpole at Strawberry Hill and purchased for Queen Victoria. Now at Windsor Castle, but lacking its original movement. Casework and driving weights original. (Britten.)

A.D 1574. The second Strasbourg Clock. Complicated astronomical and other movements. (The "Third Clock" is a reconstruction of this, completed in 1842.)

A.D. 1581. "Galileo" (Galileo Galilei) discovers the principle of "isochronism" (*see* text).

A.D. 1631. The Company of Clockmakers incorporated by Royal Charter of Charles I.

A.D. 1641. Richard Harris, London, is later claimed as the first to use the pendulum as a controller, which he is said to have accomplished in this year.

A.D. 1649. Vincenzo Galilei (son of Galileo Galilei) has partly-constructed a clock, using the pendulum, from his father's instructions, given him earlier.

A.D. 1657. Christian Huygens de Zuylichem (1629–1695), Dutch scientist, mathematician and astronomer, employs the pendulum in a clock which he presents to the States of Holland. He had adopted the pendulum as a controller earlier (1656) in a clock which he used personally in connection with his astronomical studies, as is proved by the references to this in his letters. Huygens is usually accorded the honour of being the first (through the clockmaker Samuel Coster) to apply the pendulum to clocks in a marketable manner, as distinct from purely experimental applications. Instances of the latter kind are plentiful, probably beginning with Leonardo da Vinci (1452–1519). *See* Pendulum (Glossary) and text.

A.D. 1658. A. Fromanteel introduces the Huygens pendulum, as a general controller for clocks, into England.

A.D. 1660 (*circa*). The first known Long-case Clocks.

A.D. 1666. Probable date at which Robert Hooke introduced the " anchor " escapement if, as seems likely, his claim to its invention is valid. This, however, he may have invented as early as 1656, as there exists inferential evidence which suggests the earlier date as possible.

A.D. 1671. William Clement (Bro. C.C. 1677) constructs a turret clock for King's College, Cambridge, employing the anchor escapement and a long wooden-rod pendulum. At present the earliest known use of the " royal " pendulum.

A.D. 1675. The " royal " pendulum (a long, or " seconds " pendulum *with anchor escapement*) becomes established as a generally used controller for all " up-to-date " house clocks. *See* Chapter Two, and Pendulum in Glossary.

A.D. 1676. Thomas Tompion (1638–1713) applies the invention of the rack repeating mechanism for striking clocks.

A.D. 1715. About this time George Graham (1673–1751) invented the "dead-beat" form of escapement.

A.D. 1721 Graham begins his experiments with mercury for temperature compensation, resulting in his mercury-compensated pendulum a few years later.

A.D. 1726. John Harrison introduces the 'gridiron" (compensating) pendulum. His "going-ratchet" (maintaining power) probably first used by him about this time—the exact date not certain.

1786–1788. Crotch arranges music by Handel suitably for quarter-chimes for the clock at Great St. Mary's, Cambridge. The "Cambridge quarters" more widely known as "Westminster chimes" after their use at the Houses of Parliament about the middle of the following century.

A.D. 1800 (*circa*). Regarded by many as latest date for beginning of the decline in artistic clockmaking in England. Long-case clocks after this date are usually debased in materials and design, although there are the inevitable exceptions, notably in that type of clock now known as "regulator" timepieces.

Appendix Four

List of Most Eminent Makers[1]

ARNOLD, JOHN. 1736–1799. C.C. (Clockmakers' Company) 1783. Warden 1796 Chiefly famous as a maker of marine chronometers and repeating watches. Captain Cook's ship *Resolution*, in which he made his second voyage (1772), carried a chronometer made by Arnold. A long-case month "regulator" (inscribed "No. 1") by him is illustrated in *Old English Master Clockmakers and their Clocks* by Herbert Cescinsky. This "No. 1" and also Arnold's regulator "No. 2" probably superseded the Tompion year time-pieces at Greenwich Observatory in 1774. The pallets are rubies and it has been stated that "No. 1" was two years in building. The "gridiron" compensating pendulum of Harrison type is employed, together with a large and heavy "bob".

BANGER, EDWARD. C.C. 1695. Apprenticed to Joseph Ashby for Thomas Tompion 1687. Married a niece of the latter, with whom he was later in partnership, their clocks bearing the inscription, "Tho. Tompion, Edw. Banger, London".

BARNETT, JOHN. C.C. 1682. "At ye Peacock in Lothebury." Apprenticed 1675 to John Ebsworth (q.v.). Several fine long-case clocks by this maker in existence, with marquetry casework.

BOWYER, WILLIAM. C.C. 1631. Subscribed for incorporation of the C.C., and possibly one of the earliest members. A good maker of early lantern clocks. Presented a "great chamber clock" (probably a large lantern clock) to the Company in 1642 in consideration of his being thereafter exempted from all office and service, including "quarterage" and other fees.

---

[1] Many of the particulars concerning Makers mentioned in this List have been obtained from F. J. Britten's work *Old Clocks and Watches and their Makers*. In one or two instances, where the dates given appear to present inconsistencies, these have been omitted or amended.

CLEMENT, WILLIAM. Bro. C.C. 1677. Master 1694–1699. Celebrated London maker. Probably the first *clockmaker* to use the anchor escapement, together with the long pendulum (turret clock, 1671). Some consider that the anchor escapement is, in fact, his invention, and not that of Robert Hooke, but this is debatable. He was certainly not the first horologist to use a long (or "seconds") pendulum (*see* text), although he may well have been the first to use the "royal" pendulum, i.e., a long pendulum with Hooke's (or his own) anchor escapement, as a "standard" application to clocks. He may have invented the suspension *spring*, the use of which became practically universal. Several interesting long-case clocks by him are in existence. Sometimes used the Latin form of inscription upon his dials, thus—"Gulielmus Clement, Londini, fecit."

CLOSON, PETER. C.C. 1631. Another subscriber to the incorporation of the C.C. in 1630. *Senior Warden* 1636–1638. A noted maker of early lantern clocks.

COXETER, NICHOLAS. C.C. 1646. Apprenticed 1638 to John Pennock. Master C.C. 1671 and 1677. Cescinsky illustrates a lantern clock by him, inscribed "Nicholas Coxeter at ye 3 Chaires Lothbury, Londini, Fecit". There was a small long-case clock by this maker in the Wetherfield Collection, olive and laburnum veneer inlaid with star marquetry.

EAST, EDWARD. 1602–1696. The dates of his birth and death are variously given, and it has been sometimes held that there were two Edward "Easts"—father and son. This because of the long period over which records exist, regarded as too great for the lifetime of a single maker. In an article which appeared in the *Horological Journal* for May and June, 1950, Mr. H. Alan Lloyd endeavours to prove that there was, in fact, but one maker of this name, living to the great age of 94. In this article ("*The one and only Edward East*") the author gives the dates of birth and death as at the head of this short notice. Much purpose will hardly be served in quoted opinions of other writers and, since the evidence appears good and the inferences sound, I have preferred the dates given by the author of the article mentioned to those more usually quoted.

East was Court Horologist to both Charles I and Charles II, and one of the ten original Assistants of the Clockmakers' Company.

He carried on business in Pall Mall, later in Fleet Street, and later still (according to some) "at the Sun, outside Temple Bar". An ingenious and noted maker of all kinds of clocks and watches.

EBSWORTH, JOHN. C.C. 1665. Master 1697. Apprenticed in 1657 to Richard Ames. Business "at ye Cross Keys in Lothbury", later "New Cheap Side". On dial of long-case clock by him, the inscription "John Ebsworth, Londini, Fecit". An excellent maker.

ELLICOTT, JOHN. 1706–1772. In business about 1728 at Sweeting's Alley, near Royal Exchange. Fellow of the Royal Society, 1738. Inventor of a compensating pendulum, little used since. Conducted many useful horological experiments, some of which he made the subjects of papers read before the Royal Society. A very fine long-case clock by Ellicott (*circa* 1760), in the possession of Mr. E. Beaven, is shown in Britten's work, indicating hours of day and night by sliding annular segments in the dial centre, and displaying a large secondary dial below the hood giving the Equation of Time. Main dial divided into twice twelve hours. Ellicott was a fine maker of clocks, including the later types of those in long-case form.

ETHERINGTON, GEORGE. C.C. 1684. His shop was in Fleet Street, at the sign of the Dial, and he was Master of the C.C. in 1709. In 1714 he moved his business to "the Dial over against the New Church in the Strand, London". A famous maker of clocks and watches.

FROMANTEEL, JOHANNES. C.C. 1663. "Ye Mermaid, at Lothbury". Apprenticed to Thomas Loomes (Bro. C.C. 1649). The family of Fromanteel, of Dutch extraction (and more particularly, it would appear, this John Fromanteel) are to be credited with the introduction of the practical adaptation of the pendulum into England. This would be in 1658, the year following its successful application by Huygens to a clock made for him by one Samuel Coster, of The Hague, to whose service John (Johannes) Fromanteel bound himself for some eight months from September 1657. Several early long-case clocks, with crown-wheel escapements and short pendulums, dating from 1660 to 1670 are in existence, made by J. Fromanteel. Some are illustrated in the works of Britten and Cescinsky.

FROMANTEEL, AHASUERUS. C.C. 1663. The third of this name in the family of Fromanteel. Was apprenticed to Simon Bartram, who was Master of the C.C. in 1646. An ingenious and advanced maker of splendid clocks, both long-case and mantel. His business address appears to have been the same as that of Johannes Fromanteel, and both usually inscribed their dials in the customary Latinized form of the period, following the name with the words ' Londini, Fecit ".

FROMANTEEL and CLARKE. London, *circa* 1680.

GARON, PETER. C.C. 1694. A fine London maker of beautiful clocks and watches. A watch by him is in the British Museum, and a number of long-case clocks in handsome marquetry cases are extant, some of which are of month duration, others being chiming clocks on six or eight bells. In the *London Gazette* of 31st October, 1706, appeared a notice of Garon's bankruptcy.

GOULD, CHRISTOPHER. C.C. 1682. A noted maker. Britten mentions several fine long-case clocks by him which were at one time in the Wetherfield Collection.

GRAHAM, GEORGE. 1673–1751. F.R.S. 1720. Master of the C.C. 1722. Apprenticed to Henry Aske, 1688. Pupil-assistant to his uncle, the celebrated Thos. Tompion, and succeeded to the business after managing it for some years before Tompion's death in 1713. Invented the mercurial compensating pendulum and the dead-beat escapement. Next to Tompion, probably the most famous of all clockmakers, a fact which may be partly due to the burial of both these eminent horologists in Westminster Abbey.

GRETTON, CHARLES. C.C. 1672. At " The Ship, Fleet Street ". Apprenticed to Lionel Wythe in 1662. Master of the C.C. in 1700. An eminent maker of long-case and other clocks.

HARRISON, JOHN. 1693–1776. A famous horologist. Chiefly known for his remarkable series of marine chronometers, designed to improve the accuracy of longitude calculation at sea. To him is perhaps mainly due the earliest realization of the " familiar method " referred to in Lowthorp's Abridgment of the *Philosophical Transactions* (1705) in his dedication to " His Royal Highness The Prince, Lord High Admiral of England ": " . . . and by some familiar method deliver the anxious *Seamen* from the *fatal Accidents* that frequently attend their mistaken *Longitude*." Harrison's numerous inventions include the " grasshopper " form of escapement action, the " gridiron " (compensating) pendulum, and the type of maintaining power sometimes referred to as " Harrison's Going-Ratchet ". Long-case clocks by Harrison are at the Science Museum, South Kensington, and the Guildhall Museum.

JONES, HENRY. 1632–1695. Inner Temple Gate, London. Clock dial inscribed " Henry Jones in ye Temple ". Apprenticed to Edward East (q.v.) in 1654. C.C. 1663. Master 1691. A really first-class maker, and probably the first Englishman to construct barometers, or Torricellian tubes, as they were then called.

KNIBB, JOSEPH C.C. 1670. One of a family of noted clockmakers, of which the others were Samuel, C.C. 1663, Peter, C.C. 1677, John, and Edward (apprenticed 1693 to Joseph) C.C. 1700. There was also a Joseph Knibb, Junior, who was admitted to the C.C. in 1717. The most famous maker would appear to be Joseph Knibb the Elder (C.C. 1670). He was probably first in business at Oxford (he is mentioned as " of Oxford " in the records of the C.C.) but later moved to London, where he had premises first " At the Dyal, near Serjeants' Inn, in Fleet Street " (1691), and then at " The Clock Dyal, in Suffolk Street, near Charing Cross " (1697). Britten records long-case dials engraved " Joseph Knibb, of Hanslope " and " Joseph Knibb att Hanslop " (*see* text). Knibb was a very fine maker, notable for his system of " Roman Numeral Striking " which is described in the body of this book. This system was apparently occasionally used by Daniel Quare (q.v.), an equally famous contemporary.

LISTER, THOMAS. 1745–1814. One of the later makers of long-case clocks. Son of Thomas Lister, Luddenden, Yorkshire (1718–1779). The son was in business at Halifax, where in 1774 he contracted to make, for £60, Halifax Church clock. In 1801 he made an orrery (star-machine) for the Anderson College, Glasgow, to the order of Dr. Birkbeck. Now in the Glasgow University Museum. This machine had been designed by Joseph Priestley, of Bradford. It appears that Lister was so highly regarded as a clockmaker that (it is said) he was engaged to regulate and keep in order the clock at St. Paul's Cathedral, London, to effect which duty he travelled by coach between Halifax and London. (*Chats on Old Clocks*, by Arthur Hayden). If this story is not apocryphal it is remarkable that a Northern maker should be chosen for such work in connection with the Metropolitan Cathedral in the eighteenth or early nineteenth centuries, no doubt in competition with London Horologists of repute, and is an excellent testimonial to the skill and reputation of at least one of our Northern clockmakers. at this period. Lister made for Illingworth Church, in 1802, a clock having a pendulum 30 feet long, vibrating twenty times per minute. He seems to have been a good mechanician, fond of introducing unusual features into his movements and, as he appears always to have employed an excellent cabinet-maker for the construction of the casework, his clocks seldom fail to express a decided individuality.

LYONS, RICHARD. C.C. 1656. Apprenticed 1649 to William Almond. Master of the C.C. 1683. A fine early maker.

MUDGE, THOMAS. 1715–1794. An eminent clock and watchmaker. He seems to have been chiefly concerned with the production of chronometers, watches, and clocks of the "regulator" type. C.C. 1738 (livery 1766). Apprenticed to George Graham (q.v.), to whose business he succeeded. About 1755 entered into partnership with William Dutton, another of Graham's apprentices.

NORTON, EARDLEY. (Flourished 1760–1794.) A famous maker of clocks and watches of all kinds, including long-case clocks. He was one of the finest of the later makers, and particularly excelled in the production of astronomical, chiming and musical clocks. In Buckingham Palace is an astronomical clock with four dials which he made for George III. He made a remarkable musical clock especially for the Empress Catherine of Russia. His business address was 49 St. John Street, Clerkenwell, London.

QUARE, DANIEL. 1648–1724. Admitted to the C.C. in 1671, and Master in 1708. A Quaker. In business at St. Martin's le Grand, London, and from 1680 at the "King's Arms, Exchange Alley". A fine long-case timepiece by Quare, constructed to go for a year between windings, is at Hampton Court Palace. During his later life Quare took into partnership Stephen Horsman (or Horseman) who had been apprenticed to him in 1701 (C.C. 1709), and the business was continued at the King's Arms under the title of Quare and Horseman. Quare was clockmaker to George I. Britten gives details of the difficulty respecting the taking of an oath (Quare being a member of the Society of Friends) in connection with this office.

TOMPION, THOMAS. 1638–1713. The most famous of English clock and watch makers. Bro. C.C. 1671, Warden 1700 and Master 1704. In business at Water Lane, corner of Fleet Street, Blackfriars (the Dial and Three Crowns) at an early age. "By adopting the inventions of Hooke and Barlow, and by skilful proportion of parts, he left English watches and clocks the finest in the world and the admiration of his brother artists." (Britten.) Famous long-case month timepiece presented by Tompion to the Grand Pump Room, Bath, in 1709. Long-case clock made by him for William III brought approximately £4,000 at sale of Wetherfield Collection. Two other fine long-case clocks (one by Tompion and Banger) at Buckingham Palace. Tompion was buried in Westminster Abbey; his grave was later re-opened to receive the remains of George Graham (q.v.).

In 1676 Tompion constructed for Sir Jonas Moore, F.R.S., Surveyor General of Ordnance to Charles II, the two fine *year* timepieces which Sir Jonas presented to John Flamsteed, the first Astronomer Royal, and which were set up in the Octagon Room of the original Greenwich Observatory. These movements were not cased, their dials being inset into the panelling of the Octagon Room, as shown in a contemporary print. Pendulums beating two seconds (13 feet long) and, of course, anchor escapements, were features of the original design. The movements are still in existence; one in private ownership, encased in oak at some period early in the eighteenth century, and the other at the British Museum. Both have now *seconds* pendulums and modified 'scape-wheels. Their interest is great as being the first clocks to be used for astronomical observations by a British Astronomer Royal at Greenwich. They were probably not superseded until the Arnold "regulators" were acquired in 1774 (*see* Arnold, John).

WHEELER, THOMAS. C.C. 1655. Apprenticed to Nicholas Coxeter 1647. Master of the C.C. 1684. Died 1694. His existing work would appear to be chiefly in the form of lantern clocks. Britten describes one of these as bearing the inscription "Thomas Wheeler, near the French Church in Londini". The same authority ascribes a beautiful marquetry long-case clock with square dial and high domed hood with carved gilt ornaments, which was in the Wetherfield Collection, to another Thomas Wheeler, and puts the date of the clock at *circa*

o

1700. The clock is illustrated in Hurcomb's book of the Wetherfield Collection, and the present writer would be inclined to regard it as being the work of that Thomas Wheeler who died in 1694.

WILLIAMSON, JOSEPH. Master, C.C. 1724. Died in office 1725. A distinguished horologist and mechanician. Held the office of Watchmaker to Charles II of Spain, for whom he made a 400-day long-case equation clock. He appears to have been better appreciated in the trade than otherwise famous, which is not surprising when it is remembered that he was probably responsible for the making of many of the more unusual and complicated movements for better-known contemporaries. Thus, it is a fact that the equation work (and possibly the entire movement) of the twelve-month equation timepiece at Hampton Court which bears the name of Daniel Quare, was made by Joseph Williamson for him. Williamson's dials are often inscribed in Latin—" Josephus Williamson, Londini, Fecit "; Britten illustrates one which also bears Latin mottos, engraved upon scrolls in the dial-centre.

WINDMILLS, JOSEPH. C.C. 1671. Master of the C.C. 1702. His address was St. Martin's-le-grand, and later in Mark Lane, London. A fine maker. In the British Museum is a watch by him, a representation of the Sun indicating the hour by day, and another of the moon showing the nocturnal hours. In the famous Wetherfield Collection, according to Britten, was a long-case clock by Windmills, with 10-inch dial, bolt-and-shutter maintaining power, and inlaid laburnum and olivewood case with spiral-pillared hood, dating from about 1690. Joseph appears to be the earliest recorded representative of the name; there was also Thomas Windmills (apprenticed to Joseph in 1686, C.C. 1695, Master of the C.C. 1719). J. and T. Windmills (of which firm the above Thomas was probably one of the partners) had business in Great Tower Street, and were responsible for many fine long-case clocks, 1710–1740. There were also Windmills and Wightman, Windmills and Bennett, and Windmills and Elkins, all of London and working *circa* 1725.

Appendix Five

Notes on the Clocks Illustrated in this Book

PLATE 1. Thirty-hour Striking Lantern Clock by William Coward, *circa* 1685. Height to top of central spire, 15 inches. Dial, 6 3/16 inches diameter.

The movement of this clock is illustrated in the view given by Plate 2 (side door removed).

It will be noted that the escapement is effected by a horizontal crown-wheel engaging the pallets of a verge passing over it. A short pendulum is hung by a small suspension spring from the jaws of a brass "cock", and there is a crutch provided, working in a slot in an attachment to the pendulum rod, as in many modern clocks. The pear-shaped pendulum "bob" is of lead, adjustment being by a fine thread cut at the lower end of the rod.

The handsomely brass-cased driving weight is unusual, but may be original.

The minute hand (without complementary dial-markings) suggests an addition at a later date, and this conclusion is corroborated by the hand itself, which has been shortened to fit the dial. The supports for the clock platform are seventeenth-century work, the remainder of the carved woodwork of the dark oak bracket is modern. The rose and tulip engraving of the clock dial is typical of the period, as is the inscription thereon: "Willm. Coward, Fecit". Coward was apprenticed to the famous clockmaker Johannes Fromanteel in 1673, and was admitted to the C.C. in 1681.

PLATE 3. Small Thirty-hour Lantern Clock with Alarm. Anonymous, *circa* 1710. Height to top of central spire, 8¼ inches. Dial 45⁄8th inches diameter.

Plate 4 shows the movement, a side door being removed for this purpose.

This clock is interesting because of several characteristic "lantern" features. It will be noticed that the pendulum is directly attached to the verge, without a crutch, unlike the clock illustrated by Plates 1 and 2. Then, too, the spikes for " distancing " the clock from a wall will be observed in Plate 4, screwed into the rear pair of feet and projecting backwards. Also in connection with this method of hanging the timekeeper will be seen the extension rearward of the top plate, so as to form an attachment designed to slip over a hook in the wall.

The movement follows the same arrangement as the larger clock in so far as the going train is concerned, but there is no striking train or " clock ", its place being taken by the alarm mechanism, consisting of a second (but vertical) crown wheel engaging the pallets of an upright verge, to the top of which is attached the hammer. The revolution of the crown wheel, when the alarm is let off at the appointed time, causes the verge to vibrate rapidly with a to-and-fro motion, thus bringing the hammer into contact with alternate inner sides of the bell surmounting the structure. The arrangement is similar to a balance-controlled going-train, but, of course, much faster in operation, and there is only the " escape " wheel present, the remaining wheels of the train not being required for the operation of an alarm.

Of necessity, two weights and two click-pulleys are used, with separate chains for each; a small brass counterbalance is provided for the " going " weight. The method of setting the alarm, and its mode of release is explained in the body of this work. *See* Chapter One, *Horology in the Sixteenth and Seventeenth Centuries.*

The dark oak bracket would appear to be modern.

PLATE 5. Thirty-hour Friesian Clock with Alarum. Dutch, early eighteenth century. Height overall, 21 inches. Dial, 8¾ inches by 6½ inches.

This is the Dutch equivalent to our English lantern clocks. The brass movement (unfortunately the photograph of this is not particularly suitable for blockmaking) has nicely turned decorative pillars (as in Plate 9) and the pinions are held between bars as in the English lantern movements.

The escapement is by *vertical* verge and crown wheel, similar to a balance-control English clock of early date, but a thin wire crutch from the verge projects rearwards and engages in a loop formed in the pendulum rod.

The pendulum is attached, not to the movement itself, but to the bracket supporting the entire timepiece, from the top of which wooden bracket it is suspended. The hours are sounded upon the usual large bell at the top of the clock proper, as in English clocks of this lantern type.

The dial is of painted sheet iron, and the side doors of the movement are also of iron, with glass panels. Gilded cast lead is used for the decoration around the dial and on the hood of the bracket.

An alarm-disc will be noticed, the alarm being set by means of the small pointer in the centre, in conjunction with the numerals marked on the disc itself. *See* also Plate 8 for a similar arrangement. The rope and weight operating the alarm mechanism is not now present.

There is but one hand, a large, counterpoised indicator, minute motion-work not being provided in this clock, although some Friesian clocks are equipped with two hands and corresponding motion-work. It is possible that such clocks are rather later in date than this one, but this is not always the case, much to the confusion of collectors, as variations in style and quality of work by different makers often accounts for some superficially chronological deviations.

A good idea of the decorative appearance presented by the turned brass pillars (and certain arbors) of the movement may be gathered by referring to Plate 9, which illustrates a somewhat later type of Dutch clock.

I am indebted to Mr. G. P. Lancaster, of Ulverston, Lancashire, for permission to include his interesting example of the Friesian clock in this Essay, and also for the provision of the photograph, reproduced by Plate 5.

PLATE 6. Thirty-hour Striking and Chiming Lantern Clock by Henton Brown, London, *circa* 1740. Height to top of central spire, 15 inches. Diameter of dial, 6 inches.

The movement is illustrated by Plate 7.

Henton Brown was apprenticed in 1714, admitted to the C.C. 1726, was Master of the Company in 1753, Livery 1766, and died in 1775 (*vide* F. J. Britten and G. H. Baillie).

This clock chimes the quarters on eight bells, and precedes the striking of each hour by the performance of a quaint little tune of some length— about eight bars of quick tempo—to which I cannot ascribe a title. In listening to this tune it seems probable that the time of certain bars has been disturbed by slight variations in the length or positions of the pins in the chime-barrel, due to the age of the mechanism, but on the whole one must confess the effect to be charming and quite musical.

The dial is inscribed " Henton Brown, Londini, fecit ". Hour and minute hands are provided, and corresponding dial-markings. With a good glass, it should be easily possible to appreciate the very fine engraving displayed in the centre portion of the dial, which is very clear in the photograph, although some detail may be lost in the blockmaking. The hands, as will be seen, are handsome examples of the period.

The brass side doors of the clock are also engraved, though not so elaborately as the dial.

As will be seen by referring to the next illustration (Plate 7) a crown-wheel escapement is used horizontally here, in conjunction with the usual " bob " pendulum. For non-technical readers we may explain that the first train (that next the dial) is the " watch " or going-train, that in the middle of the movement, showing the pinned chime-barrel, is the chiming train, and the rearmost series of wheels the striking train or " clock ".

The larger (and heavier) driving-weight is for going and chiming, and the smaller weight is utilized for the striking train at the back. Maintaining-power according to the Huygens system is provided in the manner of attaching the endless rope over both " watch " and chime pulleys, the same weight thus driving both trains.

The bracket on which the clock stands is modern.

PLATE 8. Thirty-hour, Quarter-striking Mural Clock with Alarum, Dutch, *circa* 1760. The dimensions are: Total height of case, 48 inches. Extreme width, 16¼ inches. Dial, 16¼ inches by 11⅜ inches.

The movement of this clock is illustrated by Plate 9.

This example is of decided interest to the antiquarian. The style of " lantern " movement employed (*see* Plate 9) is strikingly similar to that of the Friesian clock illustrated by Plate 5, and is thoroughly Dutch in the characteristic turnery of its pillars and certain arbors.

That its date must be subsequent to *circa* 1675 is evident, as the long pendulum is used with an anchor escapement; it also displays a variation from earlier Dutch clocks of the Friesian type in that the pendulum is suspended from the movement (note the " back-cock " projecting from the rear of the upper plate), whereas the early clocks had pendulums attached to the wooden brackets.

The movement is rather unusual. One bell and *three hammers* are used for the striking and alarum. The hammer for the latter is arranged to vibrate against alternate inner sides of the bell, as usual in alarm work, being double-ended for this purpose. Its operation is effected by a very small vertical verge and crown-wheel (as the *escapement* of a balance clock). The alarm escapement can just be discerned in the photograph reproduced by Plate 9, the verge being attached to the front bar of the movement, as also is the stud for the little crown-wheel actuating its pallets. A small weak spring looped around the horizontal portion of the verge terminating in the hammer controls to some extent in its to-and-fro vibrations.

The striking is peculiar. At the hour—let us say six o'clock—the larger and heavier hammer is operated to strike the bell; at a-quarter-past six the smaller hammer gives *one* stroke; half-past six is indicated by *seven* blows by the smaller and much lighter hammer; a-quarter-to-seven is sounded by *one stroke of the heavy hammer*; seven o'clock in the same way as at the previous hour, and so on.

This arrangement is interesting, and very unusual in England, but is open to one objection at least. The situation *after* twelve o'clock is aurally confusing. It will be appreciated that a series of *single strokes* by different hammers is then delivered, beginning with the smaller striker at a-quarter-past twelve, followed by a stroke of the same hammer at half-past, then by the larger hammer's single stroke at a-quarter-to one, succeeded by another single blow by this at one o'clock, the small hammer finally ending the series by another single stroke for a-quarter-past one. There are thus five single sounds in the space of one hour at mid-day, and during this period the aural indications are very indefinite. Matters improve greatly following this bad period, the system working well thereafter.

The method of striking employed in this clock, outlined above, with its use of but one bell, is clearly designed to obviate the necessity for two; the use of hammers of widely differing weight producing a somewhat comparable effect. That it will not give *the same* result is obvious, since the *pitch* of sounds remains constant, only the *intensity* varying with the different hammers. It will be seen, therefore, that another possible objection arises here, in that a person hearing the striking of the bell by the small hammer might conceivably attribute its faintness to distance, or to closed doors. These conditions, naturally, would affect the intensity of the sound *as heard*, and their calculation would be something of a problem under varying circumstances.

The very large locking-plate will be noticed at the back of the movement. I have ascertained by an examination of the pulleys that this clock was not designed for the endless *chain* shown in the Plate, but for a *rope*, the spiked pulleys lacking the middle groove for the alternately edgewise links of a chain. This is true also of the crown-wheel pulley of the alarm escapement, a temporary plaited string affair served for its operation when the clock came into my possession. A rope of hemp is the correct driving medium here for all pulleys, and such ropes have now been procured and fitted.

The pin wheel (which is also the great wheel) has a double circle of pins for the two striking hammers.

Throughout the movement the wheels are of large diameter and heavy construction.

The dial of this clock is not original, but decidedly handsome. The original hands are of solid cast brass and very heavy. It will be noticed that the style of these hands is not suggestive of a very early date, thus supporting our ascription of middle eighteenth-century fabrication for the clock.

The present dial has been substituted for the original painted iron plate at some quite modern period. It is " made up " from an old chapter-ring bearing the name " Edward Gattland, Cuckfield ", this being attached to the dial-plate *by screws*. The corner-pieces, and also the figure of Chronos (or Saturn), apparently upholding the hour-circle, appear to have been made especially for the brass dial, and are well-finished with the graver, the whole being decidedly effective, as may be seen by Plate 8. The dial is attached to the movement by two little bolts, which pass through the top-plate and into small projections or " angle-pieces " soldered to the dial at the back. A screw from the front (near the figure of Chronos) passes into a wooden block under the seat-board to complete the fixing.

Arabic numerals for the hours are engraved around the alarm-disc, and the alarm is set by means of a little brass pointer, quite discernible in the photograph from which Plate 8 is derived.

The clockcase is very light walnut, inlaid with rather crude designs of marquetry, quite well executed. A feature common in Dutch clocks is the embossed leaden covering to the pendulum window in the lower part of the case. This once more displays Chronos with his scythe and sand glass, and doubtless suggested the dial-ornament.

Those who possess the work, and are interested in the comparison should consult Willis I. Milham's *Time and Timekeepers* (New York, 1923), Fig. 131, which is described as a " Friesland Hood Clock ". The case of this is practically exact with that of my clock, and has similar decoration over the pendulum orifice in its lower portion. It does not appear to be marquetry inlaid, but the illustration is only small. The dial would appear to be painted white or some light colour, and is probably of the sheet-iron variety, but there are indications on the hood of my clock that it once bore three spires similar to those on the case illustrated by Dr. Milham. The term " Friesland " (or " Friesian ") clock is also applied to those such as are illustrated by Figs. 132 and 133 of Dr. Milham's book and Plate 5 of this volume.

PLATE 10. Small Thirty-hour Hooded Clock by Edward Russell, Catton, *circa* 1790. Height overall, 19⅝ inches. Width, 6¾ inches. Dial, 7 inches by 4⅞ inches.

The dial is illustrated to an enlarged scale by Plate 11, and a view of the movement is given by Plate 12.

This interesting little clock is in the possession of Mr. G. P. Lancaster, to whom my thanks are due for the photographs illustrating it, and for permission to reproduce them.

As will be seen, the movement has a plate frame and bob pendulum, the escapement is crown-wheel, disposed horizontally as to working plane.

This is practically the same kind of movement that was used—but with key-winding and eight-day duration—for the early long-case clocks, before the application of the anchor escapement and long pendulum. It is possible that it may have been intended for a tall case, the " spurs " on the back-plate, in this event, may be later additions, also the loop or " stirrup " which is to be seen fitted directly beneath the pendulum cock. (Plate 12.) These attachments, as in lantern clocks, were used for hanging the clock upon a wall.

Two points which are in my opinion against this supposition are (*a*) the very late date, and (*b*) the tiny dial (less than five inches in width).

As to (*a*) G. H. Baillie gives 1795 as a date for Edward Russell, *Norwich*, and as Catton is a village near Norwich, and unless there were *two* makers named Edward Russell, working at different dates in the Norwich district, we may fairly safely take 1790 as an *approximate* date for this movement.

It may be argued that the entire character of the movement is that of an earlier age than the ascribed period, to which I unhesitatingly agree; it must be remembered, however, that provincial makers (and especially provincial *village* makers) used forms for long discarded in the chief clock-making centres until (sometimes) nearly the end of the eighteenth century. This may—and often does—explain the retention of the single hand at a late date in many country village productions, and it may also be remarked that the *arched dial*, especially when employed (as here) by a provincial village maker, is hardly suggestive of an early date. We must acknowledge its use by London makers as early as 1710, although it was not by any means general at that date. Difficulties of communication, and therefore of artistic and trade intercourse generally, would tend to prevent its adoption by the distant village maker until quite late in the century.

Proceeding to point (*b*) it is quite true that dials of very small size were used for the early tall-case clock by London makers, but these were always *square* dials, and the smallest size recorded (in my own knowledge) is *seven inches;* this is the dial size quoted for a clock by Edward East, London, *circa* 1665, in a case standing only five feet five inches high, and very slender in proportion. The dial of the Russell clock, as Mr. Lancaster informs me, is but four-and-seven-eighths inches wide! It must be remembered, also, that in the arch-dial period the size of the dials had increased considerably, so much so that eleven or twelve inches for the width was common, even for those dials belonging to the earlier tall-case clocks having this feature.

We may therefore assume that this movement and its dial was *not* intended for a long case, and in this event the spurs and loop became quite probably original attachments. What then are we to say about the bracket and hood? The former attachments become redundant if the movement was designed as a hanging clock *to be enclosed in a hooded case.*

Three possible explanations are suggested here; the first a straightforward one, advanced by the owner, and perhaps the correct solution to the enigma. It is that the hooded bracket is a later addition by someone who conceived the enhanced appearance and greater protection for the clock thus treated.

The second possibility is more involved in its implications, and therefore less probable.

It is that the clock was originally designed for alternative use either as a simple hanging clock (hence the spurs and loop) *or* as one to be enclosed by a hood and stood upon a bracket, as in the illustration (Plate 10).

This theory receives some little support when one reflects that a customer of the period might wish to use his clock in different positions, i.e., he might decide to move it from its daytime position to his bedroom (it must not be forgotten that the movement has an alarum) at night, and thus the attachments on the backplate would be be of significance. This, of course, was the reason for their provision in lantern clocks, especially early lantern clocks, for in the period that these latter were the representative English chamber clocks, such timepieces were expensive items, and it is reasonable to suppose that the less wealthy members of the community could then afford the luxury of but one such clock, which would be conveniently movable for use in more than one apartment of the house.

A different imaginary customer of the same clockmaker might already have one or more timepieces, and in this event he would not necessarily require the portability mentioned above. Such a customer would probably view with favour the provision of a case for his hanging clock, an appurtenance rendering the clock somewhat cumbersome for frequent transposition, but enhancing its appearance and protecting the movement and dial. It is unlikely that the clockmaker would trouble to remove the spurs and loop provided at the back of his clock in such instances; they would do no harm, and their retention might at some time be useful.

Against this somewhat elaborate theory, the owner would seem to urge the fact that the movement is provided with covers or casings between the plates at top and sides. One such cover is visible in the Plate (No. 12) between the plates beneath the bell. I am, of course, unable to judge whether these " covers " have the appearance of originality, since I have not examined the movement personally. Mr. Lancaster, however, has kindly provided several photographs showing the movement in side views, and I am inclined to doubt their provision by the original maker. Should all[1] be original, and as two are obviously intended as protection against

---

[1] One " cover " or side-plate is utilized for mounting the verge operating the alarum, which indicates originality *in this instance*. The others may have been suggested by this.

the ingress of dust to the movement, their use *with a hooded bracket* would appear supererogatory. Even if not original, their presence seems to indicate that at some period the movement was otherwise unenclosed, in which event one is bound to arrive at the conclusion that the hooded bracket is a later addition, made especially for the clock, as such a small arch dial makes it extremely unlikely that the case has been " picked up " somewhere, just " happening " to fit the unusual dial!

Developing this approach, we may decide that the " spurs " and loop, etc., are subsequent attachments after the movement was made. The former, in particular, have some suggestion of additional work in their method of attachment to the back-plate. In this event it is probable that the *original case* was lost or done away with at some time, the " lantern type " hanging attachments then added to the movement and, finally, a *new case* provided, the spurs and loop being left *in situ*, together with the previously mentioned dust excluders. Personally, I favour *this* theory.

The usual type of alarm-work is employed (as in the small lantern clock, the movement of which is illustrated by Plate 4). A description of this mechanism will be found in Chapter One—*Horology in the Sixteenth and Seventeenth Centuries.*

No separate hour-striking is used, the bell being intended only for alarm-sounding, as in the lantern clock referred to above, and illustrated and described earlier.

The dial is shown to an enlarged scale at Plate 11, and it will be noted that the single hand (in its " overlength " character) again bears out my earlier exposition concerning the originality of this type of indicator, as well as lending further support to our ascription of *late* eighteenth-century origin for the clock.

It may appear to some that I have written of this small clock by Edward Russell to far greater length than its comparative importance warrants.

In so far that it stimulates the imagination and the critical faculties to a very large extent, it must be admitted, however, that this particular example is perhaps the most interesting in the entire Essay. It is because of survivals of this nature that those horologists and antiquarians who can succeed in preserving an open mind on all matters which admit of more than one interpretation, gradually attain the ability to reason logically and progressively, to the advancement of knowledge generally and the reputation and accuracy of historical domestic horology.

PLATE 14. Eight-day Striking Clock by Peter Walker, London, *circa* 1690. Dial inscribed: " Peter Walker, Wild Street end ". Height, 7 feet ¾ inches. Width of trunk, 12½ inches. Length of trunk door, 42½ inches. Dial, 12 inches by 12 inches.

Plate 15 illustrates the trunk door opened, so that the brass-cased driving-weights and the pendulum may be seen. The dial and hood are shown enlarged in the Frontispiece.

This is a fine example by a London maker of a typical seventeenth-century long-case clock in marquetry inlaid casework.

The latter is walnut veneer of well-defined " figure " overlaid on oak, which is used for the carcase throughout. The earlier type of marquetry is employed, displaying Dutch influence in its designs of birds and flowers in coloured woods inset into panels of ebony, these having the characteristic rounded ends of this style of inlay. The base is plain, i.e., not inlaid, but the beautiful figuring of the walnut veneer is here accentuated in the choice golden-yellow wood. A narrow plinth formed into tiny square feet at the corners completes the base at the bottom. All is original, there has been no " cutting-down " of the base to make the clock suitable for a very low ceiling here, nor has rotting of the original woodwork necessitated repairs of any kind, as, unfortunately, is often the case. The lack of inlay in the base is rather unusual; I have seen only one other case similar, enclosing a clock by Joseph Knibb.

A thin line inlay is used to mark off the sides of the trunk into "panels", as is customary though not invariable with walnut marquetry casework. The trunk door has the very usual inset window of convex bottle-glass which has come to be known as a " bull's-eye ", framed by a circular ebony moulding of half-round section. The door itself is also framed by a moulding of similar section, carried out in " cross-banded " walnut, characteristic of the period.

The hood (Frontispiece) has pilasters of *solid* yellow walnut, having ebony or ebonized capitals and bases. These pilasters are applied to the hood door itself, as is usual in early casework, and move with it. Glazed windows are inset into the hood sides, and quarter-round pilasters, ebony capped and based, are added to the angles of the hood at the back.

As may be seen by the Frontispiece and Plate 14, practically all the mouldings of the case are veneered with or formed from " cross-banded " walnut, i.e., with the well-marked grain running *across* the length of the moulding for decorative effect. This method of enhancing the appearance of good-quality furniture was employed fairly generally in the walnut period, difficulty in working being defied for the sake of effect.

Plate 15 illustrates the oaken interior of the trunk, and shows some of the many holes in the backboard, formed by a succession of owners over the two-and-a-half centuries of the clock's existence. The original brass-cased weights should be noticed; these serve to define the very different appearance of genuine old weights to that of modern replacements. The form of the old driving-weight differs from that of the modern type in that the former has a *rounded* base, whereas modern weights are usually flat here, unless they are attempts to imitate antique examples. Another point of divergence is that the genuine old weight has but a thin shell of brass, which covering the course of time and rough handling has pitted with innumerable small indentations, which may be seen by referring to Plate 15.

The pendulum will also be observed in this picture, and with the aid of a good magnifying glass it should be possible to make out the graduated scale engraved upon the flat brass termination to the rod which passes through the bob, the latter sliding on this brass extension for regulation, up or down, by means of the rating-nut beneath. This scale is not very common in early clocks, nor is it a usual feature of *any* antique examples other than regulator clocks and timepieces. We should, however, duly note the comment of Derham (*Artificial Clockmaker,* 1700 edition) in this connection:

"If therefore the Ball runs upon a Rule divided into inches, and tenths of an inch, 'tis easy to see how much, or how little, the Ball needeth to be altered."

The movement is a typical example of those produced in the last quarter of the seventeenth century.

Striking-work is the usual form employed at this period, the locking-plate being attached to the great wheel (an " inside " locking-plate, i.e., between the plates of the movement).

In this clock the escape wheel is a solid disc, with long and fine teeth. The plate-pillars are decorated with " fins " in the turnery, and the lower pair are drilled and tapped for the seat-board screws.

On the *back* of the chapter-ring is some curious engraving; a series of initials in pairs and singly, and the inscription " William Chissell, 1700 ".

The dial and hands are particularly handsome, as may be verified by the reproduction, Frontispiece. They should be studied (as also those of the remaining plates in this volume) in conjunction with Chapter Five (" Dials and Hands ").

Peter Walker was apprenticed in 1681 to Andrew Savory, C.C.

A seven-year period was usual as an apprentice, followed in most instances by a further period of two years as a " journeyman ". The construction of a " masterpiece " (the term does not here imply a work of surpassing excellence, in the modern sense) then followed, and if this was deemed to possess sufficient merit on examination, the maker was then admitted to membership of the guild and given " freedom " to practise his craft.

This procedure would bring the date of Peter Walker's entry into the clockmaking trade, as a " master ", to 1690, and this is the date I attribute to this particular example of his work.

It is undoubtedly an early clock by this maker, as it has been stated that the dial is inscribed " Peter Walker, Wild Street end " *not* " Peter Walker, London ". The exact address of his business (" London " being omitted as redundant, as at this early period in his trade he could not expect to receive other than local custom) proves this completely.

Mr. G. H. Baillie (*Watchmakers and Clockmakers of the World*) before stating that Walker was apprenticed in London, gives his location as " Holland ", and also provides the dates 1681–1730 for this maker.

I do not know from what source Mr. Baillie obtained his information in this instance, but as he is no doubt accurate in his details this may be taken as further evidence that the clock we have been examining is an early specimen of Peter Walker's work.

PLATE 16. Eight-day Striking Clock by Robert Clement, London, *circa* 1690.
Height, 7 feet 1½ inches. Width of trunk, 12½ inches. Length of trunk door, 44 inches. Dial, 12 inches by 12 inches.

Plate 17 illustrates the marquetry of the trunk door in detail, and Plate 18 shows an enlargement of the dial and hood.

This splendid example of clock and casemaking in the seventeenth century is a specimen of the type produced by good makers in London with almost unfailing " taste " and artistry during the latter years of the century.

Superseding the style displaying inlay in panels of ebony surrounded by walnut was that known subsequently as marquetry of " all-over " type.

This, as its designation implies, presents a perfect riot of colourful flowers, birds, vases, foliage and occasionally human figures completely covering the front of a clock-case, in some few instances also extending to the sides of trunk and base.

The styles overlapped in date, as may be observed by studying the examples presented by Plates 14 and 16, both ascribed to the same period of construction, viz., *circa* 1690.

Plate 14, therefore, illustrates a case of earlier *style* inlay than does Plate 16, but not of earlier *date*.

This point should be carefully considered by a beginner, as unless due recognition is accorded it one such may easily fall into the error of ascribing an earlier date to *all* panel-type inlay than is attributed to *all* that in the more luxuriant manner.

The case enclosing the Robert Clement clock (Plate 16) has had the base cut down at some time, and a new plinth has been subsequently added. This is very frequently to be seen in casework of this considerable antiquity, and is most easily detected in marquetry examples, as the border to the inlay surrounding the main design in the base will be observed to be narrower at the bottom than at top and sides.

As to the events necessitating or responsible for this mutilation we can only guess.

Three theories are (*a*) the small height of cottage ceilings in the eighteenth and very early nineteenth centuries, and (*b*) the destructive effect of constant immersion in water caused by the frequent swilling of flagged floors in the aforesaid cottages. (*a*) and (*b*) together form the " Cescinsky Theory " (*c*).

As to how or why such expensive and magnificent clocks ever came into the hands of cottagers, for whom they certainly cannot have been made originally, the argument occasionally advanced (cf. Cescinsky—the later book) is the alleged unpopularity of the long-case clock during the two mysterious decades 1740–1760. That the clocks *did* not infrequently pass to such humble abodes is no doubt quite true; I find it difficult to credit the " reasons " advanced for their " unpopularity ". *See* Chapter Three, " The Later Long-Case Clocks, 1740–1800 ".

In order to add a semblance of extreme probability to his theory, Mr. Cescinsky adduces the " proof " provided by the multitudinous perforations in the backboards of old clocks. These, according to the " Cescinsky Theory " were made by the same class of owner before-mentioned, in successive endeavours to find " fixings " in " wattle-and-daub " cottage walls, and were necessitated by pronounced instability occasioned by the vandalistic operation on the base of the casework.

It must be confessed that the theory is ingenious, and also displays a more lively and plastic imagination than is often evinced by purely horological specialists, the writings of whom frequently present a complete lack of understanding in quite elementary details affecting the cabinet-work of clocks. If we decide to discount the very improbable argument as to the *cause* of expensive marquetry-cased clocks passing into the hands of peasants, the remaining part of the hypothesis may quite conceivably " have something in it ". We must therefore feel some obligation to Mr. Cescinsky for his very original theory. It may be remembered, however, that the especially pronounced insecurity presented by a case with roughly cut-down base is not essential to an appreciation of the desirability of some form of fastening. John Smith, in his *Horological Disquisitions* of 1694 particularly mentions that a clock-case should be " fix'd fast and firm " and he, of course, was referring to a *new* clock of the period, and giving advice to the owner as to the " setting up " of his recent acquisition. Thus the numerous holes in the backboards of old " grandfather " clocks were not *necessarily* the result of Mr. Cescinsky's imaginary conditions, and, indeed, many long-cases exist having these dozens of perforations, the bases of which are perfectly intact. An example is presented in the clock by Peter Walker, illustrated by Frontispiece and Plates 14 and (especially) 15.

The movement of the Robert Clement clock is practically the same as in the Walker example (Frontispiece, Plates 14 and 15), except that the solid form of 'scape wheel is not used, this one having a " cross " (or arms) as is usual. Original brass-faced driving weights are present; the pendulum, however, lacks the graduated scale commented upon in the notes on the clock by Peter Walker.

The dial, inscribed " Robert Clement, London ", has cornerpieces of the same design as those used in the Walker clock (Frontispiece) and in

P

addition has a nicely-engraved border (*see* Plate 18). The hands are fine examples, the minute hand being rather unusual. Compare the engraving and turning around the winding holes in Frontispiece with the turning round those depicted by Plate 18.

Reverting to the casework, it will be noticed that the hood is made without pilasters to the door-framing. Examples of such are not exactly rare, and it must, I think, be admitted that the effect is better when the pilasters are present. The hood has unfortunately lost its cornice at some time, and the outline is therefore somewhat peculiar (*see* Plate 18).

Glass windows occupy their usual positions in the hood sides, and the "figure" of the walnut veneer here as also in that of the trunk sides, is very pronounced. The colouring of the walnut in this casework is decidedly darker in tone than that of the case enclosing the clock by Peter Walker (Plate 14). There may be artistic treatment evinced in this point, as the inlay of the Walker case is displayed in ebony surrounded by golden walnut, whilst here the marquetry is "set off" by the dark colour of the walnut itself.

Line inlay of box or holly divides the trunk sides into a "three-panel" effect.

If the plate should be comparable to the photograph at present before me, an excellent idea of the splendid marquetry-work may be gathered from Plate 17, which presents an enlarged picture of the trunk-door alone.

PLATE 19. Month Striking Clock by Abraham Farrer, Pontefract, *circa* 1695.
    Dial and hands. Dial, 10⅞ inches square.
Plate 20 illustrates the movement.

In this clock the trains are reversed, i.e., the "watch" is on the *left* as one faces the dial and the "clock" on the right.

There are five plate-pillars, and the small "outside locking-plate" will be observed situated high on the backplate. This locking-plate (or "count-wheel", to use an expressive alternative name) turns upon a stud on the backplate and is driven by a pinion "squared on" to the third wheel arbor, an early method. "Third wheel" in this instance refers to the "hoop" wheel of the striking train of a clock movement, and has, of course, nothing to do with the "third wheel" of the "watch".

The collets to the wheels of this movement are of the early D-shaped type, and the 'scape-wheel is provided with 24 teeth, not 30, as the clock is equipped with a pendulum some five-and-a-half feet long, therefore beating intervals of $1\frac{1}{4}$ seconds ($24 \times 1\frac{1}{4} = 30$).

The dial and hands are very choice examples, but the seconds-circle is not the original. This may be observed with a glass to be divided in the usual way, whereas a "seconds-dial" for a $1\frac{1}{4}$ seconds pendulum clock is divided, not into $12 \times 5 \times 1 = 60$, but into $12 \times 4 \times 1\frac{1}{4} = 60$. To make this clearer, the "special" dial has the arabic numerals marking each period of five seconds in the usual way, and there are also twelve of these figured markings which, however, contain but *four* (not five) sub-divisions within each, since $4 \times 1\frac{1}{4} = 5$. Hence, the total number of sub-divisions shown on the dial is $12 \times 4 = 48$, and $48 \times 1\frac{1}{4} = 60$. Each sub-division on the dial thus corresponds to a period of $1\frac{1}{4}$ seconds, so that with a good escapement and correctly positioned hand the latter will move across one complete sub-division with each beat of the pendulum. Now with the seconds dial fitted at present this will not happen, since the sub-divisions are too small, although it is obvious that at five-seconds intervals the hand will be coincident with the engraved *numerals*.

This movement and its dial are obviously by the *father* of the Abraham Farrer, *junior* (*circa* 1760) indexed by F. J. Britten. Apparently nothing is known of Abraham *père*, and the Rev. N. V. Dinsdale in his useful book on the Yorkshire makers (*see* bibliography at the commencement of this work) does not mention him. The late Mr. Britten must have known of an earlier maker of this name, since otherwise he would not have noted "junr." after the Farrer (Abraham) he records as *circa* 1760.

The very high quality of this 32-day movement by an old Yorkshire maker is testified to in no uncertain way by a quotation giving its driving weights. These are: Watch, $20\frac{1}{2}$ lb. Clock, 15 lb. (a not exceptional weight for a normal going train of month duration is 30 lb.).

PLATE 21. Dial of Eight-day Striking Clock by Aynsworth, London, *circa* 1695–1700.

The dial is $10\frac{3}{4}$ inches square and the movement has the "inside" locking-plate striking system.

PLATE 22. Dial of Eight-day Striking Clock by "Jos. Buckingham in Ye Minories", *circa* 1700.

The dial is 11 inches square, and the movement has five plate-pillars and " outside " locking-plate. *The hands are not original.*

PLATE 23. Dial of Eight-day Striking Clock, " William Tipling in Leeds, fecit ", *circa* 1710.

The extremely beautiful hands are shown enlarged by Plate 24. Dial, 11½ inches square. A peculiarity is the seconds-circle, which is " let in ", i.e., flush with the dial-plate, although quite separate and detachable. A Tudor Rose is engraved under the elaborately pierced central portion of the hour hand, upon the dial, and the decorative outer formations of this " rose " will be noticed.

The movement is very much in the " London Style ", with locking-plate on great wheel, five pillars to the plates, and nicely file-decorated hammer spring.

PLATE 25. Eight-day Striking Clock by John Clough, Manchester, *circa* 1720. Height 7 feet 9 inches. Dial, 13 inches by 18 inches.

An enlargement of the dial will be found at Plate 26.

The clock is in a stately, well-figured oak case, with walnut veneers about the hood and walnut crossbandings to the edges of the trunk-door, trunk, and base.

The particularly handsome dial and hands should be noted.

Perhaps the most unusual feature is the small sub-dial above the hand-collet. This is engraved with the Signs of the Zodiac and sub-divided into twenty-four anatomical zones (*see* Chapter Four), quaintly named and spelt.

At the base of the dial, near the feet of the lower pair of cast corner-ornaments representing the Four Seasons, will be seen two small rectangular apertures; under each is engraved, respectively, " Sun Rifeing " (*sic*) and " Sun Setting ". The device by which these indicators were once operated is not now in existence; unfortunately all trace of the mechanism has disappeared.

The Lunar Record, or Age and Phases of the Moon, displayed by a silvered and engraved disc partly revealed through a circular aperture in the arch, is of the early type, before the introduction of the painted disc. It is operated by the usual system of jointed levers from a stud on the hour-wheel pipe, which stud also engages the teeth of the Zodiac Wheel.

The movement is fitted with the early form of rack, working between the plates, and the plate-pillars are nicely decorated in the manner of all early makers, before about 1740.

PLATE 27. Eight-day Striking Clock, with Half-hour Striking and Alarum by Jacob Hasius, Amsterdam, *circa* 1720. Height to top of central spire, 8 feet 9 inches. Dial, 16½ inches by 12⅛ inches.

Plate 28. The Hood and Dial.

Plate 29. Enlarged Dial.

Plate 30. Detail of Base and Lower Trunk.

Plate 31. View of Movement and Driving Weights.

Plate 32. Front View of Movement.

Plate 33. Side View of Movement.

This truly imposing clock is illustrated in the first plate depicting it as actually standing in the owner's residence.

Longfellow's lines:

> " Half-way up the stairs it stands
> And points and beckons with its hands. . . ." [1]

were suggested to me so strongly by the photograph that I determined to sacrifice much detail for originality and general æsthetic effect here, and illustrate the clock exactly as shown, complete with shadows and the surrounding delightfully contrasting panelling.

The heavily-shadowed hood may be seen in complete detail in the next picture (Plate 28), and Plate 30 gives a clear idea of the exquisite figuring in detail.

I am greatly indebted to the owner of this clock, Mr. Robert W. Sawyer, of Bend, Oregon, U.S.A., for much generous effort on his part to provide adequate photography, and for his extreme helpfulness generally and unfailing kindness and courtesy during our correspondence.

It is hardly possible to overpraise the case of this clock. In proportion, design, finish and detail it is near perfection. The serene simplicity of its general outline includes within itself a mass of splendid detail, in which the handsome " figure " of the veneer employed and the elaboration displayed in the carving and fret-cutting of the hood call for special comment.

The dial, too, is full of interest. It will be noticed that the arch is rather low; taken over its outer edge it does not make a semi-circle with

[1] " The Old Clock on the Stairs."

the lunar axis as a centre. This is a fairly reliable indication of an early date for an arched dial, a supposition which is supported by the form of hands used, by the quarter-markings of the chapter-ring, and by the five-seconds numbering of the sub-dial. The decoration around the main dial is unusual and effective, and the cast corner pieces, representing the Four Seasons, are practically identical with those used on the dial of the English clock by John Clough, Manchester (Plate 26).

Days-of-the-month are displayed within the sub-dial for seconds, and the triangular aperture below the alarm-disc in the dial-centre shows the days-of-the-week and corresponding symbols for each day. (*See* Chapter Four, "Mechanical Devices"). It will be observed that "Donderdag", which is Dutch for Thursday, or "Thor's Day" bears beneath its title an appropriate engraving of Thor (Jupiter) hurling his thunderbolts. In this connection the Dutch title of the day is apposite, as a literal translation gives us "Thunder-day". When "Vrydag" (Friday, or "Freya's Day") appears we are given a little engraving of Venus (Aphrodite, or the Norse Freya) and Cupid (the Greek Eros); of Chronos, or Saturn, for Saturday, Apollo for Sunday, and so on. These classical allusions are not restricted to Dutch clocks, as English examples exist having the same succession of mythological subjects, used in similar manner to illustrate the Titles of the Days, but the Dutchmen may certainly be said to have employed this charming conceit more generally.

A "star-spangled" form of lunation-disc decoration is used, *painted* upon the metal, not engraved, which latter method is used for the adornment of the lunar record of the clock shown by Plate 26. There would appear to be fairly good evidence for concluding that the starry firmament was decidedly of earlier use than the painted scenes decorating the lunar records of other clocks. (*See* Chapter Five.)

Details of the hands are unfortunately lost against the background of the matted centre in the illustration of the dial (Plate 29). They may be seen better by referring to Plates 31 and 32, displaying the movement, but still not with all the clarity desirable. Enough can be gathered to show their general character, which is good but not, in my opinion, comparable in effect to those in Frontispiece, Plates 18, 19 and (perhaps especially) 24, which are very beautiful examples by English makers. The Dutch hands (particular reference is intended to the hour indicator) are too thickly constructed, lacking the delicate grace produced by fine scrolling of the metal into very thin bridges of material, sometimes varied (as in Frontispiece) by pronounced portions of designedly heavier appearance.

The very interesting movement of this clock has had several points already commented upon in earlier portions of this Essay, where a part of the general text makes a position for appropriate reference. Special features are the "latchets" for holding the plates together (repeated in the form of dial attachment used) and the alarm mechanism, already described (*see* Chapter One, "Horology in the Sixteenth and Seventeenth Centuries").

Two bells are employed in this movement, the smaller being used for sounding the half-hours. Aural recognition of any particular half-hour is attained by the clock striking upon the small bell the *succeeding* hour, not, as is more usual, repeating the preceding. This is the Dutch method, previously described.

The unusual position of the hammer-springs will be noticed in this movement (Plates 32 and 33) in which it differs from standard English practice. The initials "I. H." (Latin form of "J", usual in Teutonic countries) will be observed on the lifting-piece for repeating, to the right of the photograph, Plate 32.

PLATE 34. A typical Dutch Long-case Clock, with Marquetry Inlaid Casework, *circa* 1725.

This clock is illustrated (by kindness of Mr. J. W. Needham, Manchester) to show points of similarity, and also of variance, with the preceding example.

The inlay is of a different and coarser type to that shown by Plates 14 to 18 and Plates 41 to 44, partaking more in character to that illustrated by Plate 8, although more brilliant than the latter.

In design of base the two Dutch long-cases are quite different, and it must be admitted that the Hasius clock is distinctly the superior to English eyes. A bombè base, or some such variant of the form as that illustrated by the inlaid example we are now considering, is a very frequent detail in Dutch tall cases of the period 1725–1750.

The hood of the case depicted by Plate 34 has some general resemblance to that illustrated by Plate 28, and is certainly effective. The figure of Atlas upholding the earth on his shoulders, flanked by trumpeters, adds a certain regal effect to the whole, but here, again, my personal preference is for the more restrained and simple spires of Plate 28.

Inlaid decoration extends to the trunk-sides of the marquetry tall clock, as can just be discerned in the illustration, Plate 34, and a very nicely painted scene occupies the dial-arch.

PLATE 35. Thirty-hour Striking Clock by Jonathan Lees, Bury, *circa* 1760. In Earlier case of about 1730. Height, 7 feet 2½ inches. Dial, 12 inches square.

Plate 36 gives an enlargement of the dial.

This clock is contained in a pleasingly proportioned case of earlier date (*circa* 1730) than the movement. The general effect of " earliness " is produced by its slenderness of outline, canopied hood, squared trunk corners, and the really beautiful pierced-work of the hour hand. The cornerpieces, however, help to fix the date of the dial with tolerable certainty, as also does the general design of the movement, which is typical of such made about 1760. A plate frame with locking-plate striking of the usual 30-hour type is provided, together with the pull-up wind by endless chain devised by Huygens in 1658, this latter effecting " maintaining-power " during the act of winding.

The woodwork of the well-made case is oak, veneered with pollard oak and tastefully cross-banded with the same material, the only inlay being a little simple " stringing " about the doors of the hood and trunk carried out in some dark red wood within lines of box or holly. The plinth to the base of the casework is not original, but added later to repair a cut-down base.

The movement is solidly and carefully made; the " hoop-wheel " is really a hoop and not merely a pin-locking wheel, as in most later types of the 30-hour clock, and the front-plate bears circular scribings on its face corresponding in diameter to the various wheels. These scribings are without doubt the original markings of the clockmaker himself.

This clock and its earlier case are dealt with very fully from the standpoint of the horological antiquarian in the chapter on " Cases " to which the interested reader is referred.

PLATE 37. Eight-day Striking Clock by Edward Samm, Linton, *circa* 1760. Height to top of central spire, 7 feet 8¼ inches. Dial, 12 inches by 16 inches. Plate 39 gives an enlargement of the Hood and Dial.

This clock is provided with a case of Virginian walnut, of graceful and simple design.

The movement retains its original brass-covered weights (now bearing signs of their age in many indentations of the surfaces) and is in fine order, the clock being an excellent timekeeper. The pendulum " bob " is encased in *copper,* which is unusual and the lock of the trunk door (apparently original) is also made of this material.

It should be noted that the pretty sub-dial for seconds is sunk below the surface of the main dial, so as to allow free passage of the hour hand over the smaller indicator. The vibrating figure of Father Time in the arch is operated by the motion of the pendulum. This device was a favourite from quite early in the eighteenth century, in conjunction with the appropriate motto " Tempus Fugit ".

The Dutch style of wavy minute-band will be observed on this particular dial, and the cast corner-pieces are representative of the Four Seasons—Flora, Ceres, Bacchus and Saturn being the allegorical equivalents in classical mythology. This pattern corner-piece was also a favourite with the Dutch makers; an example of its use on a Dutch dial is illustrated by Plate 29. These particular " corners " follow more closely in detail those illustrated by the John Clough dial, Plate 26. The Edward Samm ornaments may possibly be a rather later variant of those exemplified by Plates 26 and 29.

PLATE 38. Eight-day Striking Clock by John Allen, Macclesfield, *circa* 1770. Height to top of central spire, 7 feet 5¼ inches. Dial, 12 inches by 16½ inches.

The dial is illustrated to an enlarged scale in Plate 40.

This is a well-made but not unusual type of clock, with an effective brass dial displaying calendar, moon's phases, and seconds, enclosed in a case of oak with walnut crossbandings, etc.

PLATE 41. Eight-day Striking Clock by Nathaniel Brown, Manchester, *circa* 1770. Height, 7 feet 10 inches. Width of trunk, 14¼ inches. Length of trunk door, 40 inches. Dial, 17¾ inches by 13 inches.

Plate 42. Dial and Hood.

Plate 43. Detail of Inlay, Trunk Door.

Plate 44. Detail of Inlay, Base of Casework.

The undoubtedly graceful proportions of the earlier clocks, by London makers in particular, has set a standard for some considerable time past by which modern connoisseurs are tempted to judge long-case examples exclusively. It is true that not all collectors adopt this rather biased attitude in criticism, but most would agree that decided preference is generally evinced for this type of casework. That the preference is founded upon sound principles is not to be denied; architecturally as well as on general æsthetic grounds there is much justification for its expression.

The Northern provincial makers of the later period in long-case clock construction, striving for originality at a time when, broadly speaking, London makers were becoming rather casual in the quality and individuality of their productions, did not continue the " London Style ". Instead, they offered examples, often admirable in quality, finish and progressive spirit, which set the type for their successors in that manner. Some few of these Northern makers carried the characteristics of the style to extremes, and others were not above the construction of mere " pot-boilers " of the baser type. The latter instances were no doubt consequent upon the popularity of the long-case style, and a demand for cheaper clocks, available to the many, not only to the few with educated taste and means to gratify it.

To the spreading popularity of the long-case clock in the period at which the Northern makers were chiefly working, and introducing their characteristic styles, may be attributed the very large number of so-called " cottage clocks " to be found by these makers.

These " cottage clocks " (an apparently usual term for them nowadays) were generally of oak as to cases, although mahogany was also employed, those in the former wood being often inlaid with mahogany at the edges of the base, trunk door, hood, etc. The mahogany cases of this type frequently displayed inlay of shells, flowers and similar objects in suitable parts of the structure, this inlaying being usually of good but not elaborate workmanship. A white, painted dial with brass hands (steel hands were also used) and either 30-hour or 8-day movement, frequently of very good but not highly-individual type completed the clock.

That this kind of clock, acceptable as it no doubt was (and apparently still is) to a certain section of the purchasing community, should not be at all inspiring to a collector is obvious and quite understandable.

There must not be forgotten, however, the very different productions by Northern makers which, though mostly of an entirely varying type, bear complete comparison with the many splendid clocks constructed by London makers of an earlier period.

To compare, for instance, the clocks illustrated by Plates 14 and 50 would be to acknowledge at once the entirely different styles, in large degree consequent to their totally differing periods, as well as to the localities of the makers. But an examination of the actual clocks would certainly result in the conclusion that, although one might have a strong preference for one or other example, each is a perfect clock *in its own style and of its particular period.*

The Northern maker of cases from, say, 1750 to 1780 did not disdain, on occasion, to largely copy earlier London styles, if only to show that he, too, could produce (for instance, although this is rare) walnut marquetry inlay in every way comparable with the best work by London casemakers of an earlier period.

His customer the clockmaker, also, occasionally revived early types of dials and hands to accompany his movement, apparently especially where such movement was intended for a case of reversionary design.

To such practices of clock and case maker we may attribute the fine clock by Nathaniel Brown, Manchester, *circa* 1770, illustrated by Plates 41 to 44, inclusive.[1]

The casework of this clock is of *solid* English walnut, lacking the often very decorative "figure" of veneered work, but of beautiful surface and light golden colour, shading off into darker tones here and there. Marquetry inlay of splendid quality and no little intricacy of design is used for the decoration of the long door and the base. Inlay of simpler kind (as in the borders to the panels of marquetry referred to above) is used for front *and sides* of hood and for the sides of the trunk and base; the square bases to the pilasters of the trunk also bear inlaid decoration.

Compared with the generality of Northern casework about this period or a little later, which is open to the possible objection of emphasized width in relation to height, this case is notably slender and graceful. In this respect, as in the wood used and its manner of inlay, the case may be said to provide one of those instances of reversion referred to earlier, an instance perhaps the more striking by reason of its rarity.

It may be noticed that the dial as illustrated (Plate 42) is not occupying its correct position. The maker's name around the arch should be lower,

[1] H. Cescinsky (*English Furniture of the 18th Century* and *English Domestic Clocks*) illustrates another fine clock by this maker, in splendid *mahogany* casework of totally different style, 1780–1785.

so as to show a slight margin of brass above the silvered nameplate. The clock was set up temporarily for photography, and there was no time to alter the very thick seatboard some previous owner had fitted, probably to replace an unsound original. The sinister hood-pillar, also, is slightly departing from the vertical, and requires fastening at the capital. These small faults are inclined to mar the effect of what is undoubtedly an extremely rare and beautiful employment of walnut marquetry casework by a Northern clockmaker at a very late date.

The engraving in the dial-centre, upon a matted background, is typical of much Northern work up to about 1775, after which date the silvered centre seems to have become popular. The chapter-ring bears engraving for quarter-hours (a late instance of this practice) and the lunation disc is decorated with a spangling of stars in a painted firmament. The hands are of a type fairly common 1760–1770, used with equal frequency by London makers at this period.

The movement retains its original brass-cased driving weights.

PLATE 45 Eight-day Striking Clock by Thomas Lister, Halifax, *circa* 1780.
    Height, 7 feet 5 inches. Dial, 13¼ inches by 18 inches.
    Dial enlarged in Plate 47.

The clock is a straightforward piece of work by a fine maker, having nothing remarkable about either movement or dial, but enshrined in a very beautiful case of finely inlaid mahogany, veneered upon solid oak carcase-work.

The illustration cannot adequately convey the very striking effect produced by the elaborate inlay of coloured woods, an effect not unlike that seen in some of the larger kinds of marquetry, but without the coarseness of execution sometimes apparent in the earlier specimens of this type of inlay. The cabinet-work of the case is in every respect equal to that employed in the best furniture of any period; in particular the clustered columns of the hood and trunk, with their cappings of delicately inlaid satinwood, and the pretty ogee feet to the base of the case should be noticed. The mouldings throughout are finely designed and made, and the solidity of the oaken carcase-work is immediately suggested by its appearance when the trunk door is opened so that the interior of the case may be seen.

PLATE 46. Eight-day Striking and Chiming Clock by Thomas Lister, Halifax, *circa* 1780. Height to top of central spire, 8 feet 4¼ inches. Dial, 14 inches by 21 inches.

An enlargement of the dial of this clock is given in Plate 48, and a side view of the movement in Plate 49.

This beautiful example of English clockmaking was probably produced about 1780.

It has so many interesting and unusual features that the sum of these perhaps constitute its title to be exceptional in English domestic horology.

It is an 8-day, three-train, quarter-chiming clock on six bells, with a seventh and larger bell for indicating the hour. The tune played upon the quarter-bells at the hour is susceptible of alteration by means of a small lever at the back of the movement, acting upon a spring-controlled sliding barrel. A locking-plate is used for the control of the chime part, and a rack provided for the striking train. The rack itself is not spring-loaded, a small brass counterbalance being attached to the rack-stem to certify its fall when released by the rack-hook rising.

The arrangement of the escape-wheel and pallets is unusual, necessitated by the placing of the subsidiary dial indicating seconds to the left of the normal central position. The pallets, of the anchor type, assume a place to the right of the escape-wheel instead of directly above it, and the 'scape-wheel itself is brought well over to the left of the movement, viewed from the dial.

The day-of-the-month dial has a hand or pointer connected to a wheel fitted to the back of the main dial, which wheel engages, through a pinion, with another of " star " form, moved every twelve hours by a stud fixed to the hour-wheel pipe. Two such movements constitute a division marked upon the sub-dial, or one complete " day " of twenty-four hours. At the end of the short months (as February, September, etc.), the hand of this sub-dial must be moved forward manually, in the usual way.

Upon the uppermost segment of the dial-arch will be found engraved a chapter-ring, or, more correctly, a chapter-arc. This is used in conjunction with the revolving wheel, a segment of which appears immediately beneath these chapters. The rim of this wheel is engraved with the names of twenty-four different countries or places in various parts of the globe. The time by the main dial being noted, the comparative time (indexed to within a quarter-of-an-hour) can then be read off for any of the place-names then appearing in the revolving register above. It should be observed that whenever Great Britain appears in the upper dial, the time there indicated corresponds with that of the main dial of the clock.

The chapters to the right of the central XII in the world-time dial are those *after* mid-day, and those to the left *before* mid-day, the XII before-mentioned indicating noon. The nominal hours of darkness are not shown,[1] thus, if Great Britain (for example) is not visible, it is dark at the time in the British Isles, and similarly in the case of any other named country or countries which are not visible.

Great Britain is marked on the register by a tiny gilded Sun, with rays, and therefore serves to show the apparent position of the luminary in the heavens at any time during the hours of daylight.

A special wheel at the top of the movement, turning once in 365 days, actuates a sliding frame which ascends and descends in a year, climbing in six months and falling again in a similar period. This frame operates pointers moving from a central axis which indicate on the chapter-arc the approximate times of sunrise and sunset throughout the year. These pointers are not shown in the illustration, Plate 48, as they were missing when the clock came into my possession, as was also one of the wheels for operating the Lunation Disc.

The year-wheel at the top of the movement, and the edge of the sliding frame, which moves against pulleys, can, however, be clearly discerned in the illustration given by Plate 49. (Side view of movement.)

It will be noted that the sunrise and sunset times are given as *approximate*. The latest sunrise and earliest sunset, for example, do not in actual fact occur upon the same day, nor do the times advance or recede by an *exactly* equal period day-by-day, so that a somewhat complex system of equation-work (which this movement does not possess) would be necessary to indicate the precise astronomical times.

The annular circle engraved with the place-names is rotated by a separate special pinion driven off the minute-wheel stud. This special pinion, rotating (like the minute-wheel and pinion) once per hour, is arranged to revolve the world-time circle once in twenty-four hours. The pinion has fifteen leaves and the world-time circle therefore $15 \times 24 = 360$ teeth.

---

[1] The " visible times " are from 3.45 a.m., or a little earlier, to 8.15 p.m., or slightly later, i.e. approximately sixteen-and-a-half hours out of the twenty-four. The " Chapter-arc " is therefore a large one.

Attached to the back of the world-time wheel is a large brass collet with two projecting cams or studs at its rear end. Every twelve hours one of these cams engages the teeth of one of the three wheels comprising the unusually-designed mechanism for operating the Lunar Record or Age and Phases of the Moon. The disc in the dial-arch bearing two painted representations of the moon makes one revolution in two complete lunations, each of the latter being regarded as a period of 29½ days. A scale of days showing the moon's age at any particular time is provided as a narrow silvered and numbered segment immediately above the painted disc, the new moon commencing from the left and attaining its "full" in the central position when fifteen days old. A triangular mark painted just above the "forehead" of the moon serves as a pointer to the index. The old moon vanishes behind the engraved globe on the right of the dial, the new moon gradually emerging from behind the sun on the opposite side.

The clock case is of mahogany, with inlay of satinwood in the Sheraton style about the base, and veneers of satinwood below the bases of the trunk pilasters and beneath the large concave moulding which supports the hood. The capitals and bases of the trunk pilasters are of polished black wood, ebony, or pearwood stained, and a narrow band of green-stained sycamore between fine lines of holly or box decorates the case beneath the small moulding seen immediately under the broad band of satinwood above the trunk door.

The hood has cluster columns and is decorated with applied fret in the upper portion upon a background of brown silk material, and its glazed door is made with a rather unusually narrow frame. Mahogany only is used for its construction and ornamentation, without inlay. The case is supported upon ogee bracket feet.

This clock was at one time in the possession of the late Lord Rochdale.

Appended is a list of the twenty-four places the names of which are engraved on the World Time Register. This transcription from the register is *anti-clockwise*, thus giving the order in which the place-names pass the noon position of the chapter-arc. It is therefore to be regarded as progressing in a westerly direction from the British Isles around the globe.

Great Britain	Hudson's Bay	Friendly Isles	Bengal
Canaries	Mexico	Kamtchatka	Bombay
Greenland	California	New Guinea	Persia
Brazil	De Mendoca	Japan	Arabia
Peru	Otaheite	China	Turkey
Jamaica	Owhyhee	Sumatra	Germany

Great Britain is distinguished by the little "Sun" against its engraved name, and indicates (with the main dial) Greenwich Mean Time. The Canaries are one hour *slow* of G.M.T., Greenland two hours slow, and so on until we reach the Friendly Isles, which are twelve hours *fast* of G.M.T., since here we have crossed in imagination the International Date Line [the 180th meridian, but *bent eastwards* around this position for general convenience] so that with these islands we are in another day; from (for example) Sunday we enter *Monday* in our circuit of the Earth, and with this the relative local mean time changes to *twelve hours fast* of G.M.T. The difference then diminishes by hourly intervals at each succeeding place —Kamtchatka (*sic*), if G.M.T. were used here, would be only eleven hours fast—until, for instance, Germany is but one hour in advance of G.M.T. An apparent error of the clockmaker in allocating to Peru a time-difference from G.M.T. of four hours, which today is one of *five* hours, may be explained by the fact that at different periods the territorial extent of Peru has varied. Thus in *circa* 1780 part of what is now Brazil may well have been included within the Peruvian frontiers.

The order of the names on the Register, in anti-clockwise succession from Great Britain, will be followed if each of the above columns be read *downwards*, commencing with Great Britain.

PLATE 50. Eight-day Striking Clock by Peter Fearnley, Wigan, *circa* 1790
    Height to central spire-base, 8 feet 0½ inches. Dial, 14 inches by
    19½ inches.
Enlarged dial at Plate 51. Movement at Plate 52.

A fine movement with a notable dial is here enclosed in a magnificent Chippendale case of lustrous dark mahogany—San Domingo (or "Spanish").

The clock is fitted with a dead-beat escapement and centre-seconds hand, and the indicator for the circular calendar (indexed around the inner edge of the chapter-ring) is also operated from the central position. The most interesting feature of the movement, however, is the Lunation Train. The front-plate is extended upward in its middle portion, and carries a series of wheels and pinions geared upward from the hour wheel so as to finally drive the disc displaying the lunar phenomena. (*See* Plate 52.)

The dial must be regarded as a work of art in itself, the central portion being beautifully pierced into designs of foliated scroll-work bearing the engraved mottoes " The MAN is yet unborn who duely (*sic*) weighs an HOUR " and " Temp*es* Fugit ". These silvered scrolls are backed by a brass dial-plate having a facing of red plush-like material,[1] the entire effect being unusually rich and handsome. Silvered and foliated scrolls also adorn the two " hemispheres " in the upper portion of the dial, these bearing the admonition " TIME IS VALUABLE ". The cast and chased corner-pieces in the spandrels are of " flower-and-scroll " pattern.

PLATE 53. A Clock Case of Carved Oak, enclosing a Thirty-hour Eighteenth-Century Movement by " Lomax, Blackburn ".

For some comments on this type of casework the reader is referred to Chapter Six (" Cases ").

---

[1] The Tompion dials in the Octagon Room at Greenwich Observatory in Flamsteed's time had velvet facings. Drummond Robertson (*Evolution of Clockwork*) states that the dial of that movement now in the British Museum was originally faced with *Red* velvet.

Q

Index

("G" following the page numbers or alone means that the reference is to the
Glossary in its alphabetical order.)